EDGE OF DESPAIR

DEBRA DELANEY

POOLBEG

Published 2021
by Poolbeg Press Ltd
123 Grange Hill, Baldoyle,
Dublin 13, Ireland
Email: poolbeg@poolbeg.com

A catalogue record for this book is available from the British Library.

ISBN 978178199-456-6

www.poolbeg.com

Acknowledgements

I might have written this book, but you wouldn't be reading it now if it wasn't for the help I've received from some fantastic people.

First in the frame is Claire Dean of The Editing House. I feel tremendously lucky to be working with such a superb editor. Thank you for collaborating on this project, your friendship and endless hours to get the book ready.

Next up are Paula Campbell and Kieran Devlin for your faith in both the Faredene series and me as an author. Thanks also to David Prendergast, Lee Devlin and the rest of the team at Poolbeg Press Limited for all your hard work and talent in bringing the book to fruition. And our valued readers, Dawn, Shirley, Mandy, Aileen, Mary, Jean and David, for reading draft copies when Claire and I had read it so many times we could no longer see straight.

Much love and thanks to my wonderful family, Ian and Rose, for being the first to read *Edge of Despair*, and for all the support, love and belief in my abilities.

And finally, a massive thank you to all of those who read book one in the series, *Lie a Little*, and gave such fantastic reviews. Your encouragement means more than you know and has given me the confidence to keep writing. ☺

DEDICATION

For all those who have suffered loss.

Book Two of the Faredene Saga

Prologue

Faredene, November 1910

Perhaps it was experience that made Victoria Caldwell believe that nothing good could last forever. Or maybe it was her mothering instinct. But with each word she read, her heart rate increased. When she reached the end of her son's latest letter, she wafted it in her husband's direction.

"Edward, would you mind reading Sean's letter? Normally, his happiness practically jumps off the page. He doesn't *actually* say anything is wrong, but I'm sure something has changed for the worse."

She watched him, her impatience growing as he removed his wire-rimmed spectacles from his pocket and brushed a piece of fluff off one lens before placing them on his nose. From the matching armchair on the other side of the fire, he then peered over the top of his glasses, taking in his wife's expression.

"At least let me see what he has to say before you panic."

Anxiously biting the inside of her cheek, Victoria studied his face for any outward signs of concern. His expression was unreadable. She allowed her mind to go back to that Christmas Eve in an empty church where her life had *really* begun. She could picture Sean as though it were yesterday. Only a few months old, abandoned and close to death. She'd saved his life – he'd saved hers, too. He was the child she'd longed for – her gift from God.

In order to keep him, she'd crafted a past to convince everyone that she was a widow and mother. Taking her maid, Bridie, along with them, they'd moved to Faredene and it was here she'd established Centenary House, her haberdashery and dressmakers – her little empire. And along the way, she'd found love, loyal employees and lifelong friendships with members of the impoverished Gibbs clan. They were part of her family now.

That first day, two men had also come into her life – one who . . . No – she didn't want to think about him. She forced thoughts of James Brakenridge from her mind. But the other . . . what would she have done without him? Her kind, caring Edward.

Her musings halted and she looked at the man opposite. Had there been a cost to protecting the secret behind Sean's birth? Undoubtedly. She'd been a fool, wasting so many years keeping Edward at a distance. Afraid even to trust him, rejecting his love until finally he married another, fathering a daughter of his own, Katie – or Kate as she preferred to be called.

Despite the hard work, those early days were happy. Weren't they? Or was that simply the way she remembered them? Surely it wasn't wrong to focus on the good times – Sean's smiling face, his little hand in hers – and to ignore the sleepless nights, ailments and occasional tantrums. Images of her son as he thrived flashed through her mind. Yes, he'd been an amiable child. At least he had until, at the tender age of thirteen, his world had fallen apart, when he'd changed forever . . .

Dear Bridie wouldn't rest easy if she knew the damage her final delirious words had caused the boy she loved and had helped to rear. Even now, Victoria hated remembering the anguish the idea of his parents' rejection had caused him. His tear-drenched face, the pain in his eyes. And those words: my entire life has been a lie . . . I'm nothing, Mother. I was left like a piece of rubbish.

At times Victoria thought he'd never forgive her for keeping the truth from him for so long. Then a year later, for what seemed a fleeting moment, she'd finally believed she could have it all. Edward and she would marry. They'd be a family. And one day, Sean would take over her share of Centenary Mill, which she owned jointly with her business partner, Matthew Clarkson. What a fool she'd been. Plans were nothing more than dust in the wind. And life had a way of dangling happiness in front of you, only to snatch it away again.

Had the past made her bitter? No – she believed good could come from even the most terrible situations. How could she not when she'd witnessed the joy the twins, Jane and Robert, had brought into Milly's life? Yet, they were the product of an evil act – the rape of Milly's younger sister, Kitty, by *him* . . .

As much as she hated the thought, it wasn't possible to remember the past without thinking about James. She'd wanted to strike him down when she'd found out what he'd done. If she had, perhaps she'd have saved a great deal of sorrow for the people whose lives were entwined with hers.

Could she have protected everyone from James? How she hated that man. At the thought of him, she shifted uncomfortably in her seat by the crackling fire. She glanced at Edward, who was still scrutinising Sean's letter. No doubt his keen solicitor's eye was analysing every sentence.

She wasn't sure she wanted to remember any more of what had happened in the past. Even after all this time, it was too painful. But her mind had other ideas and returned to when she'd agreed to help her friend, Lydia, escape her abusive marriage to James, taking their son, Charles, with her. If Victoria had known at the time how vengeful James would be, striking out at those she loved most, would she have made a different choice?

She hadn't wanted to let Sean go to America with Matthew's brother-in-law, Claude Dupont, but what option did she have? It appeared to be the only way to protect him from James' corruptive influence. Could there have been another solution – one that kept her son by her side, yet without such devastating consequences?

Perhaps in hindsight. But how could she have known then that, unable to get to Sean, James would try to have Edward killed? Thankfully, he'd survived. Although his leg, which was malformed from birth, was now damaged beyond repair and he'd walked with a cane ever since, hiding his pain to assuage her guilt.

The image of Kitty on a stretcher, her coat saturated in her brother's blood, was etched on Victoria's mind forever. Poor Teddy, murdered for witnessing the attack on Edward. Kitty, her once beautiful face forever disfigured simply for being with Teddy at the wrong moment.

To this day, Victoria couldn't fathom why God had allowed James to survive the accident that occurred when he'd tried to kill Harry Gibbs for daring to challenge him about the attacks on his siblings. James was a wicked man and even though he'd been invalided, may God forgive her, that wasn't enough – she'd wanted him to die.

With Edward by her side and the love of their daughter, Bella, Victoria had coped with her son living so far away – that was the only way to describe it, because she'd never get used to it . . .

Edward got her attention now by handing Sean's letter back.

"He isn't exactly raving about how wonderful life is as he normally does. Your instincts are right. Something has happened. Write back asking him straight out if something is wrong. Then if you're not completely satisfied, we will travel over there. Because I know you and now you have it in your head that he is unhappy, you won't rest," he said.

That night, she tossed and turned, unable to shake the feeling that her boy was troubled.

On the other side of the Atlantic, Sean Kavanagh rubbed his stubbled chin. He'd not shaved for a week and was bleary-eyed. He knocked back his fifth bourbon. Surely this was just a nightmare. Since he'd left England eighteen years ago, he hadn't looked back. Never once regretted his decision. Life in America had been a heady mix of work and pleasure. Until now, when his world was collapsing around him.

Claude had been twenty-two, well-travelled and exciting. To Sean, fourteen, the prospect of accompanying him to the New World and escaping the shame he'd experienced after finding out he was a foundling had been irresistible. He'd worked his way up to a senior role in the Dupont Cotton Export Company and then three years ago, Claude's father, Jules, had contracted typhoid on a trip to New York, quickly followed by his death. To Sean's amazement, he'd discovered Jules had bequeathed eighty per cent and controlling interest in the company to Claude and the remaining twenty per cent to himself.

For Sean, it truly had been the land of opportunity. But now, faced with the reality of betrayal and treachery from those he cared for, he questioned when this blissful life had gone so terribly wrong. Had his world slowly been decaying without him even noticing? More importantly, what was he going to do next?

Chapter 1

New York, November 1910

With numb fingers, Sean clutched the icy handrail, mesmerised by the foaming waves and ebony ocean that beckoned him.

"Don't do it, honey. Nothing is as bad as it seems."

As a hand in a silk glove grasped his arm, Sean flinched, jolted from the pit of misery that consumed him.

"Come inside with me. We'll have a drink and talk about it. What do you say?" the woman urged, shouting over the howling wind that whipped across the *Lusitania*'s deck as she eased him backwards.

Sean shivered, suddenly aware of the dark sky and foreboding clouds.

"I-I wouldn't have jumped."

"Well, that *is* a relief. Now, how about that drink before we both freeze to death? Crossing the Atlantic in December is bad enough without spending the voyage on deck." Still holding his arm, the woman edged towards the door.

His steps faltering, Sean allowed her to lead him – someone cared.

As she guided him to a table, long since deserted by diners, she spoke to a stick-thin man hovering nearby.

"Order us two large bourbons, would you, Harry? And leave us alone so we can talk."

Sean sat with his head in his hands. Neither spoke for several minutes.

"Get that down you – it'll warm you," she said as a waiter served their drinks.

Sean's fingers burned, thawing in the warmth of the dining room. He grasped the glass, the amber liquid rippling as his hand trembled.

He remembered the woman from earlier in the day, when he'd gone out on deck to watch as the ship had sailed away. His first-class cabin was conveniently situated on the promenade deck and he'd soon found himself a space among the well-heeled passengers, cocooned in their thick coats and hats against the plummeting temperature.

The Statue of Liberty had become a needle on the shoreline as the ship had picked up speed and Sean had wiped his eyes. It was the wind making them water, he'd decided, too embarrassed to admit even to himself that it wasn't sea salt he'd tasted on his lips. He hated himself for his weakness, ashamed that he was weeping for the future that had been ripped from him.

A loud Texan drawl further down the deck had interrupted his thoughts.

"Gees, Harry, sugar. Even my sable isn't enough to keep me warm up here."

Sean had rolled his eyes before glancing in the direction of the voice. A voluptuous dark-skinned woman wearing a bright orange waggon wheel hat that billowed in the wind had clutched the collar of her fur coat.

"Let's go inside, my sweet. We can order ourselves some champagne. When we get to England, I'll buy you a dozen more furs if you want."

Her beak-nosed escort had placed his arm around her ample waist to usher her inside, away from the elements, and the couple had stared at Sean as they'd passed. He'd made a mental note to avoid the vaguely familiar-looking man and his companion during the voyage back to England, unable to face listening to people bragging about their wealth.

"So, do you want to talk about it?" the woman said now, touching his hand, bringing his attention back to the present.

"I wouldn't know where to start."

"Try telling me your name. Then you can talk about how you got those black eyes and that gash across the bridge of your nose."

"Kavanagh . . . Sean Kavanagh. I-I fought with my friend, Claude," he mumbled.

"Marvellous friend. I hope you gave as good as you got."

He grimaced, unable to put into words his horror about the beating he'd inflicted on the man whom, until a few weeks ago, he'd considered a brother.

"I've made a mess of everything. Lost my money. Even what my mother gave me out of my inheritance. And the woman I love has turned her back on me."

"She's a bloody idiot, then. Without that beard and once the swelling goes down, I bet you're a good-looking fella . . . Don't worry, honey, I'm not making a play for you. I've got my Harry – he's the only man I want."

Sean experienced a stab of envy for this Harry who had someone who loved him.

"No. I didn't assume that – really I didn't."

"I'm just teasing. Have you been out on deck since we left New York?"

Sean nodded. "I needed to think. I had hoped fresh air might help."

"It doesn't seem to have done you much good. I noticed you out of the window while we were eating. I said to my Harry it didn't look as though you'd moved since this afternoon. You've been out there for hours. It's no wonder you're half frozen."

Sean sighed. "I'm so sorry you needed to go out on deck because of me."

"Now don't be worrying about that – I've got plenty of flesh to keep me warm."

"I didn't realise I'd been there so long."

"If you'd stayed out much longer, there would have been no need to jump – the cold would have finished you." She patted his knee.

"Perhaps that would have been for the best."

"At some point, everyone feels like they'll never be happy again. Thankfully, most of us find a way."

"I hope you're right. Because right now, I can't see a clear path through this."

"Trust me – the way doesn't need to be clear. All you have to do is put one foot in front of the other and keep moving. So, why *are* you going to England, anyway?"

"I'm going home to see my mother." He brushed back his wavy dark brown hair with a bruised hand, frowning.

Despite the pain it had caused his mother, she'd still permitted him to go to America for a year. Then, realising how happy he was there, she'd agreed to let him stay indefinitely. She'd been so proud of his achievements. How was he going to explain everything to her and his stepfather, Edward Caldwell? He was dreading it. That he might embarrass them by his failure had caused him to wonder if ending it all was the best solution. Would he have jumped? He'd never know now.

The voice of the woman who had probably saved his life punctured his thoughts again.

"You're doing the best thing. We all need our family when we're in trouble."

She was right. Regardless of how his mother felt about his situation, *he* needed her. Almost as much as when she'd found him all those years ago.

The woman pushed the second glass of bourbon towards him.

"Twice my mother came to visit me in New Orleans with my stepfather and sister, but I've never been back home to see them. She's a wonderful mother and deserves better," Sean said.

"Most mothers do, love. Now, have you eaten since you got on board?"

"I'm not hungry," he lied.

"Your lips are less blue, so let's get you to your cabin and I'll have dinner sent to you. A good meal, a decent night's sleep and things will seem better in the morning."

If only that was all it took, he thought.

Sean allowed the woman to accompany him to his cabin. As she wrote the number of her stateroom, he learned that her name was Jess Gibbs.

"Knock on our door, no matter the hour, if you need to talk," she said.

"I've imposed enough."

"If you don't promise to join us for breakfast, I'll have to spend all night in your cabin watching over you. Now you don't want that, do you, honey?"

Her threat was enough to make him comply.

11

After closing the door behind her, Sean took the bottle of bourbon from the dresser and poured a measure. Despite his hunger pains, he toyed with his food. Finally, he pushed the plate to one side and drained his glass, then poured another, burning his throat as he gulped it down. He gazed around his plush mahogany-furnished stateroom. Although he was reluctant to give up the finer things in life, perhaps he'd been foolish to spend the last of his money on a first-class passage. No – steerage with a bunk the size of a coffin would have been unbearable.

He tipped the dregs of the bourbon from the bottle into his glass and knocked it back before staggering to the bed and lying on top, fully dressed. He wasn't sure what hurt most – Claude's treachery, losing his fortune or his mistress' rejection. He felt so alone. Maybe not having anyone depending on him, no one loving him, was a blessing. Self-pity wasn't an attractive quality – not one his mother would tolerate. But damn, he was hurting.

The continuous pitching of the ship dragged his thoughts to his growing nausea. After rolling off the bed, he floundered to the water closet, where he retched until he'd brought up most of the liquor. He filled the sink with water and dunked his head before drying his face on the soft white towel. Water dripped from his hair, running down his cheek.

"You need to sort yourself out before you get back to Faredene," he said to his haggard, unrecognisable reflection.

He willed the cabin to stop spinning as he flopped back on his bunk until, eventually, he fell into a fitful sleep.

The following morning, Sean woke with a throbbing head, determined to keep his bourbon intake to a reasonable level during the remainder of the brief journey.

Aboard the *Lusitania*, he'd reach home in far less time than it took him to travel to America, the ship being renowned for the rapid speed with which it could make the crossing.

The liner sped across the ocean, breaking the enormous waves on its bow, making it difficult to keep his balance. As he crossed the dining room, Sean reached out, steadying himself on ornate white pillars. When the ship lurched violently, he staggered towards an empty table. Grasping the starched tablecloth, he pulled it and the gleaming silverware to the floor with a crash. As he stooped to help the waiter pick up the scattered cutlery, Jess waved. Her heavily adorned peacock blue lace and velvet gown, although well cut, was completely out of place at the breakfast table.

Several passengers glanced disapprovingly in her direction as she called, "Sean, over here."

Sean bowed slightly to Jess, then held his hand out to the man who stood to greet him.

"Sir."

"Even with your beard, there's no mistaking you. It's been a long time," the man said, his dark eyes studying Sean's face.

"I'm sorry – have we met?" Sean asked as a memory tickled the back of his mind.

Harold Gibbs laughed quietly, without smiling.

"I told Jess you wouldn't recognise me," he said, straightening his tie ostentatiously. "It's me, Harry Gibbs. Milly and Kitty's brother."

Sean's jaw dropped slightly.

Jess laughed loudly. "Gees, Harry, you've stunned him."

Harry was the youngest of the Gibbs family. He'd been

the least friendly and likable of the nine siblings, many of whom had worked for Sean's mother at some point, either in her shops, home or mill. Shortly after Sean's own departure, Harry had fled England with only the money Milly had taken from her tea caddy and a few days' takings Sean's mother had removed from the till. Yet, if Jess' jewels were any indication, then Harry was now incredibly rich.

Sean's chest tightened. "It's, erm, it's nice to see you. My mother wrote that you'd done well."

"Aye, turns out that bugger James Brakenridge did me a favour when he pointed his rifle at me."

"You were fortunate to get away unharmed."

"He'd have used it on me, no doubt about it. I'd never been so scared in me life. That's why I grabbed for it. Even though he deserved it, I didn't mean for it to go off. I was sure he'd snuff it and I'd swing for it. How he survived, I'll never know. I've been lucky – according to Milly, the spiteful swine claims he can't remember anything about what happened."

"Aren't you worried that one day he might remember about your involvement?"

"No, 'cos I can afford lawyers now and if he tries owt, I'll make sure he pays for what happened to our Teddy and Kitty."

"Are you going home for good?"

Jess answered for her husband.

"We sure are. We're going to set up home there. I've got a hankering for an English mansion. Somewhere real pretty."

During breakfast, Harry told Sean about his time in America, with only occasional interruptions from Jess.

Initially, he'd spent two years working in New York at the docks and running a few bets on the side. Then he and a friend had set out to see more of the country, winding up in Texas, working the drill sites and expanding their gambling ring. When their clients couldn't settle their debts, Harry and his friend often accepted land or stocks and shares as payment.

"We were right there in the thick of it in January 1901, Jefferson County, when the geyser exploded. Reached over 150 feet high, it did. Covered in oil, we were!" Harry said with unusual animation.

As luck would have it, through a gambling debt they'd recently collected, Harry and his friend found themselves in possession of a small part of this largest gusher ever found and were suddenly extraordinarily rich. When his friend had died two years later with no family, he'd left his share in the oilfield to Harry.

As Harry reached the part in his story where he'd gone to a club in which Jess had been working, she took over telling Sean how it was love at first sight for Harry and he'd pursued her.

"It sounds as if you had a wonderful life in Texas. I'm surprised you're leaving."

"It was smashin', but when Jess said she wanted to live in England, I thought why the bloody hell not."

Sean felt another pang of jealousy as Harry glanced lovingly at Jess, who gazed back.

"I'm the luckiest woman alive," she said.

He's got it all, Sean thought. Jess was obviously older than Harry, but she was kind and any dunce could see she adored him.

"What about you, Sean? I expect you did well for

yourself. You moved to America with that toff, didn't you?" Harry asked.

Sean sighed. There was no point in trying to hide the truth – they'd seen the state he was in last night. He hesitated, unsure how to explain.

"Things didn't . . . they didn't go too well after Claude's father died. I . . ."

Jess put her hand on his arm. "I can see it's difficult. You don't have to tell us what happened. Does he, Harry?"

"No, but there's no need to be secretive about it. You've not been in the clink or summat, have you?"

"It's nothing like that. I'm broke, that's all. But it's complicated and I ought to tell my mother first."

"Harry, honey, leave him be. We've all got skeletons in our closets we don't want rattling."

Sean remembered how Harry used to steal his toys and would hit him, calling him a spoilt git. He expected him to appear smug now.

"Well, if the tables have turned, I'm sorry for you. Yer mam has been good to my family. She helped me when I needed to leave Faredene sharpish," Harry said, sounding sincere.

"Thanks, Harry. I'll sort things out."

Somehow, his kindness was a kick in the teeth. Perversely, he wished Harry had gloated. Then he could have hated him instead of feeling humiliated.

In Stepney, London, George Bristow stroked his daughter's blonde hair, kissed her forehead, tucked the covers around her and wandered into the larger room next door. His wife's straw-coloured hair was fanned out across the pillow. He sat on the bed, pulling the covers down to expose her pendulous breasts.

"It took her a while to drop off, but she's asleep," George said.

Pearl touched his face. "She's a good kid, our Daphne. Got your hair and looks more like you every day."

"She's gonna be a stunner."

"Don't go out tonight, George. What's the point of a posh house if you're never home?" she said, her voice wheedling as she played with the hairs on his bare chest.

George tweaked her nipple.

"Most women would be grateful to have a home with running water, three bedrooms and space in the attic for a maid. Or did you prefer living in one bleedin' room with a paper-thin wall between you and the Irish navvies coming an' going at all hours?"

"We ain't got no maid. At least there I had mates. Apart from our Daphne, I don't speak to another soul all day. I get lonely."

"Pearl, there's no point whingeing. I'm doing my best."

George pressed his nails into her nipple.

"Ow! Don't, George, that hurts. It wouldn't be so bad if yeh came home every night."

"If I were working like the rest of the morons who slog their guts out every day for a pittance, there wouldn't be enough money for food, never mind decent frocks and presents."

"I s'pose so, but do yeh have to go out tonight?"

"There's a load of gear that needs shifting."

"It would be all right stashed here for a few days. We've got plenty of room."

"Don't talk daft, woman. The customs officers and police are constantly sniffing around. If I get fingered, I need to make sure this place is clean. Because if they find

17

a load of knocked-off booze and fags, we'll both end up along the line. Then what will happen to Daphne? She'll end up in the workhouse, that's what."

"But I don't even know where you go. What if I need yeh in an emergency?"

"The secrecy is for your own protection. You won't be lonely later. I'll be bringing back a couple of punters. Give Daphne something to make her sleep if she wakes. Make sure you're dressed nice and no talking. They're paying extra to go with a silent lady, not a bit of East End baggage."

"How long have I gotta keep going with all these posh buggers? I want us to be a proper family like yeh promised."

"Don't be so bleedin' ungrateful. It's much 'arder on me than it is you. How do you think I feel letting other men hump me wife? I'm the one making the sacrifices. An' it's all for you two. Look at those Christmas presents I've bought."

"All the presents in the world don't make up for not being with you. And yer not even planning to spend the day here to see us open our presents or to see in the New Year wi' me."

"At least you'll be here with our girl, nice and cosy by the fire, whereas I'll be alone delivering a load of booze to me buyers."

"I don't see why you have to do it Christmas Day. Besides, New Year yer not working – you'll be with that stuck-up piece yer working the scam on."

"That's no bleeding pleasure, either." He pulled away, doing his best to look hurt.

"I'm sorry, Georgie. I don't mean to nag yeh."

"Look, precious, the racket I'm working on might take a year, but if it works out, I'll have enough money to last us the rest of our lives. Then we can be together all the time."

"What if it don't work out?"

"It will. The last one paid off, didn't it?"

"Well, yeah, but before she carked it, you thought the silly cow *owned* this place an' now I have to go with fellas just to pay the rent every week. You're the only man I want in me bed."

George quashed his irritation and stroked her face.

"Don't speak ill of the dead, precious one. It won't be for much longer."

Pearl smiled as she settled herself further into the pillows.

"Tell me again what the plan is."

"Her name's Bella and she's young, wealthy and gullible. The family up north are rolling in it, plus she has a rich auntie in Knightsbridge. If I'm clever, a pile o' money will come our way."

"Do you promise you'll get rid of that Bella girl as well as her family?" She drew her finger across her neck.

"Do you trust me?"

"You know I do, George."

"Good, then shut up an' come here," he said, gently running his fingers up her thigh.

Less than an hour later, as George closed the front door, he shivered as the damp air whipped around his face.

Did the silly bitch think it was easy for him, putting up with her whingeing? Women were never satisfied. He wondered how many times he'd come back here. There was no way Pearl would fit into his plans for Knightsbridge. She'd be surplus to requirements. And the sooner the better – he didn't want to catch a dose from the dirty slut. She was bound to catch something eventually if he kept getting her to go with other men. It would be a shame about Daphne. She was a great kid – and clever like him – but needs must. There was no proof she was his, anyway.

Chapter 2

In Faredene, Bella hesitated as the crash of something metal hitting the wall came from inside her stepsister's bedroom. She tapped lightly on the door.

"Kate, is it safe to come in?"

"Only if you're female." There was no trace of Kate's soft, slightly Irish lilt in her grumpy reply.

Inching the door open, Bella popped her head tentatively in the room. Kate, dressed in a black tulle evening gown, was sitting at the dressing table scowling. Her silver hairbrush lay on the floor below a mark on the wall.

"Last time I checked, I was definitely a woman, so I'm taking my chances," Bella said.

Kate gave her a small smile.

"What do you want, Sweet Pea?"

"Mother's asking where you've disappeared to, because the other guests are ready to dine and Aunt Anne is acting as though she might expire from hunger – although Mother might throttle her first if she doesn't stop complaining."

Kate threw her hands in the air. "Sure, it won't do Anne any blasted harm to wait."

"What's wrong, Sis?"

"Never trust a man, Bella, they're swines. And there's one I want to put on a spit and roast for Christmas Day."

"Why?"

"They only want one thing."

"One thing?"

"To get in your knickers, of course."

"Kate!" Giggling, Bella flopped with difficulty on the bed. The cold-shoulder design of her dress emphasised her slim frame, but the hobble skirt of the pale pink evening gown restricted her movements. "So, who's the snorter?" She did a poor imitation of a pig.

Kate smirked despite her irritation.

"Now that, Sweet Pea, is something I can't tell you."

"Whyever not? You've always said that you trust me. Didn't you mean it?"

"Of course I meant it. Hmm, all right. It's Garrett Ackerley."

"Garrett!" He and his wife were guests at tonight's dinner party. His wife was pleasant enough and attractive, so why would he attempt to get into Kate's underwear? Bella wondered. "But he's a gentleman. Surely he wouldn't behave so outrageously."

"Now away with you, little sis. You're such an innocent."

Bella pouted. She wanted Kate to regard her as a sophisticated woman.

"I'm *not* an innocent. I simply can't imagine him behaving inappropriately. He must know that a nice girl wouldn't let a man kiss her before they're engaged, let alone get involved with a married one."

"Sure, you've left school now. Tell me you don't still believe the nonsense they drummed into you. Even in rural Ireland, half the county was at it in their haylofts. Not that I've given Garrett what he's after, mind, but I might have."

22

Bella gasped. Her parents adhered to a strict moral code and having attended a local all-girls' school in Chester, she'd had limited contact with men. Some of the older girls at school had hinted at having kissed or even gone further with boys, but no one had ever suggested they'd considered having sex.

"But he has a wife, who is downstairs with him right now."

"Bella, Sweet Pea, lots of people get married and regret it. Divorce is such a fierce scandal, so people are stuck with someone they don't love or maybe even hate. Can you imagine how awful that must be?"

"But how have you managed to see him alone?"

"I love Anne, even though at times she drives me scatty, but my visits to her in London have given me the excuse to meet Garrett when he's there on business."

Bella fiddled with the sequins on her gown, hoping to hide her shock.

"So, what's he done to upset you tonight? You seemed so upbeat earlier and excited about this evening."

"I was fierce looking forward to seeing him. He's been telling me his marriage is a sham and that they live separate lives apart from the odd public appearance. But when I was chatting with his wife, she mentioned that she's pregnant. For sure, he's been lying to get me into bed." Kate grabbed her handkerchief off her dressing table.

"Do you love him?"

"No, but I could have. And I don't like being used. It's also that . . . well, no man ever seems to see me as marriage material. I'm twenty-six and sure not getting any younger."

"I thought you weren't bothered about getting married

and all that romantic nonsense, as you call it."

"What else can I tell everyone? I'd be the quare one if I wasn't afraid of being left on the shelf, but marrying for the wrong reasons is scarier. Back in Ireland, when Grandpa knew he was dying, he tried to marry me off so I wouldn't be alone. Sure now, it was incredibly humiliating. It was obvious the men were only interested in my dowry."

"Then they were fools. You're kind and funny."

"But not beautiful. You'll never understand, Bella. Life for a beautiful woman is completely different from how it is for a plain one."

"You're not plain!"

"But I'll never bowl a man over with my looks and some eejits are put off by my brains."

"I think it's wonderful that you're so intelligent."

"Clever I may be, though half the time I don't know my own mind. The thing is, I'm so mixed up in here." She tapped her temple. "Sure, I want to do something worthwhile with my life. I could never *just* be someone's wife. But I *do* want to be loved."

Bella kneeled in front of Kate.

"I love you, Sis."

Kate rubbed Bella's shoulders.

"I love you too, Sweet Pea. We'll always have each other. It's not the same as with a man though, is it? You must have realised that since you met George."

Bella nodded. "Well, I might only be seventeen, but even I know you're too good for Garrett. Promise me you'll end things with him."

Kate inspected her fingernails.

"Kate! Please tell me you will."

"Stop that anxious head of yours. I may even tip a bottle of champagne over him so he gets the message."

"That's the least he deserves, but not in front of his wife and everyone else."

"Not tonight – I don't want a bar of him."

Bella giggled. She loved Kate's Irish turns of phrase.

"And I'm off men forever. Unlike you, I don't think there's a knight in shining armour out there for me," Kate added.

"You never know when you might meet your prince."

"Away with you. I've kissed too many frogs to believe in fairy tales."

Bella smoothed Kate's blonde bob with her fingers.

"You need to come down and put on a brave face. Don't let him see you're bothered."

"Be a pet. Make some excuse and tell them I'll be down in a minute." Kate retrieved the brush from the floor. "I need a chance to tidy myself up, so he can see what he's missing out on."

Bella paused, her hand poised on the door handle.

"Were you with him last month when you cried off going to the suffragette meeting with me?"

"Yes, I'm desperate sorry, Sweet Pea. I felt terrible about lying, especially after what happened to you. Can you ever forgive me?"

"We're sisters, aren't we. Of course I forgive you."

Bella lingered on the landing. Her mind was whirring. She was shocked that Kate had considered sleeping with a married man. And despite what she'd said, she was a little hurt that Kate had lied to her and cried off going to the meeting. At the time it had been terrifying, though it had worked out well in the end.

25

A small smile curved Bella's lips as she remembered stamping her feet to warm her toes as she'd waited outside Caxton Hall, Westminster. The excitement in the jostling crowd had been palpable. She'd felt part of something important. The eighteenth of November 1910 had gone down in history – but not for the reasons she'd expected.

As the women behind had moved forwards, Bella had pitched headlong into a woman in front of her.

"I'm sorry – I lost my footing."

"That's all right. Is this your first meeting?" the woman asked.

"Does it show?"

"You do look rather startled," she laughed, but not unkindly.

"Actually, I'm excited."

The woman pointed. "You see ahead of us – her in the brown coat? That's Annie Kenney."

"*The* Annie Kenney?"

"The same."

Annie Kenney had been imprisoned in 1905 with Christabel Pankhurst for heckling Winston Churchill and Sir Edward Grey at a rally in Manchester. She was a pivotal figure in the campaign – Bella was standing near one of her heroines.

As the doors had opened, Bella had moved inside with the crowd and the suffragettes had cheered as Emmeline Pankhurst stepped to the front of the stage. Bella had listened enthralled as Emmeline announced that the prime minister, Herbert Asquith, was dissolving Parliament at the end of November and was calling a December election designed to strengthen the Liberal majority, enabling them to progress the bill to increase taxes for the wealthy.

The woman by Bella's side turned to her, shouting above the growing unrest.

"Emmeline won't stand for this. The prime minister has reneged on his promise."

Bella didn't wish to appear ill-informed but was at a loss to understand.

"Promise?"

"In January, Emmeline suspended militant campaigning because Asquith gave his word that a bill to allow women at least some voting rights would be put to Parliament before the end of the year."

Just then, shouting erupted around them as Christabel Pankhurst called for them to march on Westminster. Bella's parents would be livid if she got involved in the march. Should she go home? But that would mean letting her fellow suffragettes down. She couldn't stop at the first obstacle . . .

Now, Bella's attention was brought back to the present and she hurried downstairs as the sound of loud laughter came from the drawing room. When she re-joined the guests, Anne sauntered over, a few silver strands glistening in her once blonde hair.

"Is Kate coming? Her rudeness really isn't acceptable, especially as she knows I asked your mother to throw this dinner party for me, to help me get reacquainted with Faredene society. After all I do for Kate when she's in London, I'd have thought she'd be more considerate."

"She'll be right down, Aunt."

"I've told you before, Bella. You and Kate must call me Anne. Aunt makes me sound ancient."

"Sorry, Aunt – I mean, Anne."

"What *is* Kate doing that's taking her so long, anyway?"

"She has tummy cramps, but she won't be much longer."

27

"Poor girl. I suffered terribly with that myself. In that case, I can wait a while."

Anne continued talking, but Bella wasn't listening, her thoughts wandering back to the suffragette march once again.

As they'd reached Westminster, lines of police and crowds of male bystanders had met the hundreds of female protesters outside the Houses of Parliament. A roar went up and there was mayhem. Bella was pushed and shoved, a boot connecting with her shin, causing her to cry out. A man had grabbed her breast, squeezing viciously. Women were being arrested around her, carried or dragged in all directions.

For what seemed an age, Bella had been pressed along, frightened, unable to find a way out of the surging crowd. She was desperate to make her escape before they arrested her. She saw a gap and rushed towards it as someone behind shoved into her. Bella fell to her knees, putting her hands out to save herself. A man in large work boots had sneered as he'd stamped on the fingers of one hand. She didn't hear the crack, but the pain shot through her. As she struggled to her feet, tears stinging, she saw another suffragette in a wheelchair being tipped out.

"No, stop, it!" she roared as she tried desperately to get to the woman to help her.

But someone grabbed the back of her coat. With his hands around her waist, almost lifting her off the floor, he pulled her into a narrow alleyway. There, the man who had crushed her fingers leered as he shoved her against a wall.

"Let's see what you're keeping up here," he jeered, dragging up her skirt.

Rough hands shoved her drawers aside, his large

fingers probing. Terrified, she'd clawed at his face, even though her fingers were throbbing, but her gloves had protected him. Bella screamed and then the next moment she felt the man being hauled away. She remembered hearing him groaning loudly as he hit the brick wall on the opposite side of the alley.

A tall figure, his back to her, stood between her and her attacker.

"Clear off before I call the police, you vile thug."

Her assailant ran out of the alley, cursing loudly. The man spun round and kneeled beside her.

"My dear girl, are you all right?" he said, his voice gentle now.

Her hands trembling, Bella pulled her skirt down, desperate to cover her undergarments and torn stockings. She flinched as he placed his hand on her shoulder.

"Can you hear me? Are you hurt?"

Her head was pounding. "I don't think I'm hurt. I-I can't stop shaking. My head . . . I c-can't think straight."

"That will be the shock. You're safe now. But we need to get out of here in case he comes back. Frankly, I'm amazed that he ran off. If it occurs to 'im, he may return with others and then we might have problems."

He retrieved his hat from the floor, placing it on top of his short fair hair. With his help, Bella stood, leaning against the wall for support.

"I know you've been through an ordeal, but you're safe with me. Please allow me to support you."

Gingerly, Bella permitted him to place his arm around her and she leaned against him.

"Can you tell me your name and address so I can ensure you get home?" he said.

She recognised her own voice muttering her name and Anne's address before dizziness swamped her. As her legs gave way, she slumped again.

Strong hands caught her and the man carried her out of the narrow side street, away from the baying crowds. After several minutes, he put her on her feet, placing her hand on a railing so she could support herself. Then he instructed her not to move as he hailed a Hansom carriage.

"I'd better travel with you, if I may."

Tears leaked from her eyes. "I'd appreciate that. Thank you, Mr—"

"Bristow, George Bristow."

Outside Anne's Knightsbridge home, George paid the driver before helping her to alight. Her legs were trembling as she climbed the steps, allowing the man to support her.

The butler gasped. "Miss Bella! What on earth has happened?"

"Quickly, man! You can see the state she's in. I need to get her inside," George said.

"Yes, yes. Bring her into the morning room. I'll fetch the mistress."

Bella rested her pounding head on the back of the sofa while the man gently removed her gloves and examined her hands.

"You've broken your fingers on one hand, I'm afraid."

Before Bella could answer, Anne came running in, exclaiming in horror then issuing instructions to the butler to have her physician brought immediately.

"Heavens, what's happened to you?" Anne said.

Bella's lip quivered as she struggled to think of a reply that wouldn't land both Kate and her in trouble.

"If I may, my name is George Bristow. I came across the young lady close to where the suffragette march was happening. She was being accosted."

Anne waved her arms as she spoke.

"Suffragette march! What *were* you thinking? Where's Kate? I thought you were shopping together."

"Perhaps the young ladies got caught up in the march accidentally and became separated. It took many by surprise," George said.

"Dear God, what will your mother say? She'll blame me for not looking after you properly," Anne said.

"She won't, Aunt. I mean Anne. I'll explain."

"Well, I have no idea what I'll say to the neighbours if they saw you in this state. They might think you've been drinking. You'd better tell me the worst of it. What happened?"

"A man grabbed me."

"Grabbed!"

"Apart from my hand, I'm fine, really."

"I'll let the doctor be the judge of that. What about Kate? If you got separated, she'll be looking for you. What if she's hurt, too?"

"She'll be fine. I went the wrong way – she'll be home soon. Please calm down, Anne. My head is banging," Bella pleaded.

"I pray you're right. The doctor will be here before too long. I'll pour you a sherry. Oh dear, I'm in such a tizzy. Where are my manners? Would you care to some refreshment, Mr Bristow?"

"No thank you, madam, but I'll call again to check how Miss Caldwell is, if I may?"

"Yes, yes, of course. You've been most kind. My nieces

and I may look as though we're sisters, but not having any children of my own, Bella and Kate are like daughters to me. You can have all the money in the world, but without family, you have nothing."

"Anne, would you be a love and fetch me a shawl from my room? I'm chilly," Bella said.

"I'll send my maid." Anne hesitated. "No, on second thoughts, I'll go myself. I need my smelling salts and I don't want the girl rooting in my bedside table."

As the door closed, Bella looked to the handsome man who had put himself in danger to save her.

"Mr Bristow, thank you. I'm incredibly grateful. Not only because you saved me, but because I appreciate your discretion with my aunt."

"Think nothing of it."

Bella glanced at the clock on the mantel.

"It's a terrible cheek, but I've arranged to meet Kate at the corner of this road about now. Could you please wait for her and explain what's happened?"

"Leave it with me."

After George had departed, Anne had insisted Bella rest. The doctor had bound Bella's broken fingers and asked if there were any other injuries. She couldn't bring herself to mention her discomfort down below caused by her attacker, nor her bruised breast. Though she'd gratefully taken the sleeping draft he gave her.

Once Anne had shown the doctor out, she'd returned to her niece. Bella was drowsy and struggling to focus on her aunt's words as Anne had straightened Bella's bedcovers.

"I've telephoned your parents. They're not pleased at all and I don't blame them. It took all of my powers of persuasion to stop them from getting the next train down here. I've had to tell them I'll escort you both home far earlier than anticipated."

"Oh no! I'll probably never be allowed out again until I'm fifty . . ."

Bella's reverie was interrupted now and her attention returned to the dinner party as Anne waved her fan in front of Bella's face.

"Are you listening?" Anne said.

"Sorry, what did you say?"

"Never mind. I'll have a chat with Owain Farrell – at least he's interested in what I have to say. Honestly, child, you're such a daydreamer."

Anne walked away, shaking her head.

Bella took a drink from the tray of a passing footman as she allowed her memories to continue.

The following afternoon, Kate had sat on the edge of Bella's bed.

"Are you aching or in pain, Sweet Pea?" Kate had asked.

Bella had nodded and the corners of her mouth had lifted, her eyes heavy.

"Only from head to foot."

"Poor love. Can I get you anything?"

"Just a glass of water, please."

Kate had filled the glass from the jug on the table, placing it in Bella's unbandaged hand.

"If you need anything else, it'll have to wait a few minutes. I want you to myself before Anne realises you're awake."

"What for?"

"Many of the women have complained about the sexual nature of the assaults. So I'm sorry, Sweet Pea, but I have to ask – were you violated?"

Bella nodded.

Kate leaned forwards. "Did he . . . Could there be . . . consequences?"

"No. It terrifies me to think about it, but I believe he might have . . . you know . . ."

"Bella, do you know what sex involves?"

"Not really. My friends hinted – one girl walked in on her parents and told us about it. The truth was, I didn't really understand and never asked because I'd have looked foolish . . . He touched me where he shouldn't, but that's not it, is it?"

"No, it's not. You're not foolish, treasure, but I'll save the talk on the birds and the bees for another time, as long as you don't let on to your mother that I've told you about it."

"I suspect he'd have done more if George Bristow hadn't come along."

"Well, thank God for George. I'd never have forgiven myself if something serious had happened to you. As it is, I can't tell you how bad I feel. I'm awful sorry I let you down."

"It wasn't your fault. You had a friend in need – is she all right?"

"Er, yes. Yes, thank you."

"It was terrible, Kate. I was terrified."

"Aww, Sweet Pea, I wish I'd been there to protect you."

"You couldn't have done anything. They were so rough with us all. Do you know what happened to the women the police took away?" Bella asked.

"Apparently, over a hundred were arrested, but I've heard that the charges are being dropped."

"I'm ashamed to admit this – I still believe in the cause, but I fear I don't have the strength of conviction of the real suffragettes. I'm too afraid to attend any more meetings."

"You mustn't fret about that. We're not all destined to be heroines." The corners of Kate's mouth curled. "Your charming Mr Bristow is a dish."

Bella's cheeks flushed. "He's not *my* Mr Bristow."

"Whatever you say, but I was late and he stood on the corner waiting for me for over an hour. And he's called already this morning to ask after you. Don't worry – he's coming back tomorrow. He seems genuinely concerned about you."

Bella had failed to keep the pleasure off her face.

"Do you think so? You should have seen him. He saved me."

Kate had laughed. "Calm down, poppet, or I'll be in trouble with Anne for overexciting you."

When her sister re-joined the party, Bella's musings were interrupted for now as she watched Garrett steal a glance in Kate's direction while chatting to his wife. Kate swept past him as though she didn't know him and sought out one of the eligible guests. She appeared totally enchanted by the tall fair-haired man, no trace of her earlier annoyance visible as she touched his arm, laughing casually at something he was saying. People played such games with each other. Maybe she *was* naïve. She couldn't understand why everyone wasn't open and honest – it would make life far simpler.

George was such a wonderful handsome man. Bella's fingers were still tender, but she didn't care, because her ordeal had been the reason she'd met him. She'd only known him a short while, but she was sure *he* wouldn't behave so badly. He'd taken tea with her twice at Anne's

35

and since then, he'd telephoned her and even travelled to Faredene to visit her, staying at The Crown but dining at her home. Her parents liked him and now he was to stay with them for New Year. She pretended to everyone that it was simply friendship, though secretly she was thrilled by his interest in her.

✧✦✧

Chapter 3

Victoria gripped the door of Centenary House so the fierce gusts didn't rip it off its hinges as her staff made their way out.

"No dawdling, ladies. It could snow before the night is out."

Their replies were carried away by the wind as they battled their way towards the high street. She closed the door behind them and waited for Kitty Nelson, the workroom supervisor, to don her gloves.

Kitty paused as she placed her scarf round her neck. Unlike the rest of her siblings, she'd been blessed with abundant Titian hair, large green eyes and a rosebud mouth. Now, although her face had aged, one side was still attractive while the other had a faded, jagged scar that ran from under her left eye to her collarbone.

"Promise me you'll sort our Milly out, 'cos I've tried and me nerves are frazzled with her," Kitty said.

"I can't promise, but I'll try," Victoria replied.

The skin on Kitty's face puckered and gave her smile a twisted appearance.

"That's the spirit. I bet you feel better now you've promised and can't let me down."

"I never . . . Oh, go home, you silly mare. All I promise

is I'll do my best."

Kitty gave her a quick hug.

"I always joke when I'm upset."

"I know. Now watch how you go. The wind will have you off your feet."

Victoria closed the door behind her friend and leaned against it for a moment, weighed down by the task before her.

As was usual in December, they'd been working non-stop all day. But despite how busy she'd been, her mind had constantly flitted back to the conversation she needed to have before she went home.

As she shot the bolt across the door, the now salt-and-pepper haired Milly came through from the storeroom, peering round three hatboxes she was carrying.

"Now we've sold those two big hats, these three slightly smaller ones will look smashing with that checked satin dress, Victoria."

"The girls can replenish the window display tomorrow morning. I want us to have a chat if that's all right."

The once optimistic woman eyed Victoria with suspicion as she said, "Is summat wrong?"

"Let's go through to the kitchen and talk."

"All right, but I'll need to get supper started. Jane's home for the weekend."

Victoria had spoken to Doctor Owain Farrell at length about Milly's grief. Despite this, her nervousness increased as she led the way down the long corridor into what was originally her home and later where Milly and Bob had lived for many years.

"Jane's train won't be in for a good while yet. She's aware I want to speak to you alone."

Milly grabbed the top of the ladder-back kitchen chair, pulling it roughly from under the table.

"What's going on? Has Kitty put you up to sticking yer nose in me business?"

"She didn't need to say anything. I can see for myself that you're not right."

In truth, it had been Sara Jane, who everyone called Jane for short, not just Kitty, who had pleaded with Victoria to intervene.

Milly sat, her arms folded. "Let's have it, then."

Victoria braced herself as she gazed around the spotless room. Clearly, Milly didn't appreciate her interfering.

"Milly, dear, I know how much you loved Bob and that his passing has devastated you, but you need to take care of yourself. You can't go on in this way. You've always been slim, but now there's nothing of you."

Milly scowled. "When Jane's home at the weekend I sometimes forget it's only me an' her, so I cook for Bob and Robert, as well. Then 'cos I don't like to waste food, I stuff me face with it."

"Milly, if you *are* eating and you're this thin, that's even worse."

"Well, I suppose there are days when I don't eat owt at all. I can't be bothered cooking for just me during the week."

"I'm more bothered about your state of mind than I am your diet. And it's not only me who's worried about you. Kitty's extremely concerned."

"Aye, she told me the other day that if I didn't pick meself up an' stop acting as if I'd found a fly in my soup, she'd get her boys to move in wi' me."

Victoria smiled. Milly loved her nephews, but they were

39

like their mother as a child – you never knew what they'd do next. And there being two of them, they were a handful.

"Well, that should have been enough to sort you out."

She'd hoped Milly would return her smile, but her lip quivered.

"Life's not worth living without my Bob. I'm so lonely."

Victoria grasped her friend's bony arm. "You have your twins, the rest of your family and me."

"It's not the same, is it? When I roll over at night, there's only a cold space. He was my rock."

"I understand how much Bob meant to you – how much you meant to him – but putting yourself in an early grave is the last thing he'd have wanted."

"I don't want anybody crying over me when my time comes."

"Please don't say that, Milly. It'll be years before anything happens to you."

"More's the pity. Me mind ain't me own any more. All I can think about is Bob. Sometimes I feel like me head is about to explode."

"Perhaps you should take a holiday – visit Agnes in Blackpool."

"I don't enjoy travelling. You know that. I'm glad Agnes is happy, 'cos I never thought she'd get married, but seeing her an' her husband together won't help."

"What about visiting Robert, then?"

"Me? Go to London? Never."

"It's not the other side of the world. It might cheer you up. I'll go with you, if you prefer."

"No thanks. I'm in no mood for gallivanting."

"You've got to keep your spirits up, Milly."

"Robert might not be best pleased if I turn up in

London. I'm proud of him training to be a doctor, but me lad is wrapped up in his own world. He's ashamed of his background. We're not rich or well educated enough for him an' I don't want to embarrass him."

"If he is, then shame on him, after the sacrifices you and Bob made to educate them both—"

"It doesn't matter, anyway. I don't want to be going to a big noisy city. Manchester was bad enough that time I went with you on a buying trip. Besides, do you think a holiday is gonna stop me missing Bob?"

"Of course not."

Milly picked at her broken fingernails.

"If I could change how I feel, I would. I even get fed up with myself, moping around all the time, but there's nothing to smile about."

"All right, Milly, I'll be direct. It's been over a year and Bob's slippers are still by the fireplace, his pipe on the mantel. Even the last newspaper he read is sitting on the arm of the chair waiting for him."

"Do yeh expect me to throw everything of his away?"

"No, I didn't say that, but Jane said Bob's clothes are still in the wardrobe, his dressing gown hung behind the door, his pyjamas under the pillow."

"Jane's got no right telling you. You might own the place, but it's my home."

"She's concerned about you."

"I'm surprised at her wanting me to wipe him off the face of the earth as though he never existed."

"Nobody wants that, especially Jane. But she's even frightened to talk about him in case it upsets you. There are far better ways to remember Bob than pretending he's going to come home any minute."

41

"Could *you* be happy without Edward?"

Victoria took a deep breath. She hated even thinking about it.

"Life would never be the same, but I'd do my best to carry on and enjoy life. It's what he'd want."

"You're stronger than me, then. I'm doing my damnedest, but I'll never be happy."

"Milly, I'm not suggesting that you forget Bob and marry again – I don't imagine you'll ever do that. But you could try to take pleasure in the other people in your life. You'll have grandchildren one day – that's something to look forward to."

"I'm doing me blinking best. What more do you want?"

"You said you forget and cook too much food, but that's not the case, is it? Because I know you insist on laying a place for him every night."

Milly looked away. "Flamin' hell. Is there nowhere you won't stick yer nose? You've got no right to interfere in my life."

"No. I haven't, but I'd like to think you'd care enough to interfere in mine if you could see I was in pain."

Milly bit her bottom lip. "I'm sorry. Honestly, I didn't mean that. You've always looked out for me an' my family. The last thing I want is to have a f-face like a slapped backside. Every morning I tell myself that today I'll be better. Then after a couple of hours, I'm back in this hole. I-I-I do me best."

"I've not seen you cry since that first day. Not even at the funeral. Are you letting your sorrow out?"

"I wish I could cry at times, 'cos the grief is choking me."

"And what about constantly cleaning this place? You must be using a bottle of bleach a day. The minute I walk in here, my eyes sting. It even lingers on you."

Milly tugged at the sleeves of her black dress.

"I don't use that much. What do yeh mean?"

Victoria grasped Milly's skeletal hand.

"Look at your hands. They're red raw because of it." Victoria pushed Milly's sleeve up, exposing her arm. "Oh no, Milly! Have you been scrubbing in bleach?"

Slowly, Milly's face contorted as she nodded.

Unable to bear the anguish on her friend's face, Victoria stared at their clasped hands as she waited in the silence. Eventually, as their hands trembled, she looked up slowly. Her oldest friend's lined face was awash, her shoulders juddering. Victoria kneeled and pulled Milly into her arms, holding her until the torrent finally subsided.

"A-apart from washing meself, I've got no interest in looking decent. It takes all me strength to force meself to pull a comb through me hair, but I need to keep everything clean. Especially me."

"Milly, you're not dirty – you never have been. Even when you were living in the Rows, you were clean. Now, you can bathe every night if it takes your fancy. Can you explain to me why you're scrubbing yourself raw? Why you spend every spare minute cleaning this place, only to put everything of Bob's back where it came from?"

"I worry about passing germs on to people. Maybe I gave some germs to Bob that killed him."

Victoria fought in vain to stop her own tears.

"Milly, love, you know deep down all the hand-washing in the world couldn't have saved Bob."

"You can't be sure."

"You've been looking for a reason to explain Bob's death and there isn't one. Losing a loved one is terrible.

43

Guilt makes us think it's our fault. I did the same thing myself when my cousin, Patrick, and Bridie died. But it doesn't help. You need to focus on the fact that Bob is no longer suffering."

"Do you think he's in Heaven?"

"Bob will be there, for certain. He was a good a man. One of the best. It won't get easier overnight – I understand that – but tomorrow afternoon, Kitty will keep an eye on the shop and Jane's going to help you make a start on sorting out his things."

Victoria felt Milly's tiny frame tense.

"I can't!"

"Not all of his things . . . Wait here a moment."

Victoria went into her office, returning moments later, using both hands to carry an ornate rosewood chest inlaid with ivory.

"You were in the stockroom yesterday when this was delivered."

She placed it on the floor at Milly's feet.

"What is it?"

"It's somewhere to keep the special things that remind you of Bob. Not that you need reminding – he'll always be at your side."

"Do yeh really believe that?"

"I do, Milly. With all of my heart. I believe our loved ones never leave us as long as we remember them, but we have to let go of our sorrow so they can be at peace."

"If I could believe that, it would help me. Everyone expects me to be the strong one. I was the one they looked up to . . . The eldest of nine. Now, h-half . . . half of them is dead. I-I couldn't s-save any of them."

Victoria pulled Milly into her arms once more.

"It's not your fault that your siblings or Bob died. It's part of life." She clutched the nearest thing to hand, attempting to stem Milly's endless flow of tears with the soon sodden pot towel. "I've spoken to Jane. She wants to . . . needs to talk about her father. About the times he made her laugh, the toys he made for Robert and her. All the wonderful memories. Even in his last days, Bob was thinking of you and urging you to be happy when he'd gone. Do it for him."

Milly stroked the lid of the casket.

"It is a beautiful chest. Thank you. Bob would have liked this."

"I thought so, too. He was so good at making things. Do you remember the crib he made for the twins?"

Milly smiled. "It was oak. I passed it on to our Kitty for her boys."

"That's right. See – Bob's memory will never die while we're alive."

"I'm gonna try, but I can't stop being clean."

"But promise me you'll use Pears soap and no scrubbing brush."

"All right. Pears is my favourite."

"We can take one day at a time, you and me together."

"You'll help me?"

"Yes, Milly, I promise. When I first moved to Faredene all those years ago, I didn't let on, but the enormity of what I'd taken on terrified me. Then I met you and I realised straightaway that you were someone I could rely on and trust. We've been friends through everything. And I'm going to help you reach a place where you can enjoy however many more years the good Lord has in mind for you."

Milly nodded, no words or tears left for the moment.

45

Chapter 4

During the remainder of the voyage, Sean dined with Harry and his wife each night. He liked Jess a great deal. Her brash manner and accent were simply her way of covering up her insecurities. Over afternoon tea, while Harry played cards in the saloon, she told Sean a little about her life.

"I've made mistakes in my life too, sugar. You've just got to sort things out as best you can."

"What if it's too late to make things right?"

"It's only too late when you've got no space to move your arms."

"You've completely lost me."

"When you're dead and buried in a coffin."

Sean smiled. "What mistakes did you make, if I may ask?"

Jess looked around the saloon lounge as though expecting it to supply the right words.

"Even though I had a few male callers, I thought no one would ever ask me to marry them. It's hard for a woman when everyone else seems to be getting wed and having kiddies and they have no one. I'm no beauty, but nor were some of my friends and yet they managed to bag themselves a man. It makes you wonder what's wrong with you. The worst part is the pity in people's eyes."

Jess took a sip of her tea before continuing.

"Then one day a big good-looking fella – sailor, he was – came into the café where I worked and asked me out. The next two days before he went back to his ship were wonderful. I couldn't believe my luck. All of my friends were commenting on how handsome he was. A month later, when he was back in port, he asked me to marry him. I hoped we'd be together forever, but it wasn't to be."

"What happened?"

"I didn't have a problem with him taking a drink while at sea – even one or two when he was ashore – but then he started getting blind drunk every night and nasty with it. Handy with his fists. I put up with it for twelve years, being knocked about every night he was in dock. There were plenty of other women where we lived who got a walloping from their men, but that didn't make it any easier to live with. It makes you feel worthless. Eventually, I even started thinking maybe he was right and that he only hit me because I was stupid and did things to annoy him."

"How did you stand it for so long?"

Jess shrugged. "Why do any of us put up with stuff? Because we hate the thought of failure. Blame ourselves for what's happening. I was always telling myself things might get better . . . Stupid, really."

"No. You wanted your marriage to work. That's understandable. If I were married, I'd do everything I could to make it a success, too."

"I don't doubt it."

"There's no excuse for hitting a woman."

"You're right about that, but it was the drink that made him aggressive. One night, when his ship docked, he was paralytic before he even got home. He saw I was expecting our first child but didn't believe it was his. Knocked me down a flight of stairs . . . I lost the baby. Doctor told me I couldn't have any more."

"I'm sorry to hear that, Jess."

"That finished it for me. There was no way I could forgive him. By the time I got out of hospital, he was back on his ship, so I got my things together, borrowed the fare off my sister and took the first train out of Boston. I didn't care where it was going. I landed up in Dallas, got myself a job in a club, took on a Texan accent . . ." She smiled mischievously. "And that's where I stayed until I met Harry. I was afraid to contact my husband, so I couldn't get a divorce."

"I'm pleased you got away from him."

"You do realise what I'm saying? Harry and me – we're not married."

Sean shrugged. "I see."

"Aren't you shocked?"

Sean glanced out of the window while he considered his response.

"No. Not at all. I don't think it matters as long as you love each other, but I won't be telling anyone. It's your business and no one else's." He wondered if he should confide his own secret – that Victoria hadn't given birth to him – but kept it to himself. Even after all these years, he was still ashamed that his parents had abandoned him. "It doesn't sound to me as though you were to blame," he added instead.

"I married the wrong fella. Then once I got to Texas . . . well, I'm not proud of what I did. But I'll need to know you better before I tell you about that. The point is that you can turn things round."

48

"You have Harry now and it's clear he adores you."

"Harry's a great man. He took chances with his gambling racket, but he never cheated. Anyway, that's all behind him. He's not the best-looking fella in town, but I'm no oil painting, either, and he knows how to treat a woman."

Would anyone ever feel that way about him? Sean wondered. Right now, he couldn't imagine that things would get better, but at least he'd swallowed his pride and was going home to try to sort his life out.

Over dinner that evening, Harry spoke about his family.

"It's a bloody good job I'm going home while I've still got some family left. Half of them have snuffed it while I've been in America."

"I was sorry to hear about your mother, Cora and Sam all passing away within a year of each other."

"Aye, if you ask me, poverty kills folk. I just hope the rest of my family will let me give them a few bob to make their lives easier now."

"I can't see why they'd refuse."

"I'm not sure they even believe I've got as much brass as I have. Either that or they think I've been robbing banks."

"Well, they'll soon see for themselves how well you've done." And what a mess I've made of things, Sean thought.

"At least our Agnes let me give her the rest of the money she and her husband needed to set up a guesthouse in Blackpool."

"My mother was pleased for Agnes, but she still misses her."

"Aye, well, she would. Our Agnes was cookin' and housekeeping for yer mam for nearly thirty years. I can't understand why the others won't let me help them. Still, it's their loss. It means there's more money for me and Jess to enjoy."

Harry laughed, but Sean could see the sadness in his eyes and guessed his family's refusals hurt.

"Did you hear our Milly's husband, Bob, died? She's taking it bad. Milly was always the strong one, but this has floored her."

"I'm sure Kitty will keep her cheerful," Sean said.

"Aye, that's true. She could make the Devil smile, our Kitty. You were sweet on her, weren't you?"

There had been nothing between Sean and Kitty, but he had fallen for her. She was his first love. Then he found out by chance she was pregnant, shattering his adolescent dreams of marrying her. But Sean wasn't discussing his feelings for Kitty with Harry.

"That was a lifetime ago. And I was young," Sean said, his colour rising.

Sunday morning, straight after church, Victoria was in the study checking the accounting ledgers from Centenary House as Edward entered the room. He was wearing his hat and grey overcoat, and was followed by his golden retriever, Kirby. Victoria raised her hand.

"Just a moment. I've nearly finished adding this row . . . No, it's gone. I'll have to start again. Are you off out?"

"I am popping into the office for a short while."

"Today?"

"I am behind on a case. I won't be long. Kirby is coming with me."

"That poor dog. I'm sure he wants a day off work, even if you don't."

Edward patted the dog's head.

"I need him. Kirby has one of the best legal brains in the country. Don't you, boy?"

"Well, I'm sure he'd enjoy retirement."

"He has been to work with me every day since he was a pup and neither of us is retiring until you do, my dear. We are *not* sitting here all day with nothing to do but chase spiders."

Victoria smiled. "Is that you or him doing the chasing?"

Edward flinched. "Depends on the size of the spider. I can't stand the big ones."

"Maybe one day all three of us can put up our feet. I never imagined I'd still be working at fifty-seven, but I can't give up the mill without letting Matthew down. And I can't leave Milly and Kitty to cope with the shops, not with Milly in her fragile state."

"You'll have to leave them for a while if we need to go to America."

"Don't remind me. I telephoned Jane. Apparently, they cried together as they were going through Bob's things. At least Milly's expressing her pain now rather than bottling it up. And that's better for both of them."

"It's a start."

"I feel I should do more."

"Owain told you that you can't watch over her every minute of the day."

"I know, but if you'd seen how upset she was . . ." She quickly wiped her damp cheek. "If we end up going away, I'll feel as though I'm abandoning her."

He kissed the top of her head.

"You will think of something if you have to. Kirby and I have every faith in you."

She nodded. "I'd best get on."

"I will be home around three. Come on, boy, we have got papers to tackle."

Victoria returned to her figures. They'd completed so many gowns recently that they'd need to place orders with most of their regular suppliers in the new year for fabric and trimmings. She should order extra supplies in case she had to go to New Orleans. Normally, Milly would be perfectly capable of placing any orders, but now . . .

She leaned back from the desk, once again wondering about Sean. If she'd not heard by the first week of January confirming all was well, she was going over there. Kitty couldn't take on any more, not with running the workroom and looking after her family, but perhaps Kate and Bella would help at the shop. Milly would probably object, but it might cheer Kate up – she'd been quiet lately. Still, there was no point in planning until she knew if it was needed. A letter could arrive any day now.

Once again, Victoria forced her attention back to the task at hand until a while later, her daughter burst through the study door.

"Bella, is something wrong?"

With her thick, glossy brown hair loosely tied, wearing a white lace blouse and the latest design of hobble skirt, she tottered towards her mother.

"Everything is fine, Mother."

"That's a lovely shade of mauve you had the girls make your skirt in, but it's such a silly design. It's so tight you can barely walk."

Bella grinned, held her arms out wide and did a twirl of sorts.

"They're the latest thing. Fashion is far more important

than agility. Kitty says this skirt is the dog's—"

"I can well imagine what Kitty said, so there's no need for you to repeat it, thank you."

Bella perched on the corner of the desk.

"Mother, Kate's going to Chester for a couple of days to do her Christmas shopping. She's asked me to go with her. Father said yes before he went to the office, but only if you agree."

"That man. He came in here and never mentioned a thing. I shall have words with your father when he gets home. It's not fair of him to put the onus on me when neither of us are comfortable with you going away without us after what happened in London."

Bella slouched, jutting out her bottom lip. "Mother, that's so unfair. Kate's a grown woman and besides, we're staying at The Grosvenor."

"Even so, I'm not happy about it."

"Anne has asked to come with us." Bella grimaced.

Victoria smiled. "Mind your face doesn't stick like that."

Bella cupped her chin. "Hmm, do I need to mention that you let Sean go to America when he was fourteen? What would Emily Pankhurst and her suffragettes make of your double standards?"

"Don't smirk, young lady. You can always get me on that one. Even though I let Sean go to New Orleans, it doesn't mean you get to go gallivanting. Besides, it's your obsession with the suffrage movement that led to you being attacked. Your fingers have only just healed. And despite what you say, it could have been much worse if not for George happening by at the right moment. So, reminding me only proves my point. The world can be a dangerous place for a young woman."

Bella picked up the silver letter opener and twirled it between her fingers.

"I'm sure if you came with us, it would please Anne no end. Imagine the fun you two could have together."

"I've had quite enough of Anne over the last few weeks – I sometimes wonder if she's ever going to return home."

"I doubt there's much chance of that. She was saying yesterday that London has lost its attraction for her now she's a lonely widow."

"Hmm, I rather think she's taken a shine to Owain Farrell. If she gives him as much advice on how to run his medical practice as she offers me on running my home, then God help him."

Bella giggled. "That's very uncharitable of you. Poor Aunt Anne simply offers advice to help you be a better wife and mother."

Victoria smiled. "I'm a wicked and ungrateful woman. But you only want me to tag along to Chester to keep her out of *your* hair. I bet neither of you thought she'd ask to go with you. That's the price you pay for being so nice to her and calling her Anne so she can pretend she's a young girl and not a fifty-year-old widow." Victoria's lips curved. "It's almost worth letting you go to get a break from her. Because I don't think your father will thank me if I drown his sister in her soup over dinner."

Bella stood. "Does that mean I can go, then? I'll be good, I promise."

"Have you got your fingers crossed behind your back?"

"Mother, you have eyes that can see through walls."

Victoria's mouth twitched as she struggled not to smile. "It would do you well to remember that, young lady." She grinned. "I'll let you go if you promise to telephone me from the hotel each day."

Bella planted a kiss on her mother's cheek.

"You're the best, Mother. I'd better dash, because Stokes is waiting to take us all to the station to catch the train at quarter past one."

"You're going today? I thought you meant tomorrow. Luncheon was only going to be cold cuts, but poor Cook will already be preparing dinner."

"It's all right – we told her not to prepare anything for us."

"Wait a minute, madam. To make that train, you must have packed already. How could I have gone with you, you little minx?"

Bella stood in the doorway, her head tilted to one side, looking at her mother. "Hmm, we'd have got a later train, of course."

Victoria laughed. "Don't give me your puppy-dog eyes. I've said you can go. Remember to take your thickest coat."

Bella blew her a kiss. "I'll come and say goodbye properly before we leave."

Victoria adored her bright, playful, caring daughter who found everything in life exciting. She differed from Kate, who was an incredibly intelligent and well-educated young woman. But despite having her father's sense of humour, she seemed a little lost somehow. Victoria would miss both girls while they were away, but time without Anne . . . bliss!

⠀⠀⠀⠀⠀⠀⠀⠀⠀⠀⠀⠀⠀⠀⠀⠀⠀⠀⠀⠀⠀⠀⠀⠀⠀⠀⠀⠀

Chapter 5

A frost covered the docks and Sean turned up his collar as he once more declined a ride back to Faredene with Harry and Jess.

"I'll be fine on the train. You'll need the space for your luggage."

Harry rested his hand on the bonnet of the gleaming burgundy Rolls-Royce waiting at the dockside.

"Most of our trunks are travelling separately. Look, there's no need to feel embarrassed. I hardly had an arse in me pants when I were a kid. If it wasn't for yer mam, we'd have starved half the time. Don't let pride stop you from taking a ride with us."

Used to her tactile mannerisms, Sean smiled as Jess patted his arm.

"Harry's right, sugar. What's the point in paying for the train when we're heading to the same place? Put your trunk on the back of our motor and let's get going."

Even though travelling in their plush new automobile highlighted the disparity in their circumstances, Sean was relieved he didn't need to wait for a train on a cold station platform.

Despite his growing nervousness, the journey was pleasant enough while experiencing England through

Jess' eyes as she exclaimed at the beauty of the countryside and quaint villages. Even though most of the trees were skeletal shadows of their former glory, he realised he'd missed the rolling hills and pastures.

When they pulled up outside his mother's elegant Georgian house, the chauffeur handed Sean his valise and carried his trunk up the steps to the entrance while Sean thanked Harry for the lift, kissing Jess' gloved hand.

"Thank you, Jess, for everything. I hope you'll allow me to call on you when you're settled."

"I'll be disappointed if you don't, honey. And stop worrying. From what I've heard about your mother, she'll be so pleased you're home, she won't care about anything else," Jess said, squeezing his fingers gently.

A tall silver-haired butler opened the door.

"Yes, sir, may I help you?" he said, glancing askance at Sean's trunk.

"Are my mother and stepfather home?"

"Sir?"

"I'm Sean Kavanagh."

A slow smile appeared on the butler's face.

"I'm sure the mistress will be delighted. Please leave your trunk for the footman and I'll announce you."

"I'd prefer to surprise them."

The butler opened the morning room door for him and Sean popped his head inside, taking a moment to survey the scene. The room had a light and feminine air, no doubt orchestrated by his mother. She stood by the window arranging some flowers in a crystal vase on a rosewood table. Streaks of platinum ran through her hair, but from behind, her figure was still trim and she stood straight, defying her years.

Sean said, "You have a visitor, madam."

His mother turned her head slowly then gasped, dropping the bloom on the bright oriental rug as she tore across the room, tears already forming in her brown eyes.

Sean grinned, his concerns forgotten for a moment as she threw her arms around him. His stepfather peered, beaming, from behind the chair beside the fire, his blue eyes twinkling below bushy white brows.

"Sean, my darling! Why didn't you tell me you were coming home?" She cupped his chin, turning his face as she inspected it. "What happened to you?"

His mother's questions tumbled out, one after the other, as she pulled him towards the pale green sofa, not giving him time to answer. How long are you staying? When did you get back? Is this a holiday or business?

As Sean explained that his ship had docked in Liverpool that morning, the butler entered carrying a tray.

"I thought you might want coffee, madam. I have also taken the liberty of having the blue room prepared for Mr Kavanagh and I've explained to Cook there will now be three for dinner."

"Thank you, Taylor."

"Do you require anything else, madam?"

"Could you please bring some scones with jam and cream." She turned to Sean. "I assume you still like them?"

"Definitely."

As Taylor poured the coffee, Sean sat next to his mother, answering some of her questions. He'd come home on the spur of the moment, there was no time to write, he said. The bruises were almost gone and there was nothing to worry about – he'd explain later. With each answer, she planted another kiss on his cheek or squeezed his hand.

"What made you leave New Orleans? Are you sure nothing is wrong?" A slight furrow appeared between her eyes.

"I'm fine, Mother. How are you now, Edward? Mother mentioned in a letter you'd been unwell."

Edward smiled. "Your mother worries too much, but Owain says I am like an old door. I creak a lot, but I will go on for years."

"Your stepfather does too much."

"We both need to slow down, Sean, which is why we are home this afternoon."

"Only because we both worked Sunday," his mother laughed.

"Lucky for me you're both here, then," Sean said.

"Is your coming home anything to do with your bruises? I told Edward I thought something was wrong."

Edward spoke softly. "Victoria, my love, give him a chance to settle. He'll tell us when he's ready."

"Sorry, Sean." She pressed his hand to her face. "Is there any possibility you'll stay in England permanently?"

She'd tried to sound casual, but Sean noted the hope in her tone.

"I'm home for good," he said.

His mother covered her face and wept loudly. Sean glanced at Edward, only to catch him gulping back his own emotions.

"Your mother has waited for this day for so long," Edward said.

Eventually, after telling him several times, between sobs, that he'd made her the happiest woman alive, Victoria recovered her composure.

"So, where's Bella, Mother?" Sean asked.

"She's in Chester with Kate Christmas shopping. No doubt spending a fortune. Apparently, there aren't any shops in Faredene that meet their high standards."

"Is Bella still full of energy and enthusiasm?"

"She certainly is. Oh, and she's met a young man from London."

"Really?"

"Yes. I didn't mention it in my letter because I was more concerned about hearing how you were."

"Sorry I didn't reply. There didn't seem any point as I was coming home. Tell me about Bella's young chap."

His mother explained how Bella had met George. "He's staying with us for New Year," she ended.

"She's young to be courting," Sean said.

"What can we do? As you'll find out for yourself, although your sister's kind and caring, she's also extremely stubborn."

"Can't think who she takes after, can you, Sean?" Edward winked.

"Nope, I can't think of anyone."

"Anyway, Kate and Bella's schemes were rather scuppered, as Anne asked if she could join them and they didn't like to say no." His mother smiled. "They'll be home tomorrow evening and you'll get the pleasure of Anne's company, as well, as she's taken root here until January. She's been lonely the last five years since her husband died."

"Your mother is exceedingly kind to Anne. Especially when you consider we discovered it was her meddling that stopped us from getting married when you were still a child. She believed she was looking after my interests, but another woman would have been less forgiving," Edward said.

"I'll look forward to seeing them all," Sean said, pleased to have the opportunity to tell his mother and Edward what had happened in private before they returned. "Mother, if I can freshen up in my room before the scones arrive, I'll tell you why I'm back."

Sean settled himself in the large bedroom with mahogany furniture, cream walls and dark blue soft furnishings that gave it a masculine look. It lacked the sumptuousness of his suite of rooms in the Dupont family mansion in New Orleans, but he felt at home. He'd be happy here – or at least as happy as he could be anywhere when his life was in tatters.

Normally he'd have enjoyed the scones, but his mouth was so dry, they were sticking to his tongue.

"Mother, may I have a brandy, please?"

Victoria glanced at her watch.

Edward pulled the bell cord.

"Of course you may, Sean. It's a little early, but it's not every day you come home."

By the time Sean had finished his second brandy and nursed a third, he finally found the courage to speak.

"Mother, there's something I must tell you."

"What is it, dear? You can tell me anything. Is it that woman you were involved with?"

"Let him speak, Victoria. We agreed to let him tell us in his own time," Edward said.

Sean glanced gratefully at his stepfather then explained how it had all unravelled.

"Everything was going well at first. Claude wanted to expand the company and asked me for an additional investment in return for an extra twenty per cent of the company, which was why I asked for my inheritance."

"My darling, I've given you almost all of it already. Do you want more money? Is that why you've come home?"

"Victoria, hush now. I realise you are anxious, but he is trying to tell us," Edward said.

"No, that's not why I'm home. This is difficult to explain. The thing is, the expansion appeared to be successful. The company had never been busier. What I didn't realise was that Claude was racking up enormous personal debts."

"Where was all of his money going?" Victoria asked.

"He was running two households – one for his family and the other for his mistress. I was aware of that but assumed he could afford to fund both places. He lied about so many things, including how much he was drinking and gambling. I've learned since that when the pressure to repay his creditors mounted, he took out a large loan, giving the business as collateral, forging my signature on documents."

His mother stared at him, clearly lost for words.

"How much have you lost?" Edward asked.

"The export company now belongs to someone else. Claude still owns his plantation, whereas I lost all of my capital. I even had to sell my automobile for the price of a ticket home," Sean finished.

"Oh, Sean! What he did was a criminal act. Did you contact the police?" his mother asked.

"I couldn't bring myself to do that. It would bring shame on his family and Claude would go to prison, then what would happen to his wife and son?"

"I can understand why you'd hesitate, but is he to get away with what he's done? What do you think, Edward?"

"You are right, my darling. Claude should pay for his

mistakes. But as they say – it is an ill wind that blows no good. Sean is home because of what has happened. Before we talk of police and prisons, perhaps we should speak to Matthew and get his view on the situation. Claude is his brother-in-law, after all."

"He should sell the plantation and give Sean his money back. That's the honourable thing to do," his mother said.

"That's why we fought. I wanted him to sell up and he refused. He claims it's his only chance of recovery. Even though I was furious, I thought about it on the voyage home and now I can see his point. Eventually, perhaps he'll be able to return my investment and still have something to pass on to his son. I realise that I've been naïve and stupid."

Sean braced himself for the rollicking he felt he deserved. Finally, his mother spoke.

"Claude's father would be so ashamed of him, whereas I'm proud of you, my darling. One thing I've realised is that if our intentions are good, all we can do is learn from our mistakes. It's pointless recriminating oneself."

Relief coursed through him. He should have known she'd be on his side, as she'd always been.

"This is your home for as long as you need. You've had your share in the mill and more besides. Edward and I reorganised our finances and assets so we could give you most of your inheritance while we're still alive, so I'm afraid there's no more capital available until we've gone. Bella would give you part of the inheritance due to her when we pass away in a heartbeat, but it doesn't seem right to ask," she added.

"I wouldn't hear of it. Even if I have to work until I drop, I'll make you proud of me, I promise."

"Sean, you darling boy, I'm already proud of you. Incredibly so. And I'm thrilled to have you home. For your sake, I wish it were under better circumstances, but you have your life ahead of you."

"Thank you, Mother."

"What will you do now?" Edward said.

"I'm hoping to work at the mill, if that's all right?"

"Matthew will appreciate your help. I'm not there as much as I should be and he still works too hard. Maybe *you* can persuade him to take things a little easier, because I've never managed," Victoria said.

Sean gave a weak laugh. "Give me a chance to settle in before I tell Matthew what to do."

"When are you going to see him?"

"Tomorrow."

"Would you like me to go with you? I need to go to the shop to check on things, but I could accompany you afterwards."

"You carry on with your plans – I'm sure I can still find my way around town."

"I'd prefer being with you."

"We'll spend plenty of time together, I promise."

When his mother told him he must borrow the car, Sean said, "I don't want to be a bother."

"Nonsense. It's all settled."

Despite what his mother said, Sean still felt he was putting them out.

"I should visit Milly and Kitty, but I don't relish facing people."

"You mustn't skulk around as though you've done

64

something wrong. You'll meet half the town at Matthew and Sophia's Christmas Eve party, anyway. It'll look odd if you're not there."

"Will Milly and Kitty be there?"

"Heavens, no. Sophia regards herself far too highbrow to associate with the working classes. I'll invite them over here on New Year's Day," his mother said.

Over an early dinner that evening, they chatted and exchanged news. But no matter how hard they tried, their conversation kept returning to Claude's behaviour. Sean found it exhausting. By nine o'clock, his eyelids were drooping and he stifled a yawn.

"Thank you both for being so understanding."

"Think nothing of it," Edward said.

"I've told you, darling, you've done nothing wrong. Now, get to bed – you look shattered. It's been a long day and you've had more than enough to drink," his mother said, taking the half-empty crystal glass from him.

Bella rang home again that evening. Her parents were so loving and despite wanting to assert her independence, she hated doing anything that disappointed them. When she joined Kate and Anne in the lounge bar, she was grinning widely.

"I have big news!"

Kate placed her glass on the table.

"You have my attention. Sure, don't keep us in suspense."

"Sean's home! He arrived this afternoon. And it's not a holiday – he's home for good."

Anne placed her glass on the table. "Did your mother say why he's come home so suddenly?"

"Nope."

"No doubt there's a story for me to uncover there."

"I'm so excited about seeing him. You'll love him, Kate. Won't she, Anne?"

"Truth be told, I don't remember him that well. I was married and living in London much of the time when he was a child. Although to hear your mother talk, he can walk on water."

"Don't be like that. I've not seen him for years, but I remember he was incredibly kind – and funny. I'm sure you'll get along with him, Kate."

"Hmm, sure, we'll have to see," Kate said.

Chapter 6

Despite his mother's reluctance to let him out of her sight, Sean set off alone for the mill. He'd become accustomed to driving himself in America, but he wasn't used to icy roads. With the exception of the Great Blizzard of 1899, snow was rare in New Orleans and the car skidded several times before he reached his destination.

He turned slowly into the gates, attempting to stop Edward's Daimler without crashing into the delivery truck parked in the yard, from which huge bales of raw cotton were being unloaded. The delivery was no doubt one of the last shipments to come via the Dupont Cotton Export Company. Sean banged the steering wheel with the palm of his hand as his resentment at Claude flared.

It was a good few minutes before he felt calm enough to enter the building. The clatter from the rows of vast machines was deafening – he'd forgotten how loud they were. The office was empty, so he made his way to the spinning room and shouted to a brawny man in shirtsleeves.

"Where can I find Mr Clarkson?"

The man removed his cap, sending a spray of sweat from his lank hair in Sean's direction. He pointed towards the weaving room, immediately returning his attention to his machine.

As Sean walked away, he wiped his face on his handkerchief – he'd better get used to the dirt and grime of the place.

Eventually, he found Matthew in conversation with a weaver. When his old mentor noticed him, he bounded over, his oil-smeared hand out. As Sean stepped back rather than clasping it, Matthew laughed.

"Maybe not. Come into the office. We'll be able to talk there," Matthew shouted over the din.

Matthew poured two shots of whiskey.

"At least it's slightly quieter in here," he said.

"I see you're still getting stuck in," Sean said, taking the glass.

"It's a necessity if I want to keep things going." He clinked his glass against Sean's. "Good to see you. I'd no idea you were coming over."

"Nobody did."

"Sophia had a letter from Claude yesterday explaining he'd sold the export company, although he's still going to supply our cotton from the plantation. It all seems a bit sudden."

Sean took a swig and lit the cigar Matthew passed him.

"Come on, lad, what's going on? Claude didn't mention you in his letter, but we wondered if there was more to it than he made out. Now, you turn up with fading bruises."

"Claude didn't sell the company. He lost it."

He told Matthew everything, including how he'd come to blows with Claude.

"Sophia will be furious with him. He's decent enough, but he's never had to work for anything – business or women. We feared he'd make a mess of things when their father passed away."

"It came as a complete shock when I discovered what he was capable of."

"I'll write and give him a piece of my mind. Even though I can't force him to pay you back, I'll apply what pressure I can."

"Matthew, I'll come to the point. I need to earn a living and was wondering if I can work here."

"Of course. Your mother still owns fifty per cent."

"I don't want charity. So please only give me a job if I'll be of use. I can still remember the basics from when I used to come here after school, but I'm prepared to learn from the bottom."

"You'll soon pick things up again. It'll be good to have you back. Hopefully, you can help me put a stop to the growing trade union movement."

"Why would you want to quash it? Surely you're in favour of workers' rights."

"I am. The thing is, there are rumours of strikes to support the miners and workers from other mills. I understand the sentiment, but I don't think we should suffer for what happens elsewhere. Unlike the rest of the mills, we've even increased our wages, despite having to cut our prices to compete with cheap imports from places like Japan."

"I'm not sure how I can help with the unions. Although I'll be grateful for the job – if you're sure you want me and can afford my salary."

"Like I said – I'll be pleased to have you. Give yourself time to settle back in at home first. Spend Christmas with your family and catching up with friends. I have a meeting in Chester on the Monday, so start work on the third of January – how does that sound?" Matthew raised his glass.

"You're the boss. Whatever suits you is fine by me. How's the family – Sophia and Yvette?"

At the mention of his wife and daughter, Matthew shifted uncomfortably.

"Not great. Sophia keeps threatening to leave me. She's never settled here and since our son died of whooping cough, she's hated it even more. I can't blame her. She believes he might still be alive if we'd stayed in New Orleans."

"I'm so sorry. You must both have been heartbroken. I understand it doesn't make it easier for either of you, but I'm glad your daughter survived it."

Matthew nodded. "Yes. Yvette is a great comfort to me."

"Is she content here?"

"It's hard to tell with these young women. One minute she's smiling and laughing, the next she's moping. I don't mind admitting, though, I spoil her. Maybe I'm still compensating for leaving them in America to come here when she was so young. I thought Sophia would follow me straightaway, but she took some persuading."

"How old is Yvette now? She was a young child last time I saw her in New Orleans."

"She's twenty-one. At her age, her mother was married with a child and another on the way."

"She still has plenty of time for all that."

"Sophia thought Yvette had feelings for Peter Mason, but it came to nothing and he's about to marry. No doubt before long some young buck will sweep Yvette off her feet and I'll lose her. What about you? Why did you never marry?"

"I spent too long giving my attention to the wrong woman."

"Take my advice. Put her behind you and enjoy life

while you can. I'm sure there will be plenty of young women happy to entertain you."

"Well, I've kept you from your work for long enough. I'd better go while there's still half of that bottle of whiskey left." He hoped he'd justify Matthew's faith in him.

A short while later, Sean parked in the mews behind the house and handed the keys to Stokes. As he entered the kitchen, Taylor turned from the kitchen dresser, where he was filling a decanter.

"My apologies, sir. Did no one answer the front doorbell? You shouldn't have to use this entrance."

"I came in from the mews. Sorry, I didn't mean to disturb you all. Things are more relaxed in the States."

"Indeed, sir. The master wishes to speak with you in his study when it's convenient."

"I'll see him now."

"Come in," Edward said in answer to Sean's knock.

His stepfather was sitting at his enormous walnut desk, round spectacles balanced on the end of his nose. In his mid-sixties, his face was lined but his expression was alert.

"Sean, please, have a seat. I won't keep you a minute. I only have a couple more letters to sign."

A moment later, Edward replaced his pen in its stand and surveyed Sean.

"How did you get on at the mill?"

"Good, thank you."

"You look as though you have shared a few tipples."

"Matthew got the whiskey out. Hopefully, Mother won't notice."

"Not much chance of that, but she is so happy to have you home that I am sure you will get away with daytime

71

drinking just this once. Now, what did Matthew have to say about Claude's behaviour?"

"He's appalled and intends to write. I doubt it'll change anything."

"Are you going to be returning to the mill?"

"Yes, although Matthew has asked me to start in January."

"Right, well, in that case, you will want this."

He removed a pile of banknotes from a drawer and pushed them across the desk towards Sean using his deformed hand. With age and arthritis, it had become more twisted and swollen than Sean remembered. It must have been painful to use, but Edward hid it well.

Sean picked up the money.

"Edward?"

"It will be a while before you have an income from the mill and I understand a man doesn't want to have to ask his mother for money."

"I'm extremely grateful. It's generous of you. I wish I were in a position to refuse, but it means I can buy Christmas presents and incidentals. I used the last of my cash to settle my tailor's bill and other suppliers before leaving New Orleans."

"That says a lot for your character. There is enough there to get some new clothes, as well. Most of yours probably aren't suitable for our climate."

Sean touched the collar of his pale linen suit.

"I'll pay you back as soon as I can."

"No, you won't. It's not a loan. Never a borrower or a lender be. This way, I can forget about it without having to set Kirby on you for non-payment."

Sean returned Edward's grin as the old dog raised his eyes at the sound of his name.

"This is between the two of us, so don't insult me by mentioning it again. Just don't go spending it all on wild women and drink," Edward chuckled.

"Thank you, Edward. I won't squander it."

"Another thing. Straight after Christmas, we are going to get a second motor – one won't be enough."

"Edward, I don't want you going to that expense because of me."

"The girls and your mother will have use of it as well on occasion. It won't be anything fancy, mind."

"I'm so grateful. Thank you."

"We will need to employ someone to drive the ladies, but our footman is leaving in the new year, so maybe his replacement will be the solution."

"Edward, I don't know what to say."

"There is no need to say anything. Now, you spend some time with your mother. The girls and Anne will be home later, so I doubt you will get a word in edgeways then."

Kate couldn't help smiling at Bella's obvious excitement as they waited for Taylor to open the door. Victoria greeted them in the large hallway, pointing to the stack of parcels Stokes was placing on the parquet floor.

"If the number of packages is anything to go by, you must have cleared out the shops in Chester."

"They have worn me out," Anne said as she removed her fur-lined gloves and hat, passing them to Taylor.

Kate grinned at Victoria.

"Taylor, will you have tea brought in, please. Or do any of you ladies need to change first?" Victoria asked.

"We're all fine, Mother. Where's Sean? I'm desperate to see him and for Kate to meet him," Bella said as she thrust her coat and hat on the hall table, clearly too eager to wait for Taylor to finish assisting Anne.

"In the morning room," Victoria said as Bella shot past her.

By the time Kate reached the door, Bella was being hugged by a tall dark-haired man. She twisted from his embrace and beckoned Kate.

"Kate, come and meet Sean."

Sean bowed slightly.

"How do you do, Kate? It's lovely to meet you."

Kate struggled to find something smart or witty to say – not a problem she generally had. Nobody had told her Saint Sean was gorgeous, with thick wavy hair, large dark brown eyes and a smile to die for.

"Hello, Sean. Sure now, are you back from conquering America?"

"Far from it. There's no point in trying to hide it from my family. Unfortunately, it's the reverse – I've come home penniless."

Oh no, her big mouth – he looked crestfallen.

"Ah, Sean, I didn't know. I'm fierce sorry."

Anne pushed past them to take a chair.

"Let me get in, won't you? Goodness me! What's all this, Sean? Come and sit down and tell me what you were playing at losing all that money."

"Well, Sean, I don't know what to make of this. My daughters and sister come home and you would think I was invisible. All they are interested in is you. Not one kiss or hello from any of them," Edward said, smiling from his chair as he held out his arms to Kate and Bella.

"Sorry, Father," the girls chorused as they bent to kiss him.

Kate listened quietly as Sean told them about America. His eyes were downcast and his words halting, yet he didn't come across as self-pitying. She had to resist the urge to move to the same sofa as him and comfort him. What the hell was wrong with her? She was going all starry-eyed and she'd only known him five minutes.

"Still, I'm home now with my family *and* I have an extra sister," Sean said, jolting Kate from her musings.

"We're not *actually* brother and sister. Sure, we have no blood connection."

Why the hell had she said it so abruptly? She didn't want him thinking of her as a sister, but now she'd come across as offish.

"No, of course not. Sorry. I just meant we were family."

"Sorry, Sean. I meant nothing by it. I didn't—"

Sean excused himself, explaining he had some letters to write. There was nothing she could do for now, but she was determined to become his friend and take the sadness from his eyes.

꘠꘠꘠

Chapter 7

Victoria supervised as the servants erected a Norwegian spruce in the hallway and her family gathered to decorate it. She couldn't remember the last time she'd taken Christmas Eve off work, but she was glad Kitty had telephoned last night.

"Now, Victoria, I want no arguments," Kitty had said. "Milly and me insist you take tomorrow off and enjoy being with your family. This will be your first Christmas together."

"The shop will be busy. I might be needed," Victoria had argued half-heartedly.

"We can manage. I've already found where you've hidden the Christmas boxes for the staff – Milly will hand them out."

"But what about—"

"You don't need to worry about my present. I'm sure mine will be the biggest, else I'll want to know the reason when you come back."

"But I—"

"We're sending the gifts we've bought for you round with the delivery lad. See, I've thought of everything."

"I wasn't going to—"

Kitty laughed. "Before you ask, Milly will be fine.

Harry wanted us to go somewhere swanky for a meal, but I said to him, when you own a pub, you can't shut up shop whenever it takes yer fancy. So, the family are coming to us at The Tanner's Arms. And we'll be spending Christmas Eve and Christmas Day together, so there's nowt for you to worry about. I've told our Milly if she's fretting, as long as she doesn't use bleach, she can sit an' wash the veg to her heart's content – that should keep her busy for a while."

"Oh, Kitty, you mustn't tease her."

"I'm no doctor, but now it's out in the open, well, I've decided the best way is to make her laugh about it if I can."

"I hope Milly agrees with you. And I thought she wanted a quiet Christmas – she refused my invitation."

"I weren't taking no for an answer. I'll get a couple o' glasses of port down her an' before you know it, she'll be singin' an' dancin' the cancan by the piano. It's usually a good night in the pub on Christmas Eve."

"You seem to have it all mapped out. Thank you. And please bring Jess and Harry to ours on New Year's Day."

"You can invite her yerself. She's booked in for a fitting on Tuesday at eleven. She's yer first appointment."

Victoria hoped Kitty was right about Milly. Perhaps she had the right idea, because the girls and their teasing of Sean as though nothing was wrong certainly appeared to be helping him. The sadness never left his eyes, though. Despite not having seen him for several years, she was his mother and recognised he was putting on a brave face. Claude Dupont was lucky the Atlantic Ocean stood between him and her, because if she ever saw him again . . . well, she didn't know exactly what she'd do to him, but it would be slow and extremely painful.

She was concerned about Sean's drinking, too, which she'd tried to curtail but could only mention so many times without becoming a nag. The last thing she wanted was for him to regret coming home.

Victoria stopped her musings as Bella grinned, peering from behind the enormous tree.

"Pass that nutcracker soldier please, Sean. Hey, Sean! Or do I need to call you Tatty Head like Kitty does to get your attention?"

Sean passed the ornament to her, a mock scowl on his face.

"Don't you dare start calling me that! I escaped that name while I was in America – I was hoping Kitty had forgotten about it."

"Definitely not. She refers to you as Tatty Head whenever she mentions you."

"Great."

Kate balanced precariously on the ladder as she looked down at Sean, a crystal bauble in her hand.

"I wouldn't call his hair tatty. In fact, from up here it looks as though it's definitely thinning."

"What?" Sean's hands shot up to his hair.

Edward laughed.

"Girls, will you please stop ganging up on him. Sean, your hair is *not* thinning. It gets thicker by the day, especially with that beard. You resemble a bear growing your winter coat."

"If you'd all quit looking at my hair and making comments on my appearance, we might stand a chance of finishing this wretched tree before Christmas instead of when Bella's young man arrives for New Year."

Bella appeared again, a string of tinsel draped round her neck, grinning even wider.

"He's *not* my young man."

"George Bristow might disagree," Kate said.

Anne placed a bauble near the middle of the tree and stepped back to admire her handiwork.

"He's such a nice young man, although it would be better if he came from money. When he brought you home that day, despite my concern for you, I couldn't help noticing the inferior quality of his suit. And he didn't have a cravat pin."

Kate put the back of her hand to her own forehead and pretended to swoon.

"Good gracious! No cravat pin? The police should arrest him so he can be flogged."

Anne scowled at Kate. "At least it sounds as though he has a decent position at the dock office. I suppose you could do worse, Bella."

Bella screwed up her face. "It's such a shame George couldn't make it for Christmas. He says Dickens definitely used his employer as the inspiration for Ebenezer Scrooge."

Victoria handed Bella the ornament she was holding.

"Never mind, dear, we'll be together for New Year. Now, Anne, Edward, why don't we leave these three to their labours and go into the parlour for a sherry."

It was dusk as George strolled from the East End docks towards his ma's house. He let himself in without a key – she never locked the door. After placing his old leather valise on the cracked lino in the small hallway, he hung his hat, smart overcoat and suit jacket on the pegs, masking the dirty, peeling wallpaper.

"Ma, I'm 'ome. Get the kettle on – I'm gasping."

His mother heaved herself off her seat with the aid of two sticks.

"Sit down, boy. I got a nice piece of beef from the butcher this morning for our supper. And a big, juicy chicken for our Christmas dinner."

"Smashing, Ma."

George kicked off his shoes, moved the newspaper that lay waiting for him and sat in the battered chair by the fire while his mother brewed the tea.

"P'rhaps after tea you can read the paper to me."

"Yes, I'll do that, Ma."

"Aww, you're a good son. Few lads would come home to spend Christmas with an old dodderer."

"I've got to slip out later – there's a consignment of fags and baccy comin' in."

"No booze this time?"

"No. The load that slipped off the back of a ship last week was the last of it for a few weeks, with it being this time of year. I got a good price for it, mind – could have sold it ten times over."

"It's a shame you've got to go out."

"A man's got to work. It should have come in last night, but the lousy weather delayed the ship."

"You'll be careful, won't you, George?"

"The beauty of doing the job tonight is that the watchman will probably be too pissed to notice what's goin' on. Besides, others do the risky stuff. I'm not daft. If all goes to plan, I'll only be out a couple of hours."

"Wi' your brains, posh accent, the way you talk like a toff an' all the learnin' that teacher gave you, you could have a steady job in an office."

"I've told you before, Ma. Don't mention that pervert to me. He only gave me those extra lessons because he had his own disgustin' motives. I showed him, though.

He won't touch up another innocent lad."

Mrs Bristow turned away. "Don't talk like that, George. It's not nice. Are you still goin' up north for New Year?"

"I'm catching the early train on the thirtieth."

Mrs Bristow pulled the woollen cosy over the pot then hobbled over to George, leaning heavily on one stick. The dark tea sloshed around the tin mug as she handed it to him.

"I've got big plans that'll change my life if they come off," George said. "Yours, too. I'm gonna buy you a nice little house. I hate that you have to live here. Still, it's a good base for me to meet up with my contacts at the docks and gives me a reason to be in the area if the peelers ever get it in their heads to question me."

"I don't mind it here. This is the house me an' yer dad moved into the day we were wed, when he got a job as a docker. Even when there weren't many ships in, he always had work – he were a grafter, yer dad."

"I'm a grafter, Ma. I work hard at what I do. But there's no way I'm working myself into an early grave like me dad did."

"You ain't getting involved with a woman up north, are yeh?"

"Don't interfere, Ma."

"George, love, it's not right. Not when you've a wife an' little 'un."

His eyes darkened. "Damn it, Ma! Don't start again. It's over. I should never have married her. You know I only visit for the kid's sake."

"But she's still legally yer wife. An' I'd love to see me granddaughter. I only got to see her an' Pearl that one time when Daphne was a baby."

"Drop it, Ma."

"But yer still married."

George slammed his mug on the floor, tea slopping onto the flags.

His mother flinched.

"Sorry, Ma." George jumped up. Passing the other stick to his mother, he helped her to her chair. "Come on, Ma, sit yerself down. Your back must be givin' you gyp."

"I'm not as daft as you think I am. I know about the other one – the widow you married. You could have got locked up for that. I hate to say it, but it were a good thing that she died."

"No one can prove nothin'. I didn't even use me proper name."

"I worry about you, George, son. It's a crime. A man can't have two wives. If yeh get caught, they'll sling you in jail."

George pushed his face close to his mother's.

"I could get slung in jail for smuggling an' peddling stolen goods as well, but if you want to get on in life, you have to take opportunities that come up." He squeezed her arthritic hand, causing her to wince. "I won't get caught, will I, Ma, as long as you keep yer trap shut."

"It's all right, George. I'll say nowt – you can trust me."

George smiled as he stroked her hand.

"Now, after tea, I'll slip down the boozer for a jug of ale an' we'll make a night of it once I'm back from my job. You know I love yeh, don't you, Ma?"

"Aye, son, I know."

Sean rubbed his hand over his cleanly shaven face. He looked better and the bruises and dark circles under his eyes had gone. More like his old self. He wished he felt better. A Christmas Eve party was the last thing he was in the mood for, but his family were being incredibly supportive and he didn't want to concern them, so he did his best to hide the multitude of emotions he experienced in a single day: guilt, anxiety, hopelessness, worthlessness, pessimism, frustration. Half the time he couldn't even define his feelings to himself, let alone explain them. His head was in turmoil. The worst part was the overwhelming sadness that was like a lead weight tied to his heart. Somehow, Kate appeared to pick up on his low moments and make him laugh. He felt better around her.

No matter how miserable he was, he wouldn't ruin Christmas for his family. He straightened his white bow tie and planted a smile on his face, ready to join the others who were gathered in the hall.

"What a gaggle of beauties," Sean said.

"Wow, you've gone through a transformation yourself," Kate said.

Bella whistled.

"Don't whistle, Bella, it's not ladylike. But you *do* look dashing, darling," his mother added.

Anne nodded. "Sean, we must have a few dances together. I'm in the market for a new husband and seeing me with you might make them jealous."

"I'm glad you all approve," Sean said, taking a bow.

Edward, Anne and his mother went ahead in the Daimler. Despite his built-up shoe and walking stick, Edward found icy surfaces perilous. Sean escorted Bella and Kate arm in arm to the Clarksons' home.

83

"That's a waltz and we've missed it," Bella said as they neared the house.

"I'm sure there will be another," Sean said.

Kate nudged Sean with her elbow.

"It's your lucky night – you can have lots of dances with me."

"Lucky for whom? For all I know, you could have two left feet," Sean replied.

"I'll leave you two to your discussion, but I'm telling you now, Sean, Kate is a wonderful dancer. I'd get in quick, because when the men of Faredene see her, she'll have to fight them off with a candelabra," Bella said as she handed her fur stole to the housemaid waiting by the door.

Kate and Sean entered the enormous drawing room together. Couples were already moving around the dance floor. Kate clenched his hand, nodding towards the preened ladies sitting on chairs that lined the walls, trying not to look desperate to be invited to dance.

"Come on, Sean. You're being eyed up like a gazelle in the sights of a pride of lions. Let's see if the Americans taught you how to polka."

"Shouldn't we find our hosts and say hello?"

"Probably, but Matthew won't mind and I expect Sophia will be surrounded by a group of admirers, so she'll be too busy to notice."

Bella was right – Kate was an excellent dancer, making him look inept by comparison. She was attractive and more intelligent than most he met. Perhaps that was why she was still single – maybe she intimidated some men. Even so, he was staggered some chap hadn't snapped up his stepsister.

"How come you never married?" he blurted.

Kate gaped. "Now, is that a question to be asking a woman?"

"Sorry, is it too personal?" he added.

"Sure, I'm messing with you. I'm not offended – being half Irish, I prefer men who are direct. Never found the right man, in answer to your question. What about you?"

"Never found the right woman."

"If we don't meet the right people in the next five years, we should marry each other."

"We couldn't do that. It would ruin our friendship and we might end up one of those couples who argue constantly," Sean said.

"That would never happen to us."

"How can you be so sure?"

"I'd have murdered you long before then."

"Wonderful! That is comforting."

"At least I was giving you the benefit of the doubt – that you're not like most dunderheads I meet. And I'm even prepared to marry you."

"Is that a back-handed compliment?"

"I rather think it is, but I reserve the right to change my mind if I can't get used to your half-English, half-American accent."

"Fair enough, but I'm only agreeing to the plan if I can get used to your half-Irish, half-English accent."

"Touché." Kate grinned as they whirled around the dance floor.

During the evening, Sean danced with family, Sophia Clarkson and several young women who were practically thrust at him by their mothers. Every time he found himself free, he made a point of dancing with Kate. He felt at ease with her. His mother was right – Kate had her father's quick mind. It was a shame that society dictated that most wealthy women did little with their lives, as he was sure Kate could achieve anything she set out to do.

"What would you like to do with the rest of your life, Kate?" he asked.

"Well, I've only got five years to plan our wedding."

Sean laughed. "Shall we get a drink?" he asked as the foxtrot came to an end.

"Grand. I'd better stay with you and protect you. Don't look now, but there's a woman over there who is sizing you up and I know she has a clatter of daughters she's trying to marry off."

Sean winked. "It's all right – I'll tell her I'm already engaged to you."

As they sipped champagne and chatted, Kate groaned when an incredibly attractive, slightly haughty-looking young woman approached.

"Sean?"

"Yvette?"

By far her best features were her ebony hair and brown eyes, which she'd evidently inherited from her mother, Sophia.

"How clever of you to recognise me."

"You look so similar to your mother."

"She's *much* older."

"Well, she's hardly likely to be the same age," Kate said.

Yvette did a double take in Kate's direction.

"Kate! I hardly recognised you. You look . . . well, nice. What *have* you done?"

"What do you mean, what have I done?"

"There's definitely something different about you."

Kate's face was deadly serious.

"Ah, I've been washing my face twice a day in caterpillar milk."

"Really? It's worked wonders. Where may I buy some?"

Sean coughed to mask his laughter.

Kate raised her eyebrows at him.

"I buy it from Harrods."

"I'll get Mama to order some." Yvette turned back to Sean, almost blocking out Kate. "I have the next dance free, if you'd care to take a turn?"

"Is that alright with you, Kate?"

"Go ahead – my feet are destroyed."

Yvette kept him on the floor for three dances until Sean said, "I'm afraid I must leave you now. We don't want people talking about our dancing together too often – I wouldn't want to harm your reputation."

"It might have enhanced it. All the mothers are talking about you."

"Why?"

Yvette giggled. "They're describing you as the gorgeous rich American who is now the most eligible man in Faredene."

He was sure they'd change their minds if they knew the truth about his financial position.

"Sadly, three dances without a rest is my limit. I must be getting old."

"Shall I come with you to get some refreshments?"

Sean nodded towards a pimply youth.

"I believe that young man would like the next dance with you."

"Perhaps we can take a turn later. I expect you think that's terribly forward of me. Don't tell Mama."

"It will be our secret," he said, retreating.

He stopped and conversed with several guests who were milling around Matthew and Sophia's drawing room as he manoeuvred his way towards the exit. As he finally reached the hallway, his mother tapped him on the shoulder with her fan.

"Sean, dear, I'm glad you're out here. We oldies are going to slip away now. I realise it doesn't matter the same for young people, but I want to go to midnight Mass. Stokes will return for you all at two."

"We'll walk – it's only a few streets."

"It's far too cold."

"Are you sure you don't want me to come to church with you?"

"That would be lovely, but I'd prefer you to chaperone Bella. I sometimes believe she's never looked in a mirror. She has no clue how attractive she is. There was a boy earlier practically salivating over her and she was oblivious."

"Where's Kate?"

"Where she has been all evening – on the dance floor. It's good to see her enjoying herself."

Anne buttoned up her coat as she approached.

"Come along, Victoria. We don't want to be stuck at the back of the church and I've asked Owain to sit with us. I'm surprised Matthew agreed to have this party tonight, but Sophia generally gets her way."

"Now now, Anne, it's Christmas Eve – remember, goodwill to all men," his mother said.

Edward, who was stooping noticeably, raised his eyebrows at Sean, grinning, and mouthed over his shoulder *Save me* as the three made their way towards the door.

Sean decided he needed a break – a quiet corner where

he could give his face a rest. The effort it took to keep a false smile all night while people probed him about his sudden return from America was staggering.

He took a bottle of champagne off the table where dozens of bottles stood waiting to be served and made his way through the dining room. Eyeing the buffet of Beluga caviar, foie gras, venison, dressed salmon and clove-studded hams all sharing a table with an assortment of salads and seafood, he paused, wondering if he should get something. He hadn't eaten, instead indulging in several glasses of champagne, and the combination was having an adverse effect. Deciding against eating, he wandered into the conservatory. It was all clear – no canoodling couples.

The warmth and relative quiet were inviting. He sat, popped the cork then drank deeply from the bottle. If his mother could see him now, she'd be annoyed – it was a good thing she'd left. On the whole, he'd enjoyed the party more than he'd expected – apart from the two dances he'd suffered with Sophia. He'd found her flirtatious manner unbecoming and only asked her to dance the second time because it would have looked rude not to when she'd made it obvious that she wanted to dance with him.

"This is one of my favourite tunes, Sean. *Surely* you will not allow your hostess to miss out?" she'd said.

The way she'd looked at him put him in mind of Claude whenever he saw a young woman he'd wanted to seduce – and there had been dozens over the years. Perhaps that was the way with overly attractive people . . . they saw everyone as a conquest.

It was hardly surprising Sean had begun an affair with

89

a married woman when the man he looked up to most had regarded monogamy as something only for the lower classes. Not that Sean blamed Claude for the choices he himself had made. If he was going to turn his life around now, he had to accept responsibility for everything. He sat drinking, his mind wandering over his life, until he lost track of time and almost nodded off.

"You can't hide out here! It's incredibly rude."

He jumped at the sound of a southern drawl beside him.

"Sophia."

"Did I startle you?"

"Yes, but I'm sorry, I shouldn't be out here. I just needed a few moments' quiet."

"Then I shall join you."

The stunning woman in a low-cut purple velvet gown perched next to him on the cane sofa, gazing at him. He was grateful that the buzz of conversation and music from the adjacent rooms dulled the silence. Why did she make him so damned awkward?

Sophia leaned towards him. "You appear uncomfortable around me. Do you hate me because of what Claude did?"

"No, of course not."

Sophia inched closer.

"I am sorry for your financial loss. I am deeply ashamed of my brother. If anyone else had accused him, I would not have believed them."

"I could hardly believe it myself."

"He has no head for business – but *forgery*! That is unforgivable. Even though I didn't own the export business, our father built it from nothing and I am appalled Claude has lost it. I have written to tell him how

EDGE OF DESPAIR

disappointed I am. Claude has sullied our family name, but how can I possibly do anything when I am stuck here so far away?" Sophia continued talking about how unhappy she was living in England. Then with eyes downcast, in a soft voice, she asked, "Sean, tell me about my father – how he passed away. Claude has told me nothing."

Sean decided no good would come from letting her know how he'd suffered.

"Before he took ill, I'd never known him to be happier. His death was tragic but mercifully quick. I loved him like a father."

"I was furious with Matthew that I couldn't be there to nurse my father or be with him when he died." She paused, observing Sean before continuing. "My being here has cost me a great deal."

"Have you and Matthew considered taking a trip home?"

She gave a derisory laugh. "Leave his precious mill? He is there seven days a week, even when it is shut on a Sunday. He brought us all here and then neglected us. I raised Yvette and mourned my son alone in a country I dislike."

Her resentment of Matthew was obvious. Sean had always liked Matthew and didn't want to get caught up in their squabbles. Seeing no reason to give Sophia the excuse to use any response he might make against Matthew, he remained silent.

"You are a remarkably handsome man."

"Er, um, thank you."

"You're blushing – how adorable."

"It's, er, it's warm in here."

"There is something incredibly alluring about you. All of the ladies have noticed, including my daughter. You

91

have caused quite a stir. They are wondering who will capture you with their charms."

"If they are, it's only because they don't know how frightfully boring I am."

"I doubt that. Do you find me beautiful? Most men do."

"Er, I don't know."

She laughed softly. "That isn't very gallant of you."

"Sorry, yes, of course you're beautiful," he waffled.

"Good, because I get extremely lonely."

"Pardon?"

"I believe you understand exactly what I mean. Matthew dedicates every waking hour to that damned mill."

"I'm sure I can be of use to him. I can help with the paperwork and I'm good with my hands."

Sophia took his hands between her gloved ones and examined them.

"They *are* powerful hands. I am pleased to hear you are good with them."

Sean glanced away uneasily as she ran her tongue along her full lips.

"Don't be bashful. You're not a child."

He jerked back, snatching his hand away. Was she trying to seduce him? Surely not. He remembered that shortly after he'd arrived in New Orleans, there were rumours Sophia was having an affair with the owner of a neighbouring plantation. Consequently, her father had insisted that she join her husband in England. It was clear she hadn't changed.

"I-I . . ." He struggled to find the words.

"You admitted you find me attractive."

"Yes, but I don't see how that's relevant."

"You were servicing the needs of a married woman in New Orleans for years, I believe."

"I was in love. Her husband was a cripple. He condoned our relationship. Matthew's my friend and I'll be working with him every day. I'd never betray him in that way."

"I intend to leave Matthew and return to America once Yvette marries. Your company may be a pleasant way to pass the time."

"No. No. I'm sorry – that will never happen."

"There is no need to look so affronted. I suspect you will change your mind. When the time comes, you know where to find me, but don't leave it too long."

With that, she swept from the room.

Chapter 8

Sean took another large swig from the bottle. He wished to God Sophia hadn't said those things to him or confided that she intended to leave Matthew. He should go back to the party, but seeing Sophia or Matthew would be incredibly uncomfortable. No, he'd stay here. Jesus! Complications with his boss' wife was the last thing he needed.

By the time he'd emptied the bottle of champagne, his head was swimming. It occurred to him he'd been absent from the party for a long time and people would wonder where he was. He stood too quickly and wobbled, grasping at an enormous Kentia palm, knocking it over. Getting unsteadily to his hands and knees, he tried to scoop the soil back into the brass pot.

"There you are! What are you up to?"

Sean looked up.

"Yvette . . . I'm afraid I'm on the wrong sh-side of a few glashhes of champagne. And I've knocked over a plant – hic."

"I can see that for myself. Your sisters have already gone home. Mama told them there was no need to send the car back for you and that you could stay over in one of the guest-rooms."

"That was kind. F-fank your parents for me, but I'll go home."

There was no way he wanted to stay over, given how Sophia had behaved.

Yvette took his hand and helped him up, covering her hand in soil as well. The room was still whirling and he swayed once more, almost stumbling against her.

"Perhaps you should wait here a moment. You wouldn't want Papa or any of his guests seeing you in this state. I will be right back."

He thanked her, plonking back down on the sofa. Why did he keep drinking to excess? He knew he couldn't hold his drink.

A few minutes later, Yvette returned and put his arm around her neck so she could support him as she led him out through the conservatory door into the garden. The cold air hit with a blast, heightening his intoxication.

"Why are we going this-s-s way? Where are we going?"

"Trust me. I told you – it wouldn't be a good idea for Papa to see you in this state."

"But Matthew enjoys a drink."

"Only what he can handle. Papa never loses control. Trust me, Sean, I am trying to help you. Papa would not be pleased if he knew how drunk you are at a party where many of the guests are his business associates."

"Thanks, Yvetteee," he slurred. "Ha! Yvetteee. Oh, I'm such a twit. I'm shooow slorry . . . err, sorry, and you're sooo nice."

Yvette felt warm as she pressed against him. They nearly fell several times and she giggled. He liked the sound.

They entered the house by the back door and went up

the narrow rear staircase. Reeling, he leaned on Yvette, almost toppling them both.

"I'm shorry. You're kind. Most people aren't kind – they're mean. They throoow you away like rubbish."

"I wouldn't treat you that way, Sean. We're friends."

"Are we? We only met tonight."

"Yes, I'm your new best friend."

As they wobbled along the landing, a door opened at the end of the corridor and the butler emerged.

"I hope the green room will be to your guest's satisfaction, Miss Yvette."

"Thank you. Please don't mention anything to Mama and Papa. They won't approve that he got drunk."

"Very good, miss."

Yvette stopped at the door and glanced over her shoulder, hovering until the butler walked down the corridor and descended the stairs.

Sean's head was fuzzy, but he'd picked up on what she'd said to the butler.

"I f-fought your parents said I could shlop, schtop over?"

"They won't mind at all. You will be better off staying, given how drunk you are. Papa would never have let you walk home and he will be annoyed if he has to wake the chauffeur at this hour to take you a few streets."

"I weeelly didn't fink Matthew had a problem with people . . . taking a drink or two. Hic."

"You've not just taken a drink – you have bathed in it. Go to bed, Sean. It is late and you aren't in a fit state to do anything else."

Sean rubbed his face. She was right – he should go to sleep. A fire was roaring in the grate, taking the chill off the room. After putting his pocket watch on the side, he undressed, dropping his clothes in a heap, and climbed into bed naked, without turning off the lamp, falling asleep instantly.

In his dreams he was back in New Orleans, enjoying life. A powerful aroma of exotic perfume wafted around him. Gentle fingers stroked his face.

"My darling," he murmured.

There was a soft giggle.

Startled, he sat up, the covers falling, revealing his bare chest.

"Sophia!"

She was leaning so close to him that her breath was hot on his face.

"I hope I am far more appealing to you than Mama."

"Yvette?"

"Why did you assume it was my mother? Has she been flirting again? I should have known she would want to get her talons into you. Poor Papa."

Her long ebony hair cascaded over her shoulders. Not as sexy as Sophia, but younger, less intimidating.

"You shouldn't be here. What would your parents say?"

"Their room is on the other side of the house. That is why I asked our butler to prepare *this* one for you." She giggled again.

"Yvette, you should leave."

Without a word, she slipped her ivory dressing gown off her shoulders, revealing a matching nightgown. He felt a sudden urge to reach out and run his fingers down her bare olive-skinned arms . . . to kiss her . . . but he stopped himself – he had enough problems.

"What's wrong? Surely you aren't shy."

"No, I don't think this is a good idea. Your father will be furious."

"As Papa will be asleep, he will never find out."

"Yvette, I can't possibly take advantage of you. It's not right."

"You're not taking advantage of me – I came to you, remember? Do you think you could love me?"

"We're almost strangers." God, he wished he could stop his head from throbbing.

"We get along, do we not?"

"Yes, but . . . We only met tonight. You must have plenty of suitors. Surely you want to save yourself for one of them."

"There was someone, but that ended."

"What happened?"

"Sean Kavanagh, it isn't appropriate to ask a lady that." She tapped his hand.

"I'm sorry."

Yvette giggled. "You silly goose. I am teasing you. That *is* an enormous bed. Would you like some company?"

"What?"

"Come on, Sean. Everyone is asleep. Think of it as a Christmas present."

She stroked his chest, tracing the shape of his muscles. Her eyes glistened mischievously. It had been ages since he'd been with a woman.

"Yvette, this is wrong."

"Don't you like me?" She moved her hand down the bed. "Even through the covers, I can tell you find me attractive."

For how long was a man meant to resist such temptation? And for the second time this evening.

98

"Of course I do. You're lovely."

"Then you are a lucky man."

She took his hand, placing it inside her nightgown so it cupped her bare breast. He heard himself groan. Leaning forwards, she kissed him. Her lips were soft. He wanted her badly . . .

As memories of the night before drifted into Sean's mind, he stretched out his arm and leg to the space next to him. Thank God! There was no one there. Had it been a wonderful erotic dream?

He opened his eyes, taking in the unfamiliar bedroom. Then realisation dawned. It *had* happened. He'd bedded Matthew's daughter! Or, more to the point, she'd seduced him.

What a mess. The women in Matthew's family were dangerous. What the hell had he been thinking? That was the problem, he acknowledged. He hadn't been thinking – at least not with his head.

The lamp had gone out, so he squinted in the darkness, grasping his pocket watch. It was six thirty Christmas morning. He needed to get home before his mother got up. That way, there was a chance she wouldn't discover he'd stayed out.

He tentatively put his feet on the floor and a wave of nausea swelled within him. He gulped then slumped back down for a moment, willing his stomach to settle.

As fast as his queasiness would allow, he dressed before creeping out of the room and down the long corridor, cringing as a floorboard creaked. He hoped Matthew was ignorant to the fact that he'd stayed over. If he was aware, then his secretive departure would look rude. Although, when compared with ploughing his daughter, it paled into insignificance.

In the hallway, several staff were already clearing the debris of the party the night before. The butler bade him good morning.

"Other than Yvette, are any family members aware I stayed over?"

"No, sir. Only the young lady knows."

Sean pushed his hand in his pocket, pulled out his wallet and removed a pound note.

"Perhaps that's for the best."

The butler discreetly pocketed the note.

"If you say so, sir. I'll ensure none of the staff members mention it."

Sean rushed out of the front door, grasping the railings as his foot slipped on the icy steps. He tentatively made the short walk home, grateful the streets were quiet – it wouldn't do for him to be seen looking so dishevelled in last night's clothing. As he reached the door, he cursed himself for not taking a key. He didn't want to knock and peered through the window to the side of the door. To his relief, Taylor was crossing the hallway. Sean tapped on the window.

"Would you mind keeping it to yourself that I've been out all night?" he asked as Taylor, not looking at all surprised to see him, stood back to let him in.

"Certainly, sir. Perhaps if the family believed you returned shortly after the young ladies, the mistress might worry less."

"I'm sorry to put you in this position."

Taylor nodded, his eyes ranging over Sean's crumpled clothes and bow tie hanging askew.

"Should I send up some Epsom salts, sir?"

"Much appreciated."

Sean sighed with relief when he made it to his bedroom without being seen by anyone else. He got undressed and climbed back in bed, hoping to get some more sleep. What the hell had he done? He'd realised during the act that he hadn't been the first man Yvette had been with, but they barely knew each other.

Kate was disappointed when Sean missed breakfast, but Christmas lunch was unavoidable. She sat opposite him, stealing glances, hoping that the others wouldn't notice. He nearly always had a sadness hanging over him. Who could blame him? Today, there was something else, too. He appeared distracted, worried about something. Perhaps it was simply all the questions he'd been asked last night by the local gossip-mongers. That was enough to get anyone down.

She was definitely falling for Sean. She'd never come close to this feeling before. It was almost as if she'd been waiting for him. Get away with yourself, having those thoughts, woman! She sounded pathetic even in her own head. But they got on so well and last night when they'd danced together, she'd felt a connection between them.

Bella pointed her fork at Sean.

"So, what time did you sneak in last night? Kate and I looked for you when we were leaving, but you were nowhere to be seen. I hope you weren't lurking in a dark corner with someone's daughter."

Sean gulped. "Er. Nothing overly exciting, I'm afraid. I nodded off in the conservatory and walked home when I woke."

"Honestly, sleeping at a party! Are you ninety?" Kate laughed. "Or was that your way of escaping Sophia?"

"Why would I need to escape her?"

"Because you looked horrified when she touched your face after you'd danced with her."

"She touched your face! Why Matthew puts up with that man-eater, I'll never understand," Victoria said.

"I didn't realise you disapproved of her," Sean replied, running his finger along the rim of his wine glass.

"It's not something a mother puts in her letters to her son, but she flirts outrageously with every man she encounters, doesn't she, *Edward*?"

"Victoria, surely you're not going to drag up what happened at that party all those years ago?" asked Edward.

"I *certainly* am. When Sophia first moved over here, I held a party for her, to introduce her to society and welcome her to Faredene. You can't have failed to notice how beautiful she is. A woman like her doesn't need to try to attract men. However, she spent the entire evening flirting with Edward."

Edward's shoulders shook as he laughed.

"You can tell from your mother's tone, Sean, that I made a fatal error. I hadn't met her before and made the mistake of saying to your mother that Sophia was attractive."

"Your mouth dropped open when she walked in – and you encouraged her flirting."

Edward held up his hands in surrender.

"Sean, I was nice to the foolish woman because your mother said she wanted Sophia to settle here and not persuade Matthew to return to America. Despite years of devotion, your mother still finds it hard to accept that she has always been the *only* woman for me."

"Sure now, Father. It's a good job I'm not fierce affronted on *my* mother's behalf," Kate said.

Her father paled. "Oh, my darling. I am so sorry, Kate," Edward said.

Kate spluttered. "Your face, Father! It's a picture. I was only joking."

Sean had laughed along with everyone else, but Kate could tell he was still distracted – there was something bothering him. Was it Sophia? The thought of Sophia flirting with him irritated her. That was putting it mildly – it made her want to book Sophia on the next ship back to New Orleans.

It was only later, as he opened her gift, that his eyes brightened and his laughter erupted.

"Hair tonic?" Sean said, his head cocked to one side.

Kate moved closer.

"Ah, here, look . . . it says on the label that it restores fifty per cent hair loss, so I got you two bottles."

His hand went to his hair.

"You're giving me a complex."

Kate ruffled his hair.

"Sure, I'm only teasing – your hair is grand."

Despite longing to place her lips on his, she reluctantly removed her hand and fled back to the sofa, sure her cheeks were reddening.

"Your present next, Bella," Kate said, hoping to distract everyone.

Goodness! He'd turned her into an adolescent girl, she thought.

Later that night, Kate went into Bella's room. She needed to confide in someone or she'd burst. Bella, wearing a lace-edged cotton nightgown, was brushing her hair.

"I'm almost finished. I'm at ninety-seven . . . Kate? Is something wrong?"

"No. Do your last three brushes – not that your hair needs it. I just fancied the craic. It's been a lovely few days, hasn't it?"

"Yes. Did you see Aunt Anne dancing with Doctor Farrell last night? Then today she asked me if I'd ever noticed the green flecks in his hazel eyes!"

"Poor Owain."

"Did it upset you seeing Garrett and his wife?"

"Ah, not at all now. I'm completely over him. In fact, I realise now I didn't have any feelings for him at all. I'm only glad I didn't make a holy show of myself."

"Really?"

"Sure. Can you keep a secret?"

Bella swivelled round on her stool, her hairbrush poised. "You know I can."

"I've my eye on someone special."

"Tell me. Come on – I want all the details. You can't keep it to yourself, not now you've hinted."

"See if you can guess. He's tall, dark, gorgeous, a little insecure and he makes me laugh."

Bella leaned closer.

"I've got no idea."

"Surely you must."

"No, honestly, I've not got a clue . . . Oh my giddy aunt. It's Sean!"

"Shh. Not so loud. If your mother hears, she'll faint. Are you shocked? Because I am."

"Yes . . . well, not really. I've noticed the way you look at him sometimes."

"Clever little you. He's not noticed. Nor anyone else."

"Gosh."

"It started on the first day I met him. He stood there with that lopsided grin on his face and even with that awful beard, I loved the cut of him. Ah, he's grand."

"That's love at first sight, then – and you said it couldn't happen."

"What can I say? Sure, I'm a hypocrite. I wasn't certain until we danced. I looked into those big brown eyes of his as we joked about marriage and thought, I could die contented as I long as I'm looking at this man."

"Crikey! You have got it bad."

"Not a word now. I need to make sure he sees me as more than a stepsister, which might prove a challenge, especially if he thinks I resemble the back end of a cow."

"Don't be daft. Why would he think that?"

"He might. I'm not beautiful."

"Well, I think you are. And in case you haven't realised, this is my best impersonation of Mother's don't-argue-with-me face," Bella said, pointing to her own face.

꒰꒱

Chapter 9

In some ways, Sean wished he could simply curl up in bed with a bottle of brandy, but tonight, Charles Brakenridge, his childhood friend, had invited him to dine at The Jubilee gentlemen's club. As he entered the drawing room, his mother laid down her embroidery.

"Remember, darling, you've nothing to feel inferior about. What happened with Claude was *not* your fault. I'm incredibly proud of the way you're doing your best to move on from what happened."

"Thank you. I'm looking forward to seeing Charles."

"Edward tells me the food is excellent at The Jubilee."

"I thought you didn't approve of gentlemen's clubs," Sean replied with a slow smile.

"It's preposterous not allowing ladies in, but they're a necessary evil for men in business. If you want to make connections, they're the places to frequent. Much the same as the Women's Guild."

"I promise to protest if I hear any talk about denying women the vote." Sean smirked, knowing this was something that annoyed his mother.

Kate looked up from the book she was reading.

"I should think so. I'm better educated than many men. Your mother's a successful businesswoman who owns several properties, yet she has no right to vote on who governs our country. It's men trying to keep us in our place. They expect us to be grateful for the few rights they *have* allowed us."

Sean's eyebrows rose as he donned his gloves.

"Hold on, hold on. I support women's right to vote. You two can stop looking at me as if I'm the enemy." He glowered playfully at Bella and Kate.

"Sorry, Sean. I didn't mean to be in your ear. I'm sure you're a progressive man. Don't mind me – I'm a tyrant," Kate said.

She was incredibly attractive when she smiled, he thought.

Bella jumped up from the piano stool where she'd been sitting and came to Sean's side.

"I'm strictly an armchair supporter of the cause these days. But thanks, Sean, you're a brick." She tapped the side of his head. "Yes, definitely solid."

"Watch it, missy, or I might change my mind and start an anti-suffrage movement in the town." He cuffed her playfully. "Edward, what about you? Surely you'll stand by me."

Edward put his hands up in submission.

"I'm not stupid. I know my ladies – they're terrifying when they get riled."

"Edward's right. Now, get yourself off. Enjoy yourself and celebrate being home, but don't overindulge."

His mother turned him round and ushered him towards the drawing room door, reminding him of when he was dawdling as a child.

"Stokes will pick you up at ten thirty. Don't drink too much." She kissed him goodbye, then as he was about to leave, she pulled him back. "But have a good time, because I love you and want you to be happy."

Sean scratched his head, pretending to look confused.

"So let me get this right, Mother. I'm to enjoy myself but not too much, is that about the size of it?"

His mother laughed.

"You know full well what I'm trying to say. Now scoot before I send you to bed with no supper."

Sean took his leave to the sound of Bella teasing their mother about treating him as though he were five.

Once the formalities of Sean signing in as a visitor to The Jubilee Club were over, the short, bespectacled manager took him to meet Charles, explaining to the potential new member about the club en route. In the reading room, plumes of tobacco smoke rose from many of the Chesterfield chairs situated around the mahogany-panelled room. Side tables were neatly piled with newspapers and a portly man warmed his buttocks by the roaring fire while several others were reading or engaged in quiet conversation.

"Naturally, ladies are not permitted in the public areas – except to clean when no gentlemen are around. And of course, *they* use the rear entrance," the manager ended.

"Naturally." Sean nodded. No wonder his mother didn't like Edward coming here.

Despite the years, Sean recognised his old friend from his blond hair and similarity to his father, James. Charles stood, the skin around his blue eyes crinkling as he grasped Sean's hand, clapping him on the back with the other.

"Sean, it's good to see you again."

"It's good to see you, too, buddy."

As Sean took a seat next to Charles, a tall red-headed young waiter appeared beside them.

"A large drink for my friend, please, Max. What will it be, Sean?"

Moments later, the waiter returned and placed a brandy down. Sean had already spoken to Charles on the telephone and told him about the events resulting in his homecoming. He was glad he'd done so, as he was in no mood to go over it now.

"I am pleased you are home. I am sorry it is under difficult circumstances, but you will soon be back on your feet, I don't doubt." Charles raised his glass.

"Thank you."

"You should join the club. There is always someone to have a game of cards with. Though I would avoid playing Garrett Ackerley, if I were you. That man has dashed too much good luck, if you get my drift. I will put your name forwards."

"Er, thanks, I'd appreciate that."

It was clear Charles was still in the enviable position Sean had been most of his life before his downfall, as it hadn't occurred to him that Sean might not have the money to join. Sean didn't know how much membership cost, but it was immaterial – until he was working, he couldn't afford the fees no matter what they were.

"You mentioned on the telephone your father is difficult to live with," Sean said.

"Cantankerous is the word for him. He gets frustrated because his mind isn't as sharp any more and he isn't so able-bodied. He can walk, but if it's any distance, he uses a wheelchair. Mind you, living with him now is a damn sight better than when I was younger."

"Can't you find him a nurse?"

"It would be difficult to find one who could put up with him, given how he is with women. Besides, he has his manservant, Charnock."

"And does he manage him? Hang on, isn't Charnock the name of the men who attacked Edward, Kitty and Teddy?" Sean asked.

"Younger brother. I was for giving him the push when I came home, but he shouldn't have to take the blame for what they did. Besides, he has been with Father for years and took care of all of his personal care after the accident. Few men would do that."

"No, I suppose not." Sean grimaced.

"I don't think he is as bad as his brothers."

"By the sounds of it, they were evil bastards. All the same, I don't think I'll mention it to my mother. She never got over what happened."

"Thank you. I know your mother thinks my father was involved. Even my mother thinks he was capable of murder. He doesn't remember his accident. Or anything that happened in the weeks beforehand, for that matter."

"Do you believe him?"

"Yes. He's not the man he was. Mind you, Charnock gives me the creeps and my father is forever sending him to fetch women back to the house. How they can go with him is beyond me. Father is not a pretty sight. I am not even certain everything works as it should, because he has alluded to having women who do all the work." Charles shuddered.

Sean grinned. "We all enjoy energetic women."

Charles laughed. "I can't say I have had that much experience of them. Still, the women keep Father happy. He is disgruntled at the moment, though, because I am refusing to give him access to the fortune my grandfather on my mother's side left me."

"Why didn't your grandfather leave it to your mother?"

110

"He cut her out of his will because she left my father. I offered her the money, but she refused as Madeleine has more than enough for their needs."

"I thought your father was loaded?"

"Most of his money came from prostitution and opium dens in Manchester and Liverpool. I didn't know about it until recently, but from what I have been told, when he was injured, like-minded criminals swooped in and took over his businesses."

"It's probably best you didn't know about it."

"I have had an enquiry to buy the Hall – an American oil tycoon, apparently. I told them the Hall needs a lot of work, but the chap doesn't even want to see the place. Asked us to name our price. Father isn't keen on the idea."

Sean explained who he suspected the oil tycoon might be. Charles didn't know about Harry's involvement in his father's injuries and even though as a boy Charles had hated his father, Sean felt it prudent not to enlighten him. He'd returned to live with him, so he must care for him a little.

"Are you definitely selling, then?"

"I need my father's permission, of course – it is in his name. I can't wait to get rid of the place. It doesn't hold many pleasant memories for me."

Sean took a sip of his drink.

"So, why did you come back? When we were at school, you couldn't stand it when he was around."

"He is my father when all is said and done. Once I found out that my mother was in love with another woman most of her life, I had a modicum of sympathy for him, but I still don't condone his treatment of her or me."

"That doesn't explain why you're back."

"I am not sure I understand myself. My mother told me some things about his childhood. His father used to hit him with his riding crop. And he was even forced to rape a maid when he was fourteen."

"Jesus!"

Charles rubbed his chin. "At first after his accident, I wished he had died. But as the years went on, I realised I wanted to get to know him better. Try to understand why he treated me like he had. I suppose I didn't want him to die without my giving him a chance to show me he wasn't all bad. Besides, I am not a child any more, so he can't lash out at me."

Sean nodded. Despite loving his own mother greatly, Sean still wondered about his natural parents – what they were like, if they were still alive, but especially why they'd left him.

"I wouldn't tell your father the buyer used to work for him. I expect that would make him even less likely to agree to sell."

"You are right. He will find out eventually, but it will be too late then."

"He may refuse to sell either way."

"I doubt it. If I don't keep paying the bills, he can't afford the upkeep."

"Will you leave Faredene when the Hall is sold?"

"No. If Father moves away, that is up to him, but I am staying."

"I'm glad you got away from him when you did – at least for a while."

"So am I. My confidence certainly grew while I was in Italy, but it's too hot over there for my liking."

"So, we're both home for good, then. I start at the mill

next week. Between you and me, I'm not sure I'll take to it."

"I have got no experience at anything, but I am sick to death of sitting here every day. If you want investment and a partner to start a business, I hope you will consider me."

"Are you serious?"

"I can't think of a better way to spend my time or money, so why not?"

"Isn't your money tied up?"

"A good deal of it is in stocks, but there is still a significant amount I've not invested yet."

"How come?"

"I have recently sold off my grandfather's coal mines – it is where he made his fortune. Even though I realise I live off the money he made from them, I don't want to be involved long term in a business that requires men to spend most of their lives underground."

"Charles, I'm incredibly flattered that you're willing to back me, but I've committed to the mill now. I'll definitely consider your offer, though."

"Good. In the meantime, I will make sure I don't tie the money up in any long-term investments."

As they clinked their crystal glasses, they were both grinning. Suddenly, they jolted at the crash of breaking glass coming from a room behind the bar, disrupting the quiet hum of the reading room. The young lad who had served Sean came out of the back and scurried past. Most of the members were oblivious, having resumed their conversations or returned to reading their newspapers. He reappeared a few moments later with a mop and bucket, blushing furiously.

Sean nodded in the lad's general direction as he spoke to Charles.

"I expect someone will get it in the neck for whatever has happened," he said.

"I hope it's not Max. He is a bright lad – and honest. I lost my wallet one night and he returned it. Wouldn't take a penny for his trouble," Charles said before suggesting that they dine.

During their meal of roast mutton with all the trimmings, Sean wondered whether or not he should broach a delicate subject, knowing how Charles had married in his early twenties and that his wife had died less than two years later during childbirth, taking their daughter with her.

As he devoured his jam roly-poly and hot custard, he ventured, "Can I ask, Charles, why you never married again?"

"I haven't met anyone who can hold a candle to my wife. But I would like to meet someone, given the opportunity. What about you? You explained on the telephone that your affair didn't end as you had hoped. Has it put you off women for a while?"

Sean smirked. "I was a numbskull. When we met, I was twenty and thinking of getting myself a wife. We were both English and in a strange country. We hit it off immediately and I became her lover. Affairs are wrong, I realise that, but in my defence, I thought she loved me. Turns out she only wanted me for my body. When I lost everything, she didn't even consider me fit to be her lover." Sean shrugged. "The rest, as they say, my friend, is history."

Charles grinned. "Was there nobody else?"

"No. Claude took me to meet some obliging ladies in Storyville – the red-light district – on my sixteenth birthday, so I could dip my wick."

Charles spluttered, droplets of custard spraying as he laughed.

"Most were beautiful and I learned a lot. Surely you must have sampled some Italian ladies of pleasure?" Sean asked.

"No, I never did. I was too afraid of catching something. Weren't you?"

"Thankfully, they were clean."

"I am glad to hear it. Perhaps you can take advantage of the services of the ladies they bring in here. I am surprised the wives don't realise what some of their husbands get up to when they spend the night at the club."

"No chance! I'm not paying for it at my age. Speaking of which, I know I shouldn't talk about it, but I can trust you to keep it to yourself," Sean said, then hesitated, wondering if he should keep quiet.

"Don't stop now, just when it sounds interesting."

"That Christmas party at Matthew's house – I got drunk and stayed over. Matthew and Sophia's daughter, Yvette, came to my room."

"Blimey, old chap. You take chances. Matthew will kill you if he finds out. Let's hope she's not up the duff."

"Don't even joke about that. It was a moment of madness on my part. I didn't invite her. But I didn't kick her out, either." Sean laughed nervously.

"Well, we had both better get married soon before we go to seed. My hair is already receding." He ran his hand over his head. "Either that or some girl's father will shoot one of us."

Sean had missed his friend more than he'd realised and was pleased how quickly their years of separation had disappeared. Despite living with his father again,

Charles appeared relaxed. No trace of his childhood stammer, either, which had always been worse when he'd been nervous or upset.

Having overindulged in wine and brandy, Sean was slightly worse for wear but refused Charles' offer of a lift and stood shivering in the doorway, waiting for his mother's chauffeur to arrive. A harsh voice shouting to the side of the building caught his attention.

"You'll get no reference from here. Now clear off."

"But you stopped my pay for something I didn't do. It isn't right."

"I said get away before I set the peelers on you for causing a disturbance."

"I did nothing. It's unfair and you know it."

The voice sounded close to tears. A door slammed and seconds later, Max came round the corner, wiping his eyes as he passed the doorway.

Sean stepped forwards.

"Max, isn't it? Are you all right?"

"Sorry, sir, I didn't see you there. Yes, it's Uriah Maxwell. But everyone calls me Max."

"What's wrong, Max?"

The lad glanced warily over his shoulder as though checking no one was around.

"We're not allowed to talk about anything that happens at the club."

"Is it something to do with the crash we heard earlier?"

"Aye. The head barman blamed me, but it wasn't me at all."

"What happened?"

"I shouldn't say, but I suppose I've got nothing to lose now he's given me the push. The waiter who was in the

116

restaurant tonight – short lad with a pencil moustache – did you see him?"

"Yes, I did."

Sean remembered the youth well, as he'd almost spilt vegetable soup in his lap during dinner.

"Well, he knocked two crates of wine off the side. Broke every bottle. Some of them were good years – the decent stuff. He was panicking as the master of the reading room had already told him he was on his last warning, so the head waiter blamed me for it instead."

"Why would he do that?"

"Because he's in thick with the waiter's mam, if you take my meaning. Stays at her place most nights."

"But didn't you tell the manager it wasn't your fault?"

"I tried, but I've not been here that long and the head waiter has worked here ten years, so it was their word against mine."

"What will you do now?"

"Look for something else. It won't be easy without a reference, but I'll find something. I'll take whatever I can get."

"Is there plenty of work around?"

"No, but I need to find something quick, because my rent's due and they haven't paid me for this week to help cover the cost of the breakages. I've got a few bob saved, but I don't want to break into that." Max sniffed, looking up at the inky sky.

Sean asked how old he was and where he lived. Max explained he was eighteen and was now renting a room in Thurston Row.

"Would you be interested in an interview for a job as footman?"

117

"Thanks for thinking of me. I'm tall enough to be one, but most mistresses won't entertain the idea of a footman with red hair."

"You don't need to worry about such nonsense. My mother isn't conventional and I know the footman is leaving in the new year."

"Aww, sir, I'd snatch your hand off, but I've no experience of working in a house. Before the club, I worked at a small hotel. Started as a bellboy then worked my way up to head waiter. I came here from Liverpool after Gran died because I've no other family and the job at the club seemed a chance to progress. I had hoped I might be a master of the reading room one day – I've got ambitions."

"There are still opportunities working in a house. I can't make any promises, but if you get the job, I'm sure the butler will train you."

The lad stared at Sean for a moment.

"I can't believe my luck. Thank you for the chance, sir. Where do you want me to come for the interview?"

Sean gave the lad the address and arranged for him to see his mother at nine the following day.

⠉⠴⠪⠪

Chapter 10

Victoria shoved her pearl-capped hatpin in and carried her gloves as she hurried out of the house and into the waiting motor car.

She pushed open the door to Centenary House a short while later.

"Morning, Milly. Sorry I'm late."

"You can come an' go as you please," Milly said, leaning on the display cabinet.

Victoria clasped Milly's hands.

"Your hands look better."

"Our Kitty had me rubbing them wi' goose fat over Christmas. I'm going to get some Vaseline instead so I'm less likely to have dogs chasing me to lick my hands."

"It's nice to hear you joking. How are you? I've been worried about you."

"There's no need. It's like our Harry said – Kitty could make a stuffed bird laugh. What delayed you this morning?"

"I was interviewing a young man for the position of footman. He was a waiter at The Jubilee Club. Sean met him last night and arranged the meeting without my knowledge. Taylor said the lad was too familiar, but I liked him, so I've appointed him."

"Sometimes domestic servants are more stuck up than the gentry."

"Taylor certainly can be. The lad's name is Uriah Maxwell, but he asked to be called Max. Apparently, he doesn't like the name Uriah and his grandmother only used it when he was in lumber. He's going to be refreshing to have around. And he's keen to learn to drive, so that's another problem solved, as he'll be able to drive myself and the girls in the second car."

Milly smiled. "Second car! Very top drawer."

"We're only doing it to help Sean, as he won't be able to afford his own for a while."

Victoria made her way from the haberdashery and into the couturier next door. After placing her hat and coat on the stand, she took the large key off the hook so she could open the separate customer entrance. As she pulled back the curtain, she could see a plump woman peering back at her through the glass door. She was wearing the thickest fur coat Victoria had ever seen, a matching sable hat balanced precariously on top of her tight black curls. Victoria quickly turned the key and opened the door.

"Jess?"

"Victoria? Am I too early?"

"Not at all. Come on in. We don't stand on ceremony here. At least not unless we're dealing with clients who want to be treated as though they're visiting royalty."

Jess pulled her into a brief hug.

"Gees, sugar, it's so nice to meet Sean's mother. I feel like I know you already."

"Likewise. I've heard a lot about you."

"Well, would you look at this place! It's wonderful."

"Thank you, Jess, I'm so glad you like it."

Jess walked around the room examining the rows of dresses, suits and blouses on either side of the room before stopping to caress the bodice of a black gown.

"These are beautiful."

"They're from our ready-to-wear range for ladies who need something immediately and for clients who can't afford couture."

"Well, honey, in that case, I can't wait to see what you make when you design one-offs. Should I sit here?" she said, indicating one of the gilt chairs upholstered in red.

"Not unless you don't fancy coming upstairs. But I'd love you to see our salon. That's where we keep our selection of half-finished gowns from our exclusive designs."

"Half-finished?"

"It enables us to make finished garments quicky if required. You'd be surprised how many ladies come in desperate for a new gown for a last-minute party."

"Surely they can wear something from their closet."

"Some wouldn't wear the same thing twice if their lives depended on it."

Jess laughed. "Lead the way, doll."

Victoria showed Jess into a room that resembled an elegant lounge.

Jess smiled. "You've got a nice big place here, sugar. It's as good as anything they had in New York."

"It's not always been this large."

"I've not always been this large, either." Jess laughed and wiggled her hips.

Generally, Victoria's customers wanted to hear how slim they looked, no matter their size, so she was unsure how to respond.

"I, er, Milly and Bob lived in these rooms until I

married Edward and then it remained empty for a few years," she said at last.

"Shall I perch here?" Jess asked, pointing to a red velvet sofa.

"Please do. And I'll ring for refreshments while you peruse our designs and fabric swatches."

"This is shopping in style! What's through that door?"

"The changing room – and there's a small retiring room along the landing."

"So I don't have to leave if I get caught short, then?"

"Exactly. Kitty will be joining us. You're privileged. She's excellent at designing and runs the workroom efficiently. But to use her words, she hasn't got the patience to be tactful with some of our more challenging clients, so rarely does fittings."

"I'm happy to put myself in your hands – I've got no natural style. You make me look like a pig in bloomers," Jess said.

"Pardon?"

"I've never given a fig what people say about me, or if they don't like the way I dress. Back home, no one's got any class and half of them invent their family tree, but I can see straight off that you're a lady."

"Thank you, Jess, but I've been in the clothing business long enough to realise that what makes a woman a lady isn't the way she dresses or speaks but how she behaves. From what I've heard about you from Sean, you're a lady in my book."

"Gees, honey, you're as kind as Sean said you were. But I want to look classy. People stare at me enough as it is because of the colour of my skin. I don't want folk thinking I've opened up a cathouse."

"Cathouse?"

"Lord, you English make me laugh. A cathouse is where ladies meet the needs of men."

"We definitely don't want people thinking that about you. It would give some of the local ladies the vapours." Victoria gave a shaky laugh.

"Right, sugar, sort me out with some decent duds."

"Duds?"

"Americans think they speak English, but since I got here, I feel like I'm speaking a different language. Duds are dresses and underthings."

"I'll call Kitty and we'll start by showing you some sketches, then adapt designs to suit you."

"I'm putting myself in your hands, so I'll let you make what you think best. I want at least five gowns to start with."

The kind-eyed woman was open and amusing. Victoria liked her.

Later, as Jess tried on several styles from their ready-to-wear range, Victoria hovered outside the changing cubicle.

"Jess, do you need help to fasten the gown?"

"No thanks, honey. The day I need someone to help me dress will be the day they're dressing me for my wooden suit."

Kitty, who was sprawling on a chaise longue, let out a roar of laughter.

"At last! Someone in the family with my sense of humour."

Jess emerged from the cubicle wearing a lilac gown. Although heavily beaded, it was more sophisticated than the one she wore when she arrived.

"I'll take this one, as well as the blue and the green

one, to tide me over until you've made the ones you're starting from scratch."

Victoria began pinning the gown for the adjustments she wanted.

"It's wonderful on you, Jess. It needs altering a little on the hips."

"You're polite. It's not as if I don't know I've got plenty to jiggle," Jess said, giving a little shimmy.

"Jess, Milly said she'd put the kettle on about now. While the girls are making the alterations, why don't you come in the back for some tea?" Kitty asked.

"I'll never understand this English obsession with tea. I'd prefer coffee."

"Camp?"

Jess pulled a face. "It's not what we'd call coffee back home, but it'll do nicely, thanks."

"Well, it's like it or lump it, I'm afraid, 'cos it's all we've got," Kitty said.

"Harry won't drink anything but the best," Jess added.

Kitty laughed. "Get Mr Posh Nob. I can't believe our Harry. When we were kids, we were lucky to get clean water to wet our whistles, now he's being a fussy bugger."

"Kitty, behave! Jess is a customer," Victoria said.

"No she's not – she's family."

"Aww, that's so lovely." Jess hugged Kitty.

"How are you liking Faredene? Have you met many people yet?" Victoria asked while they waited for Jess to remove the gown again.

"Harry's been to The Jubilee Club a couple of times with some fella called Cyril Hornby-Smythe. He's put Harry forwards as a member."

"I bet the bank manager has been blabbing about how much money our Harry has got an' that's why Hornby-Smythe has made a point of befriending him. What do you do of an evening when he's out, then?" Kitty said.

"Not much. Mr Hornby-Smythe brought his wife to meet me. He said she could introduce me to people. She nearly collapsed when she saw I wasn't white."

"*That* silly old bat," Kitty said, her eyes flaring.

"She spoke to me as though I were simple. Her husband said she should take me to the Women's Guild, but she prattled on, making excuses about not everyone fitting in."

Kitty stood with her arms akimbo.

"She acts as though she and her husband run this town. It's about time somebody put her in her place. She's nowt but an egg on legs without her stays to push it all in." Kitty guffawed and as the others asked what was so funny, she flapped her hands at them, unable to speak as she was laughing so hard. Eventually, she said, "God, that cracked me up. I just got a picture in me head of the bloody big chicken that would have laid her."

Jess threw back her head, setting Kitty off again. When Jess finally recovered her composure, she said, "You're so funny – I could do with having you around all the time when I deal with people like Mrs H-S."

"That old shrew! She's got no right to look down her nose at you," Kitty said.

"It's all right."

Victoria spoke seriously.

"It's not right, though, Jess. The only consolation I can give you is that I believe Mrs Hornby-Smythe is the worst person in Faredene. She's always been a narrow-minded bigot. When a couple of working women wanted to join the Women's Guild, she and some of her cronies tried to change the name of the group to the Ladies' Guild, hoping to put off future applications from what she termed 'unsuitable types'. I had a fight on my hands to stop it from happening. If you wish to attend the Guild, I'll be delighted for us to go together."

"I'd like that, honey. Harry and me have decided we want to help folk an' until we come up with a bigger plan, that might be a good way to start."

"Great, I'll call on you before our next meeting to decide how we're going to tackle that harridan."

"Hmm, I hope she won't make me uncomfortable," Jess said, suddenly serious.

"Don't let her intimidate you, Jess. She comes from far humbler beginnings than she lets on. And she hates people knowing that her maiden name was Ethel *Butts* and that her father was a blacksmith, not a gentleman farmer as she tells everyone."

Once they were in the parlour, Milly placed a cup and saucer in front of Jess.

"You'll be a proper lady of the manor if you buy Faredene Hall, especially now you've got your new rig-outs."

"I'll be honest with you – it'll be wonderful to leave the hotel. Don't get me wrong, they're nice enough – too nice, in fact, fawning over us. And I know I told Harry that I wanted a big country house, but now I've seen the place, it seems too big. All that land . . . it stretches for miles. But Harry wants the Hall because he used to work there, so it's settled."

"I'd love all that space for my boys to run around. It's all right living above the pub, but we get no peace," Kitty said.

126

"You need to take Harry up on his offer of a house, or at least money to start up a brewery."

"My Albert would love his own brewery, but I fancy a nice little house."

"Like Harry says, the money is there when you've decided. Or you can always move in at the Hall with us. I'm sure Harry would be happy to let you. He loves telling your lads stories about America and he's taken a shine to your Albert. Besides, I'm worried we'll rattle around like two peas in a pail."

"I know they get along, but they've only just met and living together is another matter. Ta for the offer, though."

"Are you sure, sugar?"

"I'm sure of one thing – if I moved into the Hall, the place would probably crumble with the shock."

"If you change your mind, holler," Jess said.

Victoria had the feeling Jess was lonely and had been asking more for her sake than Kitty's.

"Thanks, Jess. You're ever so kind – both of you. I'd best get back in an' make sure they're finishing your dresses properly. I don't want them putting a third sleeve in one."

"Are you not stopping for a bite or a cuppa?" Milly asked.

Kitty paused in the doorway.

"Not got time. We've got loads of orders in an' I'm all behind like a donkey's tail." After a couple of seconds, her grinning face appeared again. "Save me a slice of cake, though, to have wi' me dinner."

When the haberdashery shop assistant came through to ask Milly for help with a customer, Victoria said, "Jess, you'll stay and chat with me while we wait for your gowns, won't you?"

The moment Milly closed the door and they were alone, Jess turned to Victoria, her ready smile gone.

"I wanted the chance to speak to you in private."

Victoria's eyes narrowed.

"The thing is, honey, and I know that lovely lad of yours won't thank me for betraying him, but you're his mother. And, well, I can't watch over him now."

"Jess, you've got me worried. What is it?"

"You mustn't say anything to him or act differently so he cottons on I've told you."

"I'm not sure I can promise that before I know what it is."

"Aww, honey, I want to tell you. You need to know about it, so you must promise me you won't say a thing."

Victoria nodded. What else could she do?

Jess explained her concerns about Sean on the ship.

"He might not have jumped, but I didn't take the chance."

Victoria held her breath. That her boy might have harmed himself and she hadn't been there to help him terrified her.

Jess touched Victoria's arm.

"I'm not surprised you've gone pale – it's not an easy thing to hear."

"It horrifies me to think that he was so desolate. I could tell he wasn't right – then again, I never dreamed he was so low."

"After that first night, I made sure we spent time with him every day. Ate our meals with him and such. I didn't want him to be alone. I've been low myself in the past."

"Sean's been drinking far too much, but he's said nothing about how he's feeling. I wish he'd talk to me."

128

"It's what men do – keep things to themselves. They bottle things up. They're not like women. We share our feelings and let it out. If you tell a man your problems, he's got to fix them, when sometimes all we want them to do is listen."

"That's so true. Edward will want to sort it straightaway, but this isn't something that can be fixed overnight. It's not simply a question of money. I fear it's more about his pride and his friend's betrayal."

"I'm sorry, honey. After meeting you, I had to say something."

"I am reeling, but I appreciate you telling me. Surely he wouldn't have done anything . . . I'm so torn. Don't worry – I won't break your confidence. Besides, if he realises you've told me, you'll lose his trust. At least because you've seen him at his lowest, he might turn to you if . . . if . . ." Victoria wiped her cheek with the back of her hand.

"Aww, honey, don't cry. Now there are two of us watching out for him."

"You're right. I hope you understand that I must tell Edward, but I'll make sure he doesn't say anything to Sean."

"You know best, doll."

"If there's ever anything I can do for you, anything at all . . ."

"There is something, but I feel like I'm taking advantage by asking."

"You were there for Sean when he needed someone. I'd like to assist you if I can."

"The thing is, I love Harry and his family, but I'm feeling a bit lost. I could do with a friend. Especially one who can teach me how to behave and who will help me to fit in with the town's folk. I want to learn how to act properly and do Harry proud."

"Then yes, I'm happy to help you in any way I can."

There was nothing she wouldn't do for the woman who had saved her son's life.

When Jess had left, Victoria made an excuse to spend some time alone in her office. She needed to think about her son. When her children were unhappy, it was far worse than when something was wrong in her own life. Somehow, she felt she could cope with whatever was happening to her, but watching one of them in pain was like having her heart ripped apart.

Sean appeared to be enamoured with his stepsister. Victoria was tempted to speak to her about him, but no. She'd tell no one about what she'd learned today, apart from Edward. Sean deserved his privacy.

Chapter 11

The first day of 1911 . . . Would it be a good year for her family? Victoria mused as she wandered into the drawing room.

"Sean, you missed breakfast. Are you all right?" she said, placing the back of her hand against his forehead.

"I just need a pick-me-up. Taylor's preparing one for me."

"Are you tired?"

Sean rubbed his eyes. "A bit."

"The others are coming down now. Bella and George are getting changed. They've been walking Kirby in the park before the guests arrive."

"George is a nice chap."

She sat at the table.

"What do you *really* think of him?"

"I like him. He seems on edge, as though he's thinking about every word before he speaks. But our family can be a tad overwhelming."

"With us not knowing him well, I wondered if his arrival might dampen the festive atmosphere. Thankfully, he's fitted in rather well."

"Bella seems taken with him. Would you approve if they get serious?"

"When she's older, perhaps. Anne's right – his clothes

are imitations of more expensive styles and occasionally his accent slips. But I can't blame him for trying to better himself. Maybe when the other guests arrive, he'll realise there's no need for false airs and graces and that he'll be accepted for who he is."

"If Kitty doesn't put him at ease, no one will. Do you think he's good enough for Bella?"

"At one time I'd have wanted her to marry a gentleman. If I'm honest, I'd still prefer it. But time has taught me that breeding isn't the most important thing."

"You're right. What matters most is that Bella's happy."

"And how are *you*, darling?"

"I'm doing all right. Being home helps."

"Promise you'll come to me if you're ever feeling down about anything."

"Are you worrying about me?"

"I'm your mother – it's my job to worry."

Sean nodded. "I'll talk to you if anything is concerning me."

Sean wondered why he'd just agreed to talk to his mother if he was feeling down. It hadn't been an intentional lie, but he was already low and didn't want to discuss it. He could see she was about to speak – no doubt about to press him further – when the doorbell rang.

"I bet that's Kitty. She can't abide Taylor – thinks he's got a broom somewhere unpleasant and that he looks down his nose at her – so I'd best greet her," she said.

Sean listened to the muffled voices.

"Kitty, you're bang on time. Have you been waiting round the corner until the clock struck twelve?" his mother said.

"Mam said if we weren't ready to set off in time, she'd leave us at home, 'cos she wants to see Sean before everyone else gets here," a young boy's voice replied instead.

"Good idea. Come on in. Sean's in the drawing room."

Sean stood and held his arms out to the slim woman. Kitty touched her scarred cheek self-consciously then, dropping her hand, she rushed into his arms.

"Tatty Head! Me auld mate. It's smashing to have yeh home."

Sean laughed. "Even Bella's been calling me Tatty Head, and it's your fault."

"That's me kid. I always was someone folk want to imitate."

Sean kissed her scarred cheek, hugging her again.

"I've missed you, Kitty Gibbs. You're a sight for sore eyes."

She gestured with her thumb to the burly man with a thick moustache who had followed her into the room.

"It's Mrs Nelson now, me laddo. This hunk of a man is my hubby, so you'd better watch out. He'll knock yer block off for flirting wi' me."

Sean bowed. "Begging your pardon, Mrs Nelson."

"Mind you, he has to leave early to visit his mam, so who knows what will happen then."

"Kitty! You're shocking my son. Now behave yourself," Victoria said.

Sean held out his hand to shake the man's.

"How do you do? Albert, isn't it?"

"It is. How do, Sean? I've heard a lot about you," Albert said.

"Don't be hogging Sean. I've not seen him for years," Kitty said.

"Albert, come and meet George while Kitty and Sean

133

catch up," Victoria said, smiling as she led Albert towards Bella and George, who had followed them in and were now by the piano.

Sean had thought about Kitty over the years and wondered what might have been between them if she'd not got pregnant. To his relief, because the last thing he needed was to be hankering after another man's wife, all that was left of his adolescent feelings for her was friendship and affection.

"So, what's been happening in your life, Kitty?" he asked.

"Let me bring you up to date," Kitty said. "I've got two smashing stepsons who are both grown up and signed on as sailors and—" She stopped mid-sentence and scanned the room. "Where have them two gone now? They were right behind me. Boys!"

A couple of identically dressed strawberry blond boys appeared in the doorway. The taller stood with his arms behind his back, his chin jutted out.

"Mam, our Brian has brought his catapult."

"You rotten tell-tale, Jake."

The smaller of the two shoved his older brother further into the room, Jake's cap toppling to the floor.

"These two imps are my lads," Kitty said. "This is Jake – he's eight." She patted the taller boy on the head. "And this is Brian, who is six. Boys, say hello to Uncle Sean. Like I told youse, he's been living in America an' has come home the same as Uncle Harry."

"Hello, boys," Sean said, smiling as the boys wriggled in unison to escape their mother's clutches.

"An' they're gonna behave today or they'll get their backsides tanned," Kitty added.

134

Jake laughed. "Mam, that's no threat – everybody knows you'd never smack us."

Grinning, Kitty held on to their hands, attempting to keep them still as the boys squirmed, one either side of her.

"Cor, were you in the Wild West? Did yeh get scalped?" Brian asked.

Jake tutted. "Course he didn't, yeh numbskull. You can see he's still got all his messy hair, like Mam said."

Sean threw back his head and laughed.

"There's no doubting they're your sons, Kitty."

"I'm not sure that's a blinkin' compliment." She grinned as she pulled the boys in front of her affectionately.

"It's definitely a compliment. They're a breath of fresh air."

"Our Brian can burp 'God Save the King'. Do yeh want him to do it for yeh?" Jake asked.

Brian opened his mouth, only to have his mother's hand clamped over it, with her warning, "Don't you dare, lad."

"All right. Are we gonna get some scoff soon, Mam, I'm starving?" Brian said as Kitty removed her hand.

Kitty shook her head. "Yer always starving. I'm sure you've got tapeworm."

"Mam told yeh, Brian. We have to wait until Victoria says we can have grub an' you mustn't chew wi' yer gob open, 'cos Edward's stuck-up sister's here," Jake said, wagging his finger at his brother.

Kitty cringed before gently pushing the boys in Albert's direction.

"Go an' mither yer dad while I talk to Sean."

Kitty had been such a terror as a child – now, she was finding out what it was like to cope with precocious children.

"You and your husband have a public house, I believe?"

"Aye, The Tanner's Arms. He were running it when we met. I'd invite yeh round, but it's not the sort of place for a gentleman. Mind you, we might branch out. Harry's being right generous with his money. He's offered to help Albert start a brewery. It's blooming amazing, 'cos when he were a kid, Harry could peel an orange in his pocket. Not that we could afford oranges."

"He's done well for himself."

"That's putting it mildly. I hope he doesn't waste it an' end up broke again. Jess seems to be a decent woman. Hopefully, she'll keep him in line."

"I suspect he's got that much money he'd struggle to spend it all. Though you're right about Jess. I got to know her well on the ship."

"Jess said you'd met. They're pleased yer mam invited them today."

"Are you happy, Kitty?"

"Blimey, Sean, that's a big question. Right out of the blue." Then she smiled. "Happier than I ever expected to be." Kitty touched her cheek again. "I bet you got a shock when yeh saw me."

"You're still beautiful and have the best eyes in Faredene."

"Thanks, pet. You've turned out to be a right smasher yerself."

"I'm flattered."

"Yer mam told us that Claude fella did the dirty on you. I always thought he were above himself."

"You only met him briefly a few times, didn't you? How could you know what he was like?"

"I'm a good judge o' character. It only takes me a

minute to get the measure of people – it must be all those years taking measurements for dresses."

Kitty described what she'd like to do to Claude, which involved her sharpest scissors and a delicate part of his anatomy. Sean chuckled – she'd always made him laugh.

They continued chatting until her attention was caught by Albert telling the boys to calm down, when she said she'd better help him before they disgraced her.

Since hearing about Sean's financial situation, George had been plotting. If his plan was to work, he needed to get as many of the family on his side as possible. Victoria would be easy enough – she'd clearly agree to anything if her darling daughter wanted it. Anne and Kate were women, so easily won round. Edward would take some work, but Sean was the easiest target. As Kitty moved away, he seized his chance.

"Sean, can I have a quick word before anyone else arrives?"

"Certainly, George, what is it?"

George glanced over his shoulder to where the others were laughing at something Kitty was saying. He lowered his voice unnecessarily.

"Please tell me if I'm overstepping the mark, but you've been open with me about your current financial situation and I might be able to help. As you're aware, I work at the docks and, well, occasionally we get damaged cargo that the shipping companies need to sell off quick. There's a consignment of whiskey and wine that's just come in with water-damaged labels. It can't go to the restaurants and hotels for which it was intended, but a great deal of money can be made by buying it and selling it on. I have the contacts but not the capital to invest, but if yeh have fifty to a hundred pounds, I could nearly double yer money for you in the next month."

"Is it legal?"

George stiffened, doing his best to look affronted.

"Naturally. I'd never get involved in anything that wasn't. There's not a penny in this for me."

"I'm sorry, George. I didn't mean to offend you. It just sounds too good to be true."

"We often get damaged cargo. But if you're not interested . . ."

"It's not that. The truth is, I haven't got the money. I wasn't exaggerating when I told you I'm broke. I have a little ready cash that Edward gave me, but nothing more."

"Never mind. I just thought I'd offer. You had a raw deal in America."

"Thank you for thinking of me. I desperately need to build up my capital again. Though, I'm not sure where I can get the money right now." Sean's hand strayed to his waistcoat. He felt the pocket watch under the fabric. "I have a pocket watch – it's gold. It was left to me by my mother's cousin. He died when I was young, so I don't remember him, but he meant a great deal to her. I could pawn it if you're certain I'd get my money back . . . No – I mustn't. If I lose the watch, it'll upset her terribly."

"As I see it, you trusted someone you shouldn't. You don't know me, but I'll tell you now – I think the world of Bella. I'm not going to scupper my chances with her by getting you mixed up in something dodgy."

"Even so, I'm not sure I should take any risks."

"Perhaps you're right. Even though I'm certain the goods can be sold, I'm probably best not getting involved.

I don't want anything coming between me and Bella. Forget I said anything. Someone else can make a killing."

"You're certain you can get a buyer for it?"

"Absolutely."

"I wouldn't want anyone to know."

"I've got nothing to hide, but if you prefer it that way, it would be our secret."

"Thanks. Mother wouldn't approve of my taking chances with my watch. I'm still not certain it's the right thing to do."

Now was the time to back off again and make Sean think he might lose the opportunity.

"I can see you're unsure. It's best to leave it. I don't want to influence you, but I'm here until tomorrow afternoon if you change yer mind," George said as the drawing room door opened and Milly walked in.

Sean would find the money, George was sure. Arranging for a load of booze to fall off the back of a ship would be easy. Then the prodigal son would be in his debt and they'd share a secret. If there was one thing he knew, it was how to manipulate people.

Sean swung Milly off her feet.

"Goodness, Milly, you're so light."

She planted a kiss on his cheek.

"Aww, Sean, it's smashing having you home," she said as he placed her back on the ground.

"It's nice to be home, Milly."

She gave him another hug.

"I expect it is, love. It would be better under different circumstances. I understand – yeh don't have to pretend with me. I've known yeh since you were no bigger than a dob o' spit."

Sean nodded. "I was so sorry to hear about Bob. He was a good man."

With only a connecting door separating his childhood home from Milly and Bob's accommodation, Sean had constantly been in and out of their house as a child and had seen first-hand how happy the couple had been together.

"I miss him every minute." Milly sniffed. "At times I don't think I can carry on without him. Until my time comes, I suppose I've got to keep plodding on. Anyway, there's no point harping on about it today. It's a celebration for your homecoming an' I want you to meet my Jane."

"Where is she?"

"She's nattering to Kate in the hall. Once them two get talking about teaching methods or women's rights, there's no stopping them. Jane teaches at the girls' school in Chester but comes home every weekend. She keeps saying she wants to do summat more worthwhile like teaching the poorer kids if a job comes up local.

"She's caring, is Jane. She even read up on how to work wi' deaf children and learned sign language to help one girl, but her parents took her away from the school anyway. My son, Robert, is different altogether. He's in London studying to be a doctor. He wants to get to the top of his profession an' make money."

As the drawing room door opened again, Milly glanced over her shoulder.

"Here she is."

A petite blonde followed Kate into the room. Sean was stunned. Except for her hair, which looked almost white as it caught the sunlight coming through the window, and her grey eyes, the young woman looked almost identical to Kitty at the same age with her rosebud mouth. Sean heard George catch his breath. He couldn't blame him – Jane Kellet was the most beautiful woman Sean had ever seen.

Chapter 12

Tuesday morning, Sean dragged himself out of bed at five thirty. He crossed to the window. Christ! it was still pitch-black. Once he'd washed and dressed, he tore downstairs and grabbed a slice of toast from the kitchen before jumping in the back of Edward's motor car and greeting Stokes, who was driving him on the brief journey to the mill.

As he looked out onto the dark streets, he conjured up an image of Milly's daughter, Jane. She'd been less than a year old when he'd left for America, so she wasn't much older than Bella, but she'd barely left his thoughts since they'd met. Yes, she was beautiful, but it was more than that.

When she spoke about helping children and how she longed for the opportunity to do more, her face lit up. It appeared she had Kitty's kind nature and although more refined, she had her sense of fun. He wanted to get to know her better – much better. She was the type of girl he could see himself marrying, but before he could have any more of those thoughts, he needed to get some capital behind him. While he was living at his mother's, at least he'd be able to save from his salary at the mill, but it would take a lot more than that to be in a position to propose to Jane, or anyone else. Maybe he was getting ahead of himself, but it was good to think there was hope for the future.

That's why, he reasoned, he'd slipped out yesterday morning and pawned his pocket watch to invest in George's scheme. If he wanted a wife one day soon, he needed to take some chances. George had promised him they'd keep the arrangement between the two of them. If George's plan paid off, he'd keep investing until he had enough to do something more solid with it. If it failed? Well, then he'd have a few months to find some other way to get the money and get his watch out of hock before the pawnbroker sold it.

The racket from within the mill could be heard even as the chauffeur pulled into the yard. Sean had overindulged again last night and the noise level wouldn't help his hangover. As he'd been about to go to bed, his mother had expressed her concerns about his drinking. Her face had been deadly serious.

"Sean, darling, you're a grown man and the last thing I want to do is interfere in your life."

"So that's exactly what she's about to do," Edward had said, trying to lighten the mood.

She had scowled at her husband, the fine lines around her eyes deepening.

"I'm not interfering, but I can't stand by and say nothing. It's not that you drink every day that I have an issue with. I understand that most people enjoy a glass of wine with their meal or a brandy afterwards. It's the amount you drink that bothers me. You don't appear to know when you've had enough."

"I don't drink that much. There have been a lot of celebrations and socialising since I got home. Besides, I find it difficult to relax these days. It helps me to sleep."

"Darling, it's only because I love you that I'm concerned," she'd said.

His mother had been supportive, acknowledging that he'd had a tough time, but had asked him to curb his intake now the festive season was over. He'd said he would, all the while knowing it wasn't a promise he could keep. Drinking helped him to forget. Enabled him to cope with the disappointment he felt every day at how his life had turned out. Somehow, what had happened in New Orleans had reinforced the feeling that he'd had since he'd discovered the truth about his birth – that he was a fraud and belonged in the gutter.

Matthew was already in the office and he laughed as Sean charged through the door, conscious of being late.

"Afternoon, Sean. I nearly sent a knocker-upper to wake you."

"Sorry."

"Just pulling your leg. The undermanager opens up, though I prefer to get in early a few days a week without notice. It keeps them on their toes."

"Great. So, where do I start?" Sean said, relieved that Matthew wasn't sacking him for taking advantage of his daughter before he'd even started work.

"I'm pleased to see you're so enthusiastic. You're going to spend time in each area. I've arranged for David Gibbs to take care of you – here he is now."

Sean could see a balding middle-aged man with a thick moustache that protruded over his upper lip peering through the bevelled glass panel before knocking. As the door opened, the room was swamped by the rattle of machines.

"David, you remember Mr Kavanagh," Matthew said.

144

"Nice to see you again, David," Sean shouted, holding out his hand.

"Sean. Sorry, I mean, Mr Kavanagh." David shook Sean's hand.

"Sean's fine."

"No, sir. It wouldn't do to call yeh by yer first name here."

"Right, yes, I understand."

"Mr Clarkson has asked me to spend the week with yeh, sir. Make sure no one takes advantage, thinkin' yer green. I didn't mean no offence, sir, but if they think they can get the better of yeh and take liberties, some of 'em will try."

"You can leave your jacket here, Sean. I don't think you'll need it today. I've cleared your mother's desk for you, so you can leave it on your chair." Matthew gestured towards the desk at the back of the room.

"What about Mother?"

"She's thinking you might take over her tasks."

"Right. I'm looking forward to it," Sean replied, hoping his true feelings didn't show.

He was appreciative, but he couldn't quell the dread at being stuck in the mill day in, day out. You ungrateful sod, he thought.

Once they were in the spinning room, David waved his arms to reinforce his message as he shouted over the din, explaining the function of the seventy spinning mules and how they made the raw cotton into threads.

"Each minder looks after a pair of mules. The 1,300 spindles move about four times a minute." He stopped walking. "Am I teaching me granny to suck eggs? Do you remember all this, sir?"

"Most of it, but it's been a long time, so I don't mind hearing it again to refresh my memory."

145

"Aye, all right, but stop me if I get boring."

As they were about to leave the spinning room, David pointed at one of the mules.

"That mule was where one of me mates died when we were kids. Back then, before yer mam and Mr Clarkson took over, each spinner employed two lads to work for him. I told the bastard that me mate were ill an' I'd clean under the machinery, 'cos yeh had to concentrate, but the spinner wouldn't let me. The poor sod's head got caught . . . I'll never forget what it did to him." David shuddered.

"It's not like that now, surely."

"No, yer mam ensured everyone was employed direct by the mill, so they're treated fair, like. An' she reduced the number of hours kids work to well below the ten-hour working-day law. She also insists they attend school. Won't let 'em work if they're not well, either."

Sean blinked as some fibres landed on his lashes as they walked. He'd loved coming to the mill after school, believing that one day half of it would belong to him. He'd seen himself as the dashing mill owner, kind and benevolent to his workers while raking in the profits. Now, he was nothing more than an employee, which meant that he'd be here twelve hours or more Monday to Friday and half a day on a Saturday in this sweatbox.

"Does it get you down being here every day, David?" Sean blurted.

"Aye, I wouldn't be human if it didn't. Mr Clarkson works alongside us, though – he's always here. He's respected for that."

In the weaving room, David pointed to a weaver.

"Joe will show you how to operate the looms now, but mind how you go. You can lose a finger or have yer arm snapped like a twig if you don't watch what yer doing."

"I'll be careful."

Although it was relatively early, a light film of dust covered the young man as he moved deftly between the twelve looms he looked after while the shuttles flew back and forth. After an hour of watching him, Sean took over. Joe blanched as Sean broke the yarn several times.

"Watch the belt don't break. They're a bugger to fix while the loom is moving an' stopping 'em takes up too much time," Joe cautioned.

Sean realised none of the workers wanted their machines idle for longer than necessary. Even here, workers had to hit certain targets.

"It's all right, Joe. Mr Clarkson knows yer helpin' Mr Kavanagh – you won't get yer pay cut," David explained.

"Righto, Gaffer. I were worried, like."

"Do you enjoy being a weaver, Joe?" Sean asked.

"Aye, I've been here for nine years since I were ten an' I've never once had a clout for going too slow. Some folk think I suck up to the bosses. They can say what they want – I don't care. I work hard an' I'm not interested in any o' this union stuff," Joe explained as he eagerly took back control of his looms.

Victoria couldn't seem to concentrate on any task, instead staring out of her office window at the clouds, praying for a sign that her son would find happiness. She wondered how Sean was getting on at the mill. It was worse than his first day at school. She should have gone to the mill today. No – it would have been too obvious that she was checking up on him.

147

"Are you daydreaming, Victoria? You look as though yer miles away," Milly said.

"Milly! I didn't even hear you come in."

"This will give you a shock. Mrs Hornby-Smythe has asked to speak to yeh in private. You look washed out. Shall I tell her to go away?"

"This is a first. What can she want? Normally, she blurts out whatever's on her mind. You'd better bring her through."

"Only if yer sure, love. If she gives you any trouble, holler and me an' our Kitty will drag her out by her ear."

As the large woman entered the office, she turned at a slight angle to avoid getting caught in the doorway. Breathing heavily, Mrs Hornby-Smythe sat without being invited.

"Ethel, I don't think you have an appointment for another week," Victoria said, running a finger down the appointment book.

Ethel took a heaving breath. "I'm not here for myself today. Once again, I find myself drawn to this establishment because things are not as they should be."

"Really? In what way?" Victoria said, her mouth set firm.

"It's about Millicent and her sister still working here. I heard yesterday they're related to Harold Gibbs and that wife of his. It is hardly fitting for sisters of the owner of Faredene Hall to be shop girls. As Chairwoman of the Women's Guild, it is my duty to point these things out. I could raise it at the next meeting, but these things are best dealt with privately."

Victoria bristled. "These things! The girls are hardly working in a brothel."

"There is no need to take that tone or be vulgar, Mrs

148

Caldwell. I sometimes wonder how you got elected on to the Guild's committee."

"I was voted onto it, the same way you were."

"As the wife of a prominent solicitor, it is hardly acceptable that you're still working, either. Then, you've always been different. You caused a scandal when you bought a share in the mill. It's lucky for you that you make such fine gowns, so we more refined ladies are inclined to overlook your eccentricities."

"I'm *so* grateful." Victoria hoped the sarcasm in her tone was evident.

Mrs Hornby-Smythe smiled condescendingly.

"You're welcome."

Clearly, the sarcasm was wasted. The woman had the hide of a rhino – you couldn't insult her no matter how hard you tried.

"Harold and his wife are new to their wealth. They need to adhere to the town standards if they are to fit in. So, I will ask you straight out. Are you going to dismiss the sisters?"

Victoria felt the pencil she was gripping with both hands snap as she spoke.

"Absolutely not. Both Milly and Kitty are my partners in this business, not employees."

"Hmm . . . I suppose that makes things a little more acceptable."

"Acceptable to you or not, my business partners and I are happy with our working arrangements. While we are grateful for your patronage, if you don't approve, we won't expect you to use our services again." She rose from her seat. "Now, if there's nothing more, we're expecting the new owner of The Grange for a fitting."

"Really? I've heard her husband has a senior role in the diplomatic core and they're spending a fortune renovating the place."

"Ethel, it's a policy of this establishment not to gossip about our clientele, so if you don't mind, I'll show you out."

Mrs Hornby-Smythe faltered. "I . . . well, I . . ."

Victoria yanked the office door open, her anger vanishing as she stifled a laugh when Milly and Kitty toppled in. Clearly, they'd both been listening. And judging by the look on Kitty's face, if their visitor didn't leave quickly, she might regret it.

Milly said, "I'll show yeh out. But before I do, I'll have my say. There's nowt wrong with people earning an honest living. Which is more than I can say for people who lose money they can't afford at the gambling table."

Age hadn't mellowed Mrs Hornby-Smythe, who was still overbearing and obnoxious. Her meanness of spirit was etched into her haggard face for all to see, despite her attempts to claw on to her youth, which had evidently slipped away a long time ago. She was speechless as she was escorted out.

A rare smile brightened Milly's face when she returned.

"Why did she get so flustered when you mentioned gambling?" Kitty asked.

Milly put on a posh accent.

"Her esteemed husband apparently lost a packet to one Harold Gibbs last week."

Victoria gaped. "Really?"

She reverted to her normal voice.

"An' our Harry says her other half couldn't settle his debt, either."

"What's Harry done about it?" Victoria asked.

"Nowt. He's a crafty one, our Harry. He says he's locked the IOU in his safe until he decides the time is right to call it in."

Victoria rooted in the drawer for a new pencil.

"If she comes back, maybe we should ban her from the shop," Milly said.

Kitty nodded. "I don't know why she buys new dresses when everything she orders looks like something Queen Victoria would have worn. She may as well stick with her old ones."

"Behind all that face powder, I'm sure she's hiding summat," Milly said.

Victoria laughed. "Really, Milly, you've been reading too many Penny dreadfuls. All those cheap horror stories have got you looking for sinister plots everywhere."

"You say that, but she's definitely a nasty bugger."

"She's right, though. You could both be ladies of leisure now," Victoria said.

"No, it wouldn't suit either of us," Kitty said firmly.

Victoria glanced at Milly. She suspected Milly didn't share her sister's conviction and although Milly wasn't bleaching everything in sight now, she still had dark circles under her eyes and in Victoria's opinion, she was far from being the optimistic person she once was.

After lunch, as they left to move on to another area of the mill, Sean tentatively questioned David about the growing trade union movement.

"I understand from Matthew that there was a wave of strikes across the country last year."

David's eyes narrowed.

"Don't worry. I'm in favour of unions and the rights of workers. But I know Matthew is concerned about it affecting this mill," Sean added.

"He's right to be worried. There will be a strike here before too long an' it could rip families apart. Wives an' daughters will do as their fathers or husbands tell them, but brothers, fathers and sons are already disagreeing. It's causing rifts," David replied.

"Why are you so sure they'll strike?"

"Because even though the wages and conditions here aren't bad, some say they could be better. Then there's plenty who think we should strike to support the other mills an' the miners."

"If Matthew raised wages here, would that stop it from happening?"

"No. If the union says they've got to strike, they will. We'll all have to or be marked as blacklegs. If that happens, you can forget having mates – you'll be lucky if folk don't spit on you in the street. It's them wi' large families I worry about. The few bob they get from the strike fund won't be enough to live on."

"Where do you stand on the matter?"

"It's right complicated for me an' me lad. We want to support the other mills, but yer mam an' Mr Clarkson have been good to us – an' now there's our Harry in the mix."

"Harry? What's he got to do with it?"

"I'm not sure if I should say anything yet, but yer mam has always played straight with us, so I'll chance it. Harry seems to have more money than he knows what to do with. As a kid I thought he'd end up along the line, but I guess you never can tell how people will turn out. Anyway, he's suggested a way out for us."

"A way out of the mill?"

"Aye. All we've ever known is the mill, but I love my allotment. Our Harry has offered to set us up in a business of our own, maybe even growing veg and stuff to sell."

"That's a wonderful opportunity."

"The thing is, I'm me own man. I've never been beholden to anyone an' I don't like the idea of takin' handouts, even from me bruvver."

"I'm sure Harry wouldn't see it that way."

"Maybe not. Anyway, I can't see us sticking it here with things as they are. He's only been back five minutes an' people round here have changed towards us."

"In what way?"

"Jealous. They weren't even like this when I got promoted to overseer. 'Cos they know I'm a grafter, they were glad for me."

"They're not giving you trouble, I hope?"

"No – just making digs. They seem to think we've forgotten what it is to go hungry. To be honest, it's getting us down. An' it's worse for me lad, 'cos he needs his mates. The wife says they'll settle down, but I'm not so sure. I'll give it a bit longer while I mull over our 'arry's offer."

Harry's ability to help his family when Sean needed a handout from his stepfather highlighted his inadequacies.

When the final whistle went, Sean's back was breaking and his shirt was stained with sweat. Like David, he wasn't sure that a lifetime at the mill was for him.

Chapter 13

It was almost midnight. George blew on his fingers to warm them. From his hiding place at the corner of the dock office, he had a clear view of the wharf. He waited until the sound of the night-watchman's boots on the dockside faded into the distance – it would be an hour before he passed this way again.

George pulled the torch from his pocket and gave the agreed signal: three quick flashes followed by two long ones. A van pulled up quietly on the quay alongside an old coal steamer and a man jumped out. At the same time, the hold of the boat creaked open and another two men carrying crates emerged, their eyes furtively scanning the docks.

Once all three men were helping, they swiftly transferred the cargo as George watched, counting each crate as it was placed in the van. As the final one was loaded, George handed over a roll of notes to the captain of the boat. The old man shoved it in the pocket of his duffel coat.

"You not counting it, then?" George said.

"No need, George. We've done enough deals over the years for me to know I can trust yeh. Although this is a much bigger haul for yeh. What's going on? You got yerself a rich contact? You'll make a killin' outta this lot."

"Not a penny, pal. This is part of a much bigger plan.

I'm thinkin' of my future. I don't want to be stuck in this filthy hole for the rest of me life."

"Aye, well, I hope the sun shines for yeh, 'cos most of us have nowhere else to go. We'd better shove off before the watchman comes back or we'll be somewhere worse than this if the excise bobbies catch up with us."

George removed a revolver from inside his overcoat.

"They won't take me in. There's no way I'm doing a stretch."

The older man lost his footing as he backed away, stumbling onto the boat.

"Bleedin' hell. Put that thing away. I want none o' that."

Smirking, George touched his forelock with his gun and jumped in the van, giving the driver the first address.

Within a couple of hours, the smuggled goods were hidden in the cellars of four London nightclubs. Even after paying off the driver, he'd more than doubled Sean's money. Despite what he'd told the skipper of the boat, he would take a cut for himself, but most of it would go to the soft bleeder in Faredene. He'd soon have them up north eating out of his hand.

The day of the Women's Guild meeting, Victoria climbed into Harry's Rolls-Royce, placed her purse on the seat beside her and took Jess' hand.

"I can see you're nervous, but there's no need. Trust me, Jess. I've been dealing with these women for years. Most of them are decent. There are just a few who are . . . well, horrible. If those women accept you, you won't have any problems going forwards."

"If you're sure."

"Just be yourself. Most of them will like you for who

you are. The others only appreciate one thing – money – and thankfully, you have plenty of it. Our plan will work, you'll see."

"I don't want to buy their friendship."

"Jess, that's not what you're doing. You wanted to help people and this is simply helping you at the same time. If I believed you weren't going to be made welcome once I've done what we've agreed, I wouldn't have encouraged you."

"Does Anne not belong to the Guild?"

"Heavens, no. Anne's home is in London, although she's been staying with us a while. She's considering moving back to Faredene permanently, largely influenced by her friendship with Owain Farrell, I suspect. I hope she buys a house of her own here soon, because there's only so long I can control my temper – she's constantly telling me how I should be guiding my children better."

"I got the impression she likes to take control. She offered to introduce me to Faredene society, but I told her you had that in hand."

"She was a member of the Guild before she married, though only for the social side of things. She has no interest in helping the poor."

"I thought as much," Jess said as she fiddled with her reticule.

"Is something else wrong?"

Jess leaned close to Victoria, even though the chauffeur wouldn't be able to hear through the glass partition.

"Honey, I hope you won't think badly of me, but I need to talk to someone."

"Any time, Jess. Do you need my help with something?"

"Harry and I weren't able to get married. I already have a husband."

She told Victoria about fleeing after her husband's beating. Victoria could feel her own face tightening.

"Aww, see. Now you're appalled that we're living in sin."

"No, it's not that, I promise you. It's simply that I hate to hear of women being treated badly. My friend Lydia Brakenridge suffered for years at the hands of a violent man. So did my own mother, for that matter."

"Then you understand why I'm scared, honey. Do you think Ollie will find me?"

"No, he's on the other side of the Atlantic. What's brought on your concern?" Victoria asked.

"I've had a letter from my sister. She wanted to warn me that he's looking for me."

"Jess, all I can say is that if James Brakenridge couldn't find Lydia with his money and connections, I doubt a mere sailor will be able to track you down."

"You're right. I'm probably panicking for no reason."

The automobile pulled up under the portico of the guildhall. Victoria doubted there would be any unpleasantness, but if there was, she fully intended putting the ladies of this town firmly in their place.

"Ready, Jess?"

Jess nodded, looking dubious.

The hall was set out with several large tables, most of which were already full. As Victoria led Jess to the front of the room, where the committee generally sat, conversation lulled and she had to resist reaching out to clutch Jess' hand.

Victoria introduced Jess to the white-haired lady who was already at the committee table.

"Jess, this is Norma Payne who I told you about. She's in our corner."

Jess held out her hand.

"Nice to meet you, sugar. I need all the friends I can get. This lot look like they're set to lynch me."

"Don't let them see you're worried, that's my advice. Most are all right once you get to know them. Either way, Victoria is more than a match for them."

As the two women chatted, Victoria kept her eyes on the door until Mrs Hornby-Smythe bustled in. There was only one way to tackle this – and that was direct.

Mrs Hornby-Smythe waddled over, followed by her entourage, who took their seats, all avoiding looking at Jess.

"Ethel, I believe you've had the pleasure of meeting Mrs Gibbs," Victoria said.

"I have indeed. Mrs Gibbs, the front table is generally used by the committee," Ethel said.

Victoria placed her hand on Jess' arm.

"Jess is here as my guest."

"Hmm." Ethel grunted and pulled an expression suited to someone who had swallowed a mouthful of vinegar.

As conversation around the table began, it was clear Ethel Hornby-Smythe and her cronies were avoiding talking to Jess. Thank goodness for Mrs Payne, Victoria thought. Victoria's palms were perspiring. She'd promised Jess this would work and didn't want to let her down. She kept her eyes fixed on the chairwoman and when Ethel was about to hoist herself out of her seat, Victoria jumped up.

"Ladies, if I may have your attention. I realise this isn't our normal order of business. However, I have the honour of introducing a new member, Mrs Jessica Gibbs. As you are all aware, although she will remain an esteemed member of the Guild, Mrs Payne is stepping down after many years of valuable service and I'm delighted that our chairwoman has proposed Jessica for the vacant position on the committee."

Victoria paused to allow the murmur of surprise to die down. A few ladies were smirking, as she'd broken protocol by announcing the nomination instead of Ethel.

"I'm thrilled to second the motion. Jessica and her husband, Harold, are renowned in America for their good works and philanthropy. In fact, Jessica has today matched the amount we currently hold in our relief fund for the poor, doubling the extent of the help we'll be able to give the needy over the winter months. So, if I may have a show of hands to elect Jess to the committee . . ."

As she waited, hands were slowly raised until Mrs Hornby-Smythe gestured for her friends to raise theirs, at which point there was quickly unanimous approval. Ethel's face was pinched as she accepted the members' praise for bringing Jess into the group. Even the ones Victoria considered tight-fisted welcomed Jess, no doubt pleased her large donation would reduce their need to contribute more.

Mrs Payne leaned across and whispered in Victoria's ear.

"That was inspired, my dear. Ethel has no choice now but to act as though Jessica was her find."

Victoria smiled. "I'm sure I don't know what you mean."

As they were about to leave, Mrs Hornby-Smythe pulled Victoria to one side.

"I suppose you think that was clever."

"All I did was give credit to you, which you don't deserve. Jessica will make an excellent member of the committee, unlike one of your parsimonious cronies who you might have nominated."

"I don't like your tone, Mrs Caldwell."

"Frankly, Mrs Hornby-Smythe, I like nothing about you."

Victoria marched off, her head held high.

As Kate changed her outfit that evening, she selected one of her favourite gowns. It was probably too much for a family meal, but she wanted to look her best. She moved closer to the mirror, inspecting her face closely. Yvette was right – she did look better. Perhaps it was because she could barely keep a smile off her face. She'd never been happier.

During the week, Sean was busy at the mill, so apart from dinner with the family, she saw little of him. However, at weekends she often found herself spending time with him. Or rather, she engineered it with the help of Bella. It was part of her quest to get him to see her as a woman – a wife, not as a sister.

They'd wrapped up in warm coats and gone for walks along the canal, played cards and talked. Their talks – that was the best part. There had never been anyone who she'd laughed with as much as him. But it was more than that. They understood each other. She'd even spoken to him about her own insecurities.

"It took me a long time to accept that Father loved me as much as he does Bella," Kate said.

"Surely not. It's clear he adores you," Sean said.

"It was my mother's fault. It was only after she died that I realised she'd been lying to me about him."

"Lied about him?"

"She told me over and over that they separated because

he didn't love *either* of us. Consequently, even after she died, still I rejected him. Eventually, I realised it was all nonsense. And she'd never even told me about all the times he came to Ireland in an attempt to see me."

"Why would she do that?"

"Revenge. He didn't love her. He admits that. But I accept now that he always loved me."

"At least you know the truth now."

"Yes, but it's tainted my memory of my mother. I can make excuses for her, but she was prepared to hurt me for her own ends. She used me as a weapon to punish him. I'll never forgive her for that. She can't have loved me."

It had felt good to confide in someone about her feelings towards her dead mother. When someone dies, everyone puts them on a pedestal.

"Kate, I'm sure she did."

"You'll never convince me of that. Any mother who puts her own feelings above her child in that way can't love them. She was a stranger to the truth."

"Perhaps she convinced herself it was for your own good."

"You're being kind. How could it have been for my benefit? He's a lovely man. All I know is that if she were here today, I'd give her a roasting."

"Unfortunately, we can never know why people act in a certain way. That's not much help to you. I'm so sorry, Kate."

"That's all right. At least I'm part of a family now," she'd said.

He was so gorgeous and kind. If he was to love her, she was sure she'd never ask for anything else in her life. Pushing the image of him from her mind for the moment, she pulled on her long silk gloves. She didn't need to imagine him – he was already downstairs chatting with George and waiting to dine.

Later that week, George headed towards The White Lion alehouse in Spitalfields. It wasn't a part of town he liked to visit, but he wanted to sell the contents of two large carpet bags and this was the best place to do it. He quickly made his way through the crowded bar.

"Is he in the back?" George asked the greasy-haired cellarman, who was bending over a large barrel inserting the tap.

"For you, he's always in. Go on through."

George made way to the back room, where the whale-like landlord was sitting with his feet up on his desk.

"Get off your arse, Moby, yeh lazy git, an' see what I've got 'ere for you."

Moby belched, scratching his bulging stomach through his beer- and sweat-stained vest.

"All right, George, keep yer hair on. I was just 'aving five minutes. You get no rest in this game. The pub's always busy and then there are the tarts to sort out."

"I've seen how you manage the prossies – giving them a clout doesn't take much time."

The landlord laughed. "Let's see what you've got for me, then."

Once the contents of the bags were laid out on the desk, Moby surveyed the haul.

"These here candlesticks are heavy. This is good-quality silver. And that clock's a fine piece. You didn't knock this off anywhere round these parts?"

"I don't go in for robbing, you know that. It's too risky.

But I was in a house in Knightsbridge recently and got the lay of the land first, so this was a simple job."

"You could still have got collared."

"The woman who owns it has been away for weeks and I was right to guess her servants would be knocking back a few bottles from her wine cellar every night."

"You've got backbone, I'll give yeh that."

George grinned. "I understand people. Everyone takes advantage when they get the chance."

The landlord scratched his armpit as he slowly opened the top drawer of his desk and counted out a pile of notes before passing them to George.

"This haul is worth double this," George snarled, throwing the money on the desk.

"That's as maybe, but I'm going to have to hold on to it for a while before sellin' it on. The peelers could be lookin' for this lot."

"You're a cheating bastard, but since I got away with a big load in January, they've replaced the watchman down at the docks, slowing up smuggling and such, so I've got less coming in from there. I need money now to buy a ring."

"A ring, you say. For a woman, I take it?"

George nodded.

"I might be able to help you out there." He pulled a small box out of the drawer and held it out to George. "Genuine quality, this is. Some daft bastard who wanted to marry one of my girls gave her this. Apparently, it was his mother's."

George took it.

"What happened?"

"Let's just say he was persuaded to sling his hook.

And after a few weeks in the cellar, the tart gave up her daft ideas."

George turned the box so that the ring caught the light, his mind ticking over the possibilities.

"I'll take the ring instead of the money for this lot."

"Deal."

George cupped his chin as he considered the possibility of ridding himself of Pearl. "Are you in the market for another whore?"

"I could be."

"Well, there's a chance I could supply you with a dolly-mop, if you're interested?"

"Is she clean?"

"I wouldn't bring you a filthy whore. It'll be a while yet before I can let you have her, though."

"There's no hurry. I've got enough on the go for now. But before long, one will get a dose and I'll have to let her go," Moby said.

George caught a cab to Stepney. There was no way he was hoofing it or travelling on the omnibus with the scum. His life was on the up. Robbing from Bella's aunt wasn't even a real crime. One day, if his plan worked, it would all be his anyway. The last few weeks had been hard graft and he needed a rest. He'd spend the weekend playing with Daphne and letting Pearl spoil him with some home-cooked meals and whatever else took his fancy.

Victoria guided Anne to the sofa.

"Here, sit down. Let me get you a sherry," she said.

"Sherry's no good for shock, Victoria, I need a brandy. I can hardly believe it – someone has robbed *my* home." Anne clutched her chest.

"Did your butler say how the robbers gained entry?"

"Apparently, they prised open the scullery window. How the servants didn't hear is another matter. I'll expect an explanation when I get home."

"If they were in bed in the attics, it's unlikely they'd have heard anything. Have the police been called?"

"Yes, but I doubt they'll catch them. W-why would someone steal from the home of a poor widow?"

Victoria handed Anne the glass. Anne was hardly poor – her husband had left her a large fortune – but she was clearly shaken and no one deserved to have their home broken into.

"I've done nothing to warrant this."

"Of course you haven't. I don't expect it was anything personal. It was probably an opportunist," Victoria said as she took a seat beside her sister-in-law.

"Well, it feels extremely personal."

"Have they taken much?"

"I don't know. I'll need to return home and supervise the inventory, so I can see for myself what's gone."

"Do you want Stokes or Max to drive you?"

"Thank you, but it'll be quicker by train."

"Would you like one of us to go with you? George is visiting Bella at the weekend, so she can't go, but Edward and I could go with you."

"Heavens, no. You can't leave a house with young people unchaperoned. Goodness knows what they'd get up to."

"Perhaps Kate will go with you."

"No thank you, dear. I'm not one to create a fuss. I have my maid, but perhaps if I could take Max to help with the luggage on the train. I am quite shaken."

"Of course, Anne. If you're sure you don't want a family member?"

"I don't want to miss my weekly dinner date with Owain, so I'll only be gone a few days. Then I'll be back to help you with everything here. I know how you rely on my advice."

ॐॐॐ

Chapter 14

No matter how often he told himself not to panic, Sean was certain this meeting meant bad news. The grey skies and low February sun offered no warmth as he entered the park gates. He hadn't seen Yvette since New Year's Day, when she'd touched his arm and called him Seanie, causing Bella and Kate to howl. He tugged at his stiff collar with his leather-gloved hand. The other clutched the piece of notepaper in his coat pocket. He'd read it so many times he could visualise the words written in neat copperplate handwriting:

Dearest Seanie,
Please meet me at the boating lake Saturday at eleven. It is most urgent that I speak to you.
With great affection,
Yvette

If it were anything pleasant, surely she wouldn't have asked to meet in the park on a chilly February morning. With each step down the frosty snowdrop-edged path, Sean's nausea increased. Things had been going well until the note arrived yesterday.

His mind wandered over the past few weeks. One

consequence of the long hours at the mill was that he had less time to brood. His mother had even moved the family mealtime so that he'd have a chance to wash and change before they ate. Apart from last night, when he'd been distracted, anxious about today, dining with the family had been jovial and even if he was tired, he looked forward to it. Chatting with everyone and being under his mother's gaze, he'd drunk less and wasn't waking every morning feeling as though his head were four sizes too big for his neck. Thankfully, he'd been able to get out of the house this morning without too many questions about where he was going as Anne had the house in uproar now she was returning to London.

Kate and he were becoming close friends and she'd even spoken about her insecurities surrounding her mother. If Max hadn't come in to clear the breakfast table, Sean would have shared with her that Victoria wasn't his mother and of how he'd wanted to believe that his own parents had abandoned him in the hope he'd have a better life. Even after all these years, he could still count on one hand the number of people who knew the truth about his birth, but he trusted Kate, admired her.

Even working at the mill was improving. Monday, as Sean had been about to leave for the day, Matthew had called him into the office.

"It's about time we got you involved in the management side of things. You've passed the test." Matthew had patted Sean on the shoulder and grinned.

Sean had returned his smile. "What test would that be, then?"

"I've never baulked from any task and I couldn't have respected you unless you worked in the same way.

You've tackled every job with enthusiasm, from sweeping floors in the loading bay to the most skilled roles on the mill floor."

"I've done my best."

"Even some of the old-timers have said you can operate the looms like an old hand. It's not gone unnoticed that you've been here fourteen to fifteen hours a day, either. You're a grafter, there's no doubt about that. You've even coped well with the teasing I know you've been getting from the mill lasses."

The blatant way some of them had offered to warm his bed had caused Sean's cheeks to flame.

"They can be rather crude, but it's all in jest. Or at least I hope it is," he'd replied.

Regardless of how well he'd handled the ribbing, he'd been happier the last few days, spending more time behind a desk.

Then George had arrived last night to visit Bella. He'd got Sean on his own for a few moments and had slipped him a fat envelope stuffed with notes. Again, Sean had asked George if it was completely legal and George had assured him it was, also explaining that he didn't know when there would be another chance for Sean to invest, as it was impossible to know when a shipment would get damaged. He'd promised to let Sean know if any other opportunities turned up. Still, at least the money meant Sean had managed to retrieve his pocket watch and he would deposit the rest in the bank when he got the opportunity.

His reverie halted and he slowed as he approached the bench overlooking the boating lake where she was sitting. Yvette was wearing an emerald velvet suit with a matching hat. She was staring at her kid-gloved hands, which she clutched on her lap. Even from this distance, he found her attractive – but was that enough?

As he neared the bench, she looked up.

"Seanie! Hello."

"Yvette, I'm sorry, but I don't like that name."

"I see. Well, that's me told. Do you realise you're scowling?"

"Sorry, I didn't mean to offend you. Shall we go to a tea room? You must be freezing."

"I'm fine here for now. Please, sit down, Sean. This is difficult enough as it is without you looking at me that way."

"Sorry."

He sat next to her, keeping as much distance as he could on the small bench.

"You got my note? Obviously you did – you wouldn't be here otherwise. I don't know how to say this other than to come straight out with it."

"Please do."

Beads of cold perspiration were forming on his forehead. He pulled at his collar.

"I am having your baby."

Damn! He'd been expecting it, but it still caused his body to tense involuntarily.

"I can see you are shocked, but you could say something."

He stopped himself from asking if she was certain that it was his. It would be wrong to insult her in that way. Maybe she'd made a mistake. He had to ask.

"Are . . . a-are you definitely . . . ?"

Her eyes flashed. "It is yours, if that is what you were wondering. I am *not* a hussy!"

"That wasn't what I was going to say. I was going to

ask if you were sure you're with child, but since you mention it, I wasn't the first."

"I will not allow you to insult me." She stood to leave. "I simply want you to know before I tell Papa."

"He'll be furious."

"Not with me. Apart from the mill, I am the thing he loves most – even more than Mama."

"He might not be angry with you, but he'll want to kill me. I would in his position."

"I cannot help that, I am afraid. Unless . . ." She cocked her head to one side, clearly waiting for him to interpret her meaning.

"Do you . . . ? I mean, are you suggesting . . . ? Do you want to get married? I suppose we should."

"Oh, Sean. That wasn't the most romantic proposal. I'll make it sound better when I write about it in my diary. Do you want to marry me?"

"I . . . I want to do the right thing."

"You don't have to stand by me. I will cope somehow." Yvette stared at her feet.

"Don't cry – we'll sort things out."

"Will we?"

"Yes. I want to be a father to our child. I wouldn't dream of leaving you to cope with this alone, but I can't pretend to love you. We don't know each other. We should get married, though."

He passed her his handkerchief and Yvette took it.

"Then yes, I will marry you. Don't worry – you will come to love me."

Sean nodded. He hoped she was right. He liked her – at least what little he'd seen. Whether that was enough for marriage, he didn't know. He wanted a family and it seemed he was going to get one sooner than he expected.

"Can we tell my parents now?"

"Now?"

"Yes. Don't sound so horrified. We cannot afford to waste time. We need to marry before the baby is showing. Everyone must be told it was love at first sight. Papa will be more accepting if we say that."

"You seem to have it all planned out. I've not had time to take it in."

An image of Jane's face flashed through his mind. He'd never court her now. How would his mother react to the news? What would Matthew say? Kate would think he was a fool – she'd be right. Dear God, why had he got so drunk at the party? Why the hell hadn't he staggered home? If he'd ended up spending the night drunk in the gutter, it would have been better than this . . .

"Sean, are you listening?"

"Sorry, yes."

"You will get used to the idea. I have had longer to come to terms with it than you. We can go to my house, then straight to yours to tell your mother."

Sean nodded and Yvette smiled as she took his hand. He resisted the urge to pull away. As they walked towards Matthew's house, he pondered his fate, barely hearing a word Yvette was saying.

Yvette snapped Sean's attention back to her by pulling on his hand.

"Sean, did you hear what I said?"

"Pardon, what were you saying?" He forced a smile.

Yvette instructed him that when they arrived, he should apologise to her papa for not coming to see him in private to ask for his permission to marry her. Sean didn't like the way she was dictating to him, but what choice did he have? He was bemused and in no state to think clearly for himself.

A short while later, Sean found himself on the sofa in the Clarksons' drawing room. Yvette was sitting by his side, holding his hand. The way she was rubbing her thumb on his clammy palm was incredibly irritating.

"Matthew, I apologise for not coming to see you earlier, but Yvette and I would like your permission to marry."

Matthew stared at them, dumbfounded. Sophia's dark eyes were piercing.

"I don't understand. Why so sudden? Surely you've only met twice," Matthew said at last.

Sean cleared his throat nervously.

"The thing is—"

Sophia rolled her eyes. "I suspect they cannot wait."

Matthew's eyebrows came together.

"Papa, don't be angry. It was love at first sight, as it was for you and Mama. I am expecting a baby, though – your grandchild."

Sean nodded. Love at first sight – was there even such a thing? He'd certainly never experienced it. Until Jane . . . Was that love or lust or infatuation? There was no point even thinking about it now.

Matthew ground his teeth.

"Pregnant! When the bloody hell did you get my little girl knocked up?"

Yvette pouted. "Papa, don't shout. It isn't good for the baby. It was our Christmas party, but we are going to marry, so it hardly matters."

"You play the quiet type at the mill . . . There are at least a dozen lasses there willing to give you a quick tumble, yet you took advantage of my baby girl – and in my home!"

"Matthew, calm down. Remember how you wanted me when we first met?" Sophia rose from her seat and kissed Sean's cheek. "Welcome to the family, Sean."

There was no smile on her face and her eyes were cold, Sean noticed. She moved to her daughter.

"Congratulations, dear. You have done well."

Sean wondered what Sophia meant.

"I'm livid, Sean. But, well, I suppose if you're getting married and you love her . . . In different circumstances, I couldn't have hoped for a better husband for my daughter."

"Thank you, Matthew."

Sophia pursed her lips. "The wedding must go ahead quickly. March at the latest."

Matthew scratched his head.

"Where will you live? You've no capital to buy a house."

Sean extracted his hand from Yvette's and ran his hand through his hair.

"We've not had time to talk about that. I'll look for somewhere to rent. Perhaps my mother and Edward will allow us to stay there for a while."

Yvette's forehead creased. "Papa, don't be silly. Sean is rich – of course he has the capital to buy somewhere."

Clearly, her parents hadn't told her what had occurred.

Eventually, Matthew said, "I'm afraid your uncle Claude acted dishonourably and lost Sean's money. We kept it from you because Mama is ashamed of her brother and we assumed Sean would want his affairs kept private."

Yvette stared at Sean, her eyes wide and her brows raised. "You're poor?"

"I'm afraid so, but I don't intend to stay that way."

"A hard-working, intelligent man like you is bound to progress. After you're married, you must stay here until you get sorted. Don't you agree, Sophia?" Matthew said.

Over his dead body. Even the Rows would be preferable to living under the same roof as Sophia. Sean glanced at Yvette, relieved to see that her appalled expression had faded. She rose and approached her father, gazing up at him.

"Papa, I want a home of my own. There is a delightful little house called Park Villa up for rent opposite the park. Please say you will rent it for us."

Matthew kissed the end of Yvette's nose.

"All right, if it'll make you happy. I'll rent it for a year. That will give you time to save up and find something permanent."

Yvette thanked her father, smiling sweetly. It shocked Sean to witness how easily she'd managed Matthew. He wondered if he'd be that way with his own child.

Matthew offered him a cigar and Sophia, looking anything but happy, rang for the butler to bring champagne. Sean didn't want to celebrate but hoped a drink would give him the courage he needed to tell his mother. He'd told her he'd make her proud and this wasn't what he'd had in mind.

When they arrived at his mother's house, Taylor informed them that she was with the family in the morning room. The last thing he needed was an audience. He turned to Yvette to suggest they come back later, but before he had a chance, she pressed her lips together and pulled him across the hall. When they walked into the room together holding hands, everyone except George stared – none more so than Kate, whose jaw dropped open.

"Sean. What's wrong?" his mother asked, getting to her feet.

"Nothing, Mother. We've come to tell you that Yvette and I are to marry in March."

"Papa has agreed to rent Park Villa for us, so we will be living a few doors away from you all," Yvette said.

If it wasn't such an awful situation, the expressions of surprise and disbelief on the faces of his family would have made him laugh. Edward opened his mouth, about to speak, then glanced at his wife as though gauging her reaction before remaining quiet. Kate was frowning and her disapproval bothered him – he wanted her to respect him. Sean realised his fiancée was giggling beside him, although this time there was a nervous note to the tinkling sound in the otherwise silent room.

Say something, someone, please, he thought.

Chapter 15

Bella jumped to her feet and kissed Yvette's cheek, followed by George, who shook Sean's hand.

"Congratulations to you both," George said, beaming.

Bella grinned at him appreciatively. Thank goodness he was here, helping her to break the silence in the room. Their mother's shock was understandable – after all, none of them had even been aware that Sean and Yvette liked each other, let alone that they were courting and in love. She watched as her parents, taut-faced, toasted the couple. Nobody had asked why they were marrying so soon – everyone assumed Sean had got Yvette pregnant.

The person Bella was most concerned about was Kate, who air-kissed Yvette, congratulating her, before turning to Sean.

"Well, you've wasted no time, *stepbrother*. And all this time you've played the shy one. Now, I must be off. I'm meeting a friend in town and I have messages to run."

Bella knew Kate was lying. Making an excuse, she followed her sister upstairs, where she was putting on her coat. Tears were weighing on Kate's blonde lashes.

"It's a stupid question, but are you all right, Kate?"

"He hasn't given me any encouragement, but we get on so well. I thought we had a bond," she replied.

"Perhaps Sean regards you the same as he does me – as a sister."

"I don't want to be his sister. How could I ever compete with Yvette's dark, sultry looks? If she is his type, I stood no chance."

"I'm sure he doesn't love her. I'd bet my last shilling that she's pregnant."

"For sure. It's the first time in my life I let my guard down. Allowed myself to fall in love. I've been a ninny," Kate said as she shoved on her hat.

"You're not. I like everyone – you know I do." Bella laughed self-consciously. "But Yvette's sly. I don't trust her. I believe she's trapped him."

"We can't know that, though she is a conniving strumpet."

"Poor Sean. She's always been spiteful. When we were younger, she used to pinch me when no one was looking."

"What a terrible child." Kate gave a harsh laugh.

"It wasn't only that. I can't explain it, but I'm not daft." Kate pulled Bella into her arms.

"Sure, I know you're not daft – far from it, Sweet Pea. No doubt she baited her hook and caught him. Sean had better look out. You always see the best in people, so she must be fierce bad if you don't like her."

"He must have been drunk to want her."

"As my grandma used to say, when the wine is in, the sense is out."

"Where are you going?"

"Just into town. I'll go for tea and a stack of cakes – it might make me feel better. Then maybe I'll wander round town. If I don't get out of the house, I'll end up throwing myself at him, begging him not to marry that bold baggage and to run away with me instead."

"Perhaps you should and save him from Yvette."

Kate gave a mirthless laugh. "If I thought he'd have me, I would."

"It's chilly out. Will you be long?"

"As long as it takes to get my feelings for Sean under control and to quell my desire to shove Yvette under a passing omnibus. So only a decade or two."

"Oh, Kate. Do you want some company?"

"No. You enjoy your time with George."

Bella rescued George from the tension of the morning room, suggesting they go to the park. He smiled and the skin around his eyes wrinkled attractively. Thoughtful as always, he suggested instead that they should take Kirby along the towpath, where it would be quieter for the dog. She was so lucky. Poor Kate.

George could hardly contain his rage. He couldn't ask Bella to marry him now. He'd intended to suggest a long engagement of a few years as she was so young and then get her up the duff so Victoria and Edward would marry them off quickly. Bleeding hell! He'd worked far too hard at this to let it fall apart. Think, George, think.

Perhaps this could work in his favour. If he had got Bella pregnant, that might have soured his relationship with her parents. Yes, he'd bide his time, carry on with his plan to make them trust him and then in July, ask their permission to marry – giving him time to invent a reason that would make it difficult for them to object. He glanced at Bella. She had a right face on her. What was the matter with her?

"What's troubling you, Bella, my love? Can I help?" he asked.

"The thing is, everything was so wonderful and now it'll change."

George stopped walking and looked at her, treating her to his most adoring gaze with a hint of insecurity.

"It might not be so bad. New people coming into the family can be a positive thing."

"Yvette isn't the nicest of people, but you're right – everything will be fine. I'm being silly."

"I hope one day you'll regard a new person coming into your family favourably."

He smiled as he watched Bella's eyes light up with excitement. Women! So predictable.

"I'd be thrilled to have the right person coming into our family."

George took her hand.

"Good. And I hope your parents would look more pleased if it was the right person."

"Oh, they definitely would, if it was someone they admired," Bella said, her face glowing.

When Sean left a while later to escort his fiancée home, Victoria stood behind the sofa gripping the top, her nails digging into the fabric, while Edward sat in his usual chair by the fire.

He gave her a tight smile. "Don't take it out on the upholstery, darling."

"He's not in love with that vixen."

"You're probably right, but you can't be certain, my dear."

"How could he have been taken in by her? She's expecting, I'm sure of it."

"At least if he is married to Matthew's daughter, he is more likely to remain around here – and she is attractive."

"Is that all you men ever care about?"

"No, but if your wife is getting on your nerves, it helps if she is good to look at. Although I doubt anything would make up for that false girlish giggle."

Victoria moved to stand in front of him.

"Is that how you've coped with me?"

"Now don't start making this about us. I cherish you more than anything and you know it. All I'm trying to do is point out the positives."

She kissed his cleft chin.

"Well, you keep cherishing me. I think that's my son coming in the front door. I need to speak to him and find out how that madam got her hooks into him."

"Don't be too hard on him."

Victoria guided Sean into Edward's study, still uncertain how she was going to handle the situation.

They had barely taken a seat, when she blurted, "Sean, you've got that girl with child, haven't you?"

He nodded, looking her in the eyes. "I didn't mention anything in front of the family because I wanted to tell you in private, as I can't expect you to approve."

"Is it definitely yours?"

"She claims it is, so I had to stand by her. You understand that, don't you?"

"Yes, I'm proud of you. Though I won't pretend I'm not disappointed. But only because I wanted you to marry for love. I take it from your face that you don't love her."

"No, I hardly know her."

She absent-mindedly brushed his fringe back. "My darling boy, I do hope you can be happy with her."

"I do *want* to be a father."

"Good, I'm pleased about that at least. And a grandchild

will be a blessing. But I don't like her, Sean. So, I want you to remember, darling, that even though you'll be a married man, I'll always be here should you need anything. Anything at all. Even if you just want to talk. Don't bottle things up. If you don't want to talk to me, then speak to Edward or even George."

"I will, thank you."

"Matthew will pay for the wedding, but you'll need to buy her a ring. Edward and I'll help with that."

Sean considered telling her about the money from the deal he'd made with George, but that would mean admitting he'd pawned her cousin's watch. He hated being deceitful but was desperate to avoid disappointing her any more than he must have done already. She hid it well, but surely she must be embarrassed by his failure.

"Thank you, Mother. I don't know what I'd do without you. Yvette didn't know I was broke. I think it came as a shock. She must realise by now that she can't expect a large ring. The money will only be a loan – I'll pay you back as soon as I can."

"Buy her a nice one, darling. She'll be wearing it every day for the rest of her life. There's no rush to return the money. I just want you to be happy."

"I hope we'll grow to love each other."

"Watch her, though. Those big brown eyes distract people from the lump of coal that's where her heart should be. She'll do everything in her power to control and manipulate you, as her mother does with Matthew."

"I'll be careful, Mother. I doubt Yvette is as worldly as her mother and I won't allow her to make a sucker out of me."

She pulled him into her arms so he couldn't see her face as a tear escaped her eye.

The next morning, Kate was propped up in bed with a breakfast tray.

"Thank you for arranging this, Victoria. I know you don't like to cause the maids extra work."

"It'll be our secret. Don't tell Anne when she gets back or she'll want a tray every day. Is your headache better?"

"A little."

"Is it Sean?"

"Now why would it be him?"

"Kate?"

"How did you know?"

"I saw your face when he told us they were getting married. Then you coming home and saying that you had a headache and weren't joining us for dinner confirmed it."

"Did Father or Sean notice?"

"No, of course not. Men are about as intuitive as that egg cup. And I've not mentioned anything to your father."

"Thank you. I'd prefer it if he doesn't know what a fool I've made of myself. I don't want him fretting about me."

"You're not a fool. Your father would never see it that way, but I won't say anything. It's a blessing in a way that Anne had to go back to London to sort out her home after the robbery. At least it'll give you a few days to gather your composure. You'll have to be careful around her – she has a nose for gossip."

Kate nodded as she sliced the top off her egg.

"I take it from the way Bella scuttled after you yesterday that she knows?" Victoria said.

"Yes, I told her at Christmas."

"You cared for him that soon?"

"Victoria, you must think me such an eejit. He's done nothing to encourage me."

"Love doesn't have a timetable. I'm just sorry you're hurting."

"I was hoping Sean would eventually come to see me as something more than a sister. Not much chance of that now."

She could feel the tears building again. After last night's deluge, she'd hoped she had no tears left.

By the end of the week, when Victoria arrived home from work, her sister-in-law was lounging in the drawing room like an invalid. Victoria glared at Edward, who hunched his shoulders sheepishly.

"Anne, I didn't realise you were coming back today. Are you unwell?" Victoria said.

Anne pushed herself up a little from the sofa.

"I was away far longer than I intended. I should have taken one of you with me. But that's me – always thinking of others and not wanting to be a bother. I managed to make an inventory of what had been stolen, but I couldn't settle in London. Max was helpful – I may even steal him from you when I set up my own home here."

"You're definitely moving, then?"

"Now my home has been violated, it'll never be the same. How things like that can happen in Knightsbridge is beyond me."

"Did they take much?"

"Jewellery, candlesticks, a valuable clock, trinkets. Silver. Things that were easy to carry."

"Perhaps you need to arrange for your security to be checked."

"That's in hand. New locks are being fitted everywhere. Then the butler will close up the house, keeping a few servants to look after it until I feel ready to sell it. I'll be staying here for the foreseeable. I'm sure you don't mind, do you, Victoria?"

"Erm . . . No, Anne. You're welcome to stay as long as you require."

"I thought you'd say that. Edward told me Sean's getting married in three weeks. No doubt to avoid a scandal. I'm surprised you didn't telephone to tell me."

"We didn't want to trouble you after your robbery."

"That's what Edward said, but it's clear you need my guidance with the family. That's the problem with being a working woman."

"Victoria is an excellent mother, Anne," Edward said.

"I simply meant that being so busy, she has so little time to spare that she can't always be there for them."

Victoria scowled. "I always make time for my family, Anne, including you."

"Hmm, I know you do your best, dear, but now you have me to help."

Victoria rolled her eyes. Lord, give me the strength to resist strangling my sister-in-law.

⚜

Chapter 16

At Euston Station, London, George placed his bag in the overhead rack of the third-class carriage, turned up the collar of the old, ill-fitting mackintosh that covered his best suit and pulled the peak of his cap over his eyes. Even though he'd deliberately chosen to travel with the poorer classes to reduce the chances of being recognised, it rankled. At least by feigning sleep, no one would attempt to speak to him.

Hours later, the train hissed its way into Faredene Station, slowly grinding to a halt. George waited as the rest of the passengers disembarked before peering out into the dimness of the gas-lit platform. He watched as people hurried out into the damp night.

Finally, George saw his chance when an elderly woman and her companion alighted from the first-class carriage, distracting the station master's attention by requesting help with their luggage. He picked up his bag and walked casually off the platform and into Station Road, thankful that the drizzle and March winds had kept people home or in the public houses and the streets were empty.

He cut through the park and approached the exit opposite the house that would soon be Sean and Yvette's new home. Here, he loitered in the shadows until he was certain there was no sign of life inside Park Villa. Then, skirting round the back into the mews, he counted the gates until he reached the right one. After dropping his bag over the six-foot wall, he gripped the top of the gate and clambered over, landing quietly on the flagstones in the yard.

He used his torch to locate the latch on the scullery window, then reached into his bag and pulled out a chisel, which he covered in linen to minimise any damage. Careful not to make too much noise, he jemmied the window open. It was tight, but he squeezed through and onto the wooden draining board. As his foot caught a metal water jug, sending it clattering to the floor, he stilled, listening for signs of life in the house, though he knew it would be empty.

Bella had told him Sean's new staff were spending the night at the Clarksons' to be on hand early to assist with the wedding reception tomorrow. Smirking in the darkness, he removed the key to the back door from the hook – it was just where he'd expected to find it – and retrieved his bags from the yard. He shone his torch at his watch – not long to wait now . . .

Bella's old man liked him, of that he was sure, but Edward still needed a nudge. Something that would make him think of George as the protective sort who would care for Bella. George understood people. For someone as shrewd as Bella's father, big gestures wouldn't work. And he appeared to be as straight as they came, so there was little chance of getting any damaging information on him.

Just before eleven, he removed a piece of drugged meat from its greaseproof paper, grabbed a necktie from his bag and let himself out of the back door. He opened the gate cautiously and crept into the road between the houses and the mews.

At the back gate of Bella's home, he leaned against the wall, listening, until he heard the maid opening the kitchen door.

"Off you go, Kirby. Do your business, there's a good lad."

It was good that people had routines – it made it easier for him to make plans.

He waited for the sound of the door closing then cracked the gate open.

"Here, Kirby. Come on, old boy. Good dog. Come and get the nice meat," he whispered.

Kirby ambled over, his tail wagging. George moved the meat out of reach and clasped the dog's collar, looping the necktie through it.

"That's it. Good boy. Follow George."

Once he was safely back inside Park Villa, he gave Kirby the piece of meat and sat stroking him as the golden retriever fell into a deep sleep.

"There now, you rest easy. A nice long sleep and then tomorrow you can go home."

It was cold in the scullery and he didn't relish the idea of sleeping on the floor all night. Perhaps he should find a bed in the servants' quarters – there was less chance of anyone noticing his presence in there than if he slept in the main bedrooms. Even in the dark, he was sure he could find his way. He'd absorbed every detail of the house two weeks ago when Yvette had insisted on giving them a tour from the cellar to the attic rooms. She'd cooed about how wonderful it was. He was convinced that as she'd shown them how pleasant the servants' accommodation was, she'd somehow guessed his own home didn't measure up even to her meagre servants' quarters.

"Do you think they're adequate, *George*? Even though they're only servants, one doesn't like to think of them living in squalor," she'd said.

He'd retorted quickly, suggesting that she ensure each maid had their own bed. "In the best houses, even servants are given some privacy." That had shut her up.

They mustn't suspect he'd been here, but he couldn't arrive at Bella's home with creased clothing. Then he remembered the linen store in the housekeeper's pantry. Yvette had bragged about all the new sheets and blankets it held.

Wrapped in two thick blankets and with his suit placed carefully on the table, he settled himself as best he could on the stone flags, draping his arm across Kirby. One day, he'd show her – he'd show everyone who thought they were better than him. The first step was to marry Bella. She'd accept his proposal, that much was clear. And he already had the engagement ring from Moby, which he'd claim had been his late mother's. Now, all he had to do was keep winning her family's respect and biding his time until July, when if his schemes paid off, he was sure to get her parents' approval.

Before dawn, he woke and ate the butty his ma had packed for his journey while he thought through his next steps. Then he washed and shaved in the scullery sink, splashed on some cologne and dressed before neatly folding the blankets, returning them to the linen store. He shoved his mackintosh and cap to the bottom of his bag. As Kirby stirred, he fed the listless dog another piece of drugged meat.

"Come on, eat your breakfast, Kirby. I'm sorry, old fella. I can't risk you barking or piddling. Not much longer now."

At nine thirty, a bleary-eyed Taylor opened the door of Bella's home.

"Morning, Mr Bristow. Let me announce you and have your bag taken to the guest-room. Your new suit is already hanging in the closet."

"Thank you. I'll unpack it myself."

"As you wish, sir."

"Is something amiss, Taylor? I expected the house to be filled with the buzz of excitement today."

"Unfortunately, the kitchen maid let Kirby out last night and he's gone missing. The foolish girl didn't check the back gate. The master is most upset."

"Where is everyone? Are they out looking?"

"They have looked, sir. We all have – last night and again this morning. But the family are eating breakfast now. The events of the day must go on, though I'm afraid it's rather put a dampener on things."

When George entered the breakfast room, Bella jumped up to greet him.

"George! I didn't expect you until later this morning."

"It meant changing trains, but I wanted to get here early. I got in at nine. I hope it's not an inconvenience?"

Victoria gestured to a chair.

"Of course not, George. Won't you join us? Taylor, please set another place for breakfast."

George exchanged greetings with the others as he pulled out a chair, accepting Victoria's invitation.

"Taylor told me about Kirby."

Edward shook his head as he spoke.

"I can't understand it. The gate has been open before, but he has never gone off. Not even when he was a pup. Nowadays, I have to persuade him to go for a walk, so why would he wander off? He has been out all night."

"I'm sure he'll come back, Father. Kate's best left in bed to see if she can get over her headache, but I can look for him again before I get dressed for the wedding," Bella said.

Edward smiled wanly at her.

"No, dear, thank you for offering. It looks as though it's going to rain again. I mustn't let this spoil Sean's day."

"If you don't mind, I'll search for Kirby. He's a dear old boy. I'd hate to think of him wandering around town – there are so many automobiles these days," George offered.

"We've looked everywhere again this morning," Sean said.

"Are you sure you don't mind, George? I would be so grateful. Because if I walk much more this morning, my leg will play up all day," Edward said.

George nodded. "Absolutely. I'll go as soon as I've eaten."

Victoria smiled at him.

"Thank you, George. We appreciate it. You must ensure you leave time to get ready, though."

"It won't take me long to dress and it's early yet," George reassured.

Victoria placed her hand on her husband's arm.

"There now, Edward. Please eat something, darling."

After breakfast, George took Kirby's leash and went for a stroll through the park and into town before sneaking back to Park Villa, where he sat stroking the sleeping dog.

A couple of hours later, he shook Kirby.

"Come on, old fella, time to wake up. I need you alive."

When the dog remained motionless, George shook him again, harder this time. "Come on, Kirby, don't frighten George." As Kirby staggered to his paws, George patted him. "For a minute I thought I'd given you too much. I don't want you on my conscience." He liked dogs. They never lied to you.

A heavy shower gurgled in the gutters of Park Villa as George checked the scullery to ensure there were no signs that someone had been in, then he let Kirby into the yard. The old dog lumbered out and relieved itself while George locked the back door, climbing back out of the window, pushing it tightly closed so no one would notice it wasn't locked. He rubbed the drowsy dog's head affectionately.

"Let's wait here a few minutes while we get nice and wet, shall we?"

A short while later, Edward kneeled to hug his cherished dog.

"George, I don't know how to thank you. Where on earth have you been, Kirby, old boy? You are soaked. George, you should have taken an umbrella."

"It's only just started raining again. Kirby was near a brewery – Paynes I think it's called. He was standing in the middle of the road. I grabbed him as a truck came round the corner. People drive far too fast – no consideration."

"Thank God you found him. The poor thing looks half asleep."

"He's obviously been wandering around all night," George said.

"We will get him something to eat and he can rest. I have told Taylor I want a padlock on the gate first thing tomorrow. Now, get yourself ready, George, and we can enjoy the day thanks to you." Edward gratefully pumped George's hand.

Victoria selected the elegant fawn tulle-and-satin two-piece from her wardrobe. She was mother of the groom. Goodness! that made her sound old. Her own wedding day seemed like only yesterday. She fastened the pearl buttons on the cuffs – Kitty and the girls had done an excellent job. Perhaps she was vain, but she wanted to look her best. Sophia would no doubt look spectacular in an outfit she'd chosen not to order from Centenary House. Victoria suspected she'd been to Chester to have something made so her entry might overshadow everyone, including the bride. Put your claws away, woman – Sophia will be family now.

Matthew and Sophia had wanted to throw a party at a hotel for hundreds of guests, including their friends, Matthew's business acquaintances and the affluent of Faredene. But with her support, Sean had stood his ground and the wedding was to be a smaller affair. Although to her mind, the guest list was still too large. There again, she wasn't hosting the event, so her hands were tied.

Despite the need for them to marry, Victoria prayed Sean and Yvette would find happiness together. Hopefully, now Kirby was safely home, Sean's wedding day would proceed with no further hitches. That was the second time George had saved the day – coming to Bella's aid at the suffrage march and now finding Kirby. Edward had repeatedly pointed out to Bella that it was early days and she was far too young to be involved seriously with a young man, but she was obviously smitten. Unfortunately, they suspected she was choosing not to listen, although neither of them objected to George, who was well-mannered and treated Bella with great respect. His feelings for Bella were clear to everyone and since he'd found Kirby this morning, Victoria felt sure Edward would have warmed to George even more.

Once Victoria added the pearls Edward had bought her for their tenth anniversary, she made her way to Kate's bedroom. Kate was in front of the long mirror, struggling to fasten her navy silk dress.

"Here, let me help. I forgot we might have difficulty dressing when I agreed to send the maids to Matthew's house to help with the wedding reception. There, you look lovely. I'm glad you decided on the ivory lace trim – it sets it off perfectly."

Kate turned to Victoria, smiling – though her eyes gave away her true feelings.

"Victoria, you look grand."

"Thank you, Kate. How are you, my dear?"

"How do I look?"

"Like someone who needs a hug." She embraced Kate. "Apart from Bella and I, everyone else believes you've been suffering from a severe headache for the last two days. So, if you need to slip away from the wedding early, no one will suspect a thing. In fact, we've been so convincing, Owain offered to prescribe something when he called round yesterday. However, we can't keep using that excuse, as your father is beginning to worry."

"It might be easier if I believed Sean was going to be happy."

"If God has been listening to my prayers, he will be. Sean knows I don't trust her. But she's going to be his wife, so I'm going to do my best to keep my opinions to myself from now on."

"Victoria, I think it'll be best if we don't talk about it any more or I'll end up blubbering again."

Victoria fought back her own tears. "I understand." She kissed her stepdaughter on both cheeks. "I'll leave you to finish dressing."

As she left the room, she wondered how different today would have been if Sean were marrying Kate. Her stepdaughter could be impetuous at times, but she had a kind heart and was intelligent – unlike Yvette.

Victoria tapped gently as she entered Sean's bedroom, where he and Edward were getting ready together. She thought Sean would have asked Charles to be his best man. That he'd chosen Edward meant a lot to her and Edward's pleasure at the gesture was apparent.

"Edward, darling, may I steal a few moments alone with my son?"

"Certainly, my dear. We have been having a few for Dutch courage."

"Not too many – we don't want you falling down the aisle."

"Or rolling," Sean said, grinning.

"Any more of that and I'll take Cook's rolling pin to the pair of you," Victoria said, trying to join their playful banter.

Edward pulled a face, patting Sean on the shoulder.

"Your mother is a spoilsport. I'll pop down to the kitchen and check on Kirby again. Then I will be back to rescue you in a few minutes – I am taking my duties as best man seriously."

"Thank God. Mother looks as though she's about to scold me for a bad school report."

Victoria forced a smile. Her husband and son were doing their best to lighten the mood, but despite Sean's joking, she could see he was apprehensive about what the future might bring. She smoothed the crease-free lapels of his morning suit and straightened his cravat.

"I'm wearing the mother-of-pearl hair comb Bridie bought me the Christmas I became your mother. She'd have been extremely proud of you."

"Do you really think so? I'm sure she'd have been livid that I'm having to get married," he said.

"She'd be glad you're doing the right thing – as am I."

"Thank you, Mother. To be honest, I still wonder if it is mine."

"I probably shouldn't say anything, as it'll be too late to do anything about it once you're married, but you are my son and I don't want her to hoodwink you."

"Go on."

"I understand that ladies have pretended to fall, bringing on the childbirth, in order to explain why the child was born months earlier than their husbands might expect."

"If she tries that, then at least I'll know the baby isn't mine, but as you say, it'll be too late."

"Yvette might not be my first choice as your wife. And as it appears you're the father, I'd never encourage you to abandon her, leaving her as an unmarried mother. That said, your feelings are more important to me than anything, so if you don't want to go through with this, I'll stand by you and we'll sort things out. We'll care for Yvette and the child whatever happens."

"Mother, I'd never do that."

"I assumed you'd say that, my darling. I suppose you've had your fun and now you must pay the price."

"Unfortunately, I was too drunk to enjoy it that much.

Sorry – I've shocked you. Not the sort of thing one discusses with their mother – and it changes nothing."

"You can talk to me about anything." She stroked his hair down, only for it to spring back up as it always did. A smile brightened her face. "Not even on your wedding day will your hair behave."

"I'd give up on it if I were you. I have."

"You're right. It suits you messy, anyway . . . Tatty Head," she grinned.

"Any wise words for the condemned man?"

"If she were here, Bridie would say may the road rise to meet you."

"What does that mean?"

"It's an Irish blessing, wishing you success in the road you've chosen."

"I'm not sure I picked this road."

"Sometimes in life, Sean, we make split-second decisions that can change the course of our lives. Then we must do everything in our power to make a success of the path we've taken."

As Edward returned to the bedroom, Victoria took her leave. Like Kate, if she were to discuss it any longer, she'd be blubbing.

∽☙☙∽

Chapter 17

Despite the intermittent rain, right now the sun was shining through the stained-glass window depicting Jesus surrounded by his disciples, casting a kaleidoscope of colour around the church. It was beautiful – at odds with Sean's mood. Yvette wasn't Catholic, so they couldn't marry in the church he'd attended as a child. Some would say this meant their marriage wasn't valid, but it didn't matter to him. Would God approve of Sean marrying a woman he didn't love? He doubted it. Somehow, it made a mockery of the entire thing.

"How are you holding up?" Edward asked.

"More nervous by the minute. I hope Yvette isn't late or I might combust," Sean said.

"Sophia has arrived, so not much longer now."

Sean glanced over his shoulder, catching his mother's tight-lipped expression as his future mother-in-law sauntered to her seat. Sophia was breath-taking, her gold lamé gown shimmering as she walked, clearly aware of everyone's eyes on her.

"This might not be the most appropriate time to say it, but I want you to know. I am proud to be your stepfather."

"Thank you, Edward. It means a great deal. If I can be

half the husband and father that you are, then I'll be doing well."

"You will do a great job, I am sure of it."

The pipe organ signalled Yvette's arrival. Sean pulled at his collar as he glanced down the aisle. Matthew was beaming. The Clarksons' footman was stowing large black umbrellas by the door and a maid was helping Yvette to remove her sodden cape. Well, this was it – he was about to become a married man.

Yvette was smiling as she walked towards the altar wearing a gown of ivory Brussels Princess lace, designed by his mother. The soft, flowing organic lines ensured there was no hint of a pregnancy. She was the image of sweetness and innocence – neither of which were true. She'd made it clear that she was disappointed to be marrying someone without wealth, even suggesting he'd been deceitful by keeping his financial circumstances a secret.

As she said "I do," Sean heard a catch in her voice. Her eyes were glistening, but they weren't tears of joy, of that he was certain – perhaps regret, or relief at not being an unmarried mother.

In a brief break in the rain, the wedding party posed on the steps of the church while the photographer rushed to capture their image before the next shower. The stony faces the photographer asked for required no effort from Sean – he had little to smile about as he thought of being tied to the wrong woman until death do us part.

During the past few weeks, Yvette had pulled him round Park Villa, chatting excitedly about placing every stick of furniture or knick-knack yet never once consulting him. Matthew had paid for much of the unnecessary and overpriced furniture, and Sean noticed each request she made of her father was in the voice of a three-year-old, accompanied by a peck on the cheek. It worked every time!

At the reception, Sean took another glass of champagne off the tray Max was carrying. He couldn't allow himself to get drunk today – that was what had started all this!

"I trust you didn't mind helping at the reception, Max."

"Not at all, sir. I like weddings."

"Really? Why?"

"I like the idea of two people in love committing to each other."

"Such a romantic, Max. It might be your turn before long."

"Not for me, sir. I'll never marry."

Sean erupted with laughter.

"Well, that's a bit of a contradiction. Whyever not?"

Max shifted nervously and Sean wished he hadn't probed – it was difficult for servants not to answer questions from their employers, no matter how personal.

"You don't have to answer. I didn't intend to pry," he added.

"That's all right, sir. I'm just better off single. May I wish you every happiness."

"Thank you, Max."

Could they be happy? Charles had made a joke earlier about Sean being shackled – that summed it up completely.

Yvette was smiling as she flitted from guest to guest, talking about how thrilled she was, that Sean had fallen in love with her and swept her off her feet. Anyone watching would have believed her story. Maybe she'd said it so often that *she* believed it. He'd never have the chance to get to know Jane better now. He was glad she had a prior engagement and so couldn't attend the wedding – to have her here would have been unbearable. What sort of man was he – thinking of another woman on his wedding day?

It was just that he had nothing in common with Yvette. He wasn't even sure he liked her. If she were more like Kate, he could have been content today – as he was sure that given time, their friendship could have developed into something more.

As if on cue, Kate appeared at his side.

"So, our pact to marry after five years is definitely off, then," she said.

"Sadly."

"Nothing but wedded bliss to look forward to now."

"Let's hope so," Sean replied, his voice flat.

"I'd have to be a blind donkey to miss the sadness in your eyes. Are you truly happy?"

"Is anyone?"

"Well, you know what Oscar Wilde said about marriage," she replied.

"No. What was that?"

"'One should always be in love. That is the reason one should never marry.'"

"That's reassuring."

"Or what about this one: 'Bigamy is having one wife too many. Monogamy is the same.'"

Sean laughed.

"Sure now, there are a lot more. Maybe I'll send you a list."

"Thank you. I'll look forward to it. Seriously though, Kate, thank you for coming today." He clenched her hand. "You and I haven't known each other long, but your support and friendship mean a great deal to me."

201

"I wouldn't dream of missing your wedding. I'll make sure I attend them all," she said, surprising him with an affectionate kiss on the cheek before hurrying away, blushing.

He hoped his marriage wouldn't affect their friendship.

Kitty, her sons and Milly were making their way across the room towards him. He could see from Kitty's face and the way she was holding on to her sons that the boys had been up to mischief. It brought a smile to his face.

"Hello, you four," he said.

Kitty punched him gently on the shoulder.

"You'll have upset the mothers of Faredene today, Tatty Head. Back five minutes and married before they had time to size you up as husband material for their daughters."

"I expect they think they've had a lucky escape."

Kitty glanced around to see who was close enough to hear before speaking.

"If I'd have known yeh were going to throw yourself away on that piece, I might have waited for you meself."

"Kitty, behave," Milly said.

Kitty scowled playfully at Milly.

"All right, misery guts. I'll keep meself in check. At least I made sure no one was listening."

"The wedding is over the top, but I hope you enjoyed it," Sean said.

Milly planted several pecks on his cheek.

"One kiss will do, Milly. He doesn't need you snogging his face off," Kitty said with a grin.

Milly shot her a watch-it look.

"We wouldn't have missed yer wedding, Sean. I've known yeh since you were a baby – you're part of our family," Milly said.

"You're family to me, too."

"I remember the first time I met you, when you moved to Faredene. Before I'd even got to give you a cuddle, you'd filled yer nappy. I changed yeh while yer mam showed Bridie and Edward round Centenary House."

Kitty elbowed her sister.

"Flamin' Nora, Milly. I thought I were the one who didn't know how to behave. Don't embarrass him on his wedding day, talking about him having muck up to his armpits an' in his hair."

Kitty's sons giggled as Milly folded her arms indignantly.

"I never said that."

"No, but that's what I'm imagining." She wrinkled her nose. "Eww – and I bet it stunk to high heaven."

"Kitty! Will you act yer age for once?"

"Will I heck. I have no choice about getting older, but I have no intention of growing up."

Milly smiled at her sister.

"That's probably the best attitude to have, love. Come on, let's leave Sean in peace. You've embarrassed him enough."

"We've had a lovely time, Sean, but if yeh don't mind, love, we're gonna get off before you leave for yer honeymoon. You won't believe what these two little monkeys have been up to while I turned my back for five minutes – Albert was meant to be watching them," Kitty added.

Sean adopted a stern expression.

"What have you done, boys?"

"Aww, it wasn't owt bad, honest. We wouldn't spoil yer big day. Mam warned us straight we'd get no sweets for a month if we did."

"I'm sure it wasn't bad. So, what did you do?"

"Have you heard of the Great Houdini?" Jake asked, wobbling as he balanced one foot on top of the other.

"I have, yes."

Kitty piped up, "I blame our Harry. He's been filling their heads wi' nonsense about him. I suppose I should be pleased they don't want to be bank robbers after listening to that daft bruvver o' mine."

Jake gave his mother a disgusted look.

"It's not nonsense. Uncle Harry said he'll take us to see him on stage and we've been practising, 'cos I want to be the Great Jakerini when I grow up and Brian is going to be my assistant."

"And what does that entail, might I ask?" Sean said.

The boys were amusing, but it was Kitty's look of utter exasperation that made it difficult for him to keep a straight face.

"He only took his little brother into the servants' quarters, tied him up and hung him upside down from the bannister of the back stairs to see if he could escape. Thank Christ a footman saw him before he got the ropes off or he'd have landed on his flippin' head."

"Honestly, Mam, we're not that daft! I were gonna catch him. That's why I had to tie Brian up, even though he's only the assistant, 'cos he's not big enough to catch me."

Sean knew he shouldn't – the boy could have been seriously injured or worse – but he couldn't help grinning.

"Where did they get the rope?"

"Apparently, it came off some blocks of ice that were delivered this morning. Honest to God, these two will be the finish of me," Kitty said with a smile.

Milly gestured towards Kitty with her head.

"Makes the things she got up to look tame."

Kitty grabbed Brian's hand as the lad was about to make his next escape.

"Like I said, we'll get off now. Besides, Albert will want his tea before the pub opens again for the evening session."

As Sean escorted them to the door, Yvette called him over to meet a distinguished-looking man with a thatch of curly white hair.

"Sean, this is Mr Mason."

He extended his hand to Sean.

"I know what wedding days are like. My son, Peter, married recently. He looked as though he was a man about to go to war, as well."

"He and Louise are honeymooning in Italy," Yvette said, looking pointedly at Sean.

"Yes, two months they'll be away for. Where are you lovebirds off to for your honeymoon?" Mr Mason asked.

"We are delaying our trip, as Sean is too busy at the mill at present, so we will go later in the year," Yvette said.

How easily she lied. Not a flicker to give it away, he thought. Yvette had suggested they go abroad, which Sean couldn't afford. Matthew had for once refused her request, but only because he was concerned about her travelling far in her condition.

"You're an incredibly lucky man. Beautiful wife, and supportive, as well," Mr Mason said.

"Indeed," Sean replied.

"Louise is a lovely girl though," Yvette said.

"Louise has her qualities. Now, I mustn't keep you from your guests," he said before walking away.

"Qualities, my foot. Louise is my school-friend, so I know her better than most."

"Why didn't we go to their wedding?"

"Mama and Papa attended, but I didn't want to go. Louise and I argued a few weeks before I met you, so I declined the invite. She's as dull as ditchwater – and has a face to match – but her father owns a shipyard in Liverpool. Peter was betrothed to her when she was fourteen."

"I didn't think that sort of thing still happened."

"Well, apparently it does. Their mothers were best friends and arranged it all."

Sean empathised with this Peter. And he hadn't heard Yvette gossip nastily before – he hoped this wouldn't be a feature of their conversations from now on. Excusing himself from his bride, he made his way over to Jess and Harry.

When he'd confided in her as to why he was getting married, Jess had told him love wasn't always the most important thing. Today, Jess gripped his hand and kissed his cheek.

"A happy marriage needs friendship and trust. Don't dwell on each other's mistakes and you won't go far wrong."

"Thank you, Jess. I'm sure that's excellent advice. Do you have any more wise words? I need all the help I can get."

"If it doesn't work out, you can always head for the hills. Or jump on a train and become a nightclub singer like I did."

"Maybe even better advice. Thank you, but I'm afraid I can't hold a note."

Sean hoped he wouldn't feel the need to escape from

his marriage. He'd wanted a wife and family. Now, he had a wife and their child would soon follow, so he'd get his wish – only far quicker than he'd imagined. Surely that didn't mean it wouldn't work.

After accepting Harry's congratulations, Sean moved to the next group of guests. He was finding it a trial. If anyone else told him how lucky he was, he might punch them.

Yvette was quiet on the journey to Chester and stared out of the window of the automobile without looking at him once. He suspected she was crying and took her hand in his.

"We'll be happy, Yvette. Build a life together with our child," he said.

There was no response.

When they reached their hotel room, her mood changed. She asked him to open the bottle of champagne that was waiting for them as she began opening his trousers. Maybe there was hope for their marriage . . .

The following day, Bella was glad that the only other passenger for the London-bound train was sitting in the waiting room. It meant George and she had the platform to themselves. She didn't want to share their last moments together with anyone. They'd had a lovely time at Sean's wedding, but now she was struggling to hide her disappointment. She'd hoped George would have welcomed her idea that she travel to London with him and stay at Anne's house. In her head, it made perfect sense. She and George could spend time together in the evenings when he finished work and have every weekend together. She wanted to see where he lived, where he worked, but he was having none of it.

"Bella, there's nothing attractive about the docks where I work, so there's no way I want you spending time in that district. And I definitely don't want you to meet me after work so we might walk home together. The area isn't suitable for an unaccompanied woman and the rooms I rent are unpleasant. I don't wish you to see them – bachelors don't bother about the niceties."

"Then perhaps you could come and visit me in the evenings and at weekends."

"Bella, my darling, I need you to realise. Most nights I don't know what time I'll finish work. If a ship comes in late, I can't leave until the paperwork is complete. The last thing I want is you waiting around for me."

"Isn't it possible to do it the next day? Surely you can get away early some days."

George's jaw tightened.

"Would you say that to Sean? Everyone praises him for the hours he's working at the mill. And it's part-owned by his mother, so he's hardly likely to get the push if he does something wrong. My employer doesn't care about how tired I am, whether I'm eating enough or anything else. All he's interested in is getting the work done."

"I'm sorry. You've told me before that he's disagreeable. I should have realised."

"That's all right. I can't expect you to understand. I envy Sean. Your mother dotes on him. On both of youse . . . It's difficult having no family."

"I want to be your family."

"I know and I adore you for it. But, Bella, this conversation is pointless. I couldn't possibly be happy with you staying at Anne's house after someone robbed it."

"I could stay in a hotel."

George shook his head several times.

"Bella, stop this, please. Can you imagine how that would be for me, knowing you were close but unable to see you? I'd want to stop work early every day. By the end of the month, I'd be out on my ear. Besides, I'm not a wealthy man. I can't afford to take you out all the time and it would upset me greatly not to do so."

"I have money."

Anger flickered across his face.

"I've explained to you before – I won't take your money. It was bad enough that you persuaded me to let you pay for the theatre and dinner last month, never mind buying me a suit for the wedding. I've got my pride."

"I wouldn't care if we stayed at home."

George sighed. He turned to look down the platform. Bella bit her lip.

"I'll stop. It's j-just that I'll miss you. The six weeks until I see you again will seem like a lifetime."

"For me, too. I want us to be together all the time. That's why I took the extra weekend off before the weddin' to try on the suit you bought me, but now I must work the next few weekends to make up the time."

"I-I understand. I'm sorry."

"Do you trust me?"

"Completely."

"Good, then believe me when I say I have a plan. Now, perhaps you'll allow me to kiss you before my train comes in. I need something to keep me going."

Bella couldn't believe she once thought you shouldn't allow a man to kiss you until you were engaged, never mind in public. She lived for George's kisses.

As his train pulled out of the station, she walked

alongside it, looking at him through the window until she ran out of platform. George was such a gentleman that he'd never tried to take their relationship further in terms of intimacy. She told herself that was the measure of how much he both respected and loved her. Was she disappointed? Perhaps a little.

cↄฬฬ

Chapter 18

The heatwave that had swept the country at the beginning of July was showing no sign of abating. By the time Victoria got home from Centenary House, she was exhausted. Despite leaving the curtains closed all day to keep the sun out, their drawing room was oppressively warm. Today had been challenging enough, as even the ladies who were normally pleasant had been irritable during their fittings. Now, it seemed the day was going to end on a disagreement. She fanned herself as she looked from Edward to the devastated couple opposite.

"George, dear, it's not that we don't care about you – you're a wonderful match for Bella. But she's far too young to get married. You both have your entire lives ahead of you," Victoria said, feeling terrible as her daughter's eyes glistened.

"We can see you care for Bella, George, and her mother and I are pleased, but there is no need to rush things," Edward added.

"I knew you'd react this way. Sean got engaged after knowing Yvette only a few weeks. We could have run away, but we respect you both too much and want your blessing like you gave Sean, even though he'd got Yvette pregnant."

"Bella!" Victoria said. It was so unlike Bella to be

211

argumentative. Though she could appreciate why her daughter was so distressed. "Sean's in his thirties. You're still young."

Bella clutched George's hand.

"Tell them, George. Explain why we don't want to wait."

"This is difficult, but the thing is, I have a weak heart. Apparently, I was born with the problem, but it's slowly getting worse. I hope to live another ten years, but how many of those will be good before I become an invalid, I cannot say for certain."

Victoria gasped. "Oh, my dear boy."

"That's terrible, George. Are you sure? Could you get a second opinion? Perhaps we should consult Owain Farrell," Edward said.

"I've had four opinions and with the greatest respect, Edward, I don't want to see another doctor. If you don't feel you can give your consent, I'll walk away, despite the pain it'll cause both Bella and me."

"George, no!" Bella said.

"I won't come between you and your family, Bella. Eventually, you'd resent me for it and I couldn't bear that."

Victoria blinked away the tears that were building. Regardless of whether Bella stopped seeing George or she married him, her daughter was heading for the sorrow of losing a loved one sooner than she should. Edward echoed her thoughts.

"Naturally, I am terribly sorry to hear about your condition, but you should never have got involved with Bella. This situation can only lead to heartbreak for her."

George patted Kirby's head.

"I understand why you'd say that, but I was unaware of my weakness when I met Bella. Had I been, then I'd never have allowed her to develop feelings for me. When I found out, it was too late – we were already in love."

"It's true, Father. George explained that he'd considered ending our courtship, but as he said, that would have hurt me. And he's right – I'd have assumed he'd rejected me."

"I see," Edward said.

"But it's going to be incredibly difficult for you," Victoria said.

"I realise that, Mother. I was shocked when George told me. Hopefully, it'll be years before we must face the problem of his health. Even a few joyful years with George will be better than nothing. Surely you can grasp that."

Victoria sighed. "George, I'm so sorry that you're in this situation. It's a difficult thing to cope with at any age. At twenty-five, it's tragic. But you must appreciate our first concern has to be Bella."

"Naturally – I'd have been surprised if you hadn't been worried about her. Please, speak freely."

The last thing she wanted was to be the one who kept them apart and caused them to waste time, as Edward and she had. Still, she had to express her apprehensions. Victoria chose her words carefully.

"I remember how dreadful it was for me when Edward was hospitalised after Brakenridge's cronies attacked him. To think of Bella going through that, with perhaps no hope of your recovery, breaks my heart."

"I understand, and I pray the end will be swift, so Bella won't have to spend months watching me deteriorate."

"Forgive me, George. This may sound insensitive, but she'll still have doctors and hospital visits to attend, as well as the apprehension that goes with them," Victoria added.

213

Bella moved to the edge of her seat. "No, I won't. George has already thought of that."

"Allow me to explain," George said. "I've told Bella that we can only marry if she agrees to let me attend medical appointments alone. It's a small thing, but she must permit me to protect her in any way I can."

It crossed Victoria's mind that sitting at home waiting for him to come back from seeing his physician might be worse than being there with him, but what was clear to her was that this courageous young man was trying to protect the woman they all loved.

As though proving her point, George said, "I love Bella and want the best for her, so as I said, we'll abide by your decision."

"I won't if it's the wrong decision," Bella said.

"Bella, you seem unable to comprehend our desire to shield you, which proves that you're still too young to make such a big decision," Victoria said.

"That's not fair, Mother. I'm fighting to be with the man I love, as any woman would."

George reached out for Bella's hand.

"Please don't argue with your parents, my love. They only have your best interests at heart."

Victoria gave George a small smile – thank goodness he understood their concerns.

"Thank you, George. Bella, I realise you love George, but are you ready to face such a challenging time?" Edward asked.

"I'm certain, Father. This is what I want. I love George."

Edward looked at his wife as he spoke again.

"Then there is nothing more to say. Victoria, my darling, we must give our consent. We cannot deny these two young people the chance of happiness, however short-lived it may be."

As Victoria nodded her agreement, she could see Bella's shoulders drop as she relaxed, relief appearing on both of their faces.

Edward spoke again.

"Before we celebrate, there is one condition."

Bella frowned. Victoria wondered what he was going to say – she was still reeling from the shock of learning about George's circumstances.

Edward continued calmly.

"You must live here with us. George, I realise your job is in London, but Bella's allowance will be enough for you both to live on."

"Thank you, sir. I appreciate your offer. But I've always earned my living. Doing an honest day's work is important to me. I couldn't live on charity. Bella and I can find rooms in London so I can continue working," George said.

"I wouldn't have expected any other reaction from you, George. And I admire you for it. However, I want you to enjoy what time you have together without the extra burden of you trying to earn a living. It won't be charity because you will be family. And the money will be paid quarterly into a joint account for you both."

"With the greatest respect, Edward, I must be allowed to provide for us. You have my word Bella will be happy in London."

"I'm sorry, George, but I am afraid I must insist. Because should the time come when you and Bella need emotional support, if you are in Faredene we can be here for you both."

"Then I accept your condition gladly. I have no family

of my own. My parents both died when I was fourteen and I've been fending for myself ever since. My parents weren't rich – my father was a bank clerk – but they educated me and instilled in me the importance of family. To be part of yours means a great deal. However, I have one last condition of my own," George said.

"What is that?" Edward asked.

"The money must go into an account solely in Bella's name."

Edward held out his hand to George.

"Agreed."

Bella shot up from her seat and squeezed between her parents on the sofa, throwing her arms around her father's neck.

"Thank you, Father." She planted a kiss on Victoria's cheek. "You too, Mother."

George put his hand in his pocket and got down on one knee.

"If I may, now we have your parents' agreement, I'd like to give you this ring, Bella. It's all I have left to remember my mother."

Before retiring for the evening, they agreed George would move to Faredene and stay at The Crown, for propriety's sake, two weeks before the wedding, which would take place in August.

That night in bed, Victoria spoke to Edward of her concerns.

"Surely I should speak to her again – ensure she's not acting in haste or out of compassion. We don't want a repeat of Sean's turbulent marriage."

Edward pulled her close.

"Victoria, my love, we have raised the sweetest young

woman I have ever met, but underneath, she has your iron will. We won't be able to change her mind no matter what we say. So if we don't want her eloping to Gretna Green, I suggest we do our best to help them get through their ordeal."

"George said he'd respect our decision."

"He is a man in love. I imagine Bella could persuade him if she set her mind to it."

Victoria extracted herself from Edward's arms.

"I expect you're right. Now, I'm sorry, my love, but as much as I enjoy being close to you, it's far too hot. If I'm to get any sleep tonight, I need space."

The following day, a gentle breeze from the Thames billowed Kate's coat as they walked. She glanced at her companion. Garrett Ackerley was a handsome man, but that didn't excuse how she'd behaved. There was no going back now – she'd slept with a married man. She couldn't even pretend that he'd pursued her. At Sean's wedding, Garrett's wife's pregnancy had been obvious and she'd spent much of the day sitting with Mrs Payne's daughter, who was also with child. Garrett had flirted with Kate as he always did and she hadn't discouraged him. Then last week at a dinner party, Kate had suggested they meet in London.

"London was suitable for our little rendezvous this time, but next time we'll need to find somewhere more discreet," Garrett said now as they walked along the embankment.

"There won't be any more meetings. We should never have done this. It was a moment of madness. It can't happen again," she replied.

"Whyever not? We had fun, didn't we? You certainly sounded as if you were enjoying yourself last night."

"I said it can't happen again, and I meant it. What we've done is wrong. Your wife deserves better. I deserve better."

"Don't be so righteous. This was your idea."

"I know it was. And I'm ashamed of myself. Just go, will you. Go back to your wife and forget this ever happened."

"I've told you – my marriage is a sham. This isn't a fling for me. I have feelings for you."

"You shouldn't. It's wrong."

"Don't play the virgin maid. You're being absurd. I've heard the rumours about you around Faredene."

"I don't give a damn how stupid I'm being. You're cracked if you think I care what you've heard about me. Sure, nothing you can say will make me feel any worse. I despise myself. I'm no better than a prostitute – worse, in fact. At least most of them do it because they need the money. And you're a sleeveen – nothing but a liar. Please, just leave me. I'll make my own way back to the hotel to collect my luggage and hail a cab to the station."

Kate turned her back on him and stalked off, leaving him open-mouthed.

Once she was far enough away, she found a bench and sat. Her heart was racing. If there were rumours about her, it wouldn't be long before her family picked up on them.

In the months following Sean's wedding, she'd acted disgracefully. There had been two other men before Garrett, but at least they'd been single. One had even suggested they get married. It was hardly romantic – still, it had been a proposal, just from the wrong man.

They'd been lying in bed, smoking, after having sex and he'd said, "What about it? Should we tie the knot? At least we know we'll have a good time in the bedroom."

She shouldn't have been so cruel – not have laughed in his face. Even now she felt uncomfortable remembering her words.

"Don't be ludicrous. I could never marry you."

"Whyever not? I'll inherit my father's title one day."

"Because the occasional afternoon in the sack is grand, but I need a man with more in his head than he has in his pants, title or not."

He was a decent man and she'd wounded him. Sometimes she disliked herself. Now, she'd not only betrayed another woman, but her dignity was also lost. It was clear she mustn't carry on in this manner. She needed to get off her path of self-destruction. If she didn't change things, she'd end up a bitter old spinster with a reputation for being a tramp. Either that or she'd catch a horrible disease and die alone in a filthy room.

Get a grip, woman. You're fair maudlin, she thought.

Dragging herself off the bench, she then strolled back to the hotel, thinking over the past while giving Garrett the chance to check out of their room.

Her grandparents had been extremely strict but progressive and they'd ensured she had an excellent education. As a result, she spoke Latin, French and German fluently. She'd even attended Trinity College in Dublin. Kate had assumed they'd sent her away to school simply because they wanted her out of the way, though they'd never given her any reason to surmise this. Perhaps it was a result of being told that her father hadn't wanted her that made her so insecure. If her mother had been aware of or known how worthless it made Kate feel, would she still have said those things? Kate would never know now.

It was only when her grandpa was dying that he'd told Kate how much he and Grandma both loved her. Then he'd revealed to her how many times Edward had tried to see her while her mother had been alive.

Even though she was young when her mother died, Kate had a vivid image of her staggering, giggling, towards the barn with a young farmer following a harvest ball. Kate had followed them. She hadn't a notion what they were doing, but now she was under no illusion.

It had been only days later that her mother had died in a riding accident. That was all Edward had been told. Her grandparents saw no reason to embellish the tale with the fact that she was out riding with a married man at the time of the accident, causing a local scandal.

Her mother had frequently told Kate not to worry about conventions such as marriage and have fun while she could. She was glad her mother had enjoyed herself – life was awfully brief and in her mother's case, particularly so. Perhaps that's why Kate had always defied conventional thinking of how a lady should behave. But she'd made a mistake trying to enjoy herself with Garrett and the others – all she felt was dirty and cheap.

Whatever the reason, being reckless and selfish while longing for a man she could never have was ending today, for sure. She was going to do something worthwhile with her life. Most people didn't realise that like her father, if she read something once, she remembered it. She resolved to share her knowledge and help young women to do something with their lives other than wait around for a man to choose them. It was what she'd been doing since she met Sean. Not any more!

As Kate reached the entrance to The Savoy, she pushed her introspection to one side. She was ready to find a more fulfilling path in life.

It was when she'd returned from London that Kate had scoured the magazines and newspapers for three weeks looking for advertisements for teachers. Today, there was an advert for a teacher at a girls' school, which sounded perfect. Yet, here she was, sitting at the writing bureau in the morning room, staring at a blank piece of paper. What was stopping her from writing?

As much as she sometimes wished to put distance between her and Sean, she wasn't sure she wanted to move that far away from her family – from him, if she were honest. The only thing she was certain about was that she was bored. Her father and Victoria were always so busy. They had purpose to their lives. And Bella thought of nothing but George and her wedding. No doubt she'd have a family of her own before long.

Kate looked over her shoulder as the door opened.

"Am I disturbing you?"

"Victoria! No. Sure, I was thinking of writing a letter, but it can wait."

"I was wondering if we could talk."

"Ah, of course, is anything wrong?"

"It's rather a delicate topic."

"Come on, say it. Sure, it can't be that bad."

"Mrs Payne spoke to me in confidence after this morning's Guild meeting. She's not malicious or one for gossiping. She simply wanted to warn me about something she's heard."

"Warn you?"

"It was about you, I'm afraid."

A sense of unease crept over her.

"What did she say?"

"Apparently, it involved you and Garrett Ackerley."

She knew what the answer would be before she asked.

"What about us?"

"Do you really need me to say it? His wife is friendly with Mrs Payne's daughter."

"No. No, I don't need to hear it."

"So it's true?"

Kate nodded.

"Has the rumour gone any further, do you think?"

"Not that I'm aware of. Neither Mrs Payne nor her daughter will repeat it, but I don't know about Garrett's wife. One thing I can be sure of is that if Hornby-Smythe hears about it, she'll relish telling people. Apart from enjoying a scandal, she'd love discrediting a member of my family."

"What about Father? Does he know?"

"Not to my knowledge. I'm sure he'd have mentioned it."

"I'm altogether ashamed. If Father heard, sure, I couldn't bear it."

"Perhaps you should go away for a while. If you're not here, his wife might not tell anyone else."

"I don't suppose I have much choice."

"Where will you go?"

"I'm not going anywhere until after Bella's wedding. It would hurt her if I didn't attend. Then I'll go to Anne's – if she'll allow me to stay there for a while."

"Perhaps you need to decide what you want to do

with the rest of your life. Boredom can make people behave rashly. You're such an intelligent young woman. You could do anything you chose. I'll be happy to help you in any way I can."

"I was thinking of applying for a job as a teacher."

"That's a splendid idea. Where is the school?"

"London."

"We'll miss you, but it's probably for the best. At least for a while."

"Please promise me you won't tell Father about this."

"Kate, I dislike keeping things from him."

"Please, Victoria."

"You could tell him about the teaching post."

"Sure, I'll do that, no problem. At least that's something he can be proud of."

Chapter 19

George ignored the muffled screams and banging from the cellar of The White Lion. He smirked as he tucked the two white five-pound notes in his wallet before picking up his pint. August had brought even hotter temperatures across the county and Moby's shirt clung to his rolls of fat. The landlord's frayed sleeve strained as he pulled his arm across his stubbled chin, wiping away the beer foam as he belched.

"That Pearl's a noisy bitch. I don't mind when she's wi' the punters – some o' them like that. But she'd better not give me any trouble. I've paid you good money for her."

"She'll behave. She loves Daphne. If you threaten to take her away, Pearl will settle down sharpish."

"Just before I gave her the back o' me hand, she screamed that you're her husband an' the girl's father. Not that I care, but is there owt in that?"

"Do I look as though I'd marry someone like her? No. She's a tart, nothing more. You've got a good deal. She was earning decent money for me and still has a few good years left in her."

"So why are you sellin' her on, then?"

"I'm done with this way of life. I've bagged myself a beautiful young heiress. That's who the ring was for."

"No wonder yer looking so pleased wi' yerself. Suppose yeh won't want your old wife getting in the way, then."

"I told you, that's tripe. Right, I'm off. I've got someone I need to see before I head off into the sunset."

"One last thing. Seeing how she isn't yours, I take it you'll have no objection to me setting the kid to work when she's a bit older."

George hesitated. Despite what he'd told the landlord, she was his daughter. Pearl hadn't been on the game until after she was born, when he'd persuaded her to sleep with the men he brought home.

"Erm . . ."

"What's the problem? Yeh can't expect me to feed and clothe her for years wi' no return on my investment. Are yeh sure she's not your kid?"

"No. Do what you want with her. I was thinking I'd missed a trick and should have charged you extra. You'll make a bundle with a young 'un."

"I'm handing over no more brass. Owt could happen before she's seven or eight. She could die before I make a penny off her. I'm not like some o' the dirty buggers – I won't set girls workin' any younger than that."

"Break her in easy."

Moby belched loudly.

"Don't you worry about that. I always start 'em off meself. They don't call me Moby Dick for nothin'." He cupped the front of his trousers. "If they can handle me, they'll have no trouble with the punters."

George couldn't bear to hear more. He needed to get away before he gave in and took Daphne with him.

"Right, well I'm off. And do yourself a favour – don't

tell Pearl anything about me unless you want her doing a bunk to find me."

"Where does she think yer going, then?"

George sneered. "I told her they were to stay at the pub while I was in South Africa for a few weeks on a job. She's realised now that I was lying, though."

"I'll tell her nowt. She should be popular. That's a fine pair of knockers she's got."

"Like I said, you got a bargain."

The landlord gestured towards the cellar with his bulbous thumb.

"I'm gonna get me leg over now. Help her settle in – see what me customers will be buyin'."

Within the hour, George was at his ma's, where he removed his gun from the loft and stashed it in the bottom of his bag. He was unsure where he could keep it hidden in Faredene, but he couldn't leave it in his ma's loft any longer, not now the landlord was finally promising to fix the hole in the roof. If he couldn't find anywhere suitable in the Clarksons' house for it, he'd have to find a pub in a rough part of town and sell it on. He hadn't lived with his ma for years – never spent more than a few days in any one location – but he'd always thought of this place as home.

"It's only pork pie and salad, love. It's too hot for us to eat anythin' else. Me knees have been creasing me all day," Mrs Bristow said.

"Sit down, Ma. I'll fetch the plates to the table."

Once they'd eaten, his ma used her twisted arthritic finger to push a few stray pastry crumbs around her plate.

"Don't cry, Ma. I'll be coming to London on business from time to time, so I'll slip in an' give you a few shillings. Remember – that telephone number is for the rooms that I'm renting. Don't use it unless it's an emergency," he said.

"I won't, son. I don't even know anyone with one of those telephone contraptions to ring you, anyway."

"The post office will make the call for you. But you won't need to use it, because I'll be back to see you as often as I can."

"All right, George, love. I'm glad you've got yerself a decent job. Promise me yer not gonna be with some woman."

"There's no one, Ma. While I was up north visiting that girl, I got the chance of a job in the offices of a cotton mill and took it."

"You always said workin' was for fools."

"I still keep the odd sideline going, but everyone's got to settle down sometime. This job has got real prospects."

"So, is it over with that girl?"

"Yes, Ma."

"Well, yeh seem happy, that's for sure. That's what matters to me, boy."

George kissed her sagging cheek.

"I am, Ma. One day maybe you can come and live with me."

"What about yer wife and daughter? Will you still send them some money?"

"Don't you worry about Pearl. I've done right by her. Besides, she's moved in with a fella in Spitalfields and he's taken a shine to Daphne – wants to be a father to her. So, even though it's going to be hard on me, I'm doing the decent thing by staying away from now on. That way they can be a proper family."

"She'll still be yer wife."

227

"Let me worry about that. Now, I've got to go if I'm to catch my train. I love you, Ma."

He hated it when his ma cried and it was ruining his good mood. George kissed her once more before grabbing his two cases from the hallway and closing the front door behind him.

He pushed his shoulders back and glanced around the street where he was born. Several of the doors were open, men and women sitting on their black-leaded steps, enjoying the evening sun. A group of barefoot girls played hopscotch, laughing as one toppled over.

"You're looking dapper. Done well for yerself, Georgie boy," an old crone called from her doorstep.

George nodded, smiling at his neighbour's greeting.

"This place is a shithole even when the sun is shining," he muttered to himself as he turned the corner.

He was finally on his way to the life he deserved, that he'd worked so hard for. Stage one of his plan was falling into place nicely. Bella was both beautiful and pliable. He might keep her around as long as she didn't give him any trouble . . . Yes, George, he thought, you've come good. No working yourself to death like the other clowns.

Victoria pushed loose strands of damp hair from her own face and then fastened her pearls around Bella's neck. There had been no let-up in the heat with no rain for weeks and it looked set to continue. The guests would melt at this rate, never mind the food.

"There, my pearls were the perfect choice. The front-fastening clasp complements the square neckline beautifully."

"Thank you, Mother, they're wonderful – something

borrowed. Oh, I nearly forgot. I've not put the sixpence in my shoe."

"Kate's done it for you, as you'll discover when you put them on."

A smile spread across Bella's face and then she squealed as the maid brought her wedding bouquet into the bedroom.

"It's gorgeous! Not the limp blooms I was expecting."
She rushed forwards to take the flowers.

"I realise you're excited, darling, but I need to make a couple of final adjustments to your veil," Victoria said.

Bella had chosen a simple gown of ivory satin with a high waistline trimmed with lace and a tulle veil.

"I'm so excited, I could burst," Bella said as she pretended to waltz back to her mother.

It pleased Victoria that her sweet daughter had found such an amiable young man, but how long their happiness would last was at the forefront of her mind. No couple was certain how long they might have together, but these two lovely people had a death sentence hanging over them.

Bella gulped back a tear as her father walked her down the aisle towards her husband-to-be. She'd never expected to marry a man as wonderful as George and she refused to accept he might die in as little as ten years – he appeared to be so strong. Only last week he'd chased her round the garden. She'd laughed at first then stopped, tears filling her eyes, afraid he might collapse.

He'd made her promise she wouldn't stop him from enjoying life – not waste their time together looking for signs of illness. He wanted them to have a normal marriage and she resolved to do everything she could to ensure they did. If the worst happened, she'd care for him, although she needed to believe the doctors were wrong. What was she doing thinking about this now? This was her wedding day!

Sean took another glass of champagne off the tray as the waiter passed. He was pleased for Bella – she deserved to have a good husband and George was a decent bloke. He had to admit, he'd been delighted when Yvette said she was too heavily pregnant to attend the wedding. It was a relief to be away from her for a short while. Despite both being on their best behaviour for the first few weeks, it had soon become apparent that they had nothing in common. Now, the fleeting periods where they got on reasonably well were becoming rarer.

After five months of marriage, the laugh he'd initially considered tinkling now grated on his nerves. And he'd realised that if he didn't give his wife her own way in every little matter, she'd retaliate by making his life extremely unpleasant. Unless she was flirting with other men or the centre of attention at social events, she spent her time criticising other ladies.

He grinned at his sister. "You scrub up well, Bella. Even I can see why George has taken the plunge with you."

"Why, Sean, such praise! I'm speechless."

"Are you enjoying your day?" he asked.

"It's been perfect. I'm so glad we chose Latimers like Mother and Father did for their wedding."

Kate elbowed him.

"But what about you? Are *you* enjoying yourself? You resemble a fox hiding from the hounds. Why are you so nervous?"

Kate knew him so well. Sean pulled at his tight collar, struggling to formulate an amusing answer, unable to tell the truth – that Jane's presence left him dumbstruck.

Bella rubbed her palm on the top of his head and said, "Aww, leave him alone. He's got a child on the way – it's all too much for him."

Jane grinned. "He does appear rather overwhelmed, like a spaniel when surrounded by a gaggle of schoolgirls."

He laughed. "Will you ladies kindly not refer to me as though I'm a four-legged creature – first a fox and then a puppy."

Charles came up behind them.

"You're a cheerful bunch. What am I missing out on?"

"We're teasing Sean, which is always good fun," Bella replied.

Charles raised Bella's hand to his lips.

"Congratulations, Bella, my dear. George is a lucky man."

"Thank you, Charles. Have you met Jane, Milly's daughter?"

Sean watched Charles' eyes devour Jane before he took her hand and kissed it.

"How do you do, Jane? Delighted to make your acquaintance."

Jane gave him a dazzling smile.

"Likewise."

Bella moved so that Charles was standing next to Jane. She looked from one to the other.

"Charles is back from living in Italy. He's interested in the arts too, Jane. I'm sure you'll have a lot in common. Now, if you'll excuse me, I must rescue my husband. It appears Anne has cornered him."

Sean wanted to scream. What the hell was Bella playing

at? Was she trying to matchmake? Charles and Jane together would be more than he'd be able to stand. Sean forced himself to look around the room, away from Kate's unflinching gaze – it was as though she could read his mind. As an idea came to him, he turned back to Charles.

"I'm sorry to interrupt, Jane, but if you'll excuse us, ladies, I'm afraid I must speak to Charles about a business matter."

Charles frowned. Sean understood – he didn't want to leave Jane's company, either – but the way Charles was looking at her was making him want to lash out at his friend.

"Right now? Can't it wait? This is a w-wedding, old m-man."

Sean noted his stutter. He must be nervous. No doubt Jane was making him tongue-tied, as well.

"Sorry, no time like the present."

Sean steered Charles towards the doors that led to the patio, rapidly planning what he was going to talk about. His lips curled as he pictured the newly completed warehouses on his walk by the canal last weekend. He felt a prickle of excitement. They could open a sewing factory . . . Actually, that was brilliant idea. It was amazing what the mind could come up with when under pressure. But what would he do about his job at the mill?

Holding his hand up to shade his eyes from the glaring sun, Charles caught his attention.

"Holy cow! That woman is a goddess. Why did you drag me away?"

"Who?"

"Come off it. You're married, not dead from the waist down. Is she married or engaged?"

"Who?" Sean scowled.

"Blimey, maybe you have lost the use of your nether regions. Jane, of course."

"You shouldn't pursue her."

"Whyever not? Are you worried that I am going to hurt Milly's daughter and upset everyone?"

"Erm . . ."

"Or are you worried they'll object because of my father's alleged involvement in what happened to Teddy Gibbs?"

"They, er, might."

"Don't worry – they'll see I'm nothing like him. And my intentions are entirely honourable. Well, almost – I'm only human."

Charles laughed, but Sean's emotions were warring within him. Sean was a married man, soon to be a father – there was no future, no hope of anything between Jane and him. Although he wanted his friend to be happy, he hated the idea of Charles and her together. What was wrong with him? He was a selfish bastard. Did he want to deny his best friend happiness? The answer came in a flash. If it was with Jane – yes!

Kate couldn't help feeling envious as she sat on Bella's bed watching her change into her travelling clothes for her honeymoon in Paris. Bella balanced on one foot to put on her shoe.

"I was terribly worried that you might be sad today being at a wedding, but I couldn't have enjoyed it without you."

"Sweet Pea, I'd never have let my feelings for Sean keep me from your special day. But to tell you the truth, now you're married, I can't wait to get away to London."

"I'm sorry if my being married and so happy makes it harder for you."

"I don't begrudge your happiness. We're sisters first, remember? So, even though I'm going to be in London for the foreseeable – and hopefully a working woman if my interview goes well – if you need me, I'll come home so I will."

"Thank you. I'm sure George will be fine for years to come. And as for you, any school will be lucky to have you. I would have retained a lot more with you as my teacher. At my school, they were more interested in having us learn deportment by walking around the room with books on our heads instead of reading them."

"Even if I don't get the position, I'll remain in London for a while."

"Was today totally awful for you?" Bella asked.

"It wasn't too bad. At least Yvette wasn't there ordering him around. She's so bossy! And as for that permanent sulky pout . . . sure, I remember she used to giggle all the time. Either she's become unhappy since she married him or the way she was before was fake."

"I hate to be mean, but I suspect it was part of her act. Sophia can turn on the southern charm at the drop of a hat. Yvette's had a good teacher."

"You're right there. The way Sophia flutters those long lashes at any male in long trousers is outrageous."

Bella laughed.

"Did you notice the way Sean acted around Jane?" Kate asked.

"No."

"He likes her."

"Of course he likes her. What's not to like? She's lovely. You like her, don't you?"

"Yes, but Sean *really* likes her. He's crazed when she's around."

"Don't be daft. All men go funny around women like her. Even George admits she's attractive – but he prefers me," she grinned. "Did you see Charles? He couldn't take his eyes off her. It would be nice if he married Jane."

"Sure, she'd make any man happy, the bitch," Kate laughed.

"Seriously, though, are you going to be all right, Kate?"

"I've got no choice. He's married and sees me as another sister, so all I can do is play that role."

"You'd have been wonderful together."

"Never mind about me. I've got to get on with my life. You make sure you enjoy every minute with your lovely man. Maybe one day I'll meet a George of my own who will make me forget about Sean."

They were hugging as Victoria came into the bedroom.

"Bella, are you almost ready? George is waiting in the hallway and Stokes is ready to drive you to the station. You don't want to miss your train."

Kate got busy packing for London the moment Bella and George left.

"I could have caught the same train as the newly-weds, but I didn't want to cramp their style. Mine leaves early in the morning, so I need to have my trunk ready," she explained to her father, who was hovering at her bedroom door, leaning heavily on his stick.

"Can't you stay for another couple of days?"

"Sorry, Father. My interview is in two days."

"I'll miss you. I don't understand why you want to

235

live in Anne's empty house. Surely you could find a post closer to here."

"There are still a few servants and I've told them only to open up a bedroom and the small parlour, as I'll hardly be home."

"Will you be back for Christmas?"

She moved to her father, placing her hand on his cheek.

"I'll miss you, too. But I'll let you know nearer the time. Is that all right?"

"Are you that miserable here?"

"It's not that I'm unhappy . . ."

"Do you want to talk about it?"

Kate shook her head.

"All right, my dear. I recognise that look. You'll not divulge any more. Come and join me downstairs once you've packed. We'll have a drink together and you can tell me all about the school you're hoping to work at."

There was no way she could explain to him that she loved her stepbrother so much that it broke her heart to see him with another woman.

Chapter 20

Sean woke aroused and contented. He'd been dreaming that he was married to Jane and living in New Orleans. As he opened his eyes to find Yvette snoring softly by his side, disappointment swamped him. At least when she was asleep, they weren't arguing . . .

Over breakfast, he tried to make conversation as he gazed out at the parched garden of Park Villa.

"We should be glad of the pleasant weather, I suppose, but the sun has been melting the roads these last few weeks." Although not hopeful of a reply, Sean glanced at his wife. "I'd planned to take a stroll along the towpath this morning, but it's so damned hot already, it's put paid to that idea," he added after a few moments.

Maybe he should still go. At least he'd be out of the house – away from Yvette's critical comments. She made no attempt to hide her dissatisfaction with him. He did everything he could to make her happy, including telling her he loved her. It was a lie. Did she realise he wasn't sincere? Maybe that was why she never said it back. Or perhaps she simply didn't love him, either. Was he making the mistake of overcompensating for his inability to love her by giving in to her as her father did? Probably – she was becoming even more spoiled.

At the other end of the breakfast table, she raised her eyes contemptuously before her attention returned to cutting her bacon into tiny pieces. The way she insisted on dissecting her food into minuscule fragments was one of the many things about her that irritated him. Intimacy was a distant memory – it had been months since she'd allowed him near her. Only when in the company of others did Yvette try to put on a show.

His attention came back to her sulking face when he heard her chair scrape on the parquet floor as she rose from the table.

"It's no good. I cannot possibly eat this," she said.

"Are you unwell? Is it the child?"

"Oh, if it is anything to do with your precious child, *then* you are concerned. But if I am unhappy or unwell, you don't give a damn – you've made that perfectly clear."

"Perhaps if you stopped acting like a child, I would." He regretted the words the moment they left his mouth. "I'm sorry. I didn't mean that."

"Oh, but you did!"

Yvette stomped from the room.

He wandered over to the sideboard and poured a glass of whiskey, throwing it back and pouring another before he had time to talk himself out of it. In the last few weeks, she'd become even more unbearable to live with. He didn't know how much more he could cope with. The baby was due soon, so he hoped having a child to care for would improve her mood.

This morning's tantrum was because last night, he'd not given into her whims and had refused to buy her a horse. She'd become reacquainted with her old school-friend, Louise Mason, apparently having made up following their quarrel. From what Yvette said, the two women were in competition to see which of them had the best home and lifestyle. Sean suspected this was entirely in his wife's head – Yvette was a terrible snob.

He'd tried explaining to her that even if they could afford it, there was no point buying one when she was heavily pregnant, but it made no difference. She regarded his stance as meanness, claiming he was making her life a misery.

"Yet another example of your selfishness for my diary, just like the pathetic little ring you bought me," she'd said.

Perhaps he could visit his mother. Then again, she'd notice he was down and he was doing everything he could not to cause her worry. Stop lying to yourself, Kavanagh, he thought. She was already concerned about his drinking and gambling. The real reason was that he didn't want to admit his marriage was also a failure.

The housemaid interrupted his thoughts.

"Sir, the mistress has asked to see you upstairs. She is in some distress."

Sean took the stairs two at a time.

"Yvette, what is it?"

"The baby is coming. I have had pains all morning."

"You should have told me."

She snatched her hand away and turned from him.

"I didn't think you would care."

"I'll send for Doctor Farrell."

Yvette grimaced as another pain seized her.

"Stay calm. Should I send for our mothers?"

"No! Why would I want *your* mother? She blames me for trapping her precious son. Anyone would think you didn't play a part in this. S-send for my, aaargh . . ." She couldn't finish her sentence, as cramps came once more.

He couldn't argue with that – his mother did think exactly that.

While they waited for the doctor and Sophia, Sean held her hand, her nails digging into his palm. The discomfort was irrelevant if it helped her to deliver their child – he was scared yet excited at the prospect of being the father of a son or daughter, he didn't mind which.

Once Sophia arrived, the women made it clear his presence was unwelcome in the bedroom. He retreated to his study, where he prayed that his wife and child would be all right. If he were honest, he didn't fancy seeing all the messy bits he imagined childbirth entailed – it had been off-putting enough seeing foals born on the plantation. And he never relished being in Sophia's company, especially after her recent visit.

She'd called while Yvette had been out at Centenary House having a fitting for yet more new gowns that would see her through her pregnancy. It was a Saturday afternoon and he'd just finished his ablutions after spending the morning at the mill, when Sophia had walked into his dressing room while he'd been stark-naked.

"Sean . . . I assumed you'd have finished bathing by now," she'd purred, standing in the doorway, her eyes ranging over his body.

Sean had grabbed a towel off the rail and covered himself. He wasn't embarrassed by his body, but his mother-in-law looking at him as though he were a prize bull was another matter.

"Sophia, I need to get dressed," he said.

"You have nothing to be self-conscious about. Far from it."

"What do you want?"

"I wanted to *see* my son-in-law," she laughed as she pushed the door closed and approached him.

With one finger, she followed a droplet of water towards the towel clutched in his hands. Sean freed one hand and arrested her progress, alarmed that despite how wrong it felt, he was becoming aroused.

"Sophia, you shouldn't be in here. Please leave."

"I can see that you don't *really* want me to go." She laughed softly. "Yvette has her charms. Although from what she tells me, you're not getting to enjoy them at the moment. She is a selfish young woman – takes after her father."

In Sean's opinion, Yvette hadn't inherited her selfishness off her father – she was exactly like her mother, as his own mother had warned.

"Perhaps we can provide each other with some comfort," she added.

He struggled to keep the disgust off his face.

"Sophia, I'm perfectly content with my wife. I don't wish to insult you – you're a beautiful woman – but what you're suggesting is . . . well, frankly, it's appalling. I'm married to your daughter, for goodness' sake."

"One day you will realise she played you for a fool and when that day comes, I may no longer be willing to take you to my bed."

"What the hell do you mean by that?"

Sophia had snatched at the towel, allowing it to fall to the floor. Then smiling, she'd flounced out without answering his question. Once again, he'd wondered if the child his wife was carrying was his. Surely Yvette wasn't that scheming.

Sophia was a she-devil wrapped up in an attractive package. It hadn't been his fault, but he was ashamed at

241

what had happened, so much so he'd not even joked about it with Charles. Instead, he'd kept it to himself until last week, when after a few drinks he'd confided in George. Even then he hadn't intended speaking about it, but George was easy to talk to and Sean was sure he could keep a secret – at least he assumed that he could, as it appeared George had told no one about his investment in damaged goods from the docks.

It was early evening when he held out his arms to take his son from the doctor. From the moment he looked into his blue eyes, Sean knew he'd do anything for the child. Perhaps this was why Yvette could wrap Matthew round her little finger. Sean hoped his son would be different. It was still light outside, so Sean carried him over to the window so he could get a better look. He was so tiny, so perfect.

He turned to the doctor.

"Owain, is everything as it should be? Is he healthy?"

"He's a fine boy." He closed his bag. "If you'll excuse me, I'll be off – there are a lot of babies due this week. It's about time I got myself an assistant. This is a young man's game."

Sean walked Owain to the front door and returned to his wife's bedside. She looked drained.

"Thank you for our son – our beautiful blue-eyed, blond-haired little boy."

"He has Papa's colouring. No doubt his hair will darken," Yvette said.

"I'd like my family to come round and see him, if that's all right, my dear?"

"Not tonight, Sean. I am exhausted. In a few days . . ."

"I can take him downstairs when they arrive, so we don't disturb you."

242

"Please don't be selfish, Sean. A baby should remain with his mother. Isn't that right, Mama?"

"For a week at least. Then you must allow Sean to show off his son."

Sophia's sneer made him feel idiotic for being so proud.

"I understand. What shall we call him? I was thinking perhaps Sean Matthew Edward Kavanagh," Sean said.

Sophia smirked. "How nice – all of the men of the family remembered, except my father."

"I'm so sorry, Sophia. I didn't intend to leave him out. Perhaps Sean—"

Yvette pushed herself up on her pillows, holding her arms out to take the infant.

"I want to call him Pierre Matthew."

What did it matter what they called the boy? He had a son! He kissed the top of his wife's head.

"All right. Pierre Matthew Kavanagh it is, then. Would you prefer me to leave while you feed him?"

"No. Mama has arranged a wet nurse."

"Don't you want to feed him yourself? Surely it'll help you to bond with him."

"I am *not* an animal. Ladies don't feed their own children. The wet nurse is a perfectly amiable woman who has lost her own baby. Mama has sent a message – she will be here soon. And another has been sent to the nanny, asking if she can start sooner."

Yvette and Sophia had chosen the nanny, who was due to start work once they sent for her.

"So, you'll have someone feeding him and a nanny taking care of him. When exactly will you be with him?" Sean said.

"I carried him for nine months and gave birth to him.

I am his mother – surely at least in this you can give me my own way. Why do my wishes never matter to you?"

"I don't feel handing the care of our son over to others is the right thing to do."

"That is because your mother was nothing more than a shop owner. True ladies do things differently. I am tired. We can discuss the wet nurse tomorrow. When you meet her, I am sure you will accept I am doing what is best for my child."

Her child? Sean accepted women did all the work having children, but he was *their* child, not hers. He was about to say that his mother was more of a lady than she would ever be but thought better of it, not wanting to row with Yvette moments after their son had been born, or in front of Sophia.

"Right, well, I'll give your father and my mother the good news," he said.

A short while later, Sean sat on the chintz sofa in Matthew and Sophia's drawing room, a large glass of brandy in one hand and a Havana cigar in the other.

"He's got your hair and eyes, but let's hope he ends up better looking, like his father," Sean said.

Matthew laughed. "You cheeky young devil. He could do worse than looking like his grandfather. Pierre Matthew – that's a fine name. How's my girl doing?"

"Yvette's well. Naturally, she's tired. The nanny starts any day now. I can't thank you enough for paying her salary for the first year. We could just about have afforded it, but I appreciate it."

"I know how much we pay you. Besides, I don't want you struggling, or Yvette run ragged."

"No, of course not. Neither do I. She's also arranged a wet nurse – I'm not sure that's right."

"I find these matters are best left to the ladies. Take my advice – don't interfere."

"Perhaps you're right."

"What did your mother and Edward say about the news?"

"They're thrilled. I had to stop my mother from dashing round there to see him. Yvette doesn't want visitors."

"Women can't keep away from babies. Now, I hate to bring the conversation back to the mill, but we've got a real problem brewing. The other mill owners agree there will be strikes before long. If one mill comes out, the damned union will insist they all come out."

"I can't see what we can do about it, other than persuade the other owners to increase wages in line with ours."

"They're too bloody stubborn. They won't even discuss it. But if our lot strike, it could be the finish of us."

"Are the company's cash reserves that low?"

"We had to replace the steam engine a couple of years ago – that was a significant investment. I had hoped the old one would last a few more years, as electricity will power mills before much longer." Matthew puffed on his cigar. "I say that, but English cotton mills might even become a thing of the past."

Sean and Matthew discussed the growing unrest for a while before Sean made his way home.

There had been many times when he'd wondered if the child Yvette had been carrying was his. The blond hair and blue eyes had been a shock. But when he held him in his arms, he'd experienced such a connection to the little chap, as though he were his flesh and blood. Perhaps this would be the fresh start they needed. Surely he and Yvette could make a go of things now.

Chapter 21

As Sean reached Park Villa, Sophia was leaving. She stood on the bottom step, blocking his way.

"The proud father coming home."

"Sophia, why are you always trying to needle me? I don't know what I've ever done to offend you."

"You turned me down and bedded my daughter that same night. At least I was being open and honest with you. Whereas Yvette . . ."

"Don't stop now. What were you going to say? I'm tired of your digs and hints. Are you telling me Pierre isn't my child?"

"You saw him for yourself. What do *you* think?"

Sean turned round and stormed off. Damn that woman! Damn Yvette! She'd hoodwinked him into marrying her. His mother had said as much and she'd been right.

Jumping behind the wheel of his car, he paused. He was in no mood to explain to Charles or any of the others who might be at the club that his wife had made a fool of him. Slamming his foot down on the pedal, he tore off towards The Tanner's Arms.

Yvette had been refusing intimacy. Accused him of being a poor husband at every opportunity, when all the while she'd been carrying another man's child. If he'd been born months early, there would have been no doubt in his mind that he'd been duped, but Pierre had only been born a couple of weeks early.

Sean took a stool at the bar, ignoring the shocked expressions of the potman and several mill workers, who obviously recognised him.

Albert grinned. "Sean! Well, this is a pleasant surprise."

"I surprised myself by coming here on the spur of the moment. And your customers, by the look of things. You don't mind, do you?"

"Not at all – you're welcome anytime." Albert winked at Sean before shouting to his regulars. "What's going on? Have youse been struck dumb? Mind yer own business now or find somewhere else to drink tonight."

There were several grunts and groans from around the smoky room.

Albert lowered his voice. "They won't go, 'cos we pull a good pint an' give them an occasional lock-in so they can drink after hours, if yeh get me drift. Now, what can I get for yeh?"

"A bottle of whiskey and a round of drinks for everyone else," Sean said, which brought muttered thanks from around the room.

"Serve the rest of them, will yeh, Ron, while I see to Sean." He took a fresh bottle from under the bar and placed it in front of Sean with an empty glass. "Is this a good idea?"

"This is a pub and I need a place to get drunk . . . Sorry, I didn't mean to sound so . . ."

Albert eyed him warily.

"That's all right. Here's as good a place as any, if that's yer intention."

As Sean opened the bottle, Albert went through to the back, returning with Kitty.

"Do yeh want to come through to the house, Sean?" she asked.

"Not tonight, Kitty. Can I stay here?"

"Aye, for now," she said.

By the time Sean had downed most of the bottle and bought several more rounds for the rest of the customers, he was bleary-eyed and slurring. Each time he rested his elbow on the bar and his head in his hand, it slipped off, but this didn't deter him. The atmosphere in the pub had been growing increasingly noisy and an old man flexed his fingers.

"Tonight, we need a few tunes on the old piano," he said, sitting on the stool.

As he struck the first chord, a blonde-haired woman Sean recognised as a spinner at the mill who had frequently propositioned him leaned on the bar beside him, matching his pose.

"Well, Mr Kavanagh, does your visit to The Tanner's mean yeh can't resist my charms any more?"

"I wanna drink until I can't fink any more, 'cause I'm sooo miserable."

She thrust her bosom near his face.

"Aww, darlin', if yeh wanna forget, I've got a couple o' things that'll take yer mind right off yer troubles. Cheer you up no end an' put that gorgeous smile back on yer handsome face," she said.

As laughter erupted around the room, Albert slipped through to the back room.

"You've got reeeally big breasts," Sean said, prodding one with his index finger.

The regulars sniggered.

"That I have. Come outside an' I'll treat yeh to the knee-trembler I've been offerin' yeh for months."

Kitty yanked the woman away before Sean could respond.

"Hey, Scraggy Neck. Get away from him before I pull yer bleached hair out by its black roots. Then I'll rip yer arm off an' shove the soggy end where the sun don't shine."

The woman glared at Kitty.

"Even at school yeh thought yeh could take on the whole bleedin' world, Kitty Gibbs. What's it got to do wi' you?"

"It's Kitty Nelson. An' he's me mate. So, do us all a favour an' drop it, 'cos yeh know how people gossip. That fella o' yours won't be too pleased when his ship docks if he hears you've been messin' around."

The woman tutted and sidled back to her friends.

"Albert, help me get him through to the back."

The landlord put his arm under Sean's shoulder and half carried him through to the back.

As they staggered towards the parlour, Kitty said, "Stick him on the sofa while I get a bucket. If he's going to be sick, I don't want it on me rug. Then you'd best get back to the bar. It's getting rowdy in there."

"It's almost chucking-out time, so I'll send 'em home. They've had enough for one night, courtesy of Sean."

"Righto. I'll stay down here tonight an' keep an eye on him, if yeh don't mind. If he were one of my lads, I'd like to think someone would look after him."

Albert kissed her cheek.

"Give me a shout if yeh need owt." He paused in the doorway. "What do you think caused him to want to get in such a state, 'cos it were deliberate?"

"Dunno, love. But one thing's for sure, if she saw the state he's got into, Victoria would be livid."

By the early hours, Sean was leaning over the side of the sofa, staring into the bucket, while Kitty sat watching from the armchair, shaking her head.

"That's it, Tatty Head, get it all up. There's best part of a bottle of Irish in me bucket now. What good drinking it has done you, I'll never know. Yer a blinkin' fool."

Sean lifted his head. "Kitty, don't . . ." He wretched again. "Jus' don't have a go at me, please. The bloody room won't keep still."

"I've no sympathy for yeh. An' half the wives in Faredene will be after you when their fellas turn up drunk."

"You would have, if you knew why I was . . ." He returned his head to the bucket.

"Are yeh gonna tell me, then?"

Sean wiped his mouth on the cloth Kitty handed to him.

"I can't. Be nice, please – my head is thumping."

"Sometimes, Tatty Head, you've got to be tough with those you care about, so I'm tempted to give you a clout so yeh know how much you mean to me. Now, if you've finished up-chucking in me bucket, I'll make you a fry-up. It's the best thing for yeh, if you can stomach it."

The thought of breakfast made him want to heave, but once he'd forced himself to eat a little of the two fried eggs, black pudding, three sausages, four slices of bacon and grilled tomato, he had to admit he was feeling *slightly* better. As he took a drink of the Epsom salts she'd also provided, Kitty gestured to the half-empty plate.

"Are yeh done wi' that? I'm so used to feeding Albert that I forget not all men can eat a horse at every sitting, even after getting sozzled."

Sean nodded but grabbed another sausage as she took the plate away.

"I'd best get home now."

Kitty picked up the brown sauce from the table.

"All right, pet. I can't keep this from yer mam, 'cos it'll be round the mill by lunchtime on Monday, but I'll spare her the gory details an' say people are exaggerating. Make out you only had a few an' stayed over. Whether she believes me is another matter."

Sean rubbed his stubbled jaw. "She won't be pleased."

"No, she won't. But at least it's Sunday, so Matthew won't see you in this state, 'cos you look like summat our cat spits up and you stink like our swill tray."

"Great. Don't hold back, will you, Kitty."

"Like I said last night. I've got no sympathy for yeh, getting in this state."

"Life can be so difficult."

"It's as I always say – you're born cold, wet and hungry an' it gets worse." She rubbed his head.

"*Do* you always say that?"

"I've said it now – that's enough. Come on, Tatty Head, sling yer hook an' go home. An' sort that wife of yours out, if she's yer problem."

"She gave birth to a boy last night."

"Oh, now I see – not yours?"

"I don't know for sure. Kitty, you won't say anything, will you?"

"You don't even have to ask that, but I'll tell you this. You're the only dad that little fella will know. So, you get yerself home an' love him, 'cos it ain't a few minutes in the sack that makes you a dad – it's a lifetime of love and care."

Sean smiled. "Wise words."

"I'm a wise woman. If people only took the time to listen, more o' them would notice."

"Thanks for everything, Kitty."

Sean drove home filled with self-loathing. He wasn't proud of his behaviour last night. Not that he was ready to forgive Yvette's deceit. They *would* have it out – possibly come to some arrangement where they lived separate lives.

He entered the house to the sound of wailing.

"Good morning, sir. I'm pleased you're back," their butler said.

"Morning, Harris. Is something wrong? You look concerned," Sean said.

Harris smoothed down the long strands of hair that covered his otherwise bald pate.

"The young master has been exercising his lungs."

"For how long?"

"I am afraid it has been most of the night, sir."

"Is my wife with him?"

"The mistress was fatigued after her labours and has been sleeping."

"Sleeping? Through that noise? Has the wet nurse arrived?"

"From what I understand, sir, the woman who was expected was taken ill and couldn't come. Another woman has been engaged. The child's crying has only stopped for short periods. I enquired in the nursery if there was anything amiss but was sent away."

"Is there more to this situation?"

"It is not my place to say, sir."

"I'm asking you."

"I believe the woman has been drinking."

Sean took the stairs two at a time. As he reached the

top, the crying stopped abruptly. He threw open the nursery door. The scene before him turned his blood cold. The stranger was shaking Pierre's lifeless form.

Sean snatched the now silent infant from her.

"Stop that at once!" he thundered.

"He wouldn't stop. I've fed him. Fed him loads o' times. It ain't my fault."

"Out! Harris, get rid of her. Throw her out if you have to and send for Doctor Farrell immediately," Sean bellowed at the butler.

Left alone with his son, Sean checked for signs of life – thank God he was still breathing. Whether or not he came from his loins, Kitty was right – he was the poor mite's father. Pierre was so tiny and helpless and he'd failed to protect him. He kissed his cheek.

"Come on, son. Please be all right and I'll never let you down again, I promise."

He stormed into the bedroom, where his wife was snoring quietly, strands of ebony hair across her face.

"Wake up! Get up, now! How can you sleep when your baby has been wailing all night? What sort of mother are you?"

"What is it?" Yvette mumbled sleepily.

"It's Pierre. I said get up! Dammit, Yvette. How the hell could you leave him all night?"

"Stop being so dramatic. He was with the wet nurse."

"Dramatic! You're lucky I'm holding him, because if I wasn't, my hands would be round your throat!"

Yvette's eyes widened. "Sean, stop hollering like a commoner. You're not making sense."

He ground out each word through gritted teeth. "Your son is injured."

Yvette shot up. "How?"

Sean paced the room, cradling his son.

"That stranger you entrusted with the care of our son is a drunk. I found her shaking him like a terrier with a rat!"

Yvette's face was ashen.

"I-I . . . we . . . we were let down at the last minute. I was so tired. She seemed capable. You can't blame me – it doesn't require any special skills to feed a baby. I didn't know there was anything wrong. For God's sake, stop glaring at me as though you want to kill me."

"Look at him! I don't believe he's mine after what your mother said to me last night. Regardless, I *will* be a father to him. And I swear to God, if he dies, I'll kill you."

"What did my mother say? What do you mean?"

"I've sent for Doctor Farrell," Sean said as he stroked Pierre's face while the infant lay unmoving, nestled in the crook of his arm.

"Sean, look at me."

"I can't stand the sight of you right now. God help me, but I never thought I could feel this angry."

Yvette's voice was shaky.

"Sean, answer my question. What has Mama said? You were wearing those clothes yesterday and you've not shaved. Have you been out all night? What did she say to make you stay out?"

Sean's mind was foggy. He couldn't tear his eyes away from his son's face. Pierre whimpered suddenly and then wailed loudly. Surely that was a sign that he was going to be all right . . .

"Thank God," Sean murmured.

His knowledge of babies was extremely limited, but

even he realised shaking the infant may have permanently harmed his son.

Yvette opened her nightgown.

"Give him to me. I will feed him. Maybe he is hungry." She held out her hands.

Sean kissed Pierre's forehead. "I don't even want you to touch him."

"Don't be silly. I am his mother. If he has been crying, he must be hungry. The woman mustn't have had sufficient milk."

Sean glared at her, shaking his head.

"This is ridiculous. Please, Sean, give him to me. Please. He must need feeding."

"Be careful with him. Gently."

Sean held his breath as Yvette stroked her nipple against the baby's tiny mouth. He sighed with relief as Pierre suckled.

Yvette stared at the baby as she asked, "Well, are you going to tell me what she said?"

"Who?"

"Mama," she said, her voice shaky.

He took a while to answer, his voice weary.

"I can't remember her exact words, but she implied you've made a fool of me and that he's not mine."

Yvette's face was awash, her breath hitching as she spoke.

"He *is* yours. I s-swear on Papa's life. Mama hates me because Papa l-loves me s-so much. And because I survived yet my brother died. She-she always l-loved him m-more. And she is jealous of me because she is getting older. She c-can't s-stand thinking that one day she won't be th-th-the most attractive woman in the room. You don't k-know what she is like. Have you never wondered why I don't really love her – she's a bitch."

He knew exactly what Sophia was like. Dangerous.

"You m-must believe me. P-please tell me you believe me. I know I have been awful while I have been pregnant, but I love you. I always have. Things will be different now, I promise," Yvette ended.

Sean had never seen her so contrite. What she said made sense. And his own rejection of Sophia was another reason that might explain his mother-in-law's spitefulness.

"I want to believe you," he said.

"You can." Yvette patted the covers. "Please, come and sit on the bed with us."

Sean didn't move.

"You'd better not be lying to me," he said.

"I'm not. You have my word."

"I'll give you the benefit of the doubt, but you must confront your mother about her lies. Or should I do it?"

"I'll do it, but in private. Without Papa knowing."

"She can't say such things and get away with it."

"There are things I know about Mama. The last thing I want is to hurt Papa, but the threat of exposure should be enough to silence her vicious tongue. Will you let me handle it my way?"

"Fine. But it stops now."

"Sean, I promise you – things will be better."

Surely if Pierre were unharmed, there could be hope for his marriage . . .

They sat on the bed together watching their son until Doctor Farrell arrived. When he'd finished examining Pierre, the lines on Owain's forehead deepened fleetingly before he smiled kindly and asked if they could speak privately.

Once the chambermaid had taken Pierre to the nursery, Owain rubbed his hand over his greying sandy beard.

"The problem is, there is no way of knowing at this stage if there will be any permanent damage. We still understand so little about the brain."

"What sort of problems could he have?" Sean asked, though he wasn't sure he wanted to hear the answer.

"The last thing I want to do is cause you to panic. Pierre could be completely fine. But there's a chance of complications. Anything from minor speech problems and balance issues to severe brain damage. Every baby is different. And it depends on how violently he was shaken and for how long."

Sean stared out of the window, blind to the rosy glow cast by the morning sun. If only he hadn't driven off. He should have come into the house and confronted Yvette instead of running away. Now, Pierre might be damaged for life because his daddy was a weak, selfish bastard. He turned as he heard Owain's voice again.

"There now, my dear, don't cry. There may be nothing to worry about."

Yvette stuttered, "B-b-but everyone will blame me."

Sean worked his jaw. Why was she still thinking of herself? But wasn't that what he'd been doing – feeling guilty and sorry for himself? He kneeled beside her.

"Yvette. We must forget about apportioning blame and work together to raise our son. No matter what we face in the future, we'll do it together."

Chapter 22

The breeze coming through the open windows of the Daimler did little to cool Victoria on the brief journey to Faredene Hall. Parched brown grass could be seen everywhere – evidence of the heatwave. She felt permanently drained and longed for rain.

"Morning, Mrs Caldwell. Madam is waiting for you in the library," Harry's butler said as he took her parasol.

Although a little ostentatious, with huge crystal chandeliers, gilt bannisters and ornate furnishings, the Hall was back to its former glory.

"Morning, Jess."

Jess looked up from the book she was reading.

"Morning. You look flushed."

Victoria smiled. "I look hot and haggard. Even at this hour, it's already stifling. I've hardly slept for a month. It's so humid even at night that the sheets have to be washed each day. One can only hope that as we're nearing the end of September, the weather will break."

"I must admit, I was surprised it's so hot over here."

Victoria took a seat nearest the open French doors.

"This isn't normal by any means. In fact, you've not really seen the British weather. We generally get far more rain than we have this year."

Jess gestured towards the garden, where Harry could be seen in the distance surrounded by a small army of dogs.

"That's what Harry said."

"I don't know how he can bear to be outside in this weather, especially wearing tweed."

"He'll be in soon. Every day he walks to the quarry road and back, rain or shine. Apparently, the men working there are starting at four thirty and finishing at lunch to avoid the worst of the heat."

"Perhaps we should have done the same at the mill. Sean and Matthew tell me it's unbearable."

"Have you not been in?"

"No – I get hot flushes at the drop of a hat without going to the mill."

The butler came in carrying a tea tray.

"May we have a jug of iced tea instead, please? Is that all right with you, honey?"

"Lovely, thank you."

"Do you think it's this hot where Bella and George are honeymooning in France?"

"I believe lots of countries are experiencing a heatwave. I'll be able to ask her next week when they get back."

"How's Pierre doing?"

"He's beautiful – so like Matthew – and I'm keeping my fingers and everything else crossed that there's been no permanent damage. That's all we can do. Yvette's convinced he's fine – or she's doing an excellent job of pretending. The child's barely out of the womb and she's already asking when she can leave him so she can go and stay with her friend, Louise. Apparently, Sean has agreed she can visit once Pierre is old enough to leave with his nanny for a short while. It's disturbing how little she appears to care for the child. I have to bite my tongue for fear I'll start telling her what I think as I won't be able to stop myself."

"She probably needs telling."

"Yes, but I'm doing my best not to fall out with her. As it is, she makes clear she only tolerates our family. Besides, Yvette is Matthew's little darling. She can do no wrong in his eyes and I suspect that if I interfere, Matthew and I will argue. If you ask me, Sean's pandering to her, every bit as much as her father does. The only good thing I can see right now is they appear to be getting along better. He's said that they've reached an understanding and are making a go of things for Pierre's sake. Yet, I can see Sean's beside himself."

"When he talks, I can tell that he dotes on the boy."

"He's guilt-ridden about Pierre being left in the care of that dreadful woman who shook him and won't say why he spent the night at The Tanner's Arms, but I'm sure he had his reasons."

"I reckon Harry would have made a smashing dad. I sometimes wonder if I did the right thing being with him, 'cos it's stopped him from having children of his own."

"Jess, even as a child, Harry always knew what he wanted. If he'd set his mind on you, I doubt you had much say. And any fool can see he's happy with you."

Jess touched Victoria's arm as it rested on the table.

"Thanks, honey. I would have liked to have a bunch myself, but it wasn't to be. Still, at least I've got none to fret about."

"You're right. It's worrying about Sean that keeps me awake at night, not just the heat."

"His drinking or his gambling?"

"Both. I can't prove how much he's gambling, but I have my suspicions. I've challenged him about it, but he dismissed it as harmless fun. Even Edward said that providing it isn't getting out of hand, there's no reason for concern, so there's nothing I can do about it. At the back of my mind there's always the worry that I might not realise how unhappy he is and he'll harm himself."

"Harry keeps an eye on him at the club. I'll be honest with you, honey. He knows I'll lose my rag with him if he doesn't watch out for him."

"Harry's a good man."

"He is. And he cares about his family, even though he was never that close to them when he was a kid."

"He was always quiet as a child."

"You're being nice. He was a misery and jealous of Sean – he told me himself. It was growing up the youngest of nine with barely enough to eat. He thought that all he had stretching in front of him was a life like his parents."

"Poverty is a terrible thing. I've tried to improve conditions for families in Faredene, but it's never enough."

Jess nodded. "The drought won't be helping matters."

"From what Owain tells me, crop failures over the last two months have caused sharp price rises. Even milk has gone up. It seems life for those living in poor areas is always more fragile and he says there have been several heat-related deaths. The Guild needs to do more to help."

"What are you proposing?"

"Perhaps providing food to the children at school. Maybe arrange for the baker near the Rows to supply bread at a reasonable price."

Victoria stopped speaking as the butler entered without the iced tea.

"Excuse me, madam. There is a Mr Oliver Flinn to see you."

Jess stood, covering her mouth with her hand.

"Dear God, it can't be."

"Jess?" Victoria went to her side.

Jess clutched at Victoria's arm, her doughy hand trembling.

"It's him."

Victoria realised instantly that Jess was referring to her estranged husband. She turned to the butler.

"Please show the visitor into the morning room and ask Mr Gibbs to join us in here immediately."

The butler nodded.

"Yes, madam."

Victoria helped Jess back into her chair.

"Take some deep breaths – it'll calm you. He can't harm you."

"I can't work out how he found me. My sister won't have told him anything. I can trust her – she never liked him."

Harry marched through the French doors, his face contorted, the veins in his neck pulsing. His dogs rushed around his feet, panting.

"Is it really Flinn?" he said.

"I've not seen him, but there can't be two men with the same name. Not here looking for me, anyway."

"Let's see what the bugger wants. Don't you fret, my sweet. He won't lay a hand on you."

"No violence, Harry. I don't want the police round here. You don't want to be running like you were after what happened with that Brakenridge fella."

"I was nowt but a guttersnipe then. I've got money behind me now. If I've learned anything in life, it's that people with money are treated differently by the police."

"I don't want to see him," Jess said.

Harry stalked towards the door.

"Then I'll see to him. I'll soon get rid of him."

"No, it should be all three of us. Will you come with us, Victoria?" Jess asked.

Victoria agreed to accompany them, insisting Harry leave the dogs in the library. If Harry and Flinn were to come to blows, she was concerned the dogs would become agitated.

Flinn stood by a display cabinet that housed a collection of antique snuff boxes. The cabinet doors were open and the rugged, olive-skinned man was holding a box, turning it in his hands, without a shred of embarrassment at examining someone else's property.

"You've done well for yourself, Jess. I bet one of these is worth ten years' wages to me."

Harry stepped towards Flinn, who outmatched him in height, with biceps that were straining against the cloth of his sleeves and tattoos on his thick neck.

"What do you want?" Harry said, taking the box from the man's hand and replacing it in the cabinet, closing the door with a thud.

"Friendly sort, this fella you're bunked up with, Jess. I take it that's who he is." He gestured to Victoria. "Unless you're the one who warms his bed . . ."

Harry clenched his fist. Jess rushed forwards and grabbed his arm before he could raise it.

"What do you want, Ollie? You're not welcome here," she said.

263

"That's no way to talk to your *husband*. I take it this bloke of yours knows we're married."

"Jess told me everything and whatever you want, you can deal with me."

"Told you everything, did she? Even that she was selling herself for money before she took up with you?"

"She left nothing out. Now, what the bloody hell do you want?"

Victoria stole a glance at Jess. The poor woman had tears rolling down her cheeks. Victoria stretched out her arm and gripped Jess' trembling hand.

"Not offering me a drink?"

"You'll get nothing here," Harry said, squaring up to Flinn.

"If that's how you want it. I came home after years at sea to find my wife had gone. Her sister wouldn't tell me where she'd scarpered to. But as luck would have it, I found a postcard from Texas behind the clock on the mantel that my wife had sent her," he said with a sneer.

"Get to the bloody point," Harry said in a low growl.

"I had to travel to Texas – cost me a packet – only to be told by one of the other whores that my wife had hooked herself an oil tycoon and took off to England. Little blonde piece I spoke with . . . right proud of you she was. Showed me your letter."

"She'd never do that."

"All right, so she left letters and stuff lying around in a drawer – what's a man to do? I had to find my wife. I got myself work on a ship making the journey to England and here I am."

"We're not interest in hearing your bleeding life story. This is the last time I'm going to ask before I fetch my gun. What do you want?"

"All right, fella, keep yer hair on. We've all got guns if we want them."

"We haven't all got the nuts to use 'em, though."

Flinn gave a harsh laugh.

"If you want to keep bedding my wife, I think some compensation is in order. It's only fair you pay, same as her other punters."

"How much will it cost to make you go away for good? Because if yeh come back a second time, I'll shoot you and then feed you to my dogs."

Harry's eyes were steel. Victoria had never seen this side of him.

"This is a nice little town. I might want to make a home here myself."

"Right, I've heard enough of this shite." Harry made for the door.

"Five hundred pounds – I think that's fair to ride her every night yeh fancy. Unless she wants to come back to *my* bed. I always could keep her happy in that department. But perhaps nowadays she's more bothered about all this fancy stuff . . ." He waved his arm around the room.

Harry lunged forwards, halting suddenly as Jess screamed.

"Wait here," Harry snarled, striding from the room.

Flinn turned to look at the two women, who were still holding hands.

"I still love yeh, Jess. It makes no difference to me how many fellas you've been with. If you want to come back with me, I'll gladly have yeh. Money or no money."

"You kicked any feeling out of me that I had for you the night you made me lose my baby."

"I was drunk – you know I was. Never laid a finger on you when I were sober."

"I can't stand the sight of you. Our daughter died because of you."

Harry marched back into the room, slamming the door. He thrust an envelope at the broader man.

"Here, it's all there. But mark my words. I meant what I said. If I see you again, I'll kill yeh."

Flinn touched his forelock. "Didn't even argue about the price. Perhaps I should have asked for more. Still, maybe I'll stick with the same ship going between New York and Liverpool, so I can visit again."

Harry slammed his fist on the table. "Don't push me."

"Monied people are all the same. Never done a hard day's work in yer life and you look down on ordinary folk. I'll take yer money and get out of your hair. There's no need to show me out – I know the way."

Harry followed him out into the hallway, issuing instructions to the butler that Oliver Flinn was never to be admitted again.

In the library, Victoria dried Jess' tears as they listened to what sounded suspiciously like a scuffle. Jess broke down.

"Whatever must you think of me?"

Victoria held the larger woman in her arms, rubbing her back as Jess sobbed.

"Now, Jess, don't take on. I think of you the same as I did this morning. You're a fine woman and I'm proud to be your friend."

"I can't believe h-he found me," Jess said, her voice juddering.

"He's gone now and I don't think he'll be back – not after Harry's warning."

"I'm so ashamed."

"There's no reason to be."

"I was singing at the club, but the money was lousy . . ."

"You needed to support yourself, Jess, I realise that."

"I had a few regulars, that's all. I wasn't selling myself to every bloke who could afford to pay."

"Jess, please, you don't need to explain."

"I want to make sure you understand. You're my only friend here, apart from Harry's sisters – but they're his family, so it's different. We *are* friends, aren't we?"

"Yes, Jess, we're good friends and always will be."

Jess lifted the end of the silk scarf around her neck and used it to wipe her eyes.

"I've not got a lot else to say. Except, I swear it was never a life I wanted."

"Who knows what any of us would do if we were in need. Please don't distress yourself. Nothing has changed between us. The most interesting thing I've learned is that you were a singer." Victoria smiled.

"Blues. I was good," Jess said, her lip trembling as she attempted a smile.

Harry was rubbing his knuckles when he returned to the library. He took Jess in his arms, kissing her tight curls.

"There now, baby, it's all right. Mrs Caldwell, Victoria, I'm grateful to you, but I'll take care of Jess now. Can I ask you not to say owt about this to anyone – not even family. I'm not mithered, but for Jess' sake."

"You have my word, Harry."

"You'll come back and visit again, won't you?" Jess asked, lifting her head from Harry's shoulder.

"Of course, Jess. I'll see you soon."

As Stokes drove Victoria home, she was reeling from

what had occurred. She also realised why Jess had been so keen to improve herself. The poor woman had hoped to wipe away the shame she clearly felt about her past by becoming what she considered a more refined lady. In Victoria's opinion, Jess was kind and funny, which was far more important than airs and graces – she was glad to be her friend.

⊷⊙⊙⊶

Chapter 23

George leaned his forehead against Victoria and Edward's bedroom window, suddenly saddened. It was October already – it would be Daphne's birthday tomorrow. Had she grown much? Would she still giggle if he blew raspberries on her tummy? He'd never know . . . What was the point in thinking about it? That part of his life was over. She was in the past.

As the door handle turned, he shoved the jewels he was holding into his pocket and rushed to the door, almost colliding with Max.

"What the devil!"

"Sorry, sir. Mr Taylor has gone out and I thought the house was empty apart from the kitchen staff."

"What are you doing coming in here, boy?"

Max lifted the shoes he held that had clearly just been cleaned.

"I'm sorry, Mr Bristow. I was returning these."

"Thought you'd go sniffing around while everyone was out, did you?"

"No. No. No, honest, sir. Honest."

George grasped Max's collar.

"If people find out what sort of person you are, you'll be out on yer ear. Never talk about me to anyone in this house. Is that clear? I'm warning you – don't cross me."

"I . . . er . . . Yes, sir. I didn't mean to cause offence."

George pushed Max against the wall then stalked downstairs into the morning room, where he poured himself a drink before sitting on the sofa, clutching his temples.

Blast it! What *had* he been thinking?

George pulled the string of pearls from his pocket and flung them on the sofa next to him. He scratched his head. There was no way he wanted to mess this up over a few pearls. He'd gone in their room for a look round while no one was home. You could learn a lot from looking through people's things. He hadn't intended to take anything – it was instinct. Damn. He'd put them back in a minute.

At the sound of muffled voices in the hallway, he grabbed the necklace and shoved it in his pocket as the door opened.

"Mrs Clarkson is here, sir," Max said.

"Leave us, please," George said, struggling to keep his tone pleasant.

What the devil did she want?

Sophia sauntered in. She looked stunning, in a brown velvet suit and matching hat, softened by a peach chiffon blouse.

"Sophia, I'm afraid the family are out for the day."

"Really? Most inconvenient. I wanted to talk to Victoria about Pierre." She sat close to George. "Perhaps you can tell her for me. I have seen him this morning and he is clearly gaining weight. The child is thriving. It is a lot of fuss about nothing. Sean has exaggerated what happened because he felt guilty about gallivanting the night his son was born."

"I'll tell them you called round."

"How are you, George, dear?" Sophia said softly, placing her hand on his cheek.

"I'm fine. Thank you."

"Yes, you always look so well, considering."

"I have good days and bad."

Sophia removed her hand, her eyes downcast.

"George, what are these? A little present for Bella?" she said as she pulled the string of pearls from his pocket.

George was dumbstruck – he must have left the end showing.

"Erm, yes," he said eventually.

Sophia turned them slowly in her hand.

"George, I believe you have been a naughty boy. These are Victoria's. I would recognise them anywhere because of the silver clasp. Have you stolen them?"

"No. No . . . I . . . of course not."

Sophia threw back her head and laughed.

"My dear boy, there is no point in lying – it is written all over your face."

"Sophia, please."

She stroked his hand with one finger.

"It's all right, you can stop panicking. I don't give a damn. I cannot stand the sanctimonious bitch. It will be our little secret."

George could feel the perspiration under his armpits. What the hell was he going to do about her? He was going to put the necklace back, but if she said anything, it would make life extremely uncomfortable. Ruin everything he'd worked for. Then again, she might keep his secret, but only if he had something to hold over her. Sean had told him about her making advances towards him, so clearly she was gagging for it. And she was beautiful . . . It wouldn't be a hardship.

Grasping her by the arms, he pressed his lips against hers. As she responded, he was sure he'd made the right decision. He could always tell what women wanted. George pushed up her skirt – no need to take things slowly with this one . . .

That night, Victoria closed the lid on her jewellery box and looked in the mirror at Edward, who was sitting up in bed reading.

"I'm flummoxed. They've definitely gone."

Edward peered over his book.

"What has, darling?"

"Edward, really! Were you not listening to me for the last five minutes?"

"Of course I was, my dear."

"Poppycock! If you'd been listening, you'd know that I can't find my pearls."

"That is because they are in the safe-deposit box at the bank."

"See – I knew you weren't listening. I said that after Bella wore them for her wedding, I never returned them to the bank because the hinge on the case was broken. I've been so busy that I only dropped it off last week to be fixed. The pearls were definitely in my jewellery box."

"You must have put them down somewhere. Come to bed and give your husband a cuddle. I am sure you will remember where they are in the morning."

She never left them lying around – they meant the world to her. Perhaps Bella had borrowed them. It would be unlike her to take something without asking, but there was no other logical explanation.

Before Victoria left for work, she asked Bella about the pearls – it came as no surprise when she said that she hadn't borrowed them. Then Taylor assured her he'd tactfully question the staff. She didn't believe for one minute anyone had taken them but wondered if perhaps the maids had seen them while cleaning.

That evening when she arrived home, as Max took her hat, he asked anxiously, "Do you think they've been stolen, ma'am?"

She noticed he was avoiding her eyes.

"No. Don't look so worried, Max. I'm not accusing anyone."

"Mr Taylor is in a right tear about it and I don't like to think of anyone taking advantage of you, ma'am."

"Stop worrying. I'm sure they'll turn up," she said, hoping that was true.

The last thing she wanted was unrest in the servants' hall. She was cross with Taylor.

During dinner, Max still looked uncomfortable, so when he went to the kitchen to take out the dirty soup bowls and collect the main course, she raised the matter with the butler again.

"Taylor, Max looks on edge. I specifically asked you not to make the other servants feel as though they were under suspicion about my pearls."

"I was extremely discreet, madam. If Max is concerned, perhaps that speaks of his character."

"Are you suggesting he's dishonest? A thief?"

"Not a thief, madam. I am afraid I have nothing specific I can tell you about. However, sometimes I find the lad shifty."

She picked up her glass.

"Perhaps he's nervous and unsure of himself, but that's not enough to condemn him."

"No, madam."

The rest of the family remained quiet during the exchange until George said, "Hmm . . . I agree with Taylor. There's something about Max I don't trust. The thing is, I thought some coins had gone from my dresser the other day. I can't be certain, so I said nothing. And I'm not saying it was Max. But now with your pearls . . . Maybe the two things are connected."

Victoria put her wine glass back down on the table without taking a drink.

"Edward, I don't like a member of our household's character being questioned. I feel responsible for starting this."

"Perhaps I should search the servants' quarters, madam?" Taylor said.

"Let me check with the bank first to make sure the pearls aren't in the security box," Edward suggested.

"Edward, I know they were in my jewellery box a few days ago."

Anne wafted her hand in front of her face.

"This is dreadful. I came here because I no longer felt safe in my own home, only to find myself in a den of thieves."

Victoria tutted. "Anne, please don't be so dramatic or I may have to inflict a slow, painful death on you."

"Really, Victoria, that's not in the least bit amusing."

"It wasn't meant to be."

"I've never been one to interfere. I'll just eat the rest of my meal in silence. Forget I'm here."

If only she could forget Anne was here.

"I'll try," Victoria said.

"Maybe you'd prefer it if I went back to London, now Kate has secured a teaching post there. At least I won't be alone in the house."

"There's no need for that, Anne," Edward said.

"Edward's right. I'm sorry, Anne. This business has upset me. You're welcome here."

"At least I'll be out of your way tomorrow evening when I dine with Owain," Anne added.

"It's going to be hanging over the household until we clear it up. Taylor, ask Max to finish serving and you can check the rooms now, so we can put this behind us," Edward said.

"Perhaps it's best left until tomorrow," George said.

"No – this is so unpleasant. I want it over with," Edward insisted.

Bella bit her bottom lip.

"George, you seem concerned. Is there something else about Max we should know?"

"No, I won't sully your ears or cause trouble unnecessarily."

The conversation halted as Max returned with the meat dish. His cheeks were inflamed, but that proved nothing, other than perhaps he'd overheard them. Victoria wished she'd never spoken to Taylor about it. One thing was sure – she was determined not to believe Max's guilt if there was no proof.

"Would you excuse me for a few moments?" George said.

"George, you can't leave during dinner," Bella said.

"I must, I'm sorry."

Bella rose from the table.

"George, what is it?"

"It's simply a badly timed call of nature," he said, leaving the table.

When he returned a few minutes later, Edward said, "Are you sure you're feeling all right, George? You look out of sorts."

"It's nothing. Really, Edward. I'm sorry I disturbed our meal."

"Not to worry. It has hardly been the most relaxing evening."

For the rest of the meal, Victoria played with her food, her appetite gone. If someone had stolen her necklace, the household would never feel the same again. Suspicion would always affect the way she felt about the servants – how could it not?

She didn't pretend to know the mill workers well. However, her household servants and the employees at Centenary House were trusted completely. Only once in all of her years in Faredene had she been wrong about someone who worked for her. She hoped this wouldn't be the second time she'd made a mistake.

Taylor returned as they were finishing dessert.

"Max, please return the rest of the serving salvers to the kitchen," he said.

As the door closed behind Max, Taylor went to Edward's side.

"I'm pleased to report, sir, that the servants' quarters are clear. I'm assuming you don't wish to have my rooms checked."

"Tut, of course not, Taylor," Edward said. "Right, I will pop into the bank tomorrow and check the safe-deposit box. Until then, let's try to put this out of our minds."

Once they were in bed, Edward pulled Victoria into his arms.

"Now stop this – I can see you are fretting about things."

"It's not the pearls, even though they're precious to me. It's the thought that someone could steal from us. And I'm shocked that George and Taylor don't appear to like Max."

"I am fond of George and I respect his opinions, but you and I have always believed in taking people as we find them. We will not condemn Max with no reason."

"Max seems so nice, so normal."

Edward chuckled. "Everyone seems normal until you get to know them. Before we were married, you never suspected that I became a vampire when there is a full moon," he said, pretending to bite her neck.

Despite her concerns, Victoria giggled.

"Get off, you fool." She touched his cleft chin with her index finger. "Do you want to make me happy?"

He laughed, opening the button on her nightgown.

"Now you're talking."

She stayed his hand.

"Will you do *anything* for me?"

"Mmm-hmm. Where is this leading?"

"Will you?"

"Yes, you know I will."

"Help me search the room for my necklace or I won't be able to sleep."

"Blinking heck, woman. It's a good job I adore you. I thought it was too good to be true."

Eventually, after checking the rest of the room and the drawers of her dresser, Edward pulled the bottom drawer out and placed it on the floor before crouching down so he could look inside the cavity.

"The things I do for love."

"You'll get your reward if you find them."

"I'll hold you to that." He held up the string of pearls. "You must have put them in your top drawer. Somehow, they went down the back and ended up on the floor."

"Oh, Edward, thank you. That's so strange. I never put them in the drawer. Still, I'm thrilled. The poor servants. I feel terrible about the fuss I've caused."

As Edward pushed the drawer back in, Victoria placed her jewels carefully on top of the dresser then held out her hand to help him up before climbing back in bed.

"As soon as the case is repaired, I'll return them to the bank," Victoria said.

Without his built-up shoe, Edward's gait was even more awkward than when he'd been a younger man able to balance on his toes. He looked pained as he hobbled back to bed, where he stood beside Victoria, his expression hangdog, his shoulders slumped.

"Now I've solved the mystery of the Great Pearl Robbery, are you going to take pity on your poor invalid husband and give him some love and affection? And wasn't there mention of a reward?"

Victoria patted the covers next to her.

"Come on, then."

Kirby jumped up beside her.

"I give up. At least push him down to the bottom so we can have a cuddle," Edward said.

In their bedroom further along the corridor, George lay in the darkness, his arms around Bella as she drifted off to sleep. Tonight had been a close call – too close. Taking the necklace in the first place had been an amateur's mistake. If that blasted woman hadn't come round, he'd have put them back yesterday before Bella got home. As it was, he'd no sooner got rid of Sophia than Bella had returned early and he'd had to hide them in his wardrobe inside one of his shoes.

Thankfully, he'd come up with an excuse so he could slip out during dinner tonight and shove them in Victoria's top drawer. It was too late to put them back in the jewellery box – there was no way she'd have believed she'd simply not noticed them in there. Presumably, she'd find them over the next couple of days and that would be the end of the matter.

He wasn't worried about Sophia saying anything. Though, he might have to satisfy her needs now and again – that would keep her quiet. What about the footman? The way Max had eyed him suspiciously when he'd returned to the dining room made it clear he could become a problem. One thing was certain – if that bastard was harbouring any ideas of messing things up, he'd have to be dealt with.

cᴓᴓꙄ

Chapter 24

Sean made his way through the park down the leaf-strewn path, hoping that the brief walk to the mill would clear his head. As he neared the Rows, he could hear the rumble of men's raised voices. Although he could only make out the odd word, it was clear there was a disagreement regarding the mill. He walked faster and as he turned the corner, a group of men, most of whom he recognised, were walking ahead of him, making their way to begin their shift at the mill. Then he heard David Gibbs' voice.

"You're all mad. There's been hundreds of strikes right across the country in the last couple of years, but nothing has bloody changed."

"It's all right for you with yer brother sittin' pretty in the big house on his pile o' money. Us ordinary folk have had enough of being put down, makin' the nobs even richer," a gruff voice Sean couldn't identify responded.

Sean slowed his step so he could continue listening unnoticed.

"But it isn't like that at this mill, and you know it. Food prices are through the roof – it's no time to be striking," David said.

Sean recognised the voice of a carder.

"We've got the strike fund. And the mill and pit owners will have to give in if we all stick together. It'll be over before Christmas."

"We already have the best pay and benefits compared to other mills. Mr Clarkson's stuck between the union and the mill owners," David added.

"Makes no bleedin' difference. The union says we come out tonight ten minutes before the buzzer and God help any man who tries to stand against us," one weaver said.

Sean stopped in his tracks. He wanted to allow the men to get inside the gates without realising he'd heard them. He made his way into the mill through the yard then hurried into the office, where Matthew was hunched over his desk, a pile of ledgers in front of him.

"God, Matthew, you look like shit. Have you been here all night?"

"Almost. This damned place – it'll be the death of me. I can't sleep for worrying about when the strike will be."

"It's today. They're striking ten minutes before the final buzzer."

Matthew banged his fist on the oak desk.

"Blast! This could finish us. I'd hoped David and some other moderates could stop them."

"He was trying. I heard him myself."

Matthew swept his hand across his desk, pushing a stack of papers onto the floor with a thud.

"Is everything else all right?" Sean asked.

"I think Sophia might leave me. She's threatened it enough over the years, but now I fear maybe she means it."

So, Sophia might finally go through with it, Sean thought. Matthew deserved better, although he was sure Matthew wouldn't see it that way.

281

"Surely you can change her mind."

"I thank God that she loves me or I'd have lost her years ago. A woman like her won't be put second to a mill forever."

Could Matthew be so blind to the woman his wife was? Unsure how to answer, he focused on the strike.

"So, what are we going to do about the walkout?"

"There's nothing we can do. I'm due to pay them this afternoon. I've a good mind not to give it to them. The less money they have, the quicker the strike will break."

Sean gasped. "Matthew, we can't do that – there will be a riot."

"You're right, though it's damned annoying. All I can do is talk to the other mill owners again – see if I can persuade them to match our pay and conditions. And pray it doesn't become a national strike, because then we'll have no influence at all."

"Do you think they'll listen?"

"To be honest, I don't think I stand a chance with some of them. They blame us for paying too much and making their workers want more. Particularly when we get people from their mills seeking jobs here."

"Should we let my mother know?"

"There's no point until it happens. She can't stop it any more than we can."

Throughout the morning, as Sean and Matthew made their way around the mill, some of the workers looked arrogantly in their direction. Others looked nervous or worried.

Over the lunch break, Sean stared out of the window that overlooked the yard. Generally, there would be good-natured jeering and joking, or even the occasional fight.

Today, the atmosphere was abnormally quiet. Workers huddled in whispered conversations. He caught snatches here and there, just odd words: bosses – shock coming – solidarity.

Victoria pressed her hand into the small of her back as she rose. She was getting too old to be doing the bending required for fitting gowns.

"Can you do the hem, please? It'll be good practice for you," she said to her young assistant. "Don't worry – I'll be checking it's straight, as will the sewing room," she added for the benefit of the customer.

As she stood back watching, she allowed her mind to wander. She was still upset after quarrelling with Sean the previous day. She'd called round after Sunday lunch and it had been apparent that Sean was already intoxicated.

"You're heading for a fall. And I don't just mean the drink. I'm aware that you're frequently losing money at the card tables at The Jubilee Club," she'd said.

"You're overreacting. I enjoy a drink – and everyone plays cards."

"If you believe your drinking is under control, you're deluding yourself."

"Thanks, Mother!"

"You know how much I love you, but I'm begging you – moderate the drinking and gambling, please. If something is wrong, perhaps I can help."

"You can't sort out my marriage for me."

"Darling, I thought things had improved between you and Yvette."

"That only lasted a few weeks after Pierre was born. No, that's not true. Things are slightly better. But it'll never be a marriage like yours and Edward's or Bella and George's."

"I wish I could help."

"No one can. Even mentioning George's name makes me ashamed. He knows he won't make it to old age and I'm wasting my life. I'm not half the man he is."

"Now that's enough, Sean. Stop putting yourself down and feeling sorry for yourself."

"You're right, it's pathetic."

"I didn't say that."

"No. But you should have."

"Excessive gambling and drinking won't help you sort your problems."

"I know, but it eases the guilt. No one can reassure me that Pierre is unharmed. I let him down. If I'd not stayed out the night he was born, that woman would never have had the chance to harm him."

"Why did you stay out? You said you didn't want to talk about it, but I saw how pleased you were about his birth when you called to give us the news. Something must have happened after you left to upset you so much that you'd choose not to stay home."

"I still don't want to talk about it."

"Well, you know where I am if you change your mind."

"I'm fine, really. And I'll cut down, I promise."

Victoria believed he'd try. Whether her boy had the strength to fight the demons that had hold of him, though, was another matter.

Her attention was dragged back to the shop as her assistant asked her to check the hem.

❖ ❖ ❖

Sean and Matthew watched with dismay when, as predicted, the equipment began grinding to a halt ten minutes before the final buzzers. In the eerie silence, workers right across the mill stepped away from their machines and walked towards the doors.

"What's all this? The buzzer hasn't gone yet," Matthew said, feigning surprise.

A mother grabbed the hand of a young lad who was still sweeping, causing the broom to clatter noisily to the floor.

When they'd gone, Matthew turned to Sean.

"Well, this is it. We may as well get locked up. If it doesn't break in a month, then I'll bring in some Irish labour."

"The men will never stand for it."

"Then they'll have to come back. I'm not about to lose everything I've worked for. Possibly sacrificed my marriage for."

The two men agreed they'd call on Victoria and Edward to tell them the news.

Victoria expressed her concern for the future of the mill, but she was adamant that bringing in outside labour would only inflame the situation. Matthew explained he was going to go to the nearby mills once again to reason with the other owners.

"If they looked after their workers, they wouldn't have half the problems they have. And I can't blame the workers for sympathising with the miners," she said.

Matthew massaged his temples. "The other owners don't see it that way. All they're bothered about is their profits."

"Would you like me to come with you to see them?" she asked.

"No offence, but that would only rile them. They think I'm soft in the head for having a female business partner as it is."

"That's nonsense." Victoria bristled.

"They say I pander to the whims of a woman. And to be honest, we have done things because you suggested them."

Victoria tensed, plonking her teacup down, spilling some liquid into the saucer.

"Hold on, Victoria. Everything you've proposed has been the right thing. Sophia has no interest in the mill, so she wouldn't have come up with the things you have and without you, I might not even have thought about them," Matthew added.

"How long can you hold out with no production?" Edward asked.

"It depends on what you mean by hold out. We own the building, so we could close the mill and leave it sat there. But our customers will go elsewhere, so our business will be ruined. All the local mills will be on strike, but there's nothing to stop buyers from going much further afield, even abroad."

"What cash reserves are there in the business?" Edward asked.

"A month or two – maybe three if we don't pay our suppliers," Matthew said.

"That hardly seems fair," Victoria said.

"None of this is fair, Victoria. Least of all on us," Matthew replied.

"Do you think the workers can hold out that long, with only strike pay to live on?" Sean said.

"The best we can hope for is that the weather takes a

quick turn for the worse. It'll be harder for them to hold out if they're cold and hungry," Matthew ended.

Sean's mother fiddled nervously with the ornate locket that hung round her neck. He knew she worried about the mill, but she'd never countenance allowing people to go hungry.

It was a week since production at the mill had stopped. Most of their workers were outside other mills, supporting their fellow trade union members. Only a handful of picketers stood outside Centenary Mill, deterring anyone who was considering returning to work. Although they weren't in the union, Matthew had allowed the undermanager and secretary to stay home for fear they might be attacked if they came to work.

Victoria was sitting at Sean's desk. She and Matthew had spent several hours reviewing the situation. There were plenty of orders on the books for the next three months. However, it was irrelevant now the mill wasn't producing, so they'd written to their customers explaining they could no longer fulfil any orders due in the next month.

"All we can hope is that production starts again before we have to cancel any more orders," Matthew said.

Victoria didn't answer, as there was a gentle tap on the office door. She looked up, surprised, as they were alone apart from Sean, who was down on the mill floor taking advantage of the inactivity of the looms to service them. David Gibbs was standing in the doorway. Instead of his overalls, he wore a dark jacket with a red checked handkerchief round his neck and held his cap in his hands.

"David, I hope you didn't have any trouble getting in?"

"No, I told them I needed to have a quick word with you an' the boss, so they let me through."

She glanced towards Matthew, who nodded.

"Of course, David, come in. Take a seat," Victoria said.

David rotated his cap anxiously.

"Thanks all the same, but I'll stand. The thing is, our Harry has offered me an' my lad the job of gardeners at the Hall."

"Really?" Victoria steepled her fingers.

"Aye. He's offered me handouts, but I'll never take them. I'm a working man – always have been. But when he told me his gardener had retired, I asked if he'd take us on. There are some empty cottages on the estate an' we're gonna do a couple of 'em up. The wife's right excited about it. An' our lad can have one for him and his girl when they get wed."

"I'm pleased for you, David," Victoria said.

"Yes, I'm pleased for you, as well. I'll be sorry to see you go, but good for you," Matthew added.

"That's decent of you both. I feel bad about it, 'cos you promoted me to overseer."

"You mustn't worry about us, David. You must grasp opportunities when they come up," Victoria assured.

"There's summat else you ought to know."

"Oh, what's that?" Matthew asked.

"Young Joe is in hospital."

"What's wrong with him?"

"When rumours got round that you were thinkin' of bringing in Irish labour, Joe said he were comin' back to work, 'cos he weren't risking someone taking his job permanent. That got people's backs up and from what I heard, they've given him a right kickin'. It's a shame – he's a good lad is Joe."

"Thanks for telling us, David."

Once David closed the office door, Matthew's face was grim.

"That's a bigger problem than you might think. I was relying on David to help end the strike."

"What about that poor young man?" Victoria asked.

Matthew shut the ledger he'd been perusing with a thud.

"Leave it with me."

cada

Chapter 25

December hadn't brought the usual freezing temperatures and everyone was commenting on the mild weather. For the mill owners, this was the worst possible news. They'd hoped the need to pay for fuel to keep their families warm, as well as put food on the table and afford the rent, would force people back to work. Matthew's attempts to reason with the other mill owners over the last two months had failed and the strike was holding firm.

After a long day at Centenary House, which was a flurry of activity with the usual rush of Christmas orders, Kitty commented that she was shattered and looking forward to putting up her feet. Moments later, a young lad came to the side door and explained that Ron, their potman, wouldn't be in that night as his dad had passed away, so, despite her tiredness, it looked like Kitty was spending the night behind the bar.

The strike aside, The Tanner's Arms was still busy. Even though the pub wasn't in the Rows where most of the mill workers lived, it was still popular with them and the men could be found here most nights, drowning their sorrows and discussing the strike. The taproom was darker than usual because two nights ago, someone had put bricks through both large stained-glass windows, which were now boarded up. In all the years Albert had been running the pub, there had been no trouble. His hard features and tall, muscular build meant that people thought twice about crossing him, until now.

Around nine o'clock, Kitty leaned against the wall as she pointed to the empty glass on the round table in front of an elderly man.

"This one dead, love?"

"Aye, duck." The old man stayed her hand as she reached for the glass. "That's one hell of a shiner you've got there."

Kitty touched her eye self-consciously.

"I tripped over one o' me lads' toys a couple of days ago. Hit me face on the corner of the table."

"Sure you did, love." His tone implied he didn't believe her. "Your potman not in tonight?"

"His dad died sudden, so he's got the night off."

"We've all got to go sometime, I suppose. Well, I'd best be off home to me bed."

As he squeezed between the table and Kitty, his rank body odour assailed her nostrils.

"Mind how you go – it's belting down again," she said.

"It'll take more than a bit o' rain to wash me away." He gave her a toothless grin.

Back behind the bar, Kitty put her mouth close to Albert's ear.

"That old fella thinks you've walloped me."

"He doesn't know I wouldn't bloody dare 'cos you'd kill me," Albert grinned as he smacked Kitty's backside.

Kitty chuckled. "He's never seen a bar of soap. Who is he?"

"No idea. He's only been coming in this last week. Anyone know who the old bloke was?" Albert shouted to a group of men in the corner.

As Kitty continued collecting glasses, there was a general murmuring of "Never seen him" and a shrugging of shoulders from around the pub.

A short while later, Albert glanced at his overworked wife as she took an ashtray off a table to empty it into a metal bucket. He placed the glass he was drying on the bar.

"Come on. Drink up, gents, please. We've all got our beds to go to."

"But not all of us have someone as lovely as your missus waiting for us," shouted a voice from the corner.

Laughter broke out around the smoke-fugged bar.

"All the more reason for me to chuck you lot out."

There had been a better atmosphere tonight, with fewer jibes about how they should give away free beer now that their family was rich. No matter how many times Kitty and Albert told their regulars that the money wasn't theirs, people still felt the couple were now rolling in it and resentment had fostered.

Finally, as the last of the regulars left, Kitty removed the money from the till.

"I'll lock up," Albert said.

As he reached up to shoot the bolt, something stopped the door from closing fully. He bent to pick up a stone wedged in the frame, when the door slammed into his head, knocking him back into the room. He crashed into a nearby table, which collapsed. An overflowing ashtray flew into the air, sending a cloud of ash up, fag ends scattering across the sawdust-covered floor.

Kitty screamed as her eyes focused on the gun held in

the hand of a big man wearing a cloth cap. A scarf had been pulled up to cover his mouth and nose so only his eyes were visible.

"What the hell . . ." growled Albert as he tried to stagger to his feet.

"Albert, for God's sake stay where yeh are," Kitty said.

"That's right. Do as the lady says an' lie flat on the floor, face down, or a bullet might find its way into that lovely wife o' yours. Looks as though she's been through enough in life already."

Albert prostrated himself on the floor, snarling.

All attention swung to the door leading to the back rooms as Brian appeared, wearing striped pyjamas and rubbing his eyes.

"Mam, I wanna drink . . . What's going on?"

Kitty's arm shot out and pulled her son behind her.

"Stay quiet, love. Not a peep, now."

Albert twisted his thick neck as far as he could, raising his head off the ground.

"You bastard. If you hurt my wife or son, I'll rip yer bleedin' head off an' mount it above the bar."

The intruder waved the gun around.

"Now now, big fella. There's no reason for anyone to get hurt. P'rhaps yeh haven't noticed that I'm the one holdin' the gun."

"Albert, be quiet now. Please, I'm begging yeh," Kitty rasped.

"Now, missus, I can see you've emptied the till, so give us that there money bag. Nice and slow. Just pass it to me here. Once I've got me money, I'll be out o' yer hair an' there'll be no harm done. You can get back to yer cosy lives then."

Kitty turned round to face her son, placing a finger to her lips. With a trembling hand, she picked up the cloth bag from beside the till. In the mirror, she could see the man watching her. Slowly, she turned back to face the bar and held out the bag with one hand, the other restraining Brian firmly behind her back.

As the man reached out to take it, a voice came from the corridor.

"Mam, that little bugger's outta bed again an' I can't find him. I've checked the outhouse . . ."

This time, Jake appeared, dressed in the same attire as his brother. As he took in his mother's terrified face and the gun pointed at his dad, he screamed. The man swung the gun wildly and a bullet missed Albert's head by inches.

"Hell, look what you've made me do!" the man shouted before backing to the door.

Albert tried to grab the robber's leg as the man lost his footing and another shot pierced the air. The man took off down the street, dropping the money bag. Kitty dived for her son as Jake crumpled to the ground. Albert jumped to his feet and made for the door to give chase, but Kitty's voice stopped him in his tracks.

"Let him go, Albert. Jake's bleeding . . ."

Albert stumbled over the pieces of broken table as he rushed to her side.

"Dear God, no."

Kitty held out a quivering hand.

"Quick, grab me the bar towel so I can stem the bleeding. Then run for the doctor."

Albert shoved the towel in her hand as he dropped to his knees beside his unconscious son. From behind them, Brian whimpered.

"Mam, is our Jake gonna die?"

"Aww, no, love. It's only his shoulder. You come over here – hold his hand an' talk to him. Albert, get goin', sharpish."

"Sorry, I'm not thinkin' straight," Albert said, rising.

Brian shook his brother's arm.

"Mam, is our Jake asleep? Why won't he wake up?"

"Don't shake him – he's just fainted. Pass me that other towel, will yeh?" Kitty swapped the blood-soaked towel. "I'll tell you what will help. Can you go through to the kitchen and tidy up for me?"

"Yer bloody trying to get rid o' me, Mam."

"Don't swear. But yes, love. Do it for me, will yeh?"

Left alone with her son, Kitty's tears flowed unchecked as she murmured endearments and prayed for him to live.

To Kitty's relief, Doctor Farrell barged in and took charge in his usual brisk but kindly manner.

"Let's see what we have here, then." He crouched by Jake. "It looks worse than it is. Carry him to his bedroom, please, Albert. I can't clean him up with all this sawdust around."

In the boys' room, he gestured Albert's dismissal.

"You'd best notify the police. There's nothing to worry about here."

Albert stood his ground.

"Are yeh sure, Doc?"

"I'm not in the habit of saying things I don't mean."

"Aye, all right. I won't be long, Kitty, love."

Once Owain had bandaged Jake's shoulder, he reassured Kitty.

"As long as the wound is kept clean, he's going to be

fine. The bullet went through the flesh but missed the bone. Knowing him, he'll want to keep it as a souvenir of his adventure. And he'll have a decent scar to show off."

"He could have died. I'm still trembling worse than a pig at a hog roast."

The doctor reached for his bag.

"Do you want me to give you something for your nerves?"

"No thanks, Doctor. I need to keep me wits about me. The bobbies might want to speak to me when they get here."

"Of course."

"I can't think of anything to say that will help, though. Except that maybe the old fella who was in earlier wedged the door an' tipped off the big fella with the gun that Ron wasn't working tonight."

"I'm sure even that will be helpful to the police."

"Problem is, no one knows who the old geezer was an' the one what tried to rob us had his face an' hair covered."

A groan came from the bed behind the doctor and he looked at his patient.

"Now now, young man, no milking the situation. Some bed-rest and you'll be fine in a few days. But that wound needs to stay clean, so no getting up to mischief. I still haven't forgotten when you and that scamp of a brother attempted to climb up the inside of a chimney at the Hall."

Kitty tucked the covers around her son.

"Blinking potty, they are. Kids were forced up chimneys years back an' my daft buggers did it for fun."

The boy grinned sleepily.

"We knew that, Mam. That's what gave us the idea. We were tryin' to see what it were like."

"You don't have to try every dangerous thing you hear about, love."

"We do if we're going to be famous adventurers."

"Changed your mind about being the Great Jakerini, hey, sweetheart?"

"We can do both."

She kissed his strawberry blond curls. "You get to sleep now, love."

Kitty showed the doctor out, thanking him several times for saving her son.

"I told you, Kitty, he was in no danger. Though I appreciate your thanks all the same."

"What's got into people, robbing this place? Things haven't been the same since folk found out our Harry's got money. It's madness. And there's hardly a fortune in the till since the strike started."

"There doesn't appear to be any end in sight for the strike, I'm afraid," the doctor said as he walked down the hallway.

"No, but it doesn't stop fellas from drinking while their wives and kiddies go hungry." Kitty passed him his umbrella. "You'll need this, Doctor, or you'll be soaked getting into your car – it's still tipping down out there."

"Do you want me to wait until Albert gets back?"

"No thanks, Doctor. He shouldn't be more than a few minutes."

She bolted the door behind him and leaned against it, covering her face for a moment to compose herself.

By the time the police had left, it was early morning and Kitty's sons were both fast asleep. She and Albert sat at the table in their kitchen.

"I'm never going to feel safe here again. The night our

297

Teddy died in me arms gave me nightmares for years –
this has brought it all back."

"It used to frighten the life outta me the way you'd
thrash around screaming, drenched in sweat. I don't want
you going back to that."

"I couldn't bear to lose someone else I love at another's
hands."

"If I get me hands on that bastard, he'll hurt no one again."

"No, I don't want to see you banged up. Besides, I've
told you – I've never seen him before."

Albert lifted his hands in a hopeless gesture as he spoke.

"I don't know how else to protect you."

"We don't know why he targeted us instead of one of
the other pubs in the area. We've done nowt to make
someone have a grudge against us. People round here
don't rob from their own. P'rhaps because we're part of
the family what owns the Hall, we're fair game."

"But what can we do about that?"

"Let's get away from here. Move. If you still want a
pub, maybe we can open a little country one. But one
thing is certain – I can't stay here."

"We can't do that overnight. It could take months to
sell the place an' we can't leave it empty."

"Then let Ron run it. He's worked here for years an'
knows the ropes. He's always fancied being landlord."

"Aye, all right."

"You could pop round now."

"I'll see Ron when he's had chance to wake up. I can't
go chargin' round there this early when his dad only died
yesterday."

"Hmm, I was ready to do an Irish jig when my old
fella went, but I guess we're not all the same."

"Ron's not one to sit around mopin', though. I'll just give him some breathing space."

"That's settled, then."

"But where will we go?" he asked.

"To the Hall. Jess says it's too big for the two of 'em. She doesn't want to say owt to Harry an' upset him, 'cos it were her who wanted a big place. We can stay there until we find summat suitable."

"It won't be easy living in someone else's house."

"It'll be a damn sight easier than worrying someone is going to shoot me lads. I've told you before – if anything ever happened to one of them, I won't cope, and I meant it."

"All right, love. Don't get yerself worked up again. I've said we'll sort it an' we will."

A short while later, Albert stood in the pub's doorway, a hand braced against each side of the frame.

"Are you sure you'll be all right?"

"Yes. Remember to see Milly first – tell her what's happened an' explain I'm taking the day off. Then go an' see Ron." Kitty kissed his cheek. "Go on with yeh. If that fella comes back here, he'll get me toe up his backside."

She bolted the doors behind him and returned to the boys' bedroom, where Jake was still sleeping. She was keeping both boys off school. Brian was sitting in bed with a book, pretending to read, which was a sure sign of how much the incident had shaken him. Normally, she couldn't get him to sit still for two minutes.

"Come on, let's get packing. We've moving to Uncle Harry's," she said, handing her youngest son a bag to pack.

ꝏꝏ

Chapter 26

Victoria moved her heavy basket from one hand to the other as she led her entourage through the early morning mist into the first of the streets known as the Rows.

Bella shot her a glance. "Can you manage, Mother?"

"Yes, dear. You have your own to carry and they'll be empty soon enough."

They were delivering food to the striking families for the third time this week. Each woman had an overflowing basket, and Max and two of the footmen from the Hall were carrying large jugs of milk.

Families were struggling and Matthew and she were at odds over the best course of action to stop the strike. Victoria insisted the only solution was for the other mill owners to give the workers what they demanded. Matthew, who felt betrayed by his workforce, now said there was no choice but to starve them back to work and bring over Irish workers.

Victoria realised the strike might force the mill to close, inevitably resulting in more hardship for residents of the Rows if they lost their jobs. It wasn't what Matthew or she wanted either, as they both had a great deal of money tied up in the mill that they could ill afford to lose. Victoria believed she was doing the right thing. Edward and Sean supported her decision, but when Matthew found out, she knew he'd be furious.

They split up into groups and began tapping on doors. As the first door opened a few inches, the stench from inside wrapped itself around Victoria like a damp shawl. A dishevelled woman peered out.

"Are yeh deliverin' food again?"

Kitty stepped forwards.

"Yes. Mrs Caldwell is the one who organised it all."

The woman opened the door further.

"Aww, Kitty, pet, I've not seen yeh for such a long time. Some foreign woman an' your Milly dropped off some bits a couple of days back. Is she not with yeh today?"

"That woman is my sister-in-law, Jess, and she's with Milly in the next street."

"I heard yer up at Faredene Hall now. How are yer lads?"

"They're fine. Still runnin' me ragged, as you'd expect. How are you keeping?"

The woman looked down and pulled at her stained and tattered woollen dress.

"I'm a mess. There's no money for food or coal, never mind soap."

"No need to explain owt – we understand. We've brought you the basics. It's only bread, sugar, drippin', some sausages and milk, if you've got a jug to take some," Kitty said.

"Thanks, love. I'm right grateful to yeh. And to you, Mrs Caldwell. It's decent of yeh, seeing your mill is one o' the places on strike. It's the nippers who are sufferin'. If they're not back before Christmas, this will be the worst bleedin' one we've ever had an' that's saying summat." She turned to holler over her shoulder. "Fetch me jug, one of youse."

As they moved on to the next house, Victoria was racked by guilt. She'd held off before starting the food distribution, but when her cook had asked her to agree what was to be ordered from the butchers for their festive fare, Victoria's conscience wouldn't allow her to prepare for celebrations while others starved. Despite the problems the strike was causing for her business, she was glad it had been an exceptionally mild winter, or many of them might have perished. She didn't want their blood on her hands.

Mrs Hornby-Smythe and some ladies at the Women's Guild had relished challenging her about her workers being on strike. But she'd put them in their place, pointing out that they were striking to support other mills and that they'd made no demands on Centenary Mill.

Once they'd distributed everything they had, Victoria looked through the swirling mist to where the other group were hovering outside their final stop at the bottom of the narrow street. Milly was clutching the last loaf to her chest.

"Our Milly looks upset. Summat's wrong – we'd better get over there," Kitty said.

They scurried towards the house. The battered front door was wide open and an anguished cry emitted from inside.

"Mother of God! What's wrong?" Victoria said.

Jess gulped. "It's her baby. It's dead."

"No!" Victoria pushed past Milly, who was blocking the doorway.

Inside the dark front room, an emaciated woman was

sitting on the floor in front of a long dead fire. The limp body of a baby wearing a thin filth-splattered frock lay across the wailing woman's knee. Victoria knelt beside her on the grimy rag mat and gently removed the cold form from her lap. Without hope, she pressed her ear to the child's mouth.

Was that a faint breath?

Quickly, she turned the child over and began rubbing its back, then its cold limbs. Her mind flashed back to that first night when she'd been desperate to save Sean. After a few seconds, she listened again. She was sure that was a feeble breath.

"Max! Max! Come in here."

The women moved aside to let him through.

"Ma'am?"

"Break up those chairs and get the fire going."

The woman opened her mouth as though to protest then covered her face with her hands.

"Do you have any matches?" Max asked.

The woman pointed to a scratched dresser.

"Can one of you run back to the motor cars and get Stokes to drive you to Doctor Farrell? Get him to come immediately," Victoria said.

"I'll go," Bella said, already hurrying out of the door.

"I've got no money for the doctor. As it is, me dad will go mad when he sees what you've done to his chairs. This is his house. Me and my fella had to move in here when we couldn't pay our rent what with him being on strike."

Jess put a hand on her shoulder.

"I'll pay for the chairs and the doctor, don't you fret, sugar."

Max took off his coat and Victoria wrapped the infant in it.

"How old is your baby?"

"She's five months."

The child looked much younger.

"Can you feed her?"

"Me milk's dried up. I've not had enough to eat. I thought she were dead. Is she gonna live, then?"

"She will if I have anything to do with it, but don't get your hopes up," Victoria answered honestly.

Cradling the child, Victoria moved from the floor to the settle.

"Kitty, fetch a bowl, would you, and make me a thin pap of milk and sugar."

"Give me two ticks," Kitty said, grabbing a cracked one off the table.

"Max, can you run to the corner shop to get some more food?"

"Yes, ma'am. Anything in particular?"

"Just see what they've got, please."

Victoria looked around the practically bare room. Since Max had broken up the two chairs, all that remained in the room was the battered dresser, the settle she was sitting on and a wooden table. The peeling wallpaper was blackened and furred. That people worked hard all of their lives and could attain nothing more than this made her ashamed of her wealth.

Victoria did her best to feed the infant, her anxiety increasing until Owain arrived.

"Thank goodness you were available, Doctor. I've tried to feed her. She seems hungry, but she took barely anything," Victoria said.

The doctor nodded.

"Ladies, you may have saved a life here today, but this

304

house is far too cramped for all of us. If I can ask you to leave me to my patient."

As they took their leave, Jess removed several coins from her reticule and pressed them into the astonished woman's hand.

"That's for the chairs." Jess handed over some more coins. "But this is for you and the baby. Keep it hidden from the men if you have to."

The woman dropped the coins in the large pocket of her pinny, silently nodding her thanks.

As they walked back to the waiting automobiles, Victoria said, "Bella, you go home with Stokes and Max can drive me to the mill. I'm afraid it's time I told Matthew what I've been doing. It's not fair to keep him in the dark any longer. But after seeing how thin that mother and her baby were, there's no way I can stop helping them."

The two thin picketers doffed their caps as the watchman unlocked the gates. Victoria shivered as she made her way through the unusually cold and silent mill to the office. Having told her business partner that she'd been feeding the striking workers and their families, she braced herself for his reaction.

Matthew launched his empty coffee mug across the room.

"How the bloody hell could you be so thoughtless! You've been delivering food to them all week behind my back, prolonging the strike . . . Every day they've got no food is a day closer to them coming back. They've held out another week and it's down to you," he roared.

"Matthew, there's no point shouting at me. I couldn't stand by and let them die. Some of them didn't even want to strike – they just didn't want to be labelled as blacklegs. Their families would have been ostracised or worse."

"You still shouldn't have gone behind my back. I'd have brought Irish workers in before now if it weren't for you."

"You helped that young lad Joe when someone gave him a good hiding for talking about coming back to work. You visited him in hospital and you're paying his bill."

"That's not the same. He was coming back – he deserved our help."

"You care about them, too – you may as well admit it. If you could see how thin some of the children are, Matthew . . . it's appalling. For the ones with several children, the strike fund isn't enough to live on. Surely you're not blind to that."

"We'll see if you're so bloody righteous when our grandchild is going hungry."

Victoria sighed. "I don't see any point in continuing this conversation if all we're going to do is argue."

"You don't seem to realise how serious things are."

"I do! That woman's child would have died this morning. No doubt others have. I can't live with that on my conscience, even if you can."

"You sound like your bloody son."

Suddenly, Matthew sat back down and covered his face with his hands, shaking as he broke down. Victoria placed her hand on his shoulder.

"I'm sorry, Matthew. Please try to understand – I did what I thought was right."

"Well, I can't take any more. I'm done, Victoria."

"We'll sort something out. Come back to the house with me. Let's talk to Edward and Sean and decide on a plan."

Despite the four of them doing their best to come up

with a solution, it seemed to Victoria that they'd been going round in circles. Finally, Matthew knocked back the dregs of his third whiskey.

"There's no point in any of it any more. I'm sacrificing my marriage and for what?"

"The mill has always been so important to you," Victoria said.

"It was, but I'm not getting any loyalty from the workers, or my business partner."

"That isn't fair, Matthew," Edward said.

"No, it's not. I'm sorry, Matthew, but you've always known Mother cares about the workers. She went into business with you because you felt the same," Sean added.

"I did. But look at how they've repaid us, striking to support other mills. It'll be up to you what happens now, Victoria. I'm going to take Sophia back to New Orleans."

"You can't up and leave. What about the mill?" Victoria said.

"I'll sell my share. So, you've a choice to make. Do you want to buy me out or accept another partner?"

"Does it need to come to this? Sean won't return to America after what happened with Claude. Surely you don't want to leave Yvette and Pierre," Victoria said.

"You can't speak for Sean. Perhaps they *will* return with us."

Sean glanced sideways at his mother's horrified face.

"I'm here for good, Matthew."

"Fair enough, but I'll lose Sophia if I don't do something. For too long I've pretended she's been faithful to me, but losing her is another matter."

Victoria looked down at her hands, avoiding his eyes.

"Matthew, I'm so sorry."

"I can see from your faces that you all knew."

"Suspected, perhaps, but are you serious about the mill?" Victoria asked.

"I didn't realise I was until I said it. But yes, I must try to save my marriage. Sophia isn't perfect, but I love her. If you buy me out, Sean can run it – he's capable. Or we can look for another partner for you."

"It's not a decision I can make on my own. It'll depend on what Edward and Sean have to say. Sean, do you want to run the mill, darling?"

Sean was dumbfounded. They were all waiting for him to answer her question. He should be elated at the prospect, but he wasn't.

"Come on, Sean, be honest with us. I want your mother to retire, so she can't take on any more work. Is running the place what you want?" Edward said.

"I'm really grateful for the offer, but I don't see my future at the mill. The reality of being there every day in that humidity, and with all that noise and dust. I'm sorry, Mother."

"My darling, I'd never want you to do something you don't enjoy."

He hesitated, not wanting to let his mother down.

"If you *need* me to take it on, I will."

"Of course not, but what will you do instead?" his mother said.

"Charles has offered to back me in a business and at Bella's wedding, I suggested we open a factory."

Sean didn't mention that the idea came to him as he'd tried to come up with a reason for taking Charles away from Jane.

Victoria's eyes widened. "You never said."

"There didn't seem any point mentioning it as I've been putting him off because I'd committed to the mill."

"But what business will you start?" Edward asked.

"We've discussed making clothing. The ready-to-wear market is growing and I realise that I'll be in competition with Centenary House, but our factory would focus far more on mass-produced clothing for the middle classes."

Edward nodded slowly, looking from mother to son.

"I am sure your mother understands that you don't enjoy the mill – she has never liked it herself."

"Edward's right. We can seek a buyer for the whole thing. What do you think, Matthew?"

"It'll be easier to sell that way. The strike must end first, though."

By the time the meeting broke up, they'd agreed that before looking for a purchaser, Matthew would get the word out to the workers that they were selling the mill and that if production didn't start again soon, it may shut permanently.

"Will they believe it isn't simply a ploy to get them to come back?" Victoria asked.

"We might be on opposite sides of this fight, but they know I'm a man of my word. The mill needs to be up and running again for a while if we're to find someone who wants to run it as a going concern and isn't simply interested in the building. Which means we need to win back some of our customers," Matthew said.

"Do you want to leave now, Sean? Begin your enterprise straightaway?" Victoria asked.

"Is that all right with you, Matthew? I know you managed before without me."

"Unless I get them back to work, there will be nothing

309

for me to manage. Even if production starts again, as we're selling up, I'd prefer to know you were getting on with sorting out your own future. My daughter and grandson will rely on you to support them, after all."

"It might be for the best if I get on with it as soon as possible, then," Sean agreed.

The prospect of a new venture working with Charles was enticing. Then it suddenly hit him. With Matthew intending to return to America, Yvette could no longer turn to her father to pay her expenses. Sean had no capital to put into a new factory and no income with which to keep his family until the factory was up and running. What would he do if Charles had changed his mind and no longer wanted to invest?

❦

Chapter 27

Sean met Charles that night at The Jubilee Club. Once they'd been served their drinks, he got straight to the point.

"Charles, if you were serious about starting a business together, now is the ideal time. Mother and Matthew are selling the mill. They offered me the opportunity to run it, but I find the idea of developing our own operation far more exciting. That is if you're still willing?"

Charles grinned. "Absolutely!"

"I've not even shown you a business plan yet."

"No need, old chap. It wouldn't mean a great deal to me, anyway. My only proviso is that the factory is a decent place to work. I trust you to make it profitable and will leave the decision-making up to you."

"Don't you want to be involved?"

"I might dabble, but there is no point in pretending I know the first thing about business. I will fund it and you supply the brains. How's that?"

"Do you have that much faith in me?"

"What happened in America wasn't down to you."

"That puts a lot on my shoulders, buddy. But to be honest, I relish the idea."

"Sean, I have every faith in you."

"Charles, as well as not having any capital, if I'm not working at the mill, I'll need to press ahead, as I won't have any income until it's turning a profit."

"Don't be absurd, Sean. You will take an income from day one. You will be the one doing the work, after all, so I can't expect you to do it for nothing. What we need is to find some premises."

"There are some new warehouses near the canal. If we can secure one of them and have it converted, that'll be the quickest way to get the facilities we need. And we might have to rent some office space for a while so I can interview staff and get things organised."

Over the next couple of hours, they agreed some initial figures and Sean went home, eager to start their new venture.

That night, Bella snuggled in close to George – she loved being in his arms. In the months since her marriage, she'd frequently wondered if it was a blissful dream. George was the perfect loving husband. On their honeymoon in Paris, they'd toured the sights, dined in cosy restaurants and taken walks, hand in hand, along the banks of the Seine. It had been wonderful. Even though Kate had told her it could be extremely pleasurable and she'd endured a cringeworthy, embarrassing talk with her mother about intimacy between a man and a woman, Bella had been completely unprepared for the level of physical pleasure he gave her when they were alone in their bedroom. Their wedding night had been a glorious revelation.

She kissed his stubbled cheek.

"George, are you awake?"

"I am now, beloved one."

Bella squirmed with pleasure – she loved it when he called her affectionate names.

"This will be our first Christmas as a married couple. I'd like to get you a special gift. Any suggestions?" she asked.

"I don't need presents – I have you."

"If you don't give me any hints, I might buy you something dreadfully boring. Perhaps a pair of paisley socks or a book of classical verse."

George kissed the tip of her nose.

"I'll love anything you get me. What would you like?"

"Ooo, well, since you're asking, I'm not taking any chances on ending up with bath salts. I'd like an eternity ring, please. Because I want our happiness to go on forever."

"If that's what you want, my darling, that is what you shall have. I'll go to London to get one – it should be as special as you. And I was thinking we could get your father a new chess set."

"George, you're so considerate."

"Give over – there's nothing remarkable about me. I just want to show my appreciation."

"What about the other night when Kirby was unwell and you insisted on sitting up with him all night? Father was so grateful."

"I couldn't have Edward doing it at his age and I'm fond of the dog."

"I'm serious. Everyone thinks you're wonderful, even Kitty. I can tell because she says she'd rather eat her own feet than put up with people she doesn't like."

"That's nice."

"Perhaps we could even go away for New Year."

313

"If that's what you want," George said, turning his head away.

"George, have I said something wrong?"

"No, it's not that. Give me a minute and I'll explain."

Bella spent her days trying to please George – nothing mattered to her more. It was only a few moments, but it felt much longer as she lay beside him waiting for his response.

George did his best to look upset. He needed Bella to think each word pained him.

"Bella, it's . . . I . . . well, I suddenly feel like such a leech, lying here talking about buying presents with money from *your* allowance. I'm like a schoolboy waiting for pocket money so I can buy my Christmas gifts."

"George, it's not like that."

"Like I explained on honeymoon, I wish I had my own money so I could shower you with gifts."

"All of my life I've had everything I've wanted, but I'd give it all up in a heartbeat to spend time with you. I don't need anything else."

"It's just that I'd like us to . . ."

"What? Tell me, please."

He had to take this slowly. Play her just right. She was coming along nicely, even forgetting about those foolish women's suffrage ideas. Despite finding her harem pants sexy, he'd told her he didn't like them purely to see if she'd stop wearing them – which she had. Control was all about biding your time. If he'd rushed things with Pearl, she'd never have agreed to sleep with punters for him – she'd been a virgin when he married her. You had to wait until they were so desperate to keep you happy that they'd do anything for you. Not that he had the same fate planned for Bella. No, her value lay in her rich relatives and their fortunes he was expecting them both to inherit.

"Nothing. Forget about it, my precious," he said at last.

Bella smiled.

How could women be so stupid as to put so much store in a silly nickname? Pearl had liked that one, too.

"I can't if something is bothering you. Please tell me," Bella coaxed.

"It's best if we leave it."

George pushed the blankets off and sat up, his face sullen.

They were free to spend their days at leisure and Bella thought they couldn't be happier. Although looking at George now, sitting on the edge of their bed, his head downcast, for the first time she had doubts he shared her joy.

"What is it, darling? Tell me – are you unwell?"

George didn't look at her. His voice was heavy as he spoke.

"I'm getting weaker. I can't believe it's happening so soon."

An iron fist closed around her heart. She steeled herself. George was her world and she'd do anything for him – he mustn't see how alarmed she was. She stroked her fingers over his naked back in the way he liked, struggling to keep her voice calm.

"Let's book an appointment to see a different specialist. There must be something they can do. You look so strong and well." She placed her hand over his heart. "It's hard to accept that there's something wrong inside here."

George lifted his head and twisted to face her.

315

"We've discussed this. You know that won't help. There's nothing they can do. Even if I decide to go, it will be alone. I won't allow you to go with me. We agreed that before we married, remember?"

Bella had tried to change his mind before, pointing out to him that she might find some comfort from being able to ask questions, but it had annoyed him. She hated to make him angry. The only other cross words they'd exchanged was when he'd said that she must stop wearing trousers. Even though Bella enjoyed the freedom trousers gave her, she'd agreed. In her opinion, not wearing them was a small sacrifice.

Kate had hinted that she didn't approve of him controlling what Bella wore, but Bella didn't care what others thought. George's happiness was everything. He lived with his illness so bravely – he was her life.

She put her arm around her husband's shoulders and pressed her lips to his cheek, kissing it softly.

"What do you want us to do, George?"

He caressed her face with his fingers.

"We must make the most of the time we have."

Bella hesitated for a moment, wondering if he meant in bed – they usually made the most of their time in that way. She was amazed she wasn't already with child.

"Travel, possibly . . . I'm not sure," he added.

"We can do that. Where do you want to go? We can take a trip to America. I can ask my parents for an increase in my allowance if needed."

"No! I hate asking for money. It was a mistake to give up my job. I've lost my self-respect."

"Please don't say that. They were only trying to help. Surely you don't regret marrying me."

"No, of course not, my darling. It's . . . It's that I need . . . No, I can't say it. It sounds so ungrateful and your parents are wonderful with us. They mean a great deal to me. You understand that, don't you?"

"Yes, of course. Please, tell me what it is you *really* want."

"Forget about it."

"I'm your wife – there should be no secrets between us."

"All right. It's just that I'd like us – you, really – to have some financial independence."

"Why? My parents never refuse us anything. They certainly don't make a fuss about the money they give us."

"I'll hate myself for saying this, but you're forcing me to be honest with you. Having an allowance from your parents that you then share with me is humiliating. I'm a grown man."

Bella was dumbfounded. That something was bothering this sweet man, whose life expectancy was so limited, brought tears to her eyes.

"What do you want me to do?"

"I feel terrible asking, but perhaps if they could sign over some of your assets – give you some of your inheritance as they did for Sean."

"It's not the best timing with the mill workers on strike, but once the mill is sold, I'm sure they will. We'll talk to them about it tomorrow after breakfast. Now, let's get some sleep – you mustn't worry."

"I'll sound like a thankless cad."

"They won't think that. I'll tell them it's all my idea."

"Only if you're sure, my love. At least then I'll only have to live off my wife." He pulled a face. "I guess that

317

won't be too bad, unless I want to buy you a gift or take you on a surprise trip . . ."

"That's it – I'll put the money or property in your name."

"No. That's out of the question – it's too much."

"All right, but you will have full access to it. We'll set up a joint account."

George kissed Bella lightly on the lips then pushed the strap of her satin nightgown off her shoulder, exposing her pert breast. Leaning forwards, he took her nipple in his mouth.

Her breath quickening, Bella whispered, "George, perhaps you should rest."

"If I die with you in my arms, I'll be happy. Now shh. I want to make love to my wife," he mumbled.

Manipulating women always gave him a hard-on. Refusing the joint account months back when Edward offered it was a stroke of genius. Now, she believed it was her idea. And the silly hussy was so pleased he was buying her an eternity ring. Still, getting it from London gave him the excuse he needed to visit his ma – and take her something special for Christmas.

His ma could be annoying, as well. Then again, she was bound to be – after all, she was still a woman. But he always regretted hurting his ma. He never got pleasure from controlling her, not like he did with other women. They deserved it. No matter how nice they seemed at first, eventually they became whining and demanding, not worth the effort. But if he could get rid of the people who stood in his way, Bella would bring him a lot of money, so he could tolerate her gullible ways – at least for now, because that's how he needed her to be.

❖ ❖ ❖

On Christmas Eve, Sean adjusted his bow tie in the mirror.

"It's a shame Charles already had other arrangements for this evening."

"I find his sense of humour rather infantile. I doubt he will be missed by anyone but you," Yvette said.

Sean ignored her comment. Despite her promises of how different things would be following Pierre's birth, they still rowed frequently and he didn't wish to do so before they went out to dinner.

"We'll need to set off in a minute if we're to arrive on time."

Yvette's eyes blazed. "Don't rush me. You should not have accepted the invitation without checking with me."

"I thought you'd be pleased. Louise Mason is your friend and you're always telling me how I should see their wonderful home."

"You're right. Louise is *my* friend, so I don't see why you are being so friendly with Peter."

"It was you who recommended that we use him as our architect for the factory!"

"Because he is talented and I was being a supportive wife – trying to make sure you don't mess up this opportunity."

"Do you never get tired of putting me down?"

"Unlike your mother and sisters, I don't think everything about you is wonderful. I speak the truth. If I had realised you were a pauper, I would never have—"

"Come to my bed and thrown yourself at me."

"You useless pig."

Sean sighed. "Don't worry – I'm well aware how inadequate you think I am. Now, are you almost ready, or should we telephone and cancel?"

"Don't you dare! It is your flaming fault I am not ready yet."

"Mine? What have I done now?"

Yvette glared at him through her dressing table mirror.

"It has taken me longer to get ready because my skin and hair look so dull."

"They don't. You look lovely. But I can't see how I could influence your appearance."

She threw her powder puff back in the pot, creating a dust cloud.

"By getting me pregnant again so quickly, that is how," she shrieked.

Stunned, Sean spoke sharply before her words registered.

"It takes two as I recall." As it dawned, he kneeled beside her, his voice softer. "Yvette? Another baby? That's wonderful news."

"For you, maybe," she replied through pursed lips. "I am already nauseous in the mornings, so that is my Christmas ruined. Don't be expecting me to get up early to give Pierre the ridiculous number of presents you have insisted on buying him."

"You can rest as much as you need to. And take your time getting ready – I'll wait in my study." As he got to the bedroom door, he paused. "But you needn't worry – you look beautiful."

Later that evening, Sean watched Yvette with amazement as she giggled at something Peter Mason said. There was no trace of her earlier anger or her sulking he'd endured on the journey. Did she still have feelings for Peter? Was

320

that why she came round here at every opportunity? She was beautiful, but surely Peter wouldn't carry on an affair under his wife's nose. He was a decent man.

Sean had instantly taken to their host when Charles and he had met with Peter earlier in the week, commissioning him to design and manage the repurposing of the warehouse Charles and he were purchasing. Peter had a good sense of humour and Sean was looking forward to working with him over the next few months.

Yvette had previously described their hostess as mousey-haired and utterly boring. Although she was a quietly spoken woman, he found Louise to be highly intelligent and an excellent conversationalist.

Sean nearly choked on his wine at Yvette's next words as she patted her lips with her napkin.

"Yes, I am terribly proud of Sean and his new business venture. His plans for the factory production lines are so progressive."

He had no idea she'd even listened when he'd spoken about his proposals. In fact, she'd told him she wasn't interested. He wondered what she'd do if someone questioned her about the details. Yvette caught his attention again.

"Yes, I couldn't wait any longer – I simply had to tell Sean this evening that our darling Pierre is to have a little brother or sister next July."

She was unbelievable! She should be in Hollywood starring in moving pictures. If only she was pleased about it, he'd feel more hopeful about their marriage.

Peter raised his glass to Sean.

"Congratulations, old man. That's quite a Christmas present."

"I couldn't be more pleased. But less of the old," Sean grinned.

When they arrived home, Yvette's voracious lovemaking surprised Sean even more than her ability to change her mood instantly. Once she'd fallen asleep, he lay next to her staring into the darkness, thinking about his wife's changeable behaviour. The only conclusion he came to was that he'd never understand women – particularly her.

cᒋᎧᏮᏮ

Chapter 28

Mid-January, Kate found herself in London suffering another of the headmistress' lectures on what she didn't consider suitable reading for young ladies. The middle-aged woman removed her spectacles, placing them on her desk.

"I believe you have introduced the girls to *Wuthering Heights* by Emily Brontë. Surely you do not consider it appropriate reading for our young ladies. Mr Heathcliff is hardly a respectable gentleman."

"Girls want to read something other than Jane Austen."

"And what is wrong with Jane Austen, may I ask?"

"Nothing at all. It's simply that we've already covered her works."

"And *Dracula* by Bram Stoker – are you deliberately trying to give the girls nightmares?"

"Sure, I'm simply trying to broaden their outlook."

"Not in my school. Do I make myself clear? You are an extremely competent teacher and the girls like you. But you must stick to the curriculum I prescribe. This school has a reputation for turning out well-read, accomplished ladies who will please their husbands with pleasant conversation, not spin tales of reprobates or blood-drinking monsters."

"Can't they aspire to be more than wives?"

"Miss Caldwell, you sound like Emmeline Pankhurst and her brood. I hope you've not been attending meetings on your days off. You know my opinion on the subject. No lady who is a member of the National Union of Women's Suffrage Societies will be employed here."

"I'm well aware of your views. But sure, you can't stop progress. Branches are springing up in most towns and cities. The girls should at least be taught about the movement."

"You'll be suggesting we involve the girls in arson next."

"I'd never support such direct action. Surely even you support the No Vote, No Tax campaign. How can you not when you're a business owner."

"Women participating in such radical action deserve to be locked up."

"You can't mean that."

"I most certainly do. And as for defacing the forms and boycotting the 1911 census, I would horse whip the lot of them."

"Don't you believe women have the right to live their lives as they choose – work if they want to?"

"Married ladies should never work unless they fall on hard times, as I did after my husband passed away. Then, it is acceptable to seek employment as a governess, teacher, a ladies' companion or even a seamstress."

"What about single women? You gave me the post."

"Generally, I only employ gentile young ladies without a family to support them. You were an exception, which I hope I don't come to regret. Now, I believe you have a French lesson to teach, so if you wish to remain in my employ, I suggest we leave it there."

The headmistress picked up a book from her desk, making it clear the conversation was over.

Kate's blood was boiling as she thrust open the classroom door. For the next hour, she taught the girls how to order wine and select the correct dish should their husbands choose to take them to France on holiday.

Quel est le plat du jour? What is today's special?

Je voudrais de l'eau, s'il vous plaît. I would like some water, please.

Was this all she was fit to teach?

Women wanted more than to be ornaments for their husbands. This school was in the Dark Ages. What was also abundantly clear was that she couldn't carry on teaching in this establishment, or one like it. So, what was the alternative?

By the end of the lesson when Kate dismissed her class, she'd decided. She was going to open her own school. There was a lot to consider, so she'd stick it out here, making her plans, until July and then look for suitable premises.

She considered telephoning her father to discuss her idea with him, but while she was sure he'd approve, she suspected he'd suggest Faredene. According to Victoria, Garrett Ackerley's wife was apparently now convinced she'd been mistaken in accusing her husband of infidelity, so it would be an ideal location, as the nearest girls' school was Chester. And Victoria would be sure to have several clients to whom she could recommend the school. However, there was a big problem with that location – Sean. If she were to avoid seeing him and Yvette more frequently, perhaps another area would be preferable, though she knew that no distance would stop her from thinking about him.

Since Bella's wedding, Kate's only visit to Faredene had been at Christmas. At least on the surface, something appeared to have changed in his marriage. He and Yvette were getting along better and as much as it galled Kate to admit it, clearly there must have been some extremely happy moments – at least when he'd impregnated her for a second time.

Kate had told herself she was pleased for him. After all, she wanted him to be happy. However, on New Year's Day, when Jess had invited them to Faredene Hall, Kate saw signs that things weren't as they first appeared. Was that simply wishful thinking?

Sean had been playing with Jake and Brian, who had strapped tennis rackets to their feet and were trudging across the snow-covered lawn in a re-enactment of Ernest Shackleton's expedition to the South Pole. Kate could have stood by the French doors watching him all day, but conscious of what the others might think, she'd dragged herself away and spoken to Yvette.

"Sean's so good with the boys," Kate said.

"I suppose we all have to be good at something. He comes into his own in the nursery. Although his prowess in other areas of the home has become rather boring." She gave Kate a conspiratorial nod.

Kate understood Yvette was referring to the bedroom and replied sharply, "Intimacy is like a game of tennis doubles – a player can only be as good as his partner."

Yvette's jaw dropped.

"I didn't know you were such a fan of your stepbrother. You make fun of him constantly."

"No, I don't make fun of him. I tease him – there's a difference. I don't appreciate you putting him down."

"You and Bella have always been spiteful to me. I still haven't forgotten you trying to make a fool of me about the caterpillar milk."

"Bella couldn't be spiteful no matter how hard she tried. As for making you appear foolish, sure, you make it so easy."

Yvette had opened and closed her mouth, putting Kate in mind of a goldfish.

"Look, I don't want to bicker. Why don't you try to get along with everyone instead of walking around with a face that could turn the milk sour in an udder?" Kate had added.

"I won't give you the opportunity to insult me again. In future, I'll avoid speaking to you altogether."

Kate rolled her eyes. "Is that a promise?"

With that, Yvette had flounced off towards the buffet in the dining room.

It also hadn't escaped Kate's notice that Sean was once again nervous around Jane. In her opinion, it could only mean one thing, because Jane was delightful and wouldn't intentionally make someone ill at ease – he cared for her. Would it be easier if Sean were with Jane than Yvette? She liked Jane . . .

In fact, if she opened a school, perhaps she should ask Jane if she wanted a job. Luring Jane away from Sean and introducing her to some eligible men was appealing. Now there was a thought!

Regardless of where it was to be, the prospect of running her own school was incredibly exciting. Even as Kate taught her least favourite lesson that day – deportment – she couldn't help smiling.

Sean tore the diary from Yvette's hand and launched it across the bedroom, where it landed by the fireplace. Yvette, who had been sitting up in bed writing, stared at him, aghast.

"Stop ignoring me, Yvette!"

"Sean! You might have ripped it."

"How the hell can you sit in bed writing in your diary when we've just learned that our son is completely deaf and may have other disabilities!"

"I always write in my diary."

"The question was rhetorical. For God's sake, Yvette, don't you care? What on earth were you writing? Perhaps I should read it."

She made to scramble out of bed.

"It's private – reading it would be such a betrayal."

"Stay where you are. I'll get it for you. Don't panic – I won't read the blasted thing. I get that you *claim* you didn't notice anything was wrong, but explain this – why didn't you tell me that his nanny suspected Pierre couldn't hear?"

"Because I knew you would blame me for what happened with the wet nurse, even though you have no proof it was caused by her."

"So you threatened his nanny!"

"I'm mistress of this house! She had no right to tell you. I have a good mind to dismiss her."

"Don't you dare! Pierre is used to her – he needs to take priority over everything."

"Fine. Undermine my position in the household."

"That's not what I'm trying to do. Just explain to me how you can be so dismissive. You were there when Owain examined our son. Did his words not sink in?"

"I heard him. As I said, I believe it is too early to tell."

"So you're an expert on medical matters now?"

"Owain is nothing more than a small-town quack. If you are worried, then you should take him to a proper doctor."

"Owain is a proper doctor. Nevertheless, I'm going to get him the best care. Make sure he's seen by the specialist Owain said he can recommend. Our son will get every help I can give him. Yvette, things were getting better between us, but your attitude tonight has astounded me. Do you care so little about him?"

Yvette's lip trembled. "I am his mother – of course I care – but there is nothing I can do about it. Are you so focused on him that you have no thought for what this is like for me? The stigma of birthing a deaf child is a burden I will have to bear. Yet, he could have inherited his defect from your father. There is nothing wrong with my ancestral line."

Sean rubbed the back of his neck. He was lost for words. How could she talk about stigma when their boy was trapped in a silent world? Maybe the defect *had* come from his bloodline. After all, he had no information about any of his parents. Though, thankfully, Yvette wasn't aware of that. Truth be told, he didn't blame her entirely for what happened to Pierre – he should have been home the night Pierre was born, not running from his problems and drinking himself senseless.

"His nanny takes good care of his personal needs, but Pierre is also going to have a governess or tutor. To be honest, I've not thought it through, but I'll find someone who can teach him how to make sense of his world. And teach him – all of us, the servants, family – how to use sign language. There's no way our son is going to feel isolated his entire life."

"That's ridiculous! He's far too young for you to be talking of such things."

He glared at her. "I give you your own way in almost everything, but this isn't up for debate."

There was nothing more to say on the subject. However, there was no way he could sleep.

"I'll be up later," he said before handing her back her diary and leaving the room.

Sean crept into the nursery and kissed Pierre goodnight. He was tempted to spend the night watching over him, but he could hardly do so while the nanny was waiting to go to sleep in the same room. Instead, he spent the night in his study thinking about his son and hoping to find peace in a bottle of brandy, even though it had never helped in the past.

For the next few days, his head was in a spin, trying to work out what was best for Pierre and making plans for the sewing factory. By Saturday, Sean knew what he was going to do to help his son. It would mean getting a firm grip of his own feelings towards Jane, but that didn't matter. The important thing was getting the optimum care for his boy – he was sure this was the right decision.

Once he'd dressed and shaved, he made for Centenary House. The bell over the entrance to the haberdashery announced his arrival and for the umpteenth time that morning, it struck Sean that Pierre would never hear any sound.

"Oh, Sean, love, I'm right sorry about Pierre's problems." Milly knuckled away a tear.

Sean pulled her into a hug.

"Milly, I love you for caring. You mustn't worry about him, though."

"That's easier said than done, sweetheart. Anyway, is it me, Kitty or some darning wool you're after, 'cos yer mam's not here?" she said, forcing a smile.

"Not today, Milly. If Jane's home, though, I'd like a word with her, if I may."

"Course you can. Is owt wrong? Sorry, love, that was a stupid question when you've just found out about yer lad. Jane's in the parlour. Go on through, pet."

The parlour door was ajar and Sean peered round. Jane had a book on her knee and was making notes on some loose sheets of paper. Even in his worried state, he noticed how she'd dressed her silky blonde hair so that it framed her face. Christ, she was beautiful.

That sort of thought must end now. His son's wellbeing was more important than his own desires, no matter how strong they might be. Jane was more off limits than ever. Sean cleared his throat several times before finding his voice.

"Can I have a quick chat?"

"Sean? Certainly. Please, come in. Sit down. Can I get you a drink?"

He took the chair opposite Jane.

"No. Thank you. I hope I'm not disturbing you."

"Not at all. I'm simply preparing for one of my classes next week. My older girls are learning to appreciate the differences between the Romantic poets. Next week we're looking at Keats, starting with 'Ode to a Nightingale'."

"I was never one for poetry."

"Neither are most of the girls. Sometimes I think I'm wasting my time. I'd be better off teaching at the local school here in Faredene. I'm sure the children from poor families must appreciate their education more than some of the spoilt madams I teach."

"You mentioned something about that when we first met, so what's stopping you? Sorry, that wasn't meant to sound rude."

"It's a perfectly valid question. I applied, but the education board appear to prefer male teachers." She placed the book and the papers on the side table. "I was sorry to hear about Pierre. There was a deaf girl where I teach. I was making excellent progress with her until her parents took her away from the school."

"Why send her there in the first place then remove her?"

"She wasn't deaf initially. Sadly, I think she now spends most of her time alone on their estate in Cheshire."

"I don't want that for Pierre."

"Good, it doesn't have to mean the end of the world. If he's taught well, he can still have a full life."

"I'm so glad you said that, because it's him I want to talk about."

"Really?"

"Jane, I want you to become his governess."

"Oh, I see. Well, naturally I'll consider it when he's old enough."

"No, you misunderstand me. I want you to work with him now. Teach him sign language. Help him learn to walk, talk, feed himself."

"But, Sean, I'm a teacher. I'm not sure I'm the right person."

"Jane, you could make a real difference to his life. You can help him to achieve things he might never manage without the right help."

"Perhaps he needs a nurse. He's young to have a full-time teacher."

"He needs the best possible education. Please will you at least consider it? I'd also want you to teach my family and the servants sign language. We can provide accommodation if you prefer. It's entirely up to you."

"Sean, I'm not sure. Then again, I believe the younger you educate children, the better."

"You can name your salary."

"It's not about the money. Why are you so sure I can help? There are so many teachers out there and more people are understanding the importance of sign language all the time."

"I realise that. What I can't guarantee is that they'll care about him, whereas I feel sure you will."

"Well yes, I would. Can I take the week to consider? I don't want to make a commitment unless I'm sure. I'd hate to let you and Pierre down later."

"Take as long as you need."

"I'll show you out."

Jane walked in front of him down the corridor and through the shop. She paused while Sean said goodbye to Milly before opening the shop door for him.

"I'll take the job."

"That was a quick decision. Are you sure?"

"Yes, I'm certain. I'll need to resign from my current post and give them some notice. I can start in a month if that works for you. Though I'd prefer to come home every night so I can be with Mam," she said.

As Sean drove home, he battled with his mixed emotions. Yes, he was pleased that she'd agreed to take the job and thankful that she'd be gone most days before he returned home from work. However, having to resist the temptation to make excuses to see her so that he could look at her beautiful face would be agony. Regardless, as he'd said to Yvette, Pierre came first.

⚜

Chapter 29

Victoria traced her fingers over the bevelled glass panel in the office door then turned the lock for the last time.

"Well, they say spring is the time for change and this is certainly the end of an era."

Matthew nodded. "It's a good job we've won back some customers during the last couple of months or we'd have lost even more money on the sale of the mill than we have."

They began making their way past the slumbering machines in the spinning room. Both lost in their own thoughts, they continued a nostalgic tour through the vast building.

The mill had never brought Victoria the same pleasure as running Centenary House, although she was glad that they'd improved the lives of its workers. Matthew was a good friend and she'd miss him.

He patted the end of one of the silent looms then held up his hand to show her the layer of white dust.

"I won't miss this."

"Do you regret our working together?"

"Not for one minute. We achieved a great deal over the years. You were my conscience, never allowing me to let profit come before the workers. I thought I was a caring employer, but you put me to shame. In the end, you were right to feed the striking workers. From what I deduced, it was your kindness and the actions you took to save that baby that broke the strike – more so than the threat of permanent closure."

"I didn't realise."

"The baby's granddad was the union organiser. He played a big part in getting them to return to work."

"Do you wish we'd not sold, given that they came back?"

"No. This place will be someone else's problem from tomorrow. I'm ready to devote myself to Sophia. If I'd done it years ago, as she wanted, I'd have resented her for it. And she wouldn't have been happy without the money I earned. Now is the right time."

"Perhaps if you'd not worked so many hours, she'd have been more tolerant."

Matthew threw his head back and laughed as they walked into the yard.

"Do you honestly believe that? Nothing is ever enough for Sophia. She's a wonderful woman, but she never gives in until she has what she wants. Even then, she often decides it's not good enough." He turned the large key in the studded door.

"Doesn't it concern you that the same may happen when you get back to America?"

"I half expect it. But it's getting more and more difficult to make money from a mill. I'd prefer to give it up now before things get worse."

"I hope the mill will continue for many years. Without it, I worry about what will become of the families who depend on it. I expect many of them regret striking. They got nothing out of it and now their future lies in someone else's hands."

"I may still have decided to sell up rather than risking losing Sophia."

"Really?"

Matthew laughed. "Perhaps I might have chanced a few more years."

"The new owner is a decent sort. I don't think he'll undo the safety procedures or welfare steps we put in place."

"Come on – let's get out of here. I'll no doubt see you at Yvette's. I want to spend as much time round there as I can to imprint my grandson's image in my memory before we depart for America. Do you think Pierre will be all right?"

"Only time will tell. Sean was right to ask Jane to become his full-time teacher. She's wonderful with him. And with her teaching us all sign language, at least we'll be able to communicate with him."

"It's a sad business. I hope it won't come between Yvette and Sean. There was friction between them when I was round there the other day."

"Theirs has never been an easy marriage. I'm sure they'll come through it. Though it would help if Yvette would learn sign language."

"I'm sure she will when he's older. She'll see the point to it then."

Would he ever see his daughter for the woman she was? As he was about to return to America, Victoria doubted it. Perhaps that was for the best, she thought as they wandered towards their automobiles.

"I hope so. They have another child due in July. Perhaps that'll heal the rift," she said.

He opened his car door. "Are you off home?"

"I'm going to pop in at my shop."

"Back to where your empire started."

When Max parked, Victoria instructed him to return for her in two hours. She wasn't ready to go home yet – she needed the hustle and bustle of Centenary House.

That same morning, George said, "Come in," in answer to the knock on the door of his and Bella's sitting room. It wasn't custom for servants to knock – however, George insisted on it. There had to be some privacy.

"What is it, Max?" George could hardly bear to look at the man.

"There is a telephone call for you, sir. It's your mother."

George shot out of his seat. Thank God Bella was bathing.

"I'll take it in Edward's study. Though you're mistaken about who is calling. My parents are both dead."

"As you say, sir."

"You can take that look off your face. Get out. Go on. Remember, I know what you are."

Blast. George ran downstairs. What was wrong now? Had something happened to his ma? No, she wouldn't be ringing him herself if that were the case. Sitting in Edward's chair, he held the earpiece in one hand and leaned forwards so his mouth was close to the receiver atop the long brass stem.

"Ma, what's wrong?"

"George? Georgie? Can yeh hear me?" Mrs Bristow shouted.

George jerked the receiver away from his ear.

"Flamin' hell, there's no need to scream."

"I thought you should know. The doctor says I'm not well. Can yeh come home for a visit?"

"Is it serious, Ma?"

"Yes, lad, but I'll explain when I see yeh."

"Righto. I'll get the train first thing in the morning. Love you, Ma."

"It'll be good to see yeh, son."

"I'll see you tomorrow."

Bleedin' hell! He hated the thought that his ma was sick. He should have gone home to see her more often. Or at least sent her money. Even his ma couldn't be told everything, but she was the only person he trusted.

He was unsettled. First, Sophia seeing him with the pearls. Now, Max taking the phone call. Then there was that doctor – he was far too close to the family, making comments about how well George looked. And he was always taking Anne out for dinner. If that sawbones was considering asking her to marry him, as her husband he'd probably get the lot if she pegged it, completely scuppering George's plans for Bella's inheritance. He'd have to deal with one of them soon. It was hassle he didn't need. George had hoped to take his time getting his hands on Bella's fortune and that of her family, but he'd have to speed things up if needed.

First things first, he'd go to London. It would be nice to see his ma. Maybe he'd even call in at a few of his old haunts. Bella would have to be told he was going to see his doctor.

As Bella came into the sitting room, he said, "Let's go for a walk in the park."

❖ ❖ ❖

A stunning display of bulbs edged the path, but as they passed the benches overlooking the boating lake, Bella's eyes were drawn to two nannies occupying the first bench. Their perambulators stood side by side and a child was sitting on a blanket playing with a doll. How Bella longed for a child of her own. Why had she not conceived yet? She wanted to give George a son or daughter he could play with before he was too unwell to enjoy the interaction. George had said he desperately wanted a child, too. A houseful of them. How she envied Yvette, now having a second child.

Her mind was brought back to the present when George halted.

"I need to sit down a moment," he said.

A prickle of alarm shot through her. She took his hand, studying his face as he sat.

"George, what is it?"

"Give me a moment and I'll explain."

They sat holding hands watching a little girl feeding the ducks while Bella waited for him to speak. Surely all he needed was a couple of moments' rest – he looked healthy enough. Only last week, when he'd called to take Anne to dinner, Doctor Farrell had commented that George wasn't pale like many with a weak heart.

George squeezed her hand.

"Are you unwell, darling? You're scaring me. Do you need a doctor?" she asked, dreading his reply.

"No. Or at least not yet."

Her heart skipped a beat as she waited for him to speak again. The laughter of the little girl by the pond and the chestnut seller calling people to buy his wares penetrated her panic. Bella wanted to rail at them to shut up. All she wanted was to hear George tell her he was going to be all right.

"George, you're trembling. Whatever it is, you must tell me. We can face anything together."

"That's the thing – I don't want us to do that."

"What! What on earth do you mean?" Bella held her breath.

"Bella, my darling, I love you so much. You do know that, don't you?"

She sighed. Thank God – he still loved her. She nodded.

"I think I should go away before I become too ill."

"Our money from my parents will come through any day now the mill has sold. Where do you want us to go?"

"No, not us – me."

"George, you're not making sense. You just told me you love me. Why would you want to go away without me?"

"I realised some time ago that I was wrong to marry you. I proposed because I convinced myself that once I'd found out I was ill, it was too late to leave you because you already loved me."

"You were right – you'd have hurt me terribly and you are now."

"I was selfish because I wanted to be with you. To see your smile every day I have left."

"But you can – nothing has changed."

"Yes, it has. I love you even more now than I did then. Don't you see? What I love about you is your smile, but you won't be smiling at the end, so I can't let you watch me die."

"I'll nurse you."

"No. You're still young and lovely. I won't let you waste your life. I'd hoped we might have ten, maybe even fifteen years together before I . . . before I die." George shook his head. "Now, I fear that's not the case. The doctors told me the signs to expect when the time got nearer. I suspect I have two years at most."

Bella's heart was breaking. She bit the inside of her lip to stem the tears that threatened.

"During most of that time, I'll become a cripple, wasting away. I won't be a burden to you."

A cry escaped her lips.

"No. I won't hear of it. I'll talk to my parents when I get back. We can engage nurses."

"Bella, please. You must let me do this my way. Can't you understand? That's the last thing I want."

Bella pulled her hand from his and stood up, instantly regretting letting go of him. She sat again, curling her fingers around his hand, conscious of the watching nannies but not caring.

"George, you married me. Our vows were for life. I'm your wife – let me look after you. I'm certain my parents will agree with me. We can telephone Doctor Makin in London and get him to come here."

George stiffened.

"No. Please promise me you won't do that. I don't want your parents to know. I don't want other people involved."

"They're not other people – they're our family. They care about you."

"Even so, I'm not dragging Doctor Makin up here so he can look at me pityingly and explain once again there's nothing to be done."

"I still think I should tell my parents. So I've got someone to talk to about it."

"I promise I won't go away if you give me your word

that you'll say nothing about this until absolutely necessary."

"George, must I promise?"

"Yes. They already pity me. I can't live with people watching my every move, wondering if I might collapse, constantly looking for signs that I'm tired or sad. Can you understand that?"

"I give you my word, darling. But please do something for me."

"What?"

"See your doctor."

"If you insist. For you, my love, I'll head to London tomorrow, alone."

"Thank you. You will come back to me?"

"Yes. I promise. You must stay here, though. I'll book into a hotel. Kate's good company, but I don't want to socialise."

"Anything as long as you don't leave me," she said, her voice catching.

"Good, now dry your eyes. No more being sad and talk of illness. Let's go and listen to the band." He stood, offering her his hand.

She felt weighed down with the pain. She was torn between the desire to scream and the urge to climb into bed, pull the covers over her head and never get up again, but she knew she must be strong for George. She wouldn't even have his child to comfort her when he'd gone. She dabbed at the corner of her eyes.

"Bella, my precious, are you crying again?" George asked.

"I was wondering why I'm not with child yet."

"Do you believe it's my fault?"

"Heavens, no, George. How could you think that? I feel as though I'm letting *you* down."

"If that's the case, then you mustn't worry about it. If it's meant to happen, it will."

"You still want children, don't you?"

"More than anything. That's why we practise so much." George grinned.

He was so handsome and virile, but how could she not spend every moment fretting about him? She'd always been afraid their lovemaking was too physical, but now the thought of making love terrified her. He'd insisted that was the last thing he'd abstain from. All she could do was pray God wouldn't be cruel enough to take him away from her in such a precious moment.

Come on, Bella, sort yourself out. You mustn't let George see, she admonished herself. Her darling George was going to die far sooner than expected and the pain was crushing her. She couldn't bear it. But she must.

⌒⌒⌒

Chapter 30

George was uneasy. Last month, he'd had to rush off to London to see his ma and now this. People were always trying to mess up his plans after he'd worked so hard to get a decent life – the life he deserved, he thought as he rushed up the road to Sophia's house. He'd only managed to slip out of the house without Bella by telling her that until his mother died, she'd always made him simnel cake for Easter and that it would be nice if she took up the tradition. The useless wench couldn't even boil water, but she was down in the kitchen now, probably driving the cook daft.

Sophia had never asked him to call on her before. Since that day when they'd had sex in Victoria and Edward's morning room, they hadn't repeated their indiscretion. To George's relief, she hadn't even hinted at holding the knowledge about the pearls against him and he'd hoped the matter was behind him.

When the butler showed George into the drawing room, Sophia was sitting on the sofa. She took a nibble from a slice of cake before returning it to her plate. Then she placed the plate on the side table and flicked invisible crumbs off the bodice of her lilac gown. It was only when the butler had closed the door that she spoke.

"Please, sit down, George."

He stood in front of her, his hands clasped behind his back. He wasn't here to take afternoon tea. She was a tasty piece. Maybe it wouldn't be such a bad thing if she wanted a quick tussle before she left for America.

"George, sit down. Don't panic – I won't ravish you. Would you like tea?"

He felt a stab of disappointment, causing his voice to be harsher than he'd intended.

"I'd prefer to stand. It was difficult to get out of the house and come round here without raising suspicions."

"It had to be now. Matthew has gone to the bank to complete some financial transactions – he will be back soon."

"What do yeh want?"

"Very well. You are as keen to get this over with as I am, so I will be brief. I have been indiscreet with other men over the years. Matthew suspects, but of course he cannot be certain."

"And?"

"He is finally putting me first and we are returning to America."

George was struggling to keep his temper, yet he couldn't afford to upset her. He kept his voice calm.

"I know that already, Sophia. What does it have to do with me?"

"I want it to be a new start for us, so I intend to tell Matthew about my dalliances."

George ground his jaw, his temper flaring.

"Why the hell would you do that? If he's not raised it, he probably doesn't want to know."

"Don't glare at me! I am not stupid and have thought this through. Although I have flirted with many men,

345

only four have had carnal knowledge of me, whereas Matthew believes there were far more."

"Sophia, what you're contemplating is crazy. Most men would kill you for betraying them with one man, never mind four."

"Not Matthew. He is fully aware how badly he has neglected me over the years. I don't want to live with the guilt. I thought it only fair to warn you."

"Surely you're not planning on naming us?"

"That's exactly what I propose to do."

"Why?" Flaming hell! He wanted to squeeze the life out of her.

"He deserves to know the truth."

"You're not doing it for him. This is to ease your own conscience."

"Possibly, but my motives are not your concern."

"He might hate you for it. You could ruin everything."

"That is why I don't intend telling him now. We leave for London tomorrow, for a week at The Ritz. It is my intention to ensure Matthew glimpses how wonderful our future will be. Only when we are on board the ship will I explain to him how each indiscretion happened. That way, if he is angry, I will have time to win him round before we disembark to begin our new life."

"This is madness."

"It is something I feel compelled to do."

"If he tells anyone, it will ruin my marriage. Bella will never forgive me."

"He will not wish to hurt Bella, so perhaps he won't say anything. But he may feel she should be warned about you. Particularly because of the pearls you stole."

"I put the bleedin' things back."

"There is no need for vulgar language, George."

"For Christ's sake, woman. Surely you can understand why I'm angry."

"As you returned her mother's jewels, maybe she will forgive you. She always appears to be a naïve young chit. If not, you must manage your wife."

"Even if I can sort things with Bella, if her parents find out, they'll never stand for it."

"That, I am afraid, is your problem."

"Is there nothing I can do to change your mind?"

"Nothing."

"In that case, will you promise me you'll say nowt until you're at sea?"

"You needn't worry about that."

When he left Sophia, George headed for the park. He needed time to think. There was no way he was going to lose out on a big pay-out. Bella was a nice enough girl. He was seriously considering staying with her for much longer than he'd originally anticipated. Providing they inherited enough cash to live the life he deserved.

Within the hour, he knew what he had to do and headed home.

"Bella, I'm going to take the early train to London tomorrow evening. I want to see Doctor Makin."

She jumped up, dropping the book she'd been reading to the floor as she rushed to his side.

"Again? So soon? You were only there a few weeks ago. George, what is it?"

"I'd just like to discuss one or two things with him. Nothing for you to worry your pretty head about, my precious one, I promise. We'll tell your parents it's a check-up. I don't want everyone fussing."

347

"Can I come with you? I'd like to see Kate."

"Bella, you agreed before we married that I'd go to these appointments alone."

"I don't have to go to Harley Street with you, but we could dine together in the evening. Perhaps even take in a show."

George pulled his best "I'm hurt" face.

"Bella, this isn't a pleasure trip."

"How insensitive of me. I'm sorry, darling."

"That's all right. I forgive you."

Pliable *and* naïve – that made life so much easier.

Dealing with Sophia was a bigger problem. It was a pity he'd sold his gun to that fella down The Cross Keys. Then again, shooting her might not be the smartest move. He knew where the Clarksons were staying – all he had to do was get to London and take it from there. He was good at working under pressure. He'd sort something out.

Sean and Yvette were spending the evening with her parents before Matthew and Sophia travelled to London the following morning.

Yvette pouted. "Why do you have to leave so soon?"

Matthew smiled lovingly. "Princess, I've already explained. I promised Mama we'd take in some shows and visit Crystal Palace, Kew Gardens and anything else she wants to do before we take the train to Southampton to board our ship. I'm going to make up for the years she tolerated my working long hours."

"It's terribly self-centred of you, Mama. Are shows more important than your daughter and grandson?"

Sophia tutted. "Don't behave like a spoiled child. I have been in this drab little country for years and not once has your father taken me to London. I wish to see a little of the capital before I leave it forever."

Matthew's face clouded. "This country is one of the greatest in the world."

Sophia sipped her sherry through thin lips.

"Sorry, dear, I know it is, and it is your homeland. I will make sure you don't regret your decision. We will enjoy every moment of your retirement."

The smile returned to Matthew's face.

"That's exactly what I intend for us to do, so we are travelling in style. Look at this . . ." He handed Sean a glossy brochure.

Sean picked out the highlights: *Titanic*. The biggest steam ocean liner in the world. Turkish bath, a gymnasium and swimming baths. Luxurious. Opulent. A floating city. Sailing 10 April 1912, Southampton to New York.

"Well, it certainly looks impressive. I'm glad things have worked out for you both."

"I think we're going to be happy back in America. Plenty of sunshine and fresh air – it'll make a pleasant change after the mill," Matthew said.

"We should be going with you," Yvette said.

"Our life is here. Pierre is already responding well to Jane and she's only been with him a matter of weeks."

Yvette ignored Sean's comment and looked pointedly at her father.

"You won't even get to see the new baby."

Matthew glanced at Sean.

"Perhaps you can visit us."

"Eventually, although I don't relish the idea of seeing Claude. We haven't even corresponded since I left."

Yvette scowled. "Sean, why is it always about you?"

349

Matthew moved from his seat next to Sophia and balanced on the edge of the sofa by Yvette, taking her hand.

"Now come on – this is our last night together. I'm sure Sean will bring you over when he can. We'll want to see our grandchildren. As for Claude, I'll ensure he makes good on his promise to pay Sean back the money he owes – after all, we're family now."

"There's no need for you to do that," Sean said.

"I'll not stand by and watch him squandering while you go short."

"I appreciate that – and the money you've given us."

"Think nothing of it. It'll give you time to establish your new business. How's the building work going?"

"They should finish in a couple of days. I'm looking forward to moving in. The rented offices are adequate, but we need to get started on production. Peter has done a fine job managing the alterations to the building. I like him. And the sewing machines and equipment have arrived."

"Peter is incredibly talented," Yvette said.

Matthew laughed. "You always had a soft spot for him, didn't you? She used to follow him round all doe-eyed when she was younger."

Yvette pulled her hand from her father's.

"No I didn't, Papa. We were friends, nothing more."

Matthew smiled ruefully. "I meant nothing by it, my dear. You were a child. Anyway, Peter married Louise and you have Sean."

Sophia rose. "Yvette, come with me. I have a small gift for you."

"Really. What is it?"

"One or two of my jewels."

When they were alone, Matthew said, "Sean, are you sure that you're happy to handle the sale of this place for us?"

"Yes. Edward will do the legal side of things, so there will be little I need to do other than arrange the shipment of furniture you want to keep and sell the rest."

Matthew looked more relaxed than Sean had ever seen him.

"Do you miss the mill?"

"It's been like having my leg cut off. I've heard people say you can still feel the missing limb. The mill is like that for me. I keep thinking there are things I need to do, worrying about it. Then I remember it's not mine now."

"You and Sophia seem happier."

"We are. I'm certain we're doing the right thing. Sophia looks at me with a love I never expected to see again."

"I'm pleased for you."

"Will you promise to bring Yvette and the children over one day?"

Matthew had done a great deal for him. It was impossible to refuse.

"We'll visit before our second child starts school."

"Thank you – I can't ask for more than that. Will you two be all right? I've never felt it right to interfere in your marriage, but I'd have had to be blind not to notice the tension between you on occasion."

It wasn't fair to burden Matthew on the eve of their departure with the details of how bad their marriage was.

"We've had our difficulties, but nothing too serious."

Sean felt dishonest, but what else could he say?

"I'm glad. She means the world to me. You'll look after her?"

"Of course."

351

"I know she has a temper and would spend every penny you have, given half a chance. But I'm putting my faith in you to care for her, Sean."

"You have my word."

"That's good enough for me.

A short while later, Sean and Yvette took their leave. He would miss Matthew. Sophia was another matter. Since Yvette had spoken to her mother following Pierre's birth, Sophia had made no more advances towards him and had stopped her jibes. Despite this, he'd be glad to see the back of her.

Chapter 31

A few days later, Sean helped himself to eggs and devilled kidneys from the silver salver. Since her parents' departure, Yvette had been behaving like a spoiled child.

"So, are you going to stop being so mean about the new furniture I want to buy?" she asked as he took his seat at the table.

"I've explained several times – we must live on the income I've agreed with Charles. Our savings and the money from your parents is to be put aside in case we have need at some point."

"I have need now. Louise Mason has said she will visit. You've seen how beautiful their home is."

"Naturally, they have a beautiful home – Peter's an architect. Anyway, you're always calling her dowdy. Why do you care what she thinks?"

"She always envied me. I don't want her pitying me now because I have a failure for a husband."

"That was a low blow."

"The truth hurts. You're a selfish swine. Papa has given us a large sum – I should be able to decide how we spend it."

"Regardless, you can't spend money on furniture at the moment, and that's final."

"I hardly spend anything on myself, while you drink yourself insensible and gamble."

"The last time I gambled was before the mill shut, so you can't accuse me of that. Our furniture is perfectly adequate – most of it was new when we married. Besides which, your parents said you can have your choice of what they don't want shipped over to them."

"I don't want adequate or Mama's cast-offs. I am trying to create a decent home for our family. A successful businessman has an image to maintain."

"So am I a failure or a success?"

Yvette opened her mouth to speak, but Sean interrupted.

"Frankly, I don't care what people think. I'm not prepared to have us running out of money so you can keep up appearances."

"It is too late – I have already ordered a new armoire. My old one is too small."

"Only because you've bought too many gowns. Why you need so many is beyond me."

"I have always bought new gowns in April, ready for the summer. Surely you don't expect me to wear last year's styles."

"It wouldn't kill you."

"That would suit you, wouldn't it. You would prefer me dead and buried. Why do you complain about everything I do? Charles is paying your salary. And the factory will make money. If you don't think it will be a success, why are you bothering?"

"Even if the factory makes a fortune, I want to save for the future."

"We don't have to worry about that. Our parents aren't getting any younger – one day we will inherit from them.

You might have had most of yours and lost it, but I am Papa's only child."

"That's appalling! I'm not living my life waiting for people to die."

"You are so selfish. I wish I had gone home with my parents."

He wanted to tell her that if she left his son and their second child behind once it was born, she could follow her parents with his blessing.

Instead, he said, "Your father left the money in my control. So, buy nothing else, because I won't pay the bill and then you will have to explain that to people."

"You are a failure – a pathetic excuse for a man and always will be."

"Thank you. It's nice to know how you really feel about me."

"I loathe you – and this child you have burdened me with."

That she hated him was no surprise. Although she wanted him to say it to her, she'd never said she loved him. But surely she didn't hate their unborn child . . .

"You appeared willing enough when we were making the child together."

"Does it make you feel more of a man to think that I actually wanted you?"

"You wanted sex. Or have you forgotten that you were like a bitch on heat for the first couple of months after that wet nurse nearly shook the life out of Pierre?"

"How dare you speak to me that way!"

"Why *were* you so keen to have sex? Was it guilt? Because it wasn't love or desire for me, of that much, I'm sure. And you've not let me near you since you conceived."

"You really are a vulgar little man. Is your mother sure your father was a draper and not a labourer?"

Once again, he thanked God Yvette didn't know about his birth, or she'd have used it against him. Even so, her words hurt. Sean threw this cutlery on the plate, about to storm out of the room, when the door opened.

"Excuse me, sir, but there is a police constable asking to see relatives of Mr and Mrs Clarkson," Harris said, his face showing no signs of having heard the row he couldn't have missed.

Sean stood. "Show him in, please."

The constable stared at his feet, clutching his helmet.

"Morning, sir, madam. I'm here about Mr and Mrs Clarkson."

"My wife is their daughter."

"I'm afraid I am the bearer of some unfortunate news. Last night, there was an accident on the underground railway station at Green Park. By all accounts the lady, who has now been identified as Mrs Clarkson, tripped and Mr Clarkson tried to save her. They both fell onto the line as the train was entering the station."

Sean glanced at Yvette. She was staring at the constable as though he were speaking a foreign language.

Slowly, she said, "Is Papa all right? Can I go to him?"

"I'm sorry, madam. I am afraid they were both killed outright."

Yvette's voice was little more than a whisper.

"Poor Papa."

Sean waited for her to mention her mother. Maybe it was the shock – surely she was grieving for both.

Yvette rose, folding her napkin carefully before placing it on the table. Then her legs gave way. Sean rushed to her side.

"Harris! Bring some smelling salts and send for Doctor Farrell."

His mind was whirring. Matthew and Sophia dead. Poor Yvette. His earlier anger had vanished. Perhaps he should have let her spend what she wanted. Life was too precious to waste arguing. He prayed the shock wouldn't bring on the baby.

Once Yvette had been sedated, Sean told his mother and Edward the sad news. Despite her own shock and grief, Victoria readily agreed to stay at his house with Yvette and Pierre while Sean went to London, where he'd have the terrible task of viewing what remained of the bodies.

Sean was completely drained when he returned from London. His mother kissed his cheek lightly and ushered him into the dining room, where a cold supper was already prepared. She joined him at the table.

"I thought you'd prefer this to having the servants waiting on you."

"Thank you, Mother, but I'm afraid I don't feel like eating."

Victoria went to the dresser, returning with a decanter. She poured him a measure.

"Normally I wouldn't encourage you to drink, but you must have had a difficult time and it's hardly surprising that you have no appetite."

"I can't even begin to describe how awful it was."

"It's different when someone is ill. You at least have a little time to prepare."

"Can you ever really be prepared for someone's death?"

"No. But this situation feels so surreal because we said goodbye to them thinking they were going to be happy.

They should be on board the *Titanic* now, sailing off to their new life."

Sean had had the same thoughts himself so many times. There was nothing to add. It just seemed such a waste for their lives to end now.

"Yvette had a telegram from Claude expressing his sympathies – it was brief, and formal," his mother said.

"I don't expect we'll hear from him again, as he barely knows Yvette. And my friendship with him is well and truly over. No doubt he'll forget about the money he owes me."

"With the inheritance from Matthew and Sophia's estate, you don't need it, but I still think he should repay you."

Sean shrugged. "How's Yvette?"

"She's asleep right now. Then again, she's not been out of bed since you left and hardly speaks when she's awake. I'd hoped interacting with Pierre might be a comfort to her, but when I took him in to see her, she barely looked at him."

He was too weary to lie.

"That's normal behaviour for her, I'm afraid."

"I'm aware she's not maternal, but now isn't the time to address it. She needs our support to get through this. Owain has made a point of calling every day, staying far longer than he should when he has such a busy practice. He's been wonderful. And Jane has been marvellous. She even came to be with Pierre over the weekend as you couldn't be with him."

Sean nodded. Apart from his sign language lessons, he'd tried to avoid Jane when she was at the house for fear he might give in to his desire to pull her into his arms. Though sex was the last thing on his mind, he still wished he could feel her arms around him. She was so caring with Pierre. Sean needed that right now.

His mother interrupted his thoughts.

"Did you make the arrangements?"

"Yes. There's no way I can let Yvette see their bodies, so I've ordered closed caskets."

"Good. Edward has made the rest of the funeral arrangements."

"Thank him for me, please."

"I will, of course, but there's no need – we are family."

"Before I see Yvette, there's something I need your advice about."

"And what's that?"

"The police told me that a woman had been standing next to them before it happened. She'd turned to look in their direction because Sophia and Matthew had been laughing. Apparently, Sophia was saying what fun it was, them taking an underground train for the first time, because the one in New York hadn't been open when she moved over here."

"I expect Sophia's accent might have also attracted her attention. It's some comfort to know they appeared happy."

"It's madness, but from what the police said, the woman thought a man in the crowd might have pushed Sophia."

"W-what? N-no. Why? No. She must have been mistaken."

"That's what I told them. They don't even know anyone who lives in London apart from Kate. Besides, no one would have any reason to push her."

"Have they questioned the man?"

"No. A fair-haired man was seen hurrying from the station. Unfortunately, they couldn't trace him."

"As I'm certain no one would have wanted to harm them, I don't suppose it matters."

"The thing is, do I tell Yvette?"

"No. I don't think you should. What good would it do?"

"None as far as I can see."

"Best leave it, then. There's no point in making things worse for her."

"I agree but thought it best to check with someone else."

"Now, my darling, I hate to leave you when you've only been back a short while, but it's getting late and I could do with a night in my own bed, if that's all right with you. I'll be here again early tomorrow. Even though they've told me to take as much time as necessary, I must pop into the shop to check on Milly at some point. She always looks tired and I don't want to neglect her."

"You're a good friend."

"I'm also worried about Bella."

Sean's hand was poised near his mouth, a slice of tomato dangling from his fork.

"What's wrong with her?"

"She says it's nothing, but I'm not sure if she's keeping something from us."

"Bella's not the secretive sort."

"Also, George went to London for a check-up with Doctor Makin – he was away longer than expected. And since his return, he's been on edge."

"Do you think he's had bad news?"

"Edward and I suspect it's that. Unfortunately, if they don't want to tell us, we can't interfere."

"If there's anything I can do to help, you only have to ask."

"You're a love. Let's be honest – you have your hands full here. And a new factory to get up and running. I doubt Charles will have done much in your absence. Edward's been dealing with what he can for you."

"With Yvette as she is, I may need his help for a while."

"I'm sure Edward won't mind at all. Bella's also said she'll help with Pierre or sit with Yvette if needed. And Edward said he'll handle the paperwork relating to Matthew and Sophia's wills. We'll pull together, don't you worry."

Leaving the rest of his food uneaten, Sean kissed his mother goodbye before making his way up to the nursery to see Pierre. He was sucking his thumb, sleeping soundly, blissfully unaware of the tragedy that had occurred.

When Sean climbed into bed next to Yvette and put his arms around her, she didn't stir. Whatever their differences, he was determined to take care of her. She might not love him – or he her – but she needed him now.

It was the day of the funeral before Yvette left her room. She'd barely uttered a word to Sean since his return.

Once the mourners had departed, Edward broke the shocking news of the sinking of the *Titanic*, explaining the huge loss of life was due to the lack of lifeboats. Yvette sounded almost pleased that her parents had never managed to board the ill-fated ship.

"As they didn't even fill, never mind deploy all the lifeboats that were available, if my parents had been on board, Papa would probably have died anyway. Whereas Mama might have survived, like most of the other ladies

361

in first class. At least this way they died together, so that is a blessing. I must accept that I am completely alone now."

Clearly, he and Pierre didn't count, Sean thought.

His mother held Yvette's hand.

"Yvette, dear, I know nothing will compensate for your loss, but you'll never be alone. We're your family and will take care of you in any way you need," she said.

Edward pulled a piece of paper from his pocket. "Now the funeral is over, I need to speak to you both about Matthew's will."

"Will? Surely everything is mine?" Yvette said.

"In a way, yes."

Yvette pulled her hand from Victoria's.

"What do you mean, in a way?"

"Your father bequeathed everything to Sean, entrusting him to care for you," Edward explained.

"What!" Yvette screeched.

Sean was stunned. Matthew had never told him about the will.

"Yvette, you have no need to worry. I promised your father I would take care of you, and I will."

"You devious swine. You knew about this."

"No, I swear to you – I had no idea."

"What about Mama? Has she left me anything?"

"Your mother didn't have any assets apart from her jewellery and personal affects. Naturally, she left them to you," Edward clarified.

"I feel so betrayed."

"Can I get you anything? You need to start looking after yourself. You've hardly eaten for days – it's not good for the baby," Sean said.

"I'll decide what is good for my baby. It's the only thing I have any control over."

Yvette stalked from the room, banging the door shut behind her.

Sean looked at his mother and Edward for guidance.

"Grief affects us all differently. The will is bound to have come as a shock. However, you're right – we must try to get her to eat, especially with the child on the way," his mother said.

"Be patient with her," Edward added.

"Edward, do you know why Matthew left everything to me?"

"Yes. He adored Yvette – you know that – but he believed she was like Claude and would likely squander it all."

Later that night, Sean asked Cook to make up a plate of Yvette's favourite roast honeyed ham sandwiches and some cakes. He sat on their bed, where she lay staring at the ceiling, her diary closed beside her.

Sean picked it up and placed it on the bedside table.

"Have you been writing in your diary?"

"It helps to share my feelings on a page. Paper can't judge me."

"You can talk to me, about anything."

"My thoughts are private."

"Look, I've brought us some food so we can eat together."

"I am not hungry."

"Please eat something."

Yvette tutted, pushed herself up on her pillows and took a sandwich but didn't eat.

"You and I, we'll get through this," Sean said.

"Will we? Sometimes I think you hate me because we had to get married."

"I don't hate you, I promise." He placed the plate on the bed and picked up some strands of her ebony hair, playing with them between his fingers. "Soon, we'll be a family of four, maybe more one day. Your world has fallen apart right now, but you can rely on me. I'll take care of you."

"Do you love me?"

Sean kissed her forehead. He didn't want to mislead her, but Yvette was the mother of his child and he'd promised Matthew he'd take care of her.

"Of course I love you," he lied.

"Papa adored me. He would have done anything for me. That is why I can't forgive what he did with the money."

"I'm sure it was only because he trusted me to take care of you as he did. He asked me to look after you before he left."

"It may be wrong, but I need absolute devotion."

"I love you and I'll do my best to make you happy, I promise."

Yvette bit into the sandwich, smiling wanly. She looked extremely vulnerable. Sean prayed he could live up to his promises to her and to Matthew.

Chapter 32

It wasn't yet eight o'clock, but the June sun was already warming the streets as Sean left their new home. A couple of months had passed, but it occurred to him once again that he'd always think of it as Matthew and Sophia's house. However, it would have been foolish to continue paying rent when Yvette had been so keen to move into here. Although why she felt the need to buy new crockery and begin decorating one of the spare bedrooms, he had no idea. When he'd questioned her, she'd become angry, as usual.

"Yvette, do you honestly think now is the best time to be redecorating and buying dinner services? Why not give yourself time to settle into the house. Wait until after the baby is born before you think about changes," he'd said.

"What the hell do you mean, settle in? This was my home for years. I know what needs to be done. As for spending, I'm only buying the essentials to make sure we have a pleasant home."

"Do we need another dinner service? We have three already."

"Nothing I do is ever good enough. Do you want our guests eating off cracked plates?"

They didn't have any damaged crockery, not even in the servants' hall.

"We hardly ever receive guests," he said, keeping his voice gentle because she was grieving.

"It is your fault we don't entertain more. You are always complaining you are tired."

"I am tired. The hours I'm putting in are to ensure the factory is a success. It's for us."

"That's not as important now, because Papa chose to leave *my* inheritance to you. Why he did that when you lost your capital, I don't know. I'll never forgive him."

"You saw the letter that accompanied his will. He trusts me to ensure the money is invested wisely to secure our future."

"We could be dead tomorrow. I want to live now."

"You can live a good life without being wasteful."

"What money am I wasting?"

"The green bedroom is fine as it is – we never have guests staying over, so why are you redecorating?"

"It's old-fashioned."

"Is this about competing with Louise Mason?"

"Why can't you be supportive? My parents are dead and if shopping makes me feel better, isn't that a good enough reason? You have matched Charles' investment in the factory – I suppose you don't regard that as spending. But for all we know, you might mess that up as well and lose it all," she'd said before flouncing off.

Now, as the sewing factory came into view, the usual sense of satisfaction crept over Sean. It was a two-storey brick building with large windows, sprawled over an extensive plot, its perimeter softened by a row of mature trees. Even Yvette had appeared impressed with the new factory when she'd visited the site for the final inspection. Sean had tried to persuade her to stay home, as she'd

366

been complaining of backache. However, she'd insisted on being there when Peter showed them round.

"You were the one who was trying to encourage me to get back to normal, so now I am. You cannot expect me to stay locked up like a prisoner," she'd said.

"That's not what I want. I'm simply concerned about you and the baby," he'd reasoned.

"It is always about the baby with you. What am I to you? Simply a breeding mare? The funds have come from my parents, after all, so surely I should be able to see what we have invested in."

Sean couldn't help wondering what had brought on the sudden interest. Was it Peter's presence? He remembered what Matthew had said about Yvette caring for Peter when she was younger. She was certainly full of smiles and gushing compliments for the design as Peter had escorted her round the building. Come to think of it, she was always more pleasant when Peter was around . . .

Today, the morning sun was glistening on the factory windows, casting shadows across the car park as Sean pulled into the gates. He waved at Charles, who was getting out of his own car.

"What are you doing out of bed this early, Mr Brakenridge?" Sean asked.

"I have popped in to check on how our empire is doing before I go to the golf course."

"Come on then, old man. I'll show you what we've been doing."

Charles and he walked into the reception area, where rows of framed fashion drawings that his mother had selected lined the walls. A young woman sitting behind a desk beamed at them.

"Morning, Mr Kavanagh, Mr Brakenridge. Mrs Fowles asked me to let her know when you arrived."

"That's all right. We're going straight to the shop floor – we'll see her there," Sean said.

As they entered the factory floor, Mrs Fowles – a gaunt, heavily lined grey-haired woman – appeared at their side.

"Morning, sirs. The first shipment is almost ready to go. Do you want to inspect it yourself?" she said.

"Thank you. I'll take a look once I've finished with Mr Brakenridge," Sean said.

His new supervisor would know far better than him what to inspect. So far, she hadn't put a foot wrong, but first impressions and excellent references or not, he'd check up on her until he was certain he could trust her.

Sean led the way down one of the aisles, between the rows of workers who were operating sewing machines that appeared to move at breakneck speed.

"Damned noisy in here. I don't know how you stand it, old boy," Charles shouted from behind.

Sean looked back over his shoulder as he walked.

"It's nothing compared to the mill, buddy, but it's also why our office is nowhere near the factory floor," he said as he collided with a young lad who was sweeping up waste materials around huge wooden benches where fabric was being cut from paper patterns.

In the design department, they found a young woman with a mouthful of pins attaching pieces of material together as they hung on a tailor's dummy.

"Do you think that's right?" the girl mumbled to her colleague, who was watching from the side.

"A wider sleeve, possibly," said the softy spoken young man, who was wearing a flamboyant checked suit.

Sean and Charles watched in silence as their new designer, Darius Anderson, altered the garment. Sean was confident he'd be a great success. He was calm, efficient and hardworking. He had Kate to thank for recommending Darius. After conducting a round of disappointing interviews, finding no one suitable, he'd turned to his mother in desperation to ask her to design him a collection.

"Centenary House is extremely busy, but I hate to see you stuck, especially when you've worked so hard. With Kitty's help, I'll put together a few initial designs, but you still need to find someone as soon as possible," she'd said.

Relieved that at least he had something to get the factory started with, he'd accepted it could only be a short-term solution. Then Kate had rung him. Bella had told her about the problems Sean was experiencing finding a designer and without preamble, she'd asked if he'd found someone suitable.

"No, and I'm getting desperate. Can you draw?" he'd joked.

"For sure, but it's not me I'm suggesting, you daft thing. I have a friend here in London, Darius Anderson. He's an incredibly talented designer who needs a break in the fashion industry. He's available immediately and a good sort. If he gets the job as your designer, the only problem I can foresee is that he'll be working for a tyrant."

"Highly amusing. When can he come for an interview?"

"He's free this week. But I must warn you – he's grand but he's a gentle sort."

"What *are* you talking about?"

"He's not one of the boys, if you take my meaning. That's why he lost his last position. His employer found out about his lifestyle."

369

"I don't care how he lives his life as long as he can design decent clothing."

"Then you'll adore Darius."

"Are you coming with him?"

"No, not right now. I have a business idea of my own I'm working on."

"Tell me more."

"Not yet. You'll have to wait until next month, Nosy Parker."

"Nosy who?"

"Honestly, Sean, do you never read a book? When I'm home, I need to take you in hand."

Sean spluttered with laughter, stopping when Kate remained silent on the other end of the line. He cringed. Kate must be embarrassed at her faux pas.

Sean had arranged for Darius to come for an interview, then he'd ended the call as quickly as he could.

Pushing his musing to one side for now, Sean spoke to Charles.

"If you come to the boardroom, I'll show you the rest of the winter collection Darius has designed so far. It's something else!"

"Winter! It's summer."

Sean raised his eyes to the ceiling. He'd quickly discovered that his new partner had no head for business.

"I've told you before. Everything is ordered well in advance. The sewing room is working on a small autumn range and the design team are working on a winter collection."

"It goes over my head, but as long as everything is going well."

"Yes, it's all going to plan."

Sean took Charles into the boardroom, where he laid out the design sheets.

"What do you think?" he asked.

"Looks fine to me," Charles said.

It seemed Charles' idea of working was to pop in once or twice a week for a chat. Despite his partner's lack of interest, Sean explained that the range was targeted at middle-class women aged twenty-five and upwards, to include elegant dresses and suits in quality fabrics, finished to a high standard.

"Right, well, that all sounds splendid, old chap. I will leave you to it. I am due to tee off soon," Charles said, ending his short visit.

Sean went to inspect the first shipment with Mrs Fowles and was delighted with the finished garments. His new supervisor was a real asset to the business.

Victoria dressed in a wine-coloured gown that was one of Edward's favourites. She pushed up the sash window to allow some fresh air in, smiling as the sound of church bells filled the room. As it was a Saturday, she assumed someone was about to get married. Brides liked June, as it was generally such a clement month – Bridie's favourite. But for Victoria, it was always tinged with sadness, as it was also the month Bridie had died.

As Victoria entered the breakfast room, she was pleased to find her daughter alone. She wanted the opportunity to speak to her privately and this was the one meal at which the family served themselves from salvers.

Bella stopped buttering her toast and appraised her mother.

"You look nice, Mother."

371

"Thank you, darling. It's nice to look one's best now and again, even if I'm only going to Centenary House."

Bella glanced down at her own sage green dress that hung off her.

"Fashion doesn't seem as important these days."

"I'm sure you still want to look nice for George."

"I suppose," Bella replied listlessly.

Victoria took her place at the table.

"I take it Anne hasn't been down yet."

Bella smiled. "Before eleven? It would need to be an incredibly special occasion."

"Where's George?"

"He's taken Kirby for a walk."

"He's such a dear. Why didn't you go with him?"

"I have a slight headache. Now you've established we're alone, am I in trouble?" Bella smiled.

"No, but you *are* losing weight at an alarming rate. Is there anything I should know about?"

"I'm fine, really I am."

Victoria poured herself a cup of tea. Bella's normally glossy hair looked dull and was pinned back in an unattractive bun. It seemed she'd lost interest in everything apart from George, which was understandable. She was still attractive and her eyes looked even bigger now she'd lost weight, but she clearly wasn't taking care of herself.

"Are you expecting?"

"No. I wish I were."

"If that's what's worrying you, it can take time."

"I'm not worrying."

"Is George's health deteriorating?"

Bella bit her bottom lip, shaking her head. "No, Mother."

Victoria didn't believe her. Although it had to be said, George looked healthier than his wife.

"Then what is it?"

"Nothing, honestly. Please don't fret about me, Mother. You have enough to deal with. I don't know how you do it. You've managed to juggle running Centenary House with constantly visiting Pierre and Yvette. You've even found time to help Sean with his collection."

"Kitty and Milly do more than their fair share at the shop. And Kitty helped with the designing."

"How is Milly?"

"Still out of sorts. Actually, I'm worried about her."

"Poor Milly. I thought she was coming to terms with losing Bob. Is it something else?"

"I'm not sure. She's appears tired all the time. I don't think she enjoys working in the shop any more, but when I ask her about it, she claims everything is fine . . . Very clever, young lady, you managed to distract me, but we're talking about you."

Bella grinned, providing a momentary flash of her old self.

"Honestly, Mother, I'm perfectly fine. You're much too busy to be fretting about me."

"I'll always have time for you, Bella, no matter what else is happening. You're as thin as a pipe cleaner. Isn't George concerned about you?"

"Of course not, because I'm fine. Really I am. Please don't say anything to George – I don't want him mithered."

"You want to protect him, that's understandable. I care about George, but you'll always matter more to me than he does. So don't ask me to stop worrying about you. I'm your mother and it's a job for life."

"Hopefully, I'll find out for myself one day."

"I'm sure you will. Is everything all right in the bedroom department?"

Bella giggled as she covered her face.

"I've endured the *talk* once, Mother. *Please* don't put me through it again. Everything is perfect."

"Thank goodness for that. Because I didn't relish talking about *it* again, either."

"Right, I've finished my breakfast, so I'm off to see Pierre. As it's a Saturday and Sean's at the factory, the little lamb will be stuck with his nanny. She's nice enough but hardly fun."

"What's the rush?"

"I'm making my escape before you start to interrogate me about s-e-x again."

Victoria laughed. "Go on with you. Remember, if there's anything your father or I can do to help, you must ask. Promise me you will."

Bella put her thin arms around her mother, saying simply, "Thank you, and yes, I promise."

Sometimes children needed more looking after when they'd grown up than when you could organise their lives and decide for them. She'd learned nothing new, but at least she'd reminded her girl that she cared.

Dust motes danced in the rays of sun pouring over Sean's shoulder onto his desk. It was a beautiful day outside and right now, he envied Charles, who would no doubt be strolling around the golf course before a few liveners at the nineteenth hole.

Sean needed to get out, even if only briefly, before he tackled the mound of supplier invoices that needed paying. He'd take a quick walk into town to choose something special for Pierre.

A short while later, as he was skirting his way through the department store, past cosmetics and accessories on the ground floor, a voice behind him said, "Sean! How lovely to see you."

"Jane, how are you?"

"I'm well, thank you. I haven't seen much of you at the house."

"Sorry. I'm not avoiding you." What a stupid thing to say when that's exactly what he'd been doing. "I'm busy with the factory," he added, reddening slightly.

"How's it going?"

"Good. By the way, thank you for everything you're doing for Pierre."

"He's a joy. I'm loving every minute. I even find myself missing him at weekends."

"Do you fancy helping me choose a present for him?"

"I'd love to."

Sean could barely drag his eyes off her lovely face. This wasn't a sin . . . He wasn't being unfaithful – it was purely shopping. Who was he trying to kid?

In the confined space of the lift, Jane's perfume was intoxicating. He was grateful for the presence of the boy operating the lift, preventing him from getting his face slapped for taking her in his arms.

"I was thinking of a rocking horse," Sean said as they neared the toys.

"The one you had was passed on to Robert and me. It was rather battered after he'd finished with it, I'm afraid."

"I hope he looked after Tatty Teddy better." Seriously, what was wrong with him? Why couldn't he have a

375

conversation with her without saying stupid things? "I, er, gave you my old bear."

Jane gave him such a warm smile, it took all of his willpower not to kiss her.

"He's still in my room. I'll pass him on to Pierre."

"I was only joking." He envied the bear being in her room.

"I realise that. There's a horse over there by the window."

After paying for it to be delivered, he asked Jane what she was intending to purchase.

"Nothing. I'm treating myself to tea and cake."

"If I may join you, perhaps we could talk about Pierre's progress. Or is that a terrible imposition on your day off?" Sean said, pulling at his collar nervously.

"Not at all. There were a couple of things I wanted to talk to Yvette about, but . . ." Her voice trailed off.

"She didn't want to listen. I understand. I think she finds it too upsetting." Why was he making excuses for her, when he knew full well that she had no interest in their son?

Before they'd even been served, Jane began talking about how Pierre was developing and the methods she was using to communicate with him.

After a few minutes, she asked, "Sean, why are you grinning?"

"Because I know I chose the perfect person to help my son." Even if her presence in his home was torture, it was worth it. "It kills me to know he'll never experience the pleasure of hearing birdsong or laughter," Sean added.

"Pierre will be all right. He's bright and he's definitely a giggler."

"I love his laugh. It's such a wonderful sound . . ." He

stopped, his words catching in his throat. He gulped. "I'm sorry – I nearly made a fool of myself then."

Jane shook her head slowly. "Men should never feel embarrassed about showing emotion. All that stiff-upper-lip stuff is nonsense."

Sean nodded, unable to continue speaking. As though realising, Jane carried on talking about Pierre.

"The next few months will be crucial as he learns to walk. I spoke to Doctor Farrell last time he called in and he explained that hearing issues can affect balance," she finished.

"He said the same to me," Sean answered as he studied each one of her features.

"Do I have jam or cream on my face?"

"No, why?"

"You're staring at me."

"Am I? I'm sorry. I can't get over how similar to Kitty you are."

"Everyone says that – apart from my grey eyes."

She seemed so unaware of her own beauty, which made her more alluring. If only she were Pierre's mother. She'd be wonderful with him – and he'd never have been hurt in the first place . . .

Jane said, "I've kept you far too long. I must let you get back to your factory."

"How about a tour, if you're free?"

"Why not."

He knew he was behaving inappropriately, but he couldn't help himself. After all, there was no harm in it. He wasn't ripping her clothes off, no matter how much he might want to. He was grateful to her for helping Pierre. They were simply friends and that was all they could ever be.

As Sean showed Jane round the factory, answering her questions, he realised she'd taken more of an interest than Yvette ever had. He was glad Charles hardly came near the place. If he'd been here, he'd have been fawning over Jane, as he had at Bella's wedding.

Finally, they visited the design department, where Darius asked Jane about the cut of a jacket.

"It's lovely," she said, looking slightly embarrassed.

"My darling, please don't hold back. I'd like to know what you *really* think. You might be wearing it next year," Darius said.

"Then, perhaps it needs to be slightly fuller in the bodice."

"That's interesting," Darius said.

Jane blushed again.

"Some ladies need a little more room," she added.

"Indeed, you're absolutely right," Darius said, smiling while unpinning the front of the garment, not in the least offended by Jane's observations.

Sean watched, mesmerised. Even the way she moved her hands was alluring. God, he had it bad.

"I'd better let you get back to your work now, Sean," Jane said.

"Have you got time to see the office first?"

Jane checked her watch.

"Just a quick look, then."

Sean pulled at his collar. Was it obvious that he was trying to prolong their time together?

He spread the latest designs out on the table and was relishing being close to Jane as she commented on the sketches. The door to the boardroom opened without a preceding knock and he jumped.

"Charles! Twice in one day. What are you doing back?" Sean said.

His eyes narrowed until he noticed how pale Charles was.

"I needed to see a friendly face. I've just had word from Italy. My mother passed away suddenly. She's already buried, so I can't even say goodbye to her."

"Oh, Charles, I'm so sorry to hear that," Jane said, taking Charles' hand.

"Let me pour you a drink," Sean said, taking out a bottle of whiskey, at the same time wondering why Jane looked so concerned when she barely knew him.

Had they been meeting without Sean's knowledge? You're a narcissistic bastard, Kavanagh! Your friend is grieving. But it was almost as though Sean didn't exist.

"Can I pour you a drink, Jane?" he asked, feeling as though he was interrupting.

"No thank you, Sean."

What the hell was happening? Her eyes were glued to Charles as she comforted him.

"I'm just going to make sure the factory was locked up properly when they finished their shift," Sean said, this time getting no acknowledgement.

Despite chastising himself for his selfishness as he made his way round the factory, his mood didn't improve. And when Charles and Jane hardly noticed his return to the boardroom, he only just stopped himself from telling them they had to leave so he could finish locking up.

For the next hour, Sean felt like Jekyll and Hyde, torn between concern for his friend and jealousy regarding Jane giving Charles attention. Eventually, Charles said he

379

was ready to go home, where he'd no doubt have to face his father's gloating that Charles' mother had died first.

When Jane offered to accompany him, Sean's heart sank. There was no getting away from it – she liked Charles. And given how Charles felt about her, no doubt this would be the start of a closer relationship for them. He tried to be pleased for them both but failed miserably.

After they left together, Sean struggled to concentrate, shuffling papers as he battled his resentment. Eventually, he packed up early and went to tell his mother about Lydia's passing.

Chapter 33

Monday, Victoria stood in Milly's parlour waiting for the Gibbs sisters to don their lightweight coats and hats before they visited Sean's factory.

"How's Pierre?" Milly asked as she pushed her arms into the sleeves.

"Beautiful – and I suspect he'll be full of mischief when he's older. He's certainly able to make himself understood if he doesn't want to do something."

Kitty fiddled with her hat in front of the mirror that hung over the mantel.

"What's the little fella been up to, then?"

"When I was round there yesterday, he launched his lunch across the room. I shouldn't have laughed, but I did. He helped take my mind off poor Lydia's demise. Yvette was absent once again. The baby's due next month, so she's going to have to stay home then. At least for a while."

"Are you getting along all right with her?" Milly said.

"She's grieving, so we make allowances for her. However, she's at the Mason home most of the time. In fact, far from mourning the loss of her parents, Yvette appears to be thriving. Even so, we rub along together better these days. We're all the family she has now, so she's more accepting of us when it suits her."

381

"She's always been a stuck-up mare, if you ask me, but she should appreciate all you've done for her. I'll always be grateful to Jess and Harry for taking my family in. After all these months I thought we might have been rowing, but we get on smashing and they couldn't have been kinder," Kitty said.

"It's clear Jess loves the boys," Victoria said.

"She takes everything in her stride, although she did freak out a bit when they brought nits home from school. I've told them before not to play with the ones who are scratching – mind you, half the other kids are lousy."

"Urgh," Victoria said, scratching her own head. "You've set me off itching just thinking about it."

"Jess was right good about it – even when I had to spend a whole evening doing her hair with vinegar and lard. I'm surprised she didn't give us our marching orders there and then."

"I'm sure they'd say if they didn't want you there," Victoria said, still scratching.

"Harry's offered to build a house for us in the grounds."

"They've certainly got enough land," Victoria said.

"He's right generous. I never would have believed it if I'd not seen it with me own eyes, 'cos as a kid he wouldn't share owt. He'd have nicked yer snot if he thought he could sell it."

"Kitty! That's disgusting." Victoria shook her head as she laughed. "People change," she added. "Though you clearly haven't, coming out with things like that."

"He blinkin' has."

"How's the pub doing?" Victoria asked.

"There's been no more bother. I reckon the fella that robbed us is the same one the police arrested a week ago trying to rob The Plough Inn, though the bobbies have said he's not admitting it."

"I don't suppose it matters as long as he's locked up," Milly said.

"Come along, you two. I told Sean we'd be there for twelve o'clock," Victoria said, opening the door and ushering the others out.

"What's the hurry?" Milly asked.

"He wants us there at lunchtime. Apparently, he doesn't want his machinists being distracted by us wandering round."

"They wouldn't dare swan neck if the supervisor was there, would they?"

"If you were in charge, they wouldn't," Victoria said.

"Well that's 'cos I now know how to handle people. Maybe she's a soft touch."

"Possibly, but Sean claims she's a marvel. Apparently, he couldn't have got the factory up and running so quickly without her," Victoria said.

"Where was she working before?" Milly asked.

"Manchester. He telephoned her last employer, who was sorry when she left."

"Why has she moved all the way over here?" Milly asked.

Victoria stifled a smile as they climbed into the car. Milly never could understand why people travelled. Agnes may as well have emigrated to Australia rather than moved to Blackpool, as far as Milly was concerned.

"Sean tells me her husband's the new assistant manager at the mill, so now you know as much as I do."

Sean came into the reception to greet them, leading them to the office.

"So, Tatty Head, we're here to check out the competition. Reception is swanky – and this office is right posh 'n' all," Kitty said as she surveyed his office, running her hand along the back of his black leather chair and monochrome filing cabinets.

"Come and see the boardroom," he said as he showed them into the next room.

"By heck, you've fallen on yer feet. This is a right decent set-up," Kitty said, taking a seat at the head of the long mahogany table. "I can see myself here dishing out orders."

"Fallen on my feet? I'll have you know I work incredibly hard."

"Yeah, course you do. Yeh had mine an' yer mam's designs to start you off an' yer mam told us Charles did all the legwork," Kitty laughed.

Sean chuckled. He knew full well his mother had said no such thing. In fact, she'd frequently said that Charles should help more.

"Leave him alone, Kitty. For once, stop messing around and let's enjoy the tour," Milly said, scowling.

"All right, I'll do anything you say if it stops you pulling that face again."

Kitty stuck the tip of her tongue out.

Sean showed them round the factory floor, explaining that he was using production line techniques similar to ones he'd seen in America.

"Blimey, it's fantastic. All these modern machines – and it's so light. I'd give me hind teeth to run a workroom like this."

Milly's eyes narrowed as she looked at her sister quizzically.

"Would you?"

Kitty patted Milly's thin cheek. "Course I would. I'd never leave you, though. Yeh need me to keep you in line, or you'd have the staff taking a bath twice a day."

Milly frowned at her, remaining silent.

"Cat got your tongue then, our Milly?"

"Nobody plots to murder their little sister out loud."

Kitty threw back her head. "Aww, you'd never hurt me – you love me too much. But I like it when yeh gets feisty. Blinking heck, you've got a finishing room?" she added, distracted, as she walked through the next door into the light, airy room where the garments were checked and pressed.

"They also have a separate packing and dispatch office," Victoria said proudly.

"Would you like to look at the canteen?" Sean asked.

"I'm expecting it to be as good as The Savoy after seeing all this," Kitty said.

"Well, you won't know the difference, 'cos you've not been there any more than I have," Milly quipped.

As they walked into a large room filled with tables, the chatter subsided.

"It's all right. Don't let us interrupt your lunch," Sean said, pausing just inside the room. "Not much to see in here. The next stop is the design studio and stockroom."

"Are you going to introduce me to the wonderful Mrs Fowles?" Victoria asked.

"Yes, sorry, there she is . . ." Sean pointed to a woman who was sitting alone. She had her head down and was reading a book as she ate her sandwich. "Mrs Fowles, may I introduce my mother," he said as they approached her table.

385

"Pleased to meet you," the woman said, barely looking up from her lunch.

Victoria froze.

"Sean, will you ask Mrs Fowles to come to your office?"

"Mother?"

"Now, please, Sean."

Victoria turned on her heel, pushing a confused Milly and Kitty ahead of her as she stalked out of the canteen.

"What's wrong?" Milly asked.

"Mrs Fowles is Grace Brooks, I'm sure of it."

"Flaming hell, it can't be," Kitty said.

"I'd recognise her anywhere."

"It was about thirty years ago. Wouldn't she be dead an' buried by now?" Kitty said.

"We're the same age and I'm still alive, aren't I? She looks different, but I can still see it's her. Surely *you* recognised her, Milly," Victoria said.

"No, to be honest, I didn't, but then my eyesight isn't what it was," Milly said.

"Blimey, if yer eyesight is that bad, it's a bloody good job you work in haberdashery and not the workshop," Kitty said.

"But she moved away years ago, didn't she?" Milly asked.

"She's obviously moved back," Victoria said.

By the time they'd reached Sean's office, he'd caught up with them.

"I told her to finish her lunch and come down. What's going on?"

"I'm sure your Mrs Fowles used to be Grace Brooks. She worked for me when you were a child. She was widowed and new to the area. Her work was excellent and she was hardworking, but she stole my customers, my designs and my stock. Frankly, my business nearly failed because of her. She can't be trusted."

"Yer mam's right, Sean. If it is her, she's a devious cow," Milly said.

"Blast. I thought it was too good to be true. But, Mother, I checked out her references. She's definitely been running a workroom in Manchester." He opened a filing cabinet and took out a file. "Her name's Grace, but there must be a lot of women who have that name."

"I know it's her," Victoria said.

"There's a gap of several years in her employment history, but I assumed she was raising a family. Fowles must be her new married name," Sean explained.

There was a knock on the door and the woman entered. Even though she was wearing a high-necked blouse, the blotching above her collar was visible.

"Before any of youse say anything, can I just point out that what happened at your place were a lifetime ago an' I'm doing a good job here," Mrs Fowles said.

"So, you're *the* Grace Brooks – the one who cheated my mother . . ." Sean's forehead furrowed.

"It's Fowles now and the trouble was years back. Running your own business ain't all it's cracked up to be. I just want a quiet life now."

Sean threw the personnel file on his desk.

"How the devil did you expect to get away with it?"

"I hoped no one would recognise me. Besides, I'm doing a good job – you know I am – so I suppose I hoped you wouldn't care."

"Yeh silly moo. You almost ruined his mother," Kitty said.

Grace shot her an angry look.

Milly elbowed Kitty in the ribs. "Keep yer nose out."

Victoria spoke calmly.

"I'll never forgive you, Grace. But if Sean wants to keep you in his employ, that's up to him."

Grace threw Kitty a smug look.

"I can't believe you lied to me," Sean said.

"I didn't – you never asked. Besides, my references are genuine."

"Mother, what should I do?"

"It's up to you, Sean. The only advice I can give you is to ask yourself if you can trust her."

"Of course he can't trust her," Kitty said.

Milly nudged her again.

Sean walked to the window and stared out. He turned back to the waiting women and pulled at his collar.

"It might have been a long time ago, but I won't ever be able to trust you. I'll pay you until the end of the week. If you collect your things and come back here, I'll have your money ready for you."

"I'd follow her, if I were you – she might try shoving half yer stock in her bag and a sewing machine down her drawers," Kitty said.

Grace scowled before marching out of the office, leaving the door wide open.

"What am I going to do now? I've got no one to run the workroom. Charles will have to come in and help me in the office while I sort things out in production. But then he knows nothing about the business – and he's grieving for his mother. What a mess!" he said as he opened the safe to take out some cash to pay Grace.

They turned, stunned, when Milly spoke.

388

"Give Kitty the job."

Victoria gaped. They were run ragged as it was – what would they do without Kitty? Had Milly gone mad?

"Are you serious?" Sean asked, looking hopefully from Kitty, who was staring at her sister, quiet for once, then to Milly.

"Edward wants yer mam to retire and though she's never said as much, I think she wants it as well, so we can sell Centenary House. Kitty will do a wonderful job for you here, an' me and Victoria can manage until the sale goes through. It won't take long to find a buyer – it's a thriving business."

"What about you, Milly? What will you do?" Victoria asked as she struggled to take it in, unsure how she herself felt about giving up her precious shop.

"To tell you the truth, I've had enough. If I do any sewing, it gives me a headache. An' all that bending and lifting with the fabrics ain't good for me back. I fancy buying a little cottage, like me an' Bob always dreamed of."

"Mother?" Sean said.

"This is rather sudden, although Edward has been waiting long enough for me to retire. If Milly's certain we can cope until the business sells . . ."

They turned to Kitty, who still hadn't spoken.

"Well, Kitty? What do you have to say? It affects you more than anyone," Sean asked.

"I wondered when one of yeh might get round to asking me, instead of gassing about me as though I'm not here." Her face split in a wide grin. "If you promise you're not just doing it for me, Milly, then I'd love the chance."

"I mean it when I say I've had enough of working," Milly said, a rare smile reaching her eyes.

"I don't bleedin' believe it. Yer giving me job to *that* nasty little tart?" Grace said, standing arms akimbo in the office doorway.

"That's right. And my first job is to show you the door. Have you got what she's owed, Sean?" Kitty said, stepping forwards.

"I don't need you to show me out, yeh bitch. But mark my words, I'll do for you if it kills me," Grace said, snatching the money from Sean and storming out, this time slamming the door.

That evening, when Edward arrived home from his office, Victoria handed him a glass of sherry, smiling.

"Come and sit down – we need to talk."

"Drinking before dinner – what is going on? Should I be worried?" he joked.

"I certainly hope not. But it may come as a surprise – I'm selling Centenary House and retiring."

Edward raised his eyebrows. "Well, I am flabbergasted. You always said you couldn't leave Milly and Kitty. What is going to happen to them?"

Victoria explained the events that had led to the decision.

"I'm still in a state of shock myself," she said.

"What do you plan to do? Are we going to put our feet up and grow old and fat together?"

She laughed. "Could you have made it sound less appealing?"

"So how will you spend your time, apart from pampering me, that is?"

"I'd like to do more charity work. Jess has also mentioned she wants to become more involved, but I've been so busy, we've not had time to do anything about it."

"Then I guess I will hand most of my cases over to my partner and get someone else in. But I will retain a few key clients. That way I will have something to keep me occupied if you are swamped in charity work."

"I might not be busy. I may swan around all day indulging myself," Victoria said.

Edward grinned. "Then I'll be asking who you are and what have you done with my wife. After all these years, I know you well enough to realise you will never be idle."

"Can you help me to find a buyer for the shops – someone nice?"

"I'll make it my priority." Edward raised his glass. "Here's to our more relaxing future!"

⚜

Chapter 34

George halted outside the doorway of his and Bella's sitting room, his chest heaving. The sun pouring through the window was casting the long shadow of a man across the carpet. What was that bastard doing? He stormed in.

"What the hell are you doing reading my private correspondence?" He stalked across the room, snatching the crumpled piece of paper, slamming his hand into Max's chest. "How much have you read, you nosy swine?"

Max stuttered. "It w-w-was on the floor. I-I'm sorry."

George grabbed the lad's arm, twisting it up his back so Max bent double.

"Now you listen to me. If you breathe a word of this to anyone, it will be the last thing you do. I've had enough of yeh poking your nose into my business, so I suggest you clear off before I make out that you've been on the rob." He yanked Max's arm up further.

"Arrgh, please, you're hurting me. I won't tell anyone."

George sneered. "I don't think I believe you. Perhaps it's time I tell them what I know about you."

"Please don't say anything. I swear I'll keep my mouth shut."

"Get back down to the servants' hall and stay out of my sight or you'll find out just how nasty I can be."

Alone now, George paced the room. Bloody hell, what a mess! Things were getting out of control. He'd been happy here, but all good things come to an end. At least there was a nice fat amount of money from the sale of the mill in his and Bella's joint bank account.

At the factory, Kitty's familiar voice brought a smile to Sean's face as he approached where she was talking to her new machinist.

"Abso-bloody-lutely not," she said.

"Morning, Kitty," Sean said.

"Mornin'." She gave him a wink. "Now, I dunno what they taught yeh at yer last job, but you claimed to be an experienced machinist." She pulled at the seams, which came open immediately. "Now, shove over and let me get to yer machine so I can show you again how it should be. You don't know yer born, working under me."

Sean stifled a laugh as she added, "It's a good job I've got eyes in the back o' me head, Mr Kavanagh, or this lot would have yeh outta business in a month."

"I thank God for you every day, Kitty."

He might have sounded as though he was joking, but he didn't know what he'd have done without her. She'd taken control of the workroom from her first day, leaving him to focus on managing the salesmen, negotiating contracts and balancing the books.

He watched as Kitty rapidly sewed the seam. Smiling, she handed it to the young woman.

"There, love, can yeh see how that's better?"

The young woman nodded.

"Smashing. I know you'll get the hang of it," Kitty said kindly.

393

"Can I have a quick word in the office before you finish for the afternoon, Kitty?" Sean said.

"Don't suppose I have much choice as it's you who pays me wages," she replied with a grin.

As Kitty and Sean made their way down the corridor, his eyes widened as he realised who was approaching them.

"I hope it's all right. I told the receptionist I'm a family member as I was sure it would be fine for me to come through unannounced."

"Jane, of course. You're welcome anytime," Sean said, hoping his eagerness wasn't too obvious.

"I was shopping in town and thought I'd see if Auntie Kitty fancied a spot of lunch before she goes home."

Kitty looked at her watch.

"It's quarter of an hour before we finish and Tatty Head here has just said he wants to talk to me. He can't stand the idea of me getting a half-day finish on a Saturday, so no doubt he'll have me slaving until midnight."

"It's a good job you don't forget yourself and call me that in front of the factory workers, Mrs Nelson. I am the boss, in case you'd forgotten."

"Well, Mr Big Boss, if it's all right wi' you, I need to get off on time. I love this early finish on a Saturday lark."

Sean's mind whirled – he desperately wanted to find a reason to keep Jane here, but he also didn't want to look mean. Even worse, Charles was in the office with his feet up on his desk reading *Punch* magazine, no doubt waiting for Sean's return so he could quote some more humorous anecdotes.

"It's fine, Kitty. You get off now. I'll lock up."

Early the following day, the sun peaked round the edges of the curtains and woke Bella. To her, waking up beside

George was both the worst and the best part of the day. Her secret terror was of finding him dead beside her. Each morning, she'd hold her breath until she'd touched his warm skin, relief flooding her. Then they'd made love – it was their way of christening the day. She turned, her eyes closed, her hand feeling his side of the bed. It was empty. Her eyes shot open – George never got up before her.

She opened the connecting door to their sitting room, wondering if he couldn't sleep. George would be cross if she got herself upset over nothing – her fretting about his health was one of the few things that annoyed him.

The room was empty.

Back in their bedroom, a terrible feeling of foreboding swept over her. She pulled on her cream silk dressing gown and made her way downstairs to the breakfast room, where Taylor was clearing away some dishes.

"It's all right, Taylor, I *do* realise that I've come downstairs in my night attire."

"Yes, madam."

"Has Mr Bristow been down for breakfast?"

"No, madam. Only Mr and Mrs Caldwell have been down and now they're in the master's study discussing the situation."

"What situation?"

"I am afraid the fifty pounds that I keep in my pantry to pay for incidentals went missing yesterday. I questioned the staff about it and now it appears Max has gone, taking all of his belongings."

Bella was already leaving the room.

She hesitated outside the study. Turning on her heel, she ran back upstairs instead. There's no need to panic, she told herself as her breaths came in shallow gasps.

Calm down – Max disappearing could have nothing to do with where George was.

Despite telling herself she was being ridiculous, she pulled open the wardrobe door nonetheless. His clothes were still there. She breathed a sigh of relief. But where was the suit he'd bought last month? She looked a little closer. It was missing. She began dragging drawers open. Not everything had gone, but he'd taken some items – the gold cufflinks she'd bought him, his best shirts and shoes . . .

"Mother!" she shouted, hurrying back downstairs, almost tripping in her haste.

She flung open the door. Her father was sitting behind his desk, her mother by his side, and their conversation halted as they looked at her, their eyebrows raised.

"George has gone!"

"What silliness is this? They can't both have disappeared. This isn't the *Mary Celeste*," her father said, pushing his spectacles back up his nose.

Bella flung herself at her father, dropping to her knees in front of his chair and placing her head on his lap. Through sobs, reverting to her childhood way of referring to her father, she said, "But he has, Daddy. He's gone away to die alone."

"Nonsense! Why would he do that?" her father asked as he stroked her hair.

"Because he's trying to do the gallant thing. He doesn't want me to suffer, watching him fade. His heart is getting weaker – the end will be sooner and possibly slower than expected, so he'll need more care. He doesn't want to put that burden on me."

"Here, my poor girl, wipe your eyes," her father said, pushing his handkerchief into her hand.

"Max could have left with George," Victoria said.

"I don't care who is with him. I just need him home."

Victoria kneeled beside her.

"We'll find him, darling, I promise. As for the Max situation, that'll have to take a back seat. Missing money and an absent footman are the least of our worries. We must focus on finding George."

What Victoria couldn't fathom was why Max would have vanished on the same day. Were the two disappearances even connected? So far, they hadn't even tried to locate Max. They had no proof he'd taken any money from the housekeeping, so there was no point involving the police.

After fruitless enquiries around Faredene and repeated telephone calls to Doctor Makin in Harley Street, they were still getting nowhere. Victoria didn't want to voice this to Bella, but if George didn't want to be found, she doubted they'd locate him.

Doctor Makin had refused to confirm that George was a patient, let alone divulge if he was aware of his current address. Only when Doctor Farrell rang the Harley Street clinic had he been able to ascertain that George had registered with them in June 1911 for an initial consultation but never returned. When Victoria told Bella what Doctor Farrell had learned, her daughter was stunned.

"I don't understand," she said. "He was there only weeks ago."

"Maybe he changed doctors. He had several opinions – perhaps you got the names mixed up. After all, you never attended any appointments with him," Victoria said.

"Possibly, but I'm sure Doctor Makin was the one George said he was seeing. Then again, he hates to talk about his prognosis. He doesn't see the point when they can't do anything. He only continued to see a doctor for my sake."

"Is it possible he wasn't going for appointments?"

Bella wiped her puffy eyes. The poor girl had barely stopped crying since tearing into her father's study that first morning.

"But that would mean George lied to me. I can't imagine him doing that. How could you say such a thing?" Bella said.

"We can never be certain people are telling the truth," Victoria said.

"George isn't people – he's my husband. Although, if he wanted to stop me from worrying, he might have pretended to see a doctor. That's the sort of considerate thing he'd do."

They decided they could waste no more time in Faredene – Bella and Victoria would head to London first thing the following day. Their intention was to visit all the surgeries in Harley Street. If that failed to provide any information, they'd make enquiries with the dock office where he used to work, hoping to find an old colleague who knew where he was.

Edward wanted to go with them, but Bella asked him to remain in Faredene in case George turned up. Victoria was dismayed when Anne, having finally decided to sell her house in Knightsbridge, insisted on going to London with them to arrange the sale.

After several visits to Harley Street that saw them pleading with the secretaries of various doctors and surgeons, they agreed that line of enquiry would get them no further. Now, Bella, Kate and Victoria found themselves in a cab travelling from Anne's to the East End docks.

The jovial manager of the run-down, cluttered dock office explained that the only George Bristow he'd known had worked there years back as a docker for a few weeks.

"Is there another office?" Bella asked.

"No, miss. This is the only one and I've been here over forty years, so if he'd been a clerk here, I'd have known him. I'm sorry I can't help you lovely ladies more."

"Right," Bella said, pulling her mother out of the office.

"Bella, what is it, darling?"

"I don't understand. George told me that the manager at the dock office was a tyrant."

"Let's go back to Anne's and work out a plan for tomorrow," Victoria said, her suspicion growing by the minute that George wasn't who he appeared to be. She prayed she was wrong about him.

Bella gave a slight nod as she walked, trancelike, between them.

"Hold up there a moment, would you?" Kate called to a group of dockers walking towards the gates at the end of their shift.

When they stopped, she hurried forwards.

Victoria stood holding Bella's elbow, worried if she let go, her daughter might sink to the ground. They could see a man pointing out through the gates and gesticulating as if giving directions. Kate opened her purse and handed something to two of the men before scurrying back to Bella and Victoria.

Breathlessly, Kate said, "A couple of them knew him. They've given me an address where he used to live. Apparently, it's not an area for ladies to venture alone. They said the Limehouse district is occupied by hordes of dockers, sailors, boatmen and families crammed in together. There's often ten or twelve living in one room."

"George never said conditions were that bad, but he did say his rooms were unpleasant." Bella's pale face was hopeful. "I suppose there's a chance he's gone back to the same lodgings."

"Bella, the thing is, they said his mother lives there. I thought his parents were dead," Kate said.

"They are. He told us, didn't he, Mother?"

"Yes, darling, he did," Victoria replied.

"I still think we should check it out. I'll try anything," Bella said, sighing.

The three women walked in silence, each mulling over the information Kate had gleaned as they made their way down filthy, narrow streets before turning into Glebe Street about ten minutes later. Here, the sun shone fruitlessly on grimy windows and feral cats warmed themselves on baking cobbles. A waif in a ragged dress was sitting outside number four. A large tin bucket in front of her held a washboard and her red fingers moved up and down out of the water as she scrubbed a grey garment. The mangy mongrel by her side snarled as the women passed.

Victoria couldn't fathom why George would choose to die here. Either it wasn't him or there was more to his departure. Could Max and George have gone off together? Stranger things had happened.

"If this was where George resided, perhaps he was ashamed. Before he moved to Faredene, he refused to allow me to see where he was living," Bella said.

"Try not to get your hopes up, darling, because that wouldn't explain why he told you his mother was dead,"

Victoria said, instantly regretting her words when Bella's lip quivered.

"Perhaps he was worried about us meeting her. If she is alive, I'd have wanted her at the wedding. George was conscious of our different backgrounds. I hate to think I've made him ashamed of being poor."

"If he is with his mother, then she can come home with him. We all care about George and want the best for him," Victoria added, attempting to comfort her daughter, though secretly preparing for bad news of some sort.

Bella smiled at her mother. "You've been so supportive. You too, Kate. I'm grateful and I'm sure George will be, as well."

"You don't need to be grateful – you're my daughter. There's nothing I wouldn't do for you. Or you, Kate."

"You don't have to be grateful to me, either. Sure now, I feel terrible I didn't come home straightaway," Kate said.

"Kate, I asked you not to because I thought it would embarrass George when we found him if there had been a big fuss. You've done nothing wrong," Bella said.

"This is number thirty-six. Are you ready?" Kate's hand was poised to knock on the shabby brown front door of the terraced house.

"Just give me a minute, please. I need to prepare myself for what I might find," Bella said.

401

Chapter 35

Bella dried her tears roughly with a gloved hand, took a deep breath and pushed her shoulders down to release the tension and rid herself of the pains in her chest that had been a permanent feature since George's disappearance. Made worse by the heat of summer, the combined stench from the sewers and the dockyard caused her to gag. How could George have preferred to end his days here? Surely it was the wrong place – although she prayed it wasn't. She was terrified what she might find.

"I'm ready," she said.

In response to their knock, a frail voice called from within.

"Hold yer horses."

Eventually, the door was opened by a small woman, bent almost double, who leaned heavily on two sticks. Still stooping, she angled her head upwards so she could look at them.

Her voice raspy, she demanded, "Whatcha want?"

The knot in Bella's chest tightened once again as she took in the old woman's bloodshot eyes. It was clear she'd been crying.

"We're looking for George Bristow."

"You're too late. He's gone." The woman stepped back, ready to close the door.

Bella clutched the battered door frame to steady herself. She'd come this far – she wouldn't be put off now. If George was already dead, she had to face it.

"How? When?"

"I can't help yeh. I'm sorry, duck."

"Please, I'm his wife. I need to understand what's happened to him, visit his grave."

"He's not dead."

Bella noticed her mother shoot Kate an anxious glance.

"Please, I'm begging you. I need to find George. Are you his landlady?"

"Dear God in Heaven, this is too much to cope with in me final days."

"The last thing I want to do is distress you, but I must find him. How do you know George? Please tell me."

The old woman sighed. "I'm his mother. You'd best come in and I'll tell you what I know."

They followed her through to a sparse and dingy front parlour. Bella glanced at the closed door to the right that hid stairs leading to the upper floor. Was George up there? She understood why he might be ashamed of where he lived – this place was worse than the Rows. She'd reassure him that nothing would come between them. George needed her – it didn't matter that he'd lied.

"George! George, it's me, Bella," she called.

"Aww, duck, I told yeh – he's not here."

"Then where is he? Tell me, please."

"Gimme chance, will yeh?"

Once they were in the kitchen, they refused the woman's offer of a cup of tea. Bella was fighting to keep her irritation under control. She wanted to talk to her husband now.

403

George's mother lowered herself laboriously onto a kitchen chair and gestured to the other mismatched, battered ones.

"You'd better sit down."

"Where's my husband? Is he in hospital?"

The old woman shook her head. "I don't know if I'm doing the right thing, but I don't want owt on me conscience."

"We mean George no harm," Bella said.

"There's no easy way to say this, duck."

The three of them sat silently, waiting as the wizened, careworn woman struggled to find the right words.

George's mother sighed again as she said, "What yeh need to grasp is that me boy ain't all bad."

"We know that – we're all terribly fond of him. Despite my concerns that it appears George has lied to my daughter, we wish to ensure he has the best care. We realise he's worried about Bella and we admire him for it, but her family will support her through whatever his illness brings," Victoria said.

"It's good she has a family to stand by her – she's gonna need yeh."

Bella's mouth opened, but before her words formed, her mother reached out and grasped her hand. The woman continued to talk slowly, as though she were dragging each word from somewhere deep inside that caused her pain.

"The thing is, me duck, George ain't dying, or even ill – although maybe what he does is an illness. One thing's for sure – it ain't a normal way to behave."

Bella's stomach lurched. Her mind whirled – George wasn't ill or dying. She should be elated, but something

404

told her what she was about to hear was worse. Why else was this woman looking at her with such pity?

"I guessed he'd been up to his old tricks when he moved up north, but when I quizzed him, he denied it. I weren't sure until I telephoned the number he'd given me for emergencies. I had to tell him I'm sick, you see. The postmaster made the call for me. When I asked to speak to George, some fella said he'd see if Mr or Mrs Bristow were home. That was when I knew he'd done it again. When I saw him next, he claimed it were all a misunderstanding. That the fella who answered the phone were a simpleton. Said it were his landlady's son. I could tell he were lying – I'm not as daft as he thinks I am."

Victoria asked. "When was this, Mrs Bristow?"

"Few months back."

Bella couldn't breathe – it was as if the life were being choked out of her.

"I don't understand. What old tricks?" Bella asked.

"Bella, don't interrupt. Let her explain, darling."

"He turns up here. I thought he'd come home, 'cos a neighbour wrote to him for me to tell him I've not got long now. The doctors say a couple of months at most. But last night he tells me he's going abroad to Africa, of all places. No idea when he'll be back. He said he'll come home if he can, but I doubt I'll live to see me son again."

A chill crept down Victoria's spine.

"Mrs Bristow, can you explain? This is extremely confusing. Whatever George has done, Bella needs to find her husband."

"George ain't yer daughter's husband. According to him, his wife lives in Spitalfields now with another bloke, but that could be a load o' rubbish. George and Pearl have a little girl – Daphne. Yer the second one he's pretended to marry."

"I don't understand. We were married – in church." Bella's voice was shrill.

A tear escaped the corner of the old woman's eye and ran down her wrinkled face.

"Would have been nice to see me granddaughter in me last days," Mrs Bristow said, her head down as she fiddled with her grey apron, almost unaware they were still there.

"Bella, dear, the chancer has been lying to you – to all of us," Kate said.

"No . . ." Bella murmured.

Victoria clutched her daughter's hand.

"What Mrs Bristow is trying to tell you, my dear, is that George is a bigamist, so you aren't legally married."

Victoria watched Bella shaking her head slowly. How could that man have done this to her?

"Mrs Bristow, where is this other young lady George committed bigamy with? Why didn't she go to the police?" Kate said.

"She weren't a lass – she were a widow. Died in an accident. I didn't get any details. Now, don't be lookin' at me like that, missy. None of it were my doin'," she said, pointing a thin, gnarled finger at Kate. "First I heard about it all were after it were over. He came home wearing decent clobber an' with money in his back pocket. Weeks later, I were dusting his room, when I found a marriage licence an' a death certificate. I can't read much, but I could see what they were. He denied it, but it made no difference – I knew."

"Do you have the documents?" Victoria asked.

"I get why you want them, as evidence against him, but he shoved the lot in the fire. I can't remember the woman's name, so there's an end to it. It wouldn't help yer girl, anyway."

"What about an address for his wife and child?" Victoria added.

"Spitalfields is all I know. Before that, George and her lived in Stepney."

"Mrs Bristow, I must ask you to be truthful. Did your son have a young man with him? A Uriah Maxwell? Or he may have called himself Max."

"No, he were on his own. He's not one of them, if that's what yer askin'. Max were the fella George claimed were simple. I could tell George didn't like him from the way he spoke about him. My son likes the ladies – always has. Likes 'em a bit too much, if you ask me. Likes money an' all. He always wanted more than me an' his dad could give him."

"To your knowledge, has George ever stolen from his wives?" Victoria asked.

A cry escaped from Bella.

"Mother, George wouldn't . . ."

Mrs Bristow shrugged, her face pained. "Has he stolen from yer girl?"

"A small amount of money has gone from the house, but Bella was recently given a large sum by her father and me. As George has lied about everything else, he may have taken the money," Victoria said.

Bella bit her bottom lip. "No. You're wrong, Mother. How can you say such a thing?"

"George, George, what *have* you done? I sneaked in his room an' found a big bag o' money – a fortune. He said

407

he'd had a big win on the horses – twenty pounds he gave me. It's in that jug on the mantel. It's nowt compared to what he had with him. You can take what he left me. I don't want owt if it's yer girl's money."

"You can keep the money, Mrs Bristow," Victoria said.

"I-I need to see him – ask him why he lied to me," Bella muttered.

"He's a maggot! Forget about him, Bella," Kate said.

"His ship sailed on the first tide this morning. He'll be long gone by now, duck. I wouldn't have told you otherwise. What he does is wrong, but he's me boy an' I don't want him to go to prison."

Bella pulled her hand away from her mother's grasp and covered her mouth. Dashing to the back door, she yanked it open and staggered into the backyard, where she lost the contents of her stomach. Kate rushed to her side.

"Your son has hurt my daughter terribly. She didn't deserve this. She's such a kind, trusting person," Victoria said to Mrs Bristow.

"Aye, she's pretty an' all. The thing is, we can't always do anything about the way our kids turn out. I had two sons. My oldest were a good boy – do anything for anyone. But the Lord saw fit to take him from me when he were eighteen."

"I'm sorry to hear that," Victoria said.

"He died of a weak heart. George worshiped him. I sometimes think his passing turned George's head. He started worrying about dying young an' not wanting to waste his life."

Eventually, Bella and Kate came back into the kitchen. Bella had looked pale before – now, she was ashen. Mrs Bristow filled a chipped cup with water from a bucket that stood on an old tea chest supported by two bricks and gave it to Bella.

"If it's any consolation, duck, when he's been coming home on visits since he moved up north, he's never seemed happier."

Bella took the cup but didn't raise it to her lips.

"Then why didn't he just tell me the truth that he'd been married before? He could have got a divorce."

"Aww, love, what can I say? It's like I told yeh – it's an illness with him. He's been making up stories about who he is since he were a nipper. He wants people to like him. And if you had money, there was another temptation."

"I shared everything with him."

"Now there you have it. You sharin' and givin' – that's not what he'd have wanted. If he's taken anything from you – an' I'm not saying he has – well, he can use it to start again. Make himself a new person with money in his own right. That's what he's always wanted."

"He planned this all along?" Bella said.

"I'm not sure my George plans anything out proper. If his lips are movin', he's lying. Like as not, he were drawn to you an' then things got outta hand."

"Can you tell us any more about where he might be heading once he gets to Africa?" Victoria asked.

"No. He told me he'd be in touch when he's able. I doubt I'd tell you anyhow. Like I said, he's me flesh an' blood."

Once it was clear Mrs Bristow had no more information she was able or willing to give them, Victoria and Kate supported Bella one on either side as they made their way out of the East End.

"Why, Mother? Why would he do that to me?" Bella said.

"I'm afraid I can't answer that, my darling."

"He loved me – I know he did."

"I'm sure he did. At least that's what we all assumed."

"How could I have been so stupid?"

"Sure, we're all stupid when it comes to men," Kate said.

"George took us all in. We all cared about him. I'm shocked, too. Let's just find a cab and get out of this area as quickly as possible," Victoria said.

How was she going to help Bella to rebuild her life after this?

With Kate's help, Victoria assisted her trembling daughter up the steps of the portico. As they entered the grand hallway, Anne came scurrying out of the morning room.

"What on earth has happened to Bella? Is George already dead? Oh, that poor man. They say God takes the best ones young."

"He's not dead, Anne. If you'll let us get in, I'll explain," Victoria said, leading Bella across into the morning room.

Once they were seated and nursing glasses of sherry, Victoria explained to Anne that George wasn't only a bigamist, but possibly also a thief.

"That swine! I often thought there was something shifty about him. No one is ever that nice – and his eyes were too close together," Anne said.

Kate jutted out her chin. "Aunt Anne, that's enough, now. Bella doesn't need to hear your blathering. Can't you see the state she's in?"

Anne bristled. "I was just saying . . . All right, all right, Kate. If looks could kill, I'd be stone dead now. I'll keep my opinions to myself. No one ever listens to me, anyway."

"Please don't argue. I can't cope with any more just now," Bella said as she placed her full glass on the coffee table.

"Ah, I'm sorry, Sweet Pea. Can I get you something else?" Kate asked.

"A father for my baby."

Victoria laid her hand to her chest.

"Oh, dear God. You're pregnant? My poor child. You said you weren't."

"I'm sorry, Mother. Not even George knew. I haven't lied to you – I didn't know when we spoke."

Victoria stroked her daughter's hair. "Don't worry about that, my darling."

"My goodness, what else can go wrong? The shame!" Anne said.

Kate's eyes were like flint. "Aunt, hold your tongue. Bella's in a heap. If you can't say anything helpful, please say nothing at all. You won't be alone, Bella. You have your family. And I'll do anything I can to help."

Victoria's heart was breaking. She needed to telephone Edward so he could tell her how to help their daughter. Poor Bella looked as though George *had* died. Victoria wished he had. It would have been better than this. If Doctor Farrell were close by, he'd have given Bella something to help with the shock and checked the baby was all right.

"Anne, would your physician come out to attend Bella?" she asked.

"I don't need a doctor, Mother. I'm not ill. Kate, please tell her I don't need to see anyone," Bella insisted.

"Victoria, perhaps you should let Bella decide," Kate said tentatively.

411

"All right, darling, whatever you want." Victoria knocked back her sherry.

"I thought I'd married the most wonderful man in the world. I was terrified I was going to lose him because he was dying. But it turns out he's a conman, I've never been married, he's possibly stolen the money you gave me and my child will be illegitimate."

"We're not certain he has taken the money," Victoria said.

What else could she say? It was a fortune that she and Edward had spent much of their lives earning, but Bella didn't need that guilt piled on her as well. Thankfully, they hadn't given Bella everything that was due to her. She wished she could get her hands on George – he'd look like he'd fallen down the cellar steps, hitting each one on the way down when she'd finished with him. She'd hated her own father and James Brakenridge, but never in her life had she experienced such loathing as she felt for the man who had hurt her beautiful daughter.

Bella spoke again, her voice wavering as she stroked her stomach.

"I was desperate to have his child. George told me he wanted a child, too. He said that if it was God's will, it would happen. Now I find out he had a daughter all along who he deserted. I feel utterly bereft."

The last thing Bella needed was Anne pontificating about how she suspected he was a rogue from the start. Knowing how Anne would take ages instructing her on how it was to be prepared, Victoria asked her to speak to the cook to fix a light menu for the next few days, allowing the girls some privacy. Meanwhile, she went to Anne's study to telephone Edward.

"I can hardly believe it. Poor Bella. I've been looking forward to her giving us a grandchild, but not under these circumstances," Edward said.

"It's heartbreaking. How we'll explain it to the child when it's older, I'll never know," Victoria said.

"There's plenty of time to work that out."

"Do you think he's taken the money?"

"Yes. The swine probably had it planned all along. I'll check with the bank to see if any sizeable sums of money have been withdrawn," Edward said.

"Will they tell you?" Victoria asked.

"I should think so. The manager has been a client of mine for years," Edward said. "There's something else, darling. I completed the sale of Centenary House today. I don't know if it was a blessing or a curse that you weren't here to say goodbye to your beloved shop."

"Did you ensure the staff got the bonuses I wanted them to have?"

"I did. They all send their thanks."

"How was Milly?"

"Tired and relieved the sale went through without a hitch. The purchase of her cottage was finalised, as well. And Harry and Jess sorted out her move, so you have nothing to worry about here."

Victoria choked back a tear.

"Oh, my love, are you upset about the shop going?" Edward asked.

"At any other time, I would have been, but all I can think about is Bella and what that charlatan has done to our precious girl."

"I feel so damned useless stuck here. Should I get the train tomorrow and join you?" Edward said.

413

"I want to see you, my love, but Bella is better off with just us women at the moment. If anyone can get her through this, it'll be Kate."

Next, Victoria rang Sean – for him, she had another task.

Chapter 36

The following evening, Sean parked his motor car at the end of Birch Road and made his way to the Rows on foot. If he left it parked in the Rows for any length of time, it would no doubt end up minus its mirrors or tyres.

As he walked, his mind turned to thoughts of Jane as it always did in quiet moments. To him, everything about her was perfect. He ached for her. Since the first time she'd visited the factory, she often called in on a Saturday, which had led to Charles also "just popping in to see how things were going". The question in Sean's mind was who did Jane really want to see. Kitty? That was who she said she was coming to see and was most likely the truth. Then again, she invariably stopped off in the office for a chat. Could she want to see him? He hoped so but doubted it. Or was it because – and this bothered him – Jane was actually calling in to see Charles? She always seemed thrilled to see him, smiling broadly and talking to him at length. Blast it. If she had feelings for Charles, he wished they'd get it over with and admit to it.

Sean pushed his concerns to the back of his mind as he reached Thurston Row, where Max had told him that he'd lived previously. He'd chosen to wait until evening to look for him, when he expected people to be home

415

having their evening meal before the alehouses opened.

The occupants of several houses informed him they'd never heard of Max. Although it had been some time since the lad had lived in the area, given his distinctive appearance, Sean found it unlikely no one remembered him. Perhaps he was wasting his time, but he couldn't think of another way to find him. He knocked on the next door and it was opened by a young man in his shirtsleeves, who looked confused to see Sean.

"Mr Kavanagh, sir. What can I do for yeh?"

Sean recognised the young weaver from the mill.

"Joe, isn't it?"

"Aye, sir. Is summat wrong?"

Sean hoped that having worked with him, the lad might tell him the truth.

"Joe, I'm looking for Uriah Maxwell – Max. He lived in this street at one time. I'm hoping he might be staying somewhere nearby again, but no one appears to know him. Or at least that's what they're telling me."

"I remember him. Tall red-headed lad. Not seen him recently, though. People are suspicious – they won't want to land the lad in bother. Is he in trouble?"

"No, Joe, just the opposite. I'm trying to help him."

"I believe you, but there will be plenty what won't. An' there's some as blames yer family for selling the mill, so they won't help yeh."

"Are things bad there?"

"It's all right, but it's not the same. I'd give me left leg to get outta that place, 'cos I never wanted to bloody strike an' then they put me in hospital just for trying to go back."

"I'm sorry, Joe."

"Let me get me jacket on an' tell Mam to hold me supper. I'll come with yeh. People might tell me if they've seen him."

An hour later and despite knocking on every door in the Rows, there was still no news of Max. Disappointed, Sean thanked Joe for his help, then added, "Joe, we can always use a hardworking man at the sewing factory. If you're interested, why don't you pop in for a chat tomorrow after you've finished at the mill. Say, seven?"

"Thanks, sir, I will." Joe touched his forelock as he returned to his home.

Sean was just about to get back in his car, when the thin boy who had been watching Joe and him for the last couple of streets spoke to him.

"Hey, mister, is Max in bother?"

"No, have you seen him?"

"I might have. If yeh don't mean him no harm, 'cos he were nice to me when he lived round here."

"I want to help him."

"How much is it worth to yeh?"

Sean put his hand in his pocket and pulled out a coin then showed it to the lad.

"There's some people livin' under the viaducts. I saw him going down there the other day. Yeh can't mistake him, 'cos he's a lanky carrot top."

Sean gave the lad the money and drove to the viaducts. It appalled him to see how many people were living there. Not just men, but entire families huddled against the walls. The combination of urine and excrement pervaded his nostrils and he fought the desire to heave. Unafraid of being robbed, as no one looked as though they had the strength to attack him, he checked all the way to the back

417

of each arch amid suspicious glances. In the final arch, he approached a woman and two urchins, who crouched around a fire, their eyes glued to a small animal roasting on a makeshift spit balanced over the flames.

As a train rumbled overhead, Sean bent down to speak to the woman, shuddering as he realised the much-anticipated meal was a rat. He forced himself to smile, hiding his revulsion. He was in the middle of trying to convince the mother he meant Max no harm, when Max's voice came from behind him.

"Mr Kavanagh, sir. It wasn't me. I'd never steal, even if I were starving."

Max had always been thin, but now he was painfully so, and his shirt was stained and torn.

"I know that, Max, we all do."

The woman was staring up at him through shielded eyes and Sean handed her some coins.

"Can we walk and talk in private, Max?"

As they moved away from the viaduct down a rough track, he explained to Max what they'd found out about George. The lad listened without a word until Sean asked, "Why did you just disappear, Max?"

"It's been building up between me and Mr Bristow for a long time – small things. First off, when Mrs Caldwell's pearls went missing . . . well, I saw him coming out of their bedroom that morning, but I had no proof. Then I took a phone call from his mam and he got angry, saying I was wrong and his parents were dead."

"Well, we know now his mother is still alive."

"Just before I left, he got a letter. I watched his face go pale while he was reading it. Later that morning, I found it screwed up on the floor behind the bin and I read it. I

418

know I shouldn't, but I didn't trust him. He caught me an' that's when he said he'd claim I'd been stealing and summat else . . . I can't tell you what else he said, though. But he had it in for me."

"Bastard! Max, please trust me. We want you to come back to work, but if you have a secret that you're afraid of us knowing, how can we take you back?"

Max picked at his fingers. "I never done nothing about it. Honest. I don't want to be locked up."

"You'll have to be more explicit."

Max pulled a grubby sleeve across his filthy face. He looked terrified.

"I hope I don't regret this . . . It's just . . . I've never had a girlfriend and I'll never get married – *now* do you get my drift?"

Sean stared at the lad, who was moving from one foot to the other nervously. Finally, realisation hit him.

"Good Lord! I'm shocked. I'd never have guessed, but I won't tell anyone. You can trust me."

"If I could stop feeling this way, I would, 'cos every time I look in the mirror, I'm ashamed of who I am. My gran guessed and she said she still loved me even if I am defective, so that was something. My parents never knew, thank God."

"You're not defective, Max. Don't ever feel that way. I realise that's how some people would view you, so you do need to be careful. Eventually, society might realise it's wrong to persecute people for who they are. But I'm afraid that day, if it ever comes, is a long way off."

"Thanks. I thought you might understand because you employ Darius."

"Why didn't you tell someone about George?"

419

"I couldn't work out what to do. I was scared because I felt he was always watching me. He's a bad sort, but I didn't know what his game was. Anyway, who would have accepted my word over his?"

"I understand why it was difficult for you to say anything."

"He guessed I'm different and made comments about my sort turning his guts."

"Why didn't you come to me? Especially if you suspected I might be sympathetic. I'd have given you a fair hearing."

"I was on the verge of doing that, but I was frightened. George was part of yer family. And when Mr Taylor said fifty pounds was missing, I guessed I was being set up and I legged it."

"You should have spoken up."

"I just wanted to get away. I was going to take the train to London. Even though I'd find it hard to get work without a character reference, I hoped I stood more chance there, 'cos I've heard it's a massive place."

"Why go the same day as George?"

"I left in the early hours. I didn't even know he'd gone until you told me just now."

"Why haven't you gone to London?"

"I didn't have any money to get a place to stay, never mind a train ticket. Ever since I started working, I've been saving, but when I was packing my bag the day I left, I realised the money from under my mattress were missing."

"You'll get every penny back, Max. And you need to promise me you'll always come to me if you have a problem in future."

"Thank you, sir, I will."

"My motor is over there. Come on – you're coming back with me. Mother and Edward don't need to be looking for a new footman right now. Besides, you look half starved."

"No, sir, I can't. Mr Taylor doesn't like me, either – he suspects I'm different. I'm best off out of it. I'll look for something else. Maybe I can get a job as a chauffeur somewhere. I enjoyed driving the ladies around. Employers won't be so bothered about my red hair if I'm not a footman."

Sean sighed. Damn it, he enjoyed driving himself, but he had to help the lad.

"What about being a general manservant and valet, with occasional driving?" he asked.

"Who for, sir?"

"My wife and me. She still takes a carriage. Our coachman won't drive motorised vehicles, but he's nearing retirement."

"That would be wonderful, sir."

"Good, that's settled, then. Come on."

"But I can't get in yer motor! I'm filthy, sir."

"Don't worry about that."

"I need to get me bag with me stuff."

"Is there anything important in it? Because no offence, lad, if it's as dirty as that shirt, it'll need burning."

"The only thing I have left is this picture of my gran." He pulled a photograph from his pocket. "Sold anything I had that was of any value to buy food. I'll give me bits to some of the others."

Sean watched Max saying goodbye to his fellow vagrants. How did these people end up here? These poor sods didn't even have a roof over their heads, but what could he do about it? Well, he would make a sizeable donation to the local fund for the poor first thing tomorrow. It wasn't much, but at least it was something.

His whole opinion of his supposed brother-in-law had been shattered. If he could get hold of him, he'd smash his face in for what he'd done to Bella, and for stealing from his mother and Max. As if that wasn't bad enough, that George was prepared to set up this young lad, even send him to prison because of who he found attractive, was beyond belief.

Max climbed into the car beside him. Sean placed his hands on the steering wheel and turned to Max.

"You're going to be doing some personal tasks for me, Max, so there's one thing I want to clear up. I'm definitely a ladies' man, if you get my meaning."

"No offence, sir, but you're not my type at all." A whisper of a smile played on Max's lips.

Sean roared with laughter. "You cheeky blighter."

Poor Max – he'd probably spend his life alone, never experiencing the joy of being with the person he loved. Sean knew how that felt. Would he have been better off being alone like Max? All Yvette and he ever did was bicker. If it weren't for his son, would he have preferred to be alone? Yes.

Back at Sean's home, he insisted Max accompany him through the front entrance. As Harris opened the door, he flinched at the sight of the dishevelled young lad.

"Max has suffered a great injustice. Please have a room prepared in the servants' quarters. Once he's got cleaned up and taken a couple of days to rest, he'll take up the post of my valet, chauffeur and general manservant. He'll need a suitable uniform and ask Cook to ensure he has a good meal as soon as possible," Sean said.

"As you wish, sir." Harris nodded then smiled at Max as he gestured for him to follow him.

Max stopped at the entrance to the servants' quarters.

"Thanks, Mr Kavanagh, sir."

"You're welcome, Max. And I'll ensure you're fully reimbursed," Sean said before making his way back out of the front door.

Over a couple of brandies, Sean updated Edward with Max's version of events.

Finally, Edward said, "I am stunned. George managed to dupe the entire family, not just Bella. A young, naïve girl in love could be forgiven for being gullible. After working for forty years as a solicitor, I prided myself on my ability to weigh people up, but George fooled me completely."

"You can't go through life suspecting everyone who is too nice. I'm sickened. If could get my hands on him, he'd be sorry," Sean said.

"*He* deserves to be punished, not men like Max."

"Kitty had the right idea when she heard he's a bigamist." Sean smiled mirthlessly.

"Why, what did she say?"

"She suggested that if we find him, we cut off his manhood and force-feed it to him with boiled potatoes and peas."

Edward chuckled. "I cannot argue with her there."

"How is Bella?"

"I was just on the phone with your mother before you arrived. She said Bella is like a different person." Edward gulped and turned away for a second. "I am not sure my

423

girl will ever get over this, Sean. She is saying she cannot ever come back and face people. Kate won't want to leave her, either. I might end up losing both of my daughters."

"That bastard. God forgive me, but I hope he catches some tropical disease while he's in Africa," Sean said.

"Cheers to that." Edward raised his glass.

We need to decide – shall we keep it to ourselves about Max's preferences?" Sean asked.

"Definitely. Your mother won't be bothered, but the fewer people who know, the better. We don't want him imprisoned or beaten up if it gets out."

"I don't want him ostracised by my servants, either. People can be cruel. Max said Taylor suspects and doesn't like him."

"I will speak to Taylor and make sure he keeps his suspicions to himself."

"Good, that's settled, then. I'll give Max the money back that he lost and extra to replace his belongings."

"Let me know how much I owe you."

"There's no need – I can cover it."

"I insist. I let that man into my family, so I want to pay Max back."

Sean nodded.

Edward peered over his glass. "You said he will be doing valeting duties. Are you not a little concerned about him working in such a personal role? I mean, running your bath, sorting your clothes and such."

"It crossed my mind, but no, he's told me straight – I'm not his type. I was actually quite offended."

Edward laughed, the ice in his drink clinking against the glass as his shoulders shook.

"That has put you in your place."

"It certainly has."

"You had better get home. How is Yvette doing?"

"I've insisted she stay home as the baby is overdue. Hopefully, she'll be less temperamental once it arrives."

"Pregnancy can affect women in strange ways and coming on top of the death of her parents . . . well, it cannot have been easy for her. But that doesn't help you any."

"Every time I mention it, she gets in a temper. She threw a plate at me last week. I wouldn't have minded, because her aim isn't that good, but it was full of stew – splashed all over me." He smiled ruefully.

"What has she had to say about this business with George?"

"I'm not sure I should say."

"Whyever not? I won't tell anyone else, if that is what you are worried about."

"She said George was the only member of my family she ever liked and now he's gone, she isn't bothering with the rest of you."

∽ᐠⓄⓄᐟ∾

Chapter 37

It was the end of summer when Sean's stomach clenched as Charles said the words Sean had been dreading for months.

"I have never been so happy. I am in love and I hope she feels the same way."

"You dark horse. Who is the lucky lady?"

Truthfully, he didn't care who it was – as long as it was anyone but Jane.

"It's Jane. What are you looking like that for?"

"Jane Kellet?"

"Yes. I am sure even you have noticed the beauty who comes in here to see Kitty."

"Does she have any idea how you feel about her?"

"She must have, surely. She was kind after I found out my mother had died. I couldn't believe my luck when we bumped into each other in town and she agreed to have tea with me."

"That's hardly proof of her feelings, buddy," Sean said.

"Maybe not, but she's always calling round here on a Saturday and then last Sunday, she dropped off a book I was interested in. I intend to marry her if she'll have me. Even the old man approves – he was extremely encouraging. You don't look that happy for me, though. I thought you

426

would be pleased for me."

Sean couldn't help feeling devastated. Jane had taken tea with Charles *and* she'd visited his house . . . Regardless of how wrong it was, he wanted Jane for himself. Maybe it had been his imagination, but he thought perhaps she cared for him, too.

At last, Sean said to Charles, "If you're right, I'm pleased for you. Really I am. But don't read too much into Jane being nice to you, that's all. She's kind to everyone."

"W-why are you being such a damp mop? I thought you would be in my c-corner."

Sean glanced away, running his hand through his hair. Charles rarely stammered any more. The last thing he wanted to do was hurt his friend.

"I'm sorry, buddy. Take no notice of me. I'm happy for you. She couldn't get a better man. I'm just in a lousy mood today and I've got a lot on. If you don't mind, I need to work."

Charles left looking dejected and Sean despised himself.

That evening, as Sean left the factory, the sky was a breathtaking mixture of coral-and-grey hues – the perfect summer evening for a walk along the towpath. At his car, he hesitated. He wanted to be there if Yvette's pains started, so reluctantly, he drove home. After dinner, Yvette complained that her feet were hurting and swollen, so he removed her stockings and massaged her feet for her. He wasn't a great lover of feet, but he wanted to show her that he cared.

"Have you thought of a name for the baby?" he asked.

"You can choose one. I have no preference," she said as she wiggled her toes.

"When Pierre was born, you were adamant you wanted to choose his name."

427

"Can't we talk about something else?"

"What would you prefer to talk about, then?"

"I thought Louise might come and see me now I'm imprisoned here. She claims she's too busy with her child. Honestly, she's all over him and he's so ordinary-looking, like her. Pierre may have his difficulties, but at least my son is beautiful."

That she'd referred to Pierre as *her* son wasn't lost on him. Yet, she barely saw him. Every morning if Yvette was home, Pierre was escorted down to the morning room by Jane or the nanny. All Yvette would do is kiss the top of his head, ask if he was well and then the poor boy was returned to the nursery.

Her nasty comment about her friend's child was also typical of Yvette's attitude. How was Sean meant to love her when he didn't like her? They'd dined several times with Peter and Louise, and he liked them both.

"When we dine with them, Louise speaks about their son with great affection, so to her I'm sure he is handsome," he said.

"I suppose that's your way of suggesting Louise is a better mother than I am."

"Not at all. I was merely—"

"Don't bother explaining – I'm going to bed." With that, she shoved his hands off her feet and flounced from the room.

Damn it! He was going to The Jubilee Club.

When he arrived at the club, Charles was playing poker and nodded to him in greeting. At least playing cards, they couldn't talk about Jane, Sean thought as he joined the game.

Several large brandies and three hours later, Sean,

barely able to see straight, stared over his cards at Harry on the opposite side of the table. It wasn't just his skill – Harry also had an unerring nerve that never seemed to fail him. Having lost a packet, Garrett Ackerley and Cyril Hornby-Smythe had already folded and left the club.

"I'm going home, Sean. Why don't you go, too?" Charles said.

"Why don't you mind your owwwn sodding business," Sean slurred.

Charles patted him on the shoulder. "All right, old chap, if that's the way it is with you this evening, I'm not going to argue with you when you're in this mood."

"I'll see he's all right," Harry said.

"I don't need looking afffter," Sean said.

"Right, I'm off." Charles hovered uncertainly.

He looked hurt. Sean's marriage was a disaster, but none of that was Charles' fault. Yet, without Sean's oldest friend even realising it, there was now a barrier between them – Jane. He was tormented by the possibility that they might end up together. It was irrational, because even if she didn't want Charles, someone as lovely as her was unlikely to be single for long and there was nothing he could do about it – except stamp out his feelings for her. He was failing miserably.

"Charles, I'm reeealy sorry, buddy. Don't be mad with me."

"No harm done. I'll see you soon," Charles said before walking off.

Harry pushed two more notes towards the pile of money in the centre of the table.

"Raise."

"I'll have to give you an IOU," Sean hiccupped.

Harry nodded.

Even in his inebriated state, Sean realised his full house was a good hand, but was it enough to beat Harry? How did the saying go? Unlucky in love – lucky at cards. Well, he certainly qualified for the first part. His wife hated him. Sean scribbled the promissory note.

"Come on, you've had enough. I'm taking you home," Harry said.

"I want to play my sland, er, hand," Sean said.

"All right. Let's see what you've got."

Sean laid his cards down. Harry smirked as he placed his own cards on the table.

"Royal flush. Come on – my chauffeur will drop you off."

"I can drive."

"You must be bloody joking. If you think I'm going to get it in the neck from Jess and my sisters for letting you wrap your car round a lamppost, you've got another thing coming."

Harry practically dragged Sean from the club with the help of his chauffeur and threw him in the back of his Rolls-Royce.

Outside Sean's house, Harry ripped up Sean's IOU, saying, "Stop playing poker. You're no good at it. And get a grip before you screw up yer life completely. If it were up to me, I'd give you a good kick up the arse. I used to envy you not being dragged up in the gutter, but it might have done you good, because one setback in life and you've gone to pieces."

Despite how drunk he was, Harry's words penetrated Sean's addled brain. He'd had more than one setback, but Harry wasn't to know that. Still, Harry was right, he was messing up his life.

Max opened the door.

"I'll take it from here. Come on, sir, let's get you upstairs," Max said.

"I'll shleep in my dwessing room."

"Good idea, sir," Max replied as they staggered upstairs.

Sean left for the factory the following morning before Yvette got up. He was hungover but threw himself into his work, determined to moderate his drinking from now on. He was ashamed of his behaviour the previous evening. What if the baby had been born while he was drunk? He didn't want to let this one down, as he had Pierre.

Just before close of business, Max knocked on his office door.

"Mr Kavanagh, sir. The doctor has been called and the mistress instructed me to collect you. She said to tell you that her labours begun early this morning and it's time for you to come home."

Back at the house, Sean flew up the stairs.

"No need to run, Sean. This young chap didn't waste time coming into the world. Quickest birth I've ever seen," Owain said.

Then the bundle the doctor was wrapping in a shawl mewled.

"I have another son?"

"You do indeed. A fine, strapping young man – the image of his father."

Sean took his son. His own mother was right. Love was infinite – you never ran out of capacity.

Once Owain had left, Sean sat on the end of the bed, stroking his son's tiny hand.

"Our son is wonderful. Just look at his fingers," Sean said.

"They're just fingers. Don't bother asking if I'm all right! I've only given birth to him alone and without Mama."

It was rare for her to mention needing or missing her mother, but it must be difficult at a time like this.

"Yvette, I'm so sorry. I would have come home earlier if you'd sent a message. And my mother would have been delighted to be here."

"Owain thought I was incredibly brave to cope alone."

So, it was Owain now. Not long ago, she thought he was a quack. But Sean was determined not to bicker with her today.

"He's right. How are you, darling?"

"Tired. I need to get some rest. Can you get Nanny to take him?"

"Don't you want to hold him or feed him first?"

Yvette tutted as she took the child from him. Because she was still grieving, Sean had reluctantly agreed to a wet nurse, but only after the first month, and then she'd be supervised at all times by the nanny.

"Thank you, Yvette, he's gorgeous. We have two sons now. Hopefully, we'll have a girl next."

"I don't want any more."

"We've not discussed it, but I was hoping to have more."

"That's because you don't have to put your body through carrying them or giving birth."

"We can talk about it when you've had time to recover."

"Don't think you can persuade me."

The last thing he wanted was to upset her and taint what should be a special time.

"All right, we can be careful in future."

"I will not allow you in my bed again. I am moving into the green room. It's been redecorated to suit my taste."

432

"So that's why you were redecorating it. You've been planning this for months."

"Yes, what of it?"

"We'll discuss it when you've rested."

"I mean it. You must keep your urges under control."

It was on the tip of his tongue to tell her that she had urges of her own. But no, he mustn't upset her – she'd had a tough few months. He'd be patient with her. Although how was a man expected to cope when his wife had told him he'd have to live the rest of his life without sex?

Perhaps that was why so many men took a mistress, but that wasn't something he wanted to do. He didn't want to be like Claude – unless it was with Jane. No. He didn't want her as his mistress – he loved her. Unfortunately, she liked Charles. Maybe it was more than that . . . Perhaps she loved Charles. The thought made his chest tighten.

He banished the thought from his mind, reaching out and stroking the baby's dark brown curls. He had a wife and two sons to care for – his own feelings must take second place.

"How about we name him Matthew?" he suggested, hoping that would please her.

"How can you be so insensitive?" she said.

"Insensitive?"

"Do you honestly think I want Papa's name being used all the time?"

"I'm sorry. I didn't think."

"You never do. Here . . . take him."

As he took the child from her, he realised she hadn't looked at the infant while she fed him. Saddened and worried, he took his son to the nursery and placed him in the waiting hands of Nanny.

"His name is Joshua Edward."

"He's a little love, if you don't mind my saying so, sir."

"I don't mind at all, Nanny. Thank you for taking care of them. Things haven't been easy for my wife."

"It's my pleasure, sir. Hopefully the mistress will feel better now this little one has been born. It's no fun being heavy with child in the hot weather."

"Has she been difficult? With the staff, I mean."

"I'm not sure it's my place to say, sir."

"That's a yes, then. I'd rather know."

"Well, she's not so bad with me. The housemaids get the worst of her moods. And I know the mistress has struck her personal maid a few times."

Sean sighed. "Thank you for telling me, Nanny. I'll do what I can to deal with it."

"You won't let on I've told you, will you, sir? Because they'll panic in case they lose their places. If they're dismissed without a character, they won't get taken on in another household."

"Please reassure them that no one in this house will be discharged unfairly without a reference. Tell them to come to me if they any have concerns about the way they're treated."

He peered into the cot where Pierre was sleeping. There was a little bubble at the edge of his mouth and a blond curl stuck to his forehead. Next to him was Tatty Bear. Sean picked it up and held it close to his face. When Jane had first passed it on to Pierre, it had smelled of her perfume and Sean hadn't been able to resist holding it, imagining himself burying his head in her hair. The aroma had faded – another small pleasure gone. He placed the bear back in the cot and kissed Pierre before going downstairs to eat alone.

Usually, he enjoyed roast beef, but tonight he pushed it around his plate, instead polishing off a bottle of wine. It appeared there was little hope for their marriage. Everyone had their breaking point. Had he reached his?

Taking the whiskey decanter to his study, he drank until he fell into a restless sleep in an armchair by the fire. So much for not drinking . . .

Since Bella had learned of George's deception, her father had discovered that George had taken all the money from their joint account. She'd gladly have given him every penny to make him happy if he'd loved her. Now, she had no husband and a child growing inside her. She was sure it would be a boy. A son who might grow up to look like George. Despite how difficult things were going to be, she still wanted her child. Longed for him with all of her heart. Born out of wedlock, her child would be a bastard – for that, she'd never forgive George.

She needed to get up, but the temptation to lie in bed all day was keeping her glued to the sheets. Slowly, she swung her legs out of bed and sat on the edge. Her legs trembled as she stood – she'd feel better after she'd eaten. She must keep going for the child's sake. Force herself to wash and dress. She knew she looked dreadful. He'd done this to her – made her into a drab, bitter woman. Gripping the bannister, she made her way downstairs.

Bella spooned jam onto her plate, aware her family were sneaking glances at her, watching for signs that she was about to fall apart again. She loved them all for the effort they were making to pretend things were normal. She allowed their small talk to wash over her as she took a slice of toast from the plate the footman presented to

435

her. That was when the pain caused her to clutch her stomach.

"Bella, dear, are you all right?" Her mother left her seat.

"Yes, sit back down, Mother," she replied, doubting her own words.

If only they'd stop looking at her. She picked up her knife and helped herself to some butter, forcing herself to bite into the toast – it tasted like cardboard. She tried not to scream as the pain gripped her once more and warm liquid spread between her legs.

"M-mother, I think I'm l-losing the baby," she said.

A couple of hours later, the doctor pronounced the baby was gone – that was all it took for her child, who had never taken a breath, to disappear. She was left with nothing – not even a body she could bury. It wasn't fair. None of it was fair.

She'd wept for hours after that, soaking her pillow before falling into a fitful sleep. When she woke, it was morning again. A new day where she had to face up to the reality that her dream of being a mother had been wiped away on a towel. Yvette was a terrible mother, but she now had two sons. Why had God allowed her to keep them yet taken her child?

"It was in the early stages, so as she's young and healthy, she could have a dozen more children," the doctor had said.

What did he know? She would never trust another man.

Now, she truly had lost everything. George had left her and her innocent child never got the chance of life. Bella wanted to join her child – willed God to take her – but her only release from her torment was a laudanum-induced sleep.

The next time she woke, there were voices. It seemed her mother was worried Bella had lost her reason. Had she? Perhaps. Her head was empty. She couldn't focus. There was nothing but pain. Sleep was the only release. Thankfully, it came.

The room was light, the sun shining on her face, but she didn't have the will to turn away. Voices again . . . Kate reassuring Victoria that they'd get Bella though this mess. What mess? She wanted to sleep again, to close her eyes and sleep forever – to shut out the disturbing thoughts that pervaded her mind. She didn't like being awake . . . Blackness came again.

When Bella woke next, it was dark again outside. She wanted to go back to sleep, but it wouldn't come. How long had she lain here? She could make out the outline of Kate, who was sleeping in the chair by her bedside. Either her mother or Kate had been there each night, of that she was sure.

She was being selfish. They loved her. She must pull through this. George couldn't be allowed to ruin the lives of her family. But what was she going to do with the rest of her life? All she'd ever wanted was to be a wife and mother. She couldn't lock herself away from the world forever. Her mother wouldn't allow her to give in. Her mother was strong – she must be, too. George had stolen everything else from her. She wouldn't let him take her future.

⣏⣿⣾⣹

Chapter 38

Victoria made her way up the stairs of Anne's home, intending to persuade Bella to take a walk in Hyde Park. She hoped the fresh air and the sight of the trees, which were rapidly turning a stunning mixture of golds and reds, might lift her spirits. What nonsense – it would take more than a few autumn leaves to repair Bella's broken heart.

Bella was adamant she couldn't return to Faredene and face the gossips, and Victoria was getting desperate. Every time she looked at Bella and saw how much her daughter, who had once been so fun-loving, was suffering, it was like having a knife plunged into her own heart. There was no trace of the girl who had first met George Bristow – he'd ripped her blossoming confidence away from her. For a while, Victoria had thought Bella would never recover from the loss of her child and she'd gladly have sacrificed her own life to save her daughter's sanity.

Once Bella had finally become coherent, Kate had spent a great deal of time talking to her sister, holding her, letting her cry on her shoulder, trying to get through to her. Today was no different. Outside one of Anne's guest-rooms, Victoria pressed her ear against the door. Even though she wasn't proud of herself for eavesdropping, she needed reassurance that her daughter was going to be all right.

"Look, Bella, we've been over this before, but I'm going to say it again. Broken hearts mend. It hurts like hell, but it won't kill you. Trust me – mine's broken and I'm not dead yet," Kate said.

"I'm so ashamed. What will people say when they find out?" Bella replied.

"Don't go back to Faredene, then."

Victoria stifled a gasp. She didn't want Bella to stay in London.

"Could I stay here with you?" Bella said.

"Not here, but you can come with me to wherever I decide to open my school for girls. There's a couple of properties I'm interested in."

"Where are they?"

"Ireland and Shropshire. It won't be anything grand, but it'll be somewhere that girls can realise there's more to life than finding a husband. Marriage is fine if that's what they want, but I want them to know there are options."

"You'll make a wonderful headmistress."

"Like I said, you can come with me. I can't think of a better person to provide pastoral care and teach art or music."

"You'd let me work with you?"

"Not let you. I need you. To be honest, I'm apprehensive of doing it alone."

"Why not Faredene?"

"It might be easier if I was setting it up there."

"So why not? Is it because you don't want to see Sean?" Poor Kate, Victoria thought.

"Faredene would be ideal. Because I've realised being

able to see him is better than spending every day missing him, wondering what he's doing or if he's all right. But if you want to come with me, that might not be the best place for you."

"I don't want to spoil your plans."

"You won't be. Besides, working with you is more important."

"Can you afford to open a school?"

"Sure, there's my inheritance from my grandparents. And I have the money Father and Victoria gave me after the mill was sold. You won't need to put any money in. I'll gladly share what I have with you. We'll be equal partners."

Kate was so kind, Victoria thought.

"I'd like to be with you, but I don't expect you to make me a partner. Although I'll miss home – George has stolen that from me. It's best for everyone if I don't go back to Faredene. If I'm not there, Mother and Father can give people whatever explanation they choose without being embarrassed by me."

Victoria had no intention of losing both of their daughters because Bella assumed they'd be embarrassed by her. She tapped on the door tentatively and entered without waiting to be told to come in.

"Girls, I'm sorry to interrupt. I'll not pretend that I haven't heard what you were talking about."

Kate scowled. "All I want is to help Bella. Maybe she doesn't want to go back to Faredene."

"I understand, but please hear me out."

Both girls nodded.

"Your school is a wonderful idea. There's an ideal property called The Grange, which is a mile further out from town than Faredene Hall. It's been refurbished recently, but now the owners are moving abroad because he has a new diplomatic posting."

Kate's lips moved, but Victoria cut her off.

"Please let me finish, Kate. I want to keep you both nearby. The Grange has a lodge house, which would be perfect for your father and me."

"What about your house? It was Father's childhood home – he might not want to leave," Bella said.

"Your father will love the idea. Besides, Anne said that if we ever moved, she'd want to buy our house." Victoria grinned. "Perhaps that's why she's been staying with us so much. It's part of her cunning plot to drive us out by being so difficult to live with."

"Mother, I'm not sure I can go back to Faredene," Bella said.

"If you don't like the idea, I understand. Wherever you decide to live, we'll be happy to help both of you girls financially if needed."

"I'm not sure . . ." Bella said.

"Locating the school at The Grange would mean you won't have to be in the heart of town. Not that you have anything to be ashamed about," Victoria said.

"Don't do it for the rest of us – your feelings are paramount," Kate said.

"I do want to go home, but . . ." Bella said.

Victoria took a deep breath – she was going to suggest letting history repeat itself.

"Bella, people believed George was dying, so tell them he did and that he was buried in London. If you ever choose to get married again, you can tell your husband the truth then. No one else needs to know."

"Won't there be legal paperwork to be sorted, as I was never really married?"

"I'm sure your father can sort that discreetly. Trust me – if you want to keep what's happened a secret, it can work."

"I don't see how you can be so sure. Besides, I'll never marry again. Or I suppose I should say marry, as I've never actually been married."

"You might change your mind one day. That's why I'm suggesting you tell people he's dead."

"You – the most honest person I know – you'd help me forge a lie so that I can come home?"

"Yes, in a heartbeat."

"People would find out," Bella said.

Victoria took a seat opposite Kate on the other side of Bella's bed. Even after all these years, the girls still didn't know Sean wasn't her natural-born son. She'd spoken to him last night about Bella's reluctance to come home and he'd given his permission for her to tell them both.

"I know it's possible to keep a secret because I've kept one of my own for over thirty years."

The girls were agog as she relayed the story of how she'd found Sean and moved to Faredene.

"Anne doesn't know. Neither does Yvette. It's because Sean trusts you both that he's allowed me to tell you the truth. It's important to him you still think of him as your brother," she ended.

"I do, of course I do," Bella said.

"Well, I never have thought of him that way. But sure, that's the problem – he doesn't see me as anything other than a friend or a sister," Kate said.

"As much as I believe he may have been happier with

you, he has a wife and children now and I don't think he could live with himself if he left them."

"Don't worry – he doesn't know I care for him and I'll never tell him. You know, I'd never have guessed he wasn't yours. Sure, he's the image of you," Kate said.

"Would you prefer me to keep the truth about my sham of a marriage from people?" Bella asked.

"Your father and I'll be happy with whatever you decide."

"You're not embarrassed by me?"

"Never."

Bella turned from her mother to her sister.

"Kate, do you want to go back to Faredene?"

"I'm game if you are. It'll be grand. We can throw ourselves into our new venture. It'll be more fun than being a couple of spinster sisters gathering dust."

"Kate, you definitely have Father's sense of humour," Bella said.

"Sorry, just hoping to lighten the mood. We're not going to allow you to throw the rest of your life away because of a scoundrel, are we, Victoria?"

"Absolutely not. The school will give you both something to focus on."

Bella grabbed her pillow and covered her face. Victoria stared at Kate, who shrugged her shoulders as though to say she didn't know what Bella was thinking.

Finally, Bella looked up. Her face was awash with tears again.

"Thank you for offering to assist us with the school. We'd appreciate any financial help you can give us, because I want to be a proper partner."

"And Faredene? Please say you'll come back," Victoria said.

443

"I won't lie about my marriage – I'd be too afraid someone will find out eventually."

"Do you need longer to think about it?" Victoria asked.

"No. Everyone would sympathise with me about the loss of my *wonderful* husband. I'm certain I can't face lying to people for the rest of my life. It would change who I am eventually."

"We can set up our school anywhere, Bella, if that's what you need," Kate said.

Victoria steeled herself, hoping they wouldn't move too far away. She and Edward could move, but that would mean leaving Sean and their grandchildren.

Bella bit her lip. "We'll set up our school in Faredene, but I'm going to tell people the truth. I won't live my life in shame. If they want to talk about me, they can. I expect some people will pity me and others will laugh behind my back, but that's up to them."

"Good for you," Victoria said, praying Bella wouldn't regret her bravery.

"What if my history puts parents off sending their girls to our school?" Bella asked Kate.

"Then they're not the right families for us. That's settled, then. We're going back to Faredene," Kate said.

By October, all signs of summer had vanished and the rain that clattered against the windows of Sean's office matched his mood perfectly. His head was banging. Now sleeping alone, he felt less like a married man than ever. When did a relationship stop being a marriage? They didn't have sex, there was no affection between them at all. They didn't spend time together apart from mealtimes and they certainly didn't talk about anything that mattered. He felt like the loneliest man on the planet.

Sean didn't know how much more he could cope with. He couldn't talk to anyone about his feelings for Jane, either. He thought about confiding in Kate – they'd been close before she'd moved to London. But she might think he was a cad for lusting after a woman other than his wife and he didn't like the idea of her disapproval. He was sure everyone would think he was detestable if they knew he couldn't love his wife – the woman who had given him two beautiful sons.

"Sean, you look as though you're in a world of your own."

"Charles, sorry – I didn't hear you come in. What can we do for you today?"

"You've looked down recently and as I was passing on my way back from the golf course, I thought I'd call in and see how you are."

"Thanks, buddy. I'm fine."

"We have been friends too long for me to believe that. What is getting you down, making you drink too much? Is it Yvette?" Charles asked.

Sean needed to tell someone at least part of what was bothering him.

"It's everything about my marriage. If I didn't have this place, I don't know how I'd cope. I have you to thank for backing me."

"I enjoy having something to dabble in. Besides, when I was younger and life at home was unbearable, you were always there for me."

"The last thing I want for my boys is for them to grow up in an unhappy home, but that's what's happening. I try with Yvette, really I do. But nothing is ever good enough for her and at times I feel like I'm trapped in hell. As for the intimate side of things, I can't understand it. Yvette likes sex as much as I do, but she refuses to let me near her now."

"You don't think she's got someone else, do you?"

"Don't think I haven't considered that. But no. She only goes to Peter and Louise's. From what I understand, she's with Louise most of the time – unless Yvette is out riding."

"She could be doing the groom," Charles said with a grin.

"Thanks – that's comforting. If she is, I wish she'd run off with him, leaving me free to get on with my life, because if my little friend doesn't get regular exercise, it's going to wither away," Sean said, laughing.

"If you don't want to take a mistress or use the services of the ladies that The Jubilee Club can provide, there is nothing else for it, old chap. You will have to exercise on your own."

They both laughed like a pair of adolescent boys talking about girls behind the bike sheds. It didn't solve his problems, but even joking about them with Charles helped – at least for a short while.

After his friend had left, Sean managed to focus on compiling the wages until a knock came at his door.

"Come in," he said.

"Right, Sean, they're all getting off home. You said you'd lock up, so I'm off now," Kitty said.

"Is it that time already?"

Where had the time gone? He'd been so lost in his thoughts that he'd not noticed the hours slipping by.

"You all right, Sean?"

"I'm fine. Has Harry's chauffeur arrived? If not, I can drop you off up at the Hall – it's coming down in buckets out there."

"No, love. I've got summat to do before I go home today. Besides, I'm not sure I'd get in a car wi' you. Have yeh been drinking during the day again?"

"Aww, Kitty, don't you start. I'm not driving, anyway. Max is coming back for me."

"Don't aww Kitty me. I grew up livin' with a drunk an' I know someone with a problem when I see 'em. I've told yeh before I should tell yer mam how often you drink at work."

"Don't, Kitty. Please – she worries enough."

"Well, get yerself sorted, then. I know Yvette can be a pain in the backside, but you've got everything going for you, so don't mess it up, love," she said as she left his office.

Chapter 39

Victoria had instructed Stokes to park in the street next to Sean's factory.

"There she is now," she said as Kitty came hurrying round the corner, holding her hat as her already drenched coat clung to her legs.

Falling leaves swirled around her.

"Blimey! It's awful out there. I'd better sit over here or you'll be soaked if I get too close," Kitty said, taking a seat in the back of the Daimler.

"Don't worry – my clothes are already damp."

"Thanks for this, love. I couldn't face doing it on me own."

"I felt terrible keeping it from Milly this morning," Victoria said.

"We're doing the right thing, protecting her from this. I'm convinced she doesn't know anything about what's going on."

"You're probably right. However, I find secrets always lead to more problems in the end."

"Don't say that. I've still never told Albert who raped me. If he finds out, he'll finish Brakenridge off for sure. Anyway, I don't think you've got the hang of retirement – yer always rushing around. Jane could have helped Milly to hang her new curtains."

"I couldn't refuse. Not when she coped without us both at the shop before it sold when I was busy looking after Bella."

"How is she now?"

"Kate's keeping her busy. Setting up the school will be simple enough – attracting pupils will be the main challenge. The gossip-mongering fuelled by Ethel Hornby-Smythe has been in full force. Poor Bella – she's handled it incredibly well."

"Is she getting to hear much of what's being said, then?"

"Unfortunately, a few of her so-called friends have visited to give their support, as they put it, when all they really wanted was the gossip. Kate, bless her, is fearsome when she wants to be – she's given the worst of them short shrift. One or two have proved to be genuine friends. I just hope the scandal doesn't affect the uptake at the school too much. There's no denying Bella's reputation will put some parents off enrolling their daughters, but the girls intend advertising nationally, so fingers crossed."

"Trust Hornby-Smythe to be driving the gossips."

"Hmm, I was thinking it's about time I knocked her off her unofficial throne."

"Sounds good to me. How are you planning to do that?" Kitty asked.

"That will take some thinking about. And Jess and I are keen to do something together to help the residents of the Rows, but I have too much else on at the moment. I don't mind telling you, I'll be glad to move into the lodge house. Anne's already become lady of the manor, acting as though our house already belongs to her."

"What servants are you taking with yeh, then?" Kitty said.

"Just the cook and a housemaid. I've never been comfortable with a large staff. And Anne seems happy to retain the others."

"Is there no sign of Doctor Farrell proposing to her yet?" Kitty said.

"Not that I'm aware of. And I'm sure if he'd said something, we'd all know about it. She obviously cares for him, so I hope he does return her feelings."

As the motor pulled up outside an imposing five-storey town house, the two women clenched hands before climbing out.

"Is Edward all right about what we're doing?" Kitty asked.

"Yes. He wanted to come with us until I explained it would be less embarrassing for Charles if it was just the two of us."

"You'll do all the talking, won't you?"

Victoria nodded.

When the front door opened, she asked if they could speak to Mr Charles Brakenridge, praying they wouldn't run into his father. The butler took their names.

"If you would wait in the morning room, I will see if the master is home," he said as he showed them the way.

The room was furnished in dark red and gold. It had a distinctly masculine feel. Victoria could almost hear the younger woman's heart pounding.

"Mrs Caldwell, Kitty, what a pleasant surprise," Charles said. He was smiling but he looked perplexed. "Can I get you some refreshments?"

"No thank you, Charles, my dear. I'm afraid we're here on a delicate matter. Is your father home? It would be best if we weren't disturbed," Victoria said.

"He is out and won't be back for a while yet."

"May we sit down, Charles?"

"Of course, my apologies. I am a little taken aback. Is it something to do with Sean?"

Kitty played nervously with the clasp on her bag, which opened, spilling the contents on the floor. She bent, stuffing her handkerchief and purse back in her bag.

"It's about our Jane," she said without looking up.

"I can assure you, my intentions towards your niece are honourable. I have done nothing to warrant your concern."

Victoria rested on the edge of the chair.

"The thing is, we must ask for your complete discretion in this matter. We need your word you will tell no one what we're about to discuss. Neither your father, Milly nor Jane must ever find out about our discussion."

Charles nodded, clearly bemused and uneasy.

"Charles, I believe you care for Jane," Victoria said.

"I do. I have made no advances, but I hope she returns my affections."

"The thing is, Charles, Jane isn't Kitty's niece. She's her illegitimate daughter."

"I see – though, to be honest, I don't see how that changes anything. It doesn't matter to me. I don't think any less of her."

Victoria's fingers drummed the arm of the chair.

"Charles, there's no delicate way to put this. Jane is your sister."

"M-my sister?" He held his hand to his temples. "H-how can that be? I d-don't understand."

"It were yer dad. He forced himself on me when I were a young lass," Kitty said.

"Dear God. I n-need a d-drink. If you will excuse me." Charles got up and poured himself one from the decanter on the table. "I don't know w-what to say. I'm s-s-sickened."

"Kitty wanted you to know because there can be no possibility of a relationship between you and Jane. I'm sure you understand that. Jane's unaware of the situation and we'd like it to stay that way," Victoria said.

Poor Charles – he looked crestfallen. She hated having been forced to bring him such news.

"Is t-t-there anything else?" he stammered.

Victoria stood, pulling Kitty up with her.

"No. We assume we can trust you to put a stop to whatever bond is forming between the two of you."

"You have m-my word. I understand. I'm s-s-sorry for what my f-father did to you, Kitty."

"It weren't nobody's fault but his, love. The thing is, when yer dad found out I were carrying, he threatened to kill the baby if I didn't get rid of it. It's too late now for him to do anything about it, but I still don't want him to know about the twins."

"He won't h-hear about it from me. I would like to be alone. So if it is all the s-same to you, I will s-s-s-show you out." He opened the morning room door.

Kitty's expression mirrored Victoria's. She was deeply saddened for Charles although relieved it was over so quickly. The two women scurried after Charles across the hallway. He didn't bother to ring for his butler to open the door. It was clear he wanted to be rid of them as much as they wanted to leave.

Just as Charles reached for the doorknob, the bell rang. Charles yanked the door open.

"What are you doing opening the door yourself, man?

What the devil is the world coming to?" James Brakenridge snarled as his manservant pushed his wheelchair over the threshold.

Victoria flinched. She'd seen him at a distance, but never close to. On one side of his face was a mass of mutilated flesh where his eye once was and a dented, disfigured scalp was revealed where his hair had been. The skin on the other side was like parchment and what remained of his hairline had receded, thin strands hanging past his neck.

He stared from Victoria to Kitty.

"My God, you two whores in *my* house!"

Charles' eyes flashed. "It is not your house, F-father. Do n-not insult my g-guests."

"What's the matter with you, man? F-f-forgotten how to talk properly, have you?"

"Don't be so bloody cruel," Kitty said.

James let out a mirthless laugh. "Here about our daughter, are you?"

Kitty let out a strangled cry.

"You knew Jane was your daughter?" Charles glared at his father, his face horrified.

"She's got the Brakenridge eyes, but I couldn't be certain until I saw those two interfering bitches here." He glanced back at his servant. "Wheel me further in, man, and shut the blasted door."

Charles' jaw tightened. "B-but you encouraged m-me to c-court her, you foul, evil bastard."

"What is the matter with you, you damned milk sop? That little by-blow of mine is a tasty piece, regardless of who her mother is."

"But she's my s-sister."

James removed his scarf, allowing it to fall to the floor. The tall wiry-haired manservant retrieved it, his eyes all the while fixed on Charles.

"A touch of inbreeding hurts no one – the royals do it all the time."

"Not with their sister, you ugly, filthy git," Kitty snarled.

"Don't screech at me like that. You might be dolled up like a dog's dinner, swanning around at the Hall with the rest of your tribe, but you'll always belong in the gutter."

Victoria's bile rose. Time had dampened her hatred of this man – now, it coursed through her veins, stronger than ever.

"What sort of animal are you? How could you be so cruel to your own son?" she hissed.

James nodded in her direction. "Still meddling then, you stuck-up shrew. You lost me my wife and now you're trying to stop my son from having a harmless tussle . . ."

"S-s-shut up right n-now, Father, or I swear I'll throttle you! I wanted to m-marry Jane," Charles said.

"Help me out of this thing. I'll walk," James said to his manservant.

The man helped James to stand, passing him his crutches that were leaning against the wall.

"You hateful bastard. The poor sod's heartbroken. Any fool can see that," Kitty said, gesturing towards Charles.

"I'll invite my daughter round for tea. She can get to know her father."

"You go anywhere near her an' I swear I'll swing for yeh," Kitty said, poking a finger at his chest.

"L-ladies. If you will excuse us. I n-need to speak to my f-father."

454

"Will you be all right, Charles? You know where I am if you need anything," Victoria said.

"Of course he'll be all right. The pair of you, out!"

Kitty stood her ground.

"You can't push me around any more, you dirty old bastard. We're leaving, but not because of you."

Victoria placed a restraining hand on Kitty's arm.

"What are you hanging around for, then? Do you want a rematch? Even with that scar, I'd still give you a seeing to."

Kitty snarled at him. "I never wanted to go with you in the first place. I'd rather rub me arse on a brick than come near you. Is that clear enough for you?"

He turned, sneering at Kitty. "I love women with a bit of spark. I bet that pretty girl of ours is a tigress in the bedroom."

"Father! That is enough. T-take him to his r-room now." Charles' voice echoed around the hallway.

"Don't you dare order me around, you insolent pup! I should have strangled you at birth," James roared.

Before anyone could stop her, Kitty snatched up his crutch, unbalancing James so he fell forwards, landing on his knees. She brought it down with a loud crack on his back and he lay on the floor groaning. Victoria screamed as the manservant grabbed the crutch off Kitty and raised it above her. Charles grasped the end.

"H-help him up," he said to the manservant. "Please, l-ladies, allow me to deal with this," he added.

"It's all right, Charles, we're leaving." Victoria gripped Kitty's sleeve and pulled her through the front door.

Both women were shaking. From behind, they heard James' voice roaring after them.

"You'll regret this, bitch. If you think I don't know that Harry caused my injuries, you're as simple as that dead brother of yours."

Stokes hovered by the car looking bewildered.

"Madam, may I be of assistance?"

Victoria stood on the pavement, allowing Kitty to climb in the car first, anxious to make sure her friend didn't go back to the house to continue the fracas.

"Just take us to Faredene Hall, please."

Once they were seated, Kitty said, "James Brakenridge is the bleedin' Devil. I've wanted to do that for a long time. I just wish I'd killed him."

"No you don't, Kitty. All we can do now is pray Charles can control his father and hope that James doesn't press charges against you. I've thought it before, but today has confirmed it. James is sick in the head. The way he behaves isn't normal."

"I only wish I'd smacked his man, as well."

"Why? You can't blame him for trying to protect James, although if he'd hit you, I'd have tackled him myself."

"I didn't want to land one on him because of that. He's a Charnock! One of the younger brothers – I'm not sure which he was. They all looked alike and were as thick as pig shit. Except the youngest – I don't know about him. Mind, he was probably as bad."

Victoria clutched Kitty's arm. "Kitty, dear, did you catch what James said as we were walking out of the door?"

Kitty's eyes flashed again. "Aye, I heard him. He's claiming that our Harry was responsible for his injuries."

"Surely he won't try to cause trouble. If he does, it'll be his word against Harry's. I doubt James will want to risk being charged for his involvement in Teddy's murder. All the same, it'll be best if you warn Harry and Jess."

"I'll tell him as soon as we get back to the Hall."

"We must ensure Harry doesn't go charging round there to confront James."

"He won't. Our Harry knows how to keep a secret."

"If James tries to press charges, Edward will use his legal contacts to find Harry the best barrister."

"I doubt it'll be needed. Harry will probably scarper back to America if there's any sign o' trouble."

A sense of foreboding washed over Victoria. She wondered if they'd poked a sleeping bear.

಄ᎧᎧᎧ

Chapter 40

The wheels of Kate's automobile crunched their way along the gravel driveway as she approached the entrance of Caldwell Grange Girls' School. Even when it stood below an ominous sky, to her the building was beautiful. Built over five floors, the red brick building had an attractive pillared portico and stone cornices. It gave the right impression – a solid building. Well cared for but not flamboyant.

November wasn't the ideal time to open a school, but Kate was hopeful that regular advertisements over the coming months would be successful. They'd placed them in publications aimed at ladies in the hope that mothers wanting something more than marriage for their daughters would persuade their husbands to make enquiries. They decided they needed to appeal to the more broad-minded parents, because there was no point in getting the wrong families interested – it would only lead to problems further down the line.

As she pushed open the solid oak studded door, it creaked loudly. She'd get their handyman to fix it – first impressions were important. Bella met her in the hallway.

"Wow, now would you look at you," Kate said. "Give me a twirl."

"Miss Bella Caldwell dazzled her gossipy neighbours by wearing a lilac bluebell-shaped skirt with an overskirt teamed with a white lace blouse with sloping shoulders and a wide collar," Bella said as she turned round, her arms held out.

At least she's pretending to take an interest in her appearance and fashion again, Kate thought. Although there was a long way to go before her now almost reclusive sister was back to normal.

"Anyway, forget about my outfit for now. I've exciting news – two more families are coming to view the school," Bella added.

"Marvellous. You're so good with the parents," Kate said as she removed her hat and coat.

"I love you for trying to bolster my confidence, but there's no need. I'm just grateful for the chance to be part of all this . . ." Bella gestured vaguely, indicating the school.

"You're an important part."

"I'm glad you're back from town. I've got to go there now. Mother's going to Blackpool with Milly and I offered to run them to the train station."

"They never said when I called in at the lodge house yesterday."

"It's all very last-minute. Apparently, Agnes has broken her arm and Milly's going to stay there for a few weeks to help out at the guest-house," Bella said.

"Why's Victoria going?"

"Milly doesn't fancy making the journey alone. Mother's only staying for the weekend."

"Do you want me to drive them to the station?" Kate asked.

"No. If it's all right with you, on my way back, I'm

going to check on the boys and visit for a while."

"I can't blame you for being concerned about them. That one has as much maternal instinct as a cuckoo."

"She makes Sean miserable, as well. He panders to her, but she still treats him like an inferior. And I'm sure he drinks more than any of us realise. I wish there were something we could do."

"Sometimes you have to let people sort things out in their own way."

"You're probably right. I'll see you later," Bella said as she made for the door.

"Are you all right? You're awfully pale, Sweet Pea," Kate asked.

Bella turned. "I'm doing as well as can be expected, I guess. How about you? Are you happy, Kate?"

"Of course – our school will be a triumph."

"Not about the school – with life."

"I'd like to find a man to warm my bed."

"Kate!"

"I'm just being realistic. I've accepted that I'll never find the sort of love like Father has for your mother."

"You could still get married."

"Now that would be a fine thing, but it's not going to happen while your gorgeous brother is alive and kicking."

"Is it difficult for you, knowing he can never be yours?"

"I'm getting used to it. Now, it only hurts when I breathe." Kate managed a laugh. "I'll content myself with being his friend or sister, whatever he wants. What amazes me is that I only dream about poisoning Yvette once a day."

Bella laughed. "That sounds like you've planned it."

"Only in my darkest moments. What about you? Are you getting over George?"

"I don't miss him as much as you might think. Not since I realised that I was in love with a man who was a fake."

"Are you still furious with him?"

"Only when I'm awake," Bella grinned. "No, I'm not angry. And I'm getting over the humiliation. Though, I'm not thrilled that he ruined my chances of finding a decent husband now that I'm tarnished goods."

"That's not true. Sure, any decent man would understand you were blameless."

"It doesn't matter – I won't put myself in that position again. Even though I desperately want a child, that will never happen now, either. Thankfully, I have Pierre and Joshua to lavish my affection on."

"Ah, George deserves to suffer for what he did to you. I wonder where he is now and if he's hoodwinking some other poor soul."

"I'd like to think I was the last woman he conned, although I wouldn't stake my life on it."

"Me neither. Lying for some people is a habit they can't break. George is a stranger to the truth if ever I've met one."

"I hope he's happy," Bella said.

"You're so forgiving. You were too good for him."

Bella shrugged. "I'm sure there will be another scandal before too long and things will get easier. One thing I know for certain is I'm going to come through this a stronger person. If I ever happen to meet up with George again, he'll find out I'm no longer a pushover." Bella laughed. "And I'm determined to be happy or die trying."

"Grand, neither of us will get ourselves in a heap over a man again. For you and me, Sis, our future is what we make it and together, nothing can stop us. It's going to be grand," Kate said, smiling.

Victoria paused as she packed her things into the small case that was lying on their bed.

"Do you think it'll be even colder in Blackpool? Should I pack something warmer?"

Edward moved away from the fire that was roaring in the grate, rubbed a hole in the condensation on the bedroom window and peered out.

"It is about to pour out there. With the wind coming off the sea, it is likely to be freezing, so I suggest you wrap up as warm as you can." He grinned. "Perhaps you should even take a pair of my long johns."

Victoria walked over to her wardrobe and pulled out a fur coat.

"I think I'll pass on the undergarments, but thanks for the offer."

"You are welcome. Don't blame me if you get chilblains somewhere unmentionable."

"Will you be all right without me?"

"Kirby and I will be fine, if I can prise him out of his basket by the range. That is clearly his new favourite place. And if I get bored, I will slip along to my office and interfere there. Or pop up to the school and poke my nose into the girls' business."

"I'll definitely be back Tuesday, as I can't afford to miss the Women's Guild meeting. Jess and I are going to raise the question of finding out who owns the Rows and forcing them to renovate."

"I have told you, it might not be that easy. The landlord might have other ideas."

"Then we'll just have to bring him round to our way of thinking."

"Lord help him. I've seen that determined look before."

"I hope everything else will be all right while I'm away."

"It will. You have been on edge ever since the altercation with Brakenridge and nothing has happened, so I think he was just blowing hot air."

"I hope you're right. It's not just him . . . I worry about the boys, too. Yvette seems incapable of loving them. I know it bothers Sean."

"Yvette's loss, if you ask me. They are fine boys."

"I've seen her face when Pierre tries to speak. She's embarrassed by him."

"Don't start thinking about that now. You will only get upset before you go on your little jaunt."

"Hardly a jaunt – I just didn't want to say no to Milly when she's so eager to help Agnes out."

"I'm surprised she wanted to go, given how she feels about travelling."

"Jess and Harry offered to take her over there or pay for some additional staff, but you know Milly when it comes to those she loves being in need. She wants to help Agnes herself. I wish you were coming with me, but it will be nice to see Agnes again."

"I wouldn't be much company. With my leg this bad, I couldn't be tramping around Blackpool. Now, that sounds to me as though Bella has just pulled up outside."

Victoria closed her case.

"Quick kiss, then I'd better get off to collect Milly if we're to catch our train, because unlike Kate, Bella doesn't drive everywhere at top speed."

"I am still not sure I approve of them driving," Edward said as she pulled away.

Victoria kissed him for a second time.

"They're liberated young women, so you'd best get used to it, my darling, because I don't think we'll hold our daughters back from anything they want to do."

Yvette pushed the food around her plate. Sean prepared himself for what she was about to say. She clearly had something on her mind and he was in no mood to put up with one of her tantrums.

"I'm thinking of going to see Louise," she said, breaking the silence.

"Why not invite her and their son here for a change? It'll be nice for Pierre and Joshua to have another child around," Sean said.

The shadow of an eye-roll crossed Yvette's face.

"Absolutely not. It is boring here."

"All right, you can go, but you must at least wait until Sunday so I can spend the day with the boys."

"Don't worry about me – I will just have no life. It doesn't matter if I am miserable, stuck in this house all day with nothing to look at but our pathetic little garden."

"For God's sake, Yvette. Stop overreacting. You could try looking after our sons for once."

"How dare you! I am here day in, day out looking after *your* children, running *your* household, with no thanks or appreciation. If you loved me as a husband should, you would want me to be happy."

"I appreciate what you do."

"Well, you don't show it. All you do is complain about me wanting a little time to myself and my spending.

Perhaps I should stop buying the boys clothes – maybe you would prefer them to run around naked."

"You know I don't, but while we're discussing clothes, the bill from your new dressmaker was astronomical."

"It's not my fault your mother sold her business. I don't like the designs the couple who took over her shop have, so I am forced to go to Chester or Manchester."

"No one forced you to go on a three-day shopping trip or to spend so much. You have a wardrobe full of clothes."

"So, am I not allowed to treat myself to a nightdress or slip without your permission now?"

"You're being ridiculous."

Yvette launched her plate of smoked salmon and scrambled eggs across the table at him, the plate smashing on the floor. Next, she grasped the bowl of primroses, shoving it off the table. Sean jumped up and stayed her hand as she went for the coffee pot.

"Not now, Harris," he growled as the dining room door opened. He leaned close to Yvette, his voice low. "That's enough. You're behaving like a bloody child."

"Get your hands off me." She tried to remove her hand from his grip. "Are you about to hit me now?"

Sean pulled his hand away.

"I wouldn't dream of it. Just calm down, please, this is so bloody wearing."

"That is the second time you have sworn and I won't stand for it. Papa never used bad language to Mama."

"Sorry, but you drive me to it."

"I might have known that it would be my fault, as well. I can do no right. Not like the marvellous Jane. To hear you talk, she is so blasted wonderful with Pierre that I'm surprised you don't want to marry her."

Sean stiffened. If Yvette suspected he had feelings for Jane, he'd never hear the last of it. Worse still, Jane and Charles might find out.

"Jane's an employee and I appreciate her efforts with our son, nothing more."

"Maybe if I was a servant, you would treat me better. Don't think I'm not aware you have told the servants to come to you if they have any problems. You have undermined me in my own home."

"Only because you threatened and even lashed out at them."

"I hate you, Sean Kavanagh. I wish I had never married you," she said.

Sean groaned – he'd heard this so many times. It was now depressingly clear that they'd never agree about anything – particularly not what it took to have a happy marriage. She was impossible to live with. He either gave her everything she wanted and put his own needs at the bottom of the pile, or she got angry. His breakfast uneaten again, he asked Harris to tell Max that he wanted to drive himself today.

As Sean pulled up outside the factory, he wondered why he'd even bothered coming in when the last thing he felt like doing was working. Being a Saturday, it was also half-day closing. There was no point pretending – he wanted to get away from his wife and, if she called in, he hoped to see Jane, even if it was only for a few minutes.

Since Charles had confessed his love for Jane, Sean had made far too many excuses to visit the nursery so he could talk to her . . . look at her. All of his earlier good intentions were failing. She was a drug he desperately needed. Perhaps it was the thought that if Charles had his way, Jane would be Mrs Brakenridge before long. She wouldn't carry on working, surely. Certainly not once she had a child of her own. The thought of Jane and Charles making a child together was too painful to dwell on – he needed to sort out his own marriage.

Straightening his cravat, he pushed thoughts of their argument from his mind and went inside. As he took his seat behind his desk, an envelope in Charles' handwriting caught his attention. He picked up the letter and began reading, his brow furrowing:

Sean,

Deep down, I have always known my father was evil, but I never believed he could hate me as much as he does. By the time you read this letter, it will be too late. I intend to end my life – take my father with me. That way, he won't hurt anyone else.

I can see your face and imagine you shouting at me that I am taking the coward's way out. Maybe you are right, but it is my decision.

My last will and testament is in the top drawer of your desk. I have left everything to you, my best friend.
Charles

As the words sank in, Sean dropped the letter on the desk. Jesus Christ, no!

"Is something wrong, sir?" the receptionist asked as he charged past.

"Ask Mrs Nelson to lock up at the end of the shift," Sean called as he charged through reception.

He'd not stopped to put on his hat or coat but was oblivious to the biting wind as he dragged open his car door.

Please don't let me be too late to stop him. He can't die!

What could James have possibly done to upset Charles so much? Why hadn't Charles talked to him?

Guilt hit him. Recently, whenever Charles had visited the factory, Sean had pretended to be too busy to have conversations. He'd been selfish, only thinking of himself. His preoccupation had meant he wasn't there to protect Pierre from the wet nurse. And now Charles might be dead because Sean had been so wrapped up in his own problems that he'd not noticed his friend hurting.

Thoughts flew through his mind as he jumped behind the wheel and careered out of the factory gates, heading towards Charles' house.

Abandoning the motor car, he tore up the front steps two at a time. He pounded on the door.

"Come on. Come on. Open up!"

His hands were sweating, adrenaline coursing through him. He shoved the door as it opened slightly.

ᴇᴏᴏᴏᴏ

Chapter 41

"Where's Charles? Where is he?" Sean bellowed at the maid, stopping in his tracks as she covered her face. He was too late. This time, his voice was hollow. "Where is he?"

"He's in his bedroom – third door on the right, first landing. The doctor is still up there with him," the petite maid said on a sob.

Sean ascended the stairs, his step slower, dreading what was awaiting him but knowing he had to see for himself before he could accept it. His heart was pounding, his mouth dry. Outside the bedroom door, a thick rope lay coiled. Jesus! surely there must have been an easier way than hanging . . .

Owain was standing by the dresser. He nodded his greeting to Sean.

"Sean, come in. I'm just completing the paperwork."

"Did he hang himself? Sorry, stupid bloody question."

"From the bannister. Must have been in the early hours. The poor butler got a shock. I've sent him to get a brandy for his nerves. I see a lot of death. Somehow, it's worse when they take their own lives. It seems a pointless waste when others cling to life, desperate for a few more precious days."

"Can I see him?"

"It might be best not to . . ."

Sean had already pulled back the sheet. He'd hoped his friend would look at peace. Instead, the sight horrified him.

"Aww, Charles. Not like this, buddy. I'm sorry I let you down. If I'd have known something was wrong . . ."

Sean gripped his friend's body, pulling him against him, his hand twisting Charles' shirt.

"I just w-wish there were something I could have done. If only you'd told me." Unable to bear the sight any longer, Sean laid Charles' corpse down and turned away. Tears threatened. "I'll never forgive myself for not saving him."

Owain patted Sean's shoulder, handing him a handkerchief.

"Take your time and I'll wait here until you're ready to leave."

Eventually, Sean turned back to the bed. Charles was covered again, sparing Sean further anguish.

"It appears he poisoned his father before he took his own life. His father's manservant is distraught – doesn't want to leave his side. He'll have to soon, as they'll be taking the bodies away. I understand he's been with him years."

Sean nodded.

"They've not found a note, which is unusual."

"He left one for me at our factory."

"Well, that ties things up."

"He wrote to me knowing I wouldn't see it until this morning – that it would be too late for me to stop him."

"Did you have any idea he was so low?"

"No . . . I've been too busy to talk to him recently. If

470

I'd suspected in any way, I'd have helped him – tried to do something . . . tried to help."

"I understand. The most troubled often keep it to themselves. Then again, even if we do know, we generally think people will pull through whatever it is they're facing."

"I'll never forgive myself for being so selfish – for not realising."

"Lots of people feel as though they're at the edge of despair at some point. Thankfully, most of us come back from it. But for others, things are just too much – you weren't to know."

"I should have made time for him. I've been so wrapped up in my own life, my own problems."

"Most of us are. It's always the same – people think that by ending their life, they're ending their own pain, even making life easier for others. Instead, it causes a lifetime of anguish for those left behind. You mustn't blame yourself. It's not your fault."

Sean returned to the factory to break the news to Kitty and the other staff. As Kitty groped for a chair, Sean steadied her.

"It's knocked me for six, Sean. I feel sick. Is it all right if I get off home?"

"Of course, Kitty. I'll tell them all to go home, then I'll drive you to the Hall."

At first, the news of Charles' death brought a stunned silence to the factory floor. Then Sean's irritation spiked when a woman asked if their jobs were safe. How could he blame her? Life went on – they had bills to pay and it would be Christmas soon.

Neither of them spoke on the brief journey to the Hall.

After dropping Kitty off, Sean went home and spent the rest of the day playing with his sons, taking solace from their childish innocence. He even helped to give them their tea, much to the horror of the nanny, who clearly thought it improper for a parent to stay so long in the nursery.

When she explained apologetically that it was time for the boys' baths, Sean made his way to his wife's room. If you were alive, surely there was always a chance for things to improve, no matter how bleak they looked. He'd wondered himself at one time if he had the strength to face what lay ahead. Even though his life wasn't perfect, he was glad he'd not gone through with it. Thank God Jess had noticed how low he'd been. She'd saved him. Taken the trouble to talk to him. It was more than he'd done for Charles . . .

Was there hope for his marriage?

"Can you leave us, please?" Sean said to his wife's maid, who was helping her to pack for her visit to the Mason home.

"What *is* going on, Sean. You had no right to dismiss my maid," Yvette said.

When they were alone, Sean guided Yvette to sit beside him on the bed.

"Charles is dead – he committed suicide this morning."

Her eyes were wide with interest.

"Really, why?"

"He was unhappy. I don't have all the details."

Yvette looked deflated.

"He had probably had enough of living with his father. Who is going to take care of him now?"

"He's dead, as well. Charles poisoned him."

"That will cause a scandal. Who is going to inherit Charles' fortune?"

"He left me everything, including the factory."

"Aren't you the lucky one! Someone else leaving you their fortune. Everyone is desperate to throw their money at you."

"Yvette, there's nothing lucky about this situation. Don't you understand what I'm telling you? My best friend is dead."

"I am not stupid. But don't act all upset. I mean, you hadn't seen him for years before he came back to Faredene. This is another unexpected windfall for us."

"I can't see it that way."

"Well, I think we should buy somewhere bigger. It's such a shame Faredene Hall isn't available. We could use the money to build somewhere. That would show Louise. Peter could design it for me."

Sean stiffened. "How can you be so callous?"

"Don't expect me to be crying for you. I didn't get any sympathy when Papa died."

"It wasn't just your father – it was your mother, as well. And you got plenty of compassion. I spent months trying to cosset you and support you through your bereavement."

"Always the hero."

"I know we're not close, Yvette, but I've had to look at the dead body of my friend today. Can't you show me any sympathy?"

"I'm here, aren't I? If I had my way, I'd be back in America. But my Papa betrayed me, left me penniless."

"That's not what your father was doing."

"That is easy for you to say. Your parents never let you down. You have no idea how it feels."

Sean turned away. If only she knew how his real parents

had abandoned him. But there was no way he could ever tell her and risk having it thrown back in his face constantly.

"I am still going to go to Louise's tomorrow. I hope you don't expect me to change my arrangements," she said.

"No, don't change your arrangements. Clearly, I'll not get any support here, so I'm going to spend the night at my club."

"Fine, I will just stay here and look after *your* children. It is always about what you want. It isn't only me who thinks you are tight-fisted – everyone I talk to about you agrees with me."

"That's because they listen to your biased version of our lives. By the time I get home tomorrow, no doubt you'll have left."

"Don't look at me as though I disgust you! Go on, drown your sorrows in a bottle like you always do. It is a pity you don't drown yourself and join your friend."

There was nothing to be gained from continuing the argument, so he retreated to his room, where he put a few essential items into a valise.

As he closed the front door, a thought hit him – Jane would be devasted if she'd returned Charles' feelings. He hadn't thought of her all day . . . That was a first. Normally, she was never out of his head for more than five minutes. She must be told.

In response to his knock, he listened as the key turned in the lock of Milly's front door. Sean took a step back as blond hair and large grey eyes peered through the crack in the door.

"Jane? I need to speak to you."

"Of course. Is it Pierre?"

"No. Can I come in?"

She pulled the door open further. "You look ghastly. Are you all right?"

Jane stepped aside so Sean could enter. After locking the door behind him, she led him down the corridor.

"Is Milly not here?"

"No. Mam's gone to Blackpool to see Aunt Agnes."

"May I sit down?"

"Sorry, where are my manners? I'll pour you a drink. You look like you need it. All Mam has is whiskey. I hope that's all right?"

Jane handed him a large one, which he sank and then held the glass out again. She refilled it, moved a ginger kitten out of the way and sat on the sofa next to him.

"What's wrong, Sean?"

"Sorry, Jane. I'm not sure exactly how deeply you feel about him, but I know you like him. It's Charles . . ."

"Charles Brakenridge?"

"Yes. I'm so sorry. I understand you and he were, er . . . friends. I wish there was an easy way to say this. He committed suicide and took his father with him."

Her face drained of colour.

"Are you all right? Can I do anything?" Sean asked.

She downed her own drink.

"I-I've been popping into the factory because I wanted to get to know . . . my b-brother. I hoped one day I could tell him and he'd be pleased."

Sean's mouth dropped open as her words burned into his mind.

"Charles was your brother?"

"Yes. Mam and Dad told me an' Robert before Dad

475

died. Dad was concerned that we might find out one day, so he wanted to tell us himself. That way, he could make sure we were in no doubt that he couldn't have loved us more if we'd been his natural children. We understood his reasons for telling us."

Sean's eyes were wide. "I can't believe it. It must have been difficult for Milly, you finding out that she isn't your real mother."

"I didn't realise you knew," Jane said.

"Only that Kitty was raped and your parents adopted you from her. I didn't know who attacked her."

"It was hard for Mam to tell us, but she'd have done anything for Dad. Her only request was that we keep it to ourselves, at least while she's still alive."

"God, you seem to have taken it better than I did."

"What do you mean?"

Sean explained about his own birth. Even though he'd never told his own wife, he found he wanted to share his lifelong secret – his shame – with Jane.

"Perhaps it was how you found out that made it more upsetting," Jane said when he'd finished.

"You said you tried to get to know Charles. Did Milly not mind?"

A single tear tracked down her face.

"She didn't know, as I mainly saw him at the factory when I visited town on a Saturday. She assumed I was simply calling to see Auntie Kitty at the factory, so I never mentioned he was there."

"At least you got to know him better."

Jane wrapped her arms around herself as tears swamped her. Sean wanted to embrace her but didn't trust himself to stop there.

Finally, she said, "Yes, but he developed other feelings for me – that was my fault. I shouldn't have tried to get to know him."

"He'd still have loved you, Jane."

Jane's breath hitched. "You can't be sure of that."

"I can. You mustn't blame yourself. He was attracted to you instantly."

"Thank you for that. You're always so kind. I had no idea he thought of me in that way. If I had, I'd have kept my distance."

How could she not realise that being so beautiful, most men would want to possess her? he wondered.

"Can I pour you another drink?" he asked.

Without waiting for her reply, Sean replenished the glass of whiskey in her quivering hand. He held his own hands over hers for a few seconds.

"I can't stop shaking," Jane said as tears flowed.

"It's the shock."

"You still don't understand. I've not told you the worst part. Yesterday, Charles came to see me and told me he loved me. I explained I was his sister, but he said he didn't care. He said he still loved me and asked me to run away with him. I was horrible to him. I said he was as vile as his rapist father – that he disgusted me. Now, I can't take it back."

Sean's heart was racing. Charles had considered committing incest with his sister? It sounded out of character, but he believed her. As tears seeped through her closed eyelids, he fought the desire to hold her.

"I believe that in time he'd have come to his senses – realised what he was suggesting was wrong. You mustn't blame yourself for what you said. Charles would have understood why you reacted as you did."

477

"I'm going to have to tell Robert how the half-brother he never met is dead because of me."

"Jane, I keep saying this and you're not listening. You're not to blame."

"I wish I could believe you. Will you hold me, please?"

Sean placed his arm around her shoulders. He could feel the heat from her body as she rested her head on his chest. He longed to tell her he loved her, but it would be wrong. She was hurting. They both were.

"Tell me about him, please. What was he like as a boy?" Jane said.

As he held her close, they talked about Charles, drinking whiskey until eventually, Sean said reluctantly, "I must go. I'm staying at my club tonight and I need to be there before long if I'm to get a room and a meal."

"Aren't you going home?"

"I know it's a cliché, but my wife doesn't understand me," he said with a wan smile.

"Would you stay with me? Like this, I mean. I don't want to be alone."

"I'm parked outside. It might give people the wrong impression."

"I could go to the Hall, but I'm not ready to be with them all. Please stay. I can make us some food."

"I don't think it's a good idea. I'm just concerned about what people might say."

"Not many cars come up this road and even if someone does see your car, they're unlikely to know it's yours or realise Mam isn't here. Sorry, I'm being pushy. It's just I don't want to be alone."

"If you're sure. I suppose it is pitch-black out there. And it's cold, so there won't be many people around. I'll stay," he said, at that moment wanting nothing more than to comfort her.

After they'd eaten some sandwiches, they sat on the sofa together, his arm around her shoulder, until they dozed off.

Sean woke wondering where he was. He'd taken off his jacket and kicked off his shoes at some point. Jane's head was still resting on him, her hair against his cheek. It smelled of sunshine.

How he hated himself. His best friend was dead and because of that, perversely, this had been the best night of his life. Here with Jane, he felt more loved than he'd ever done with Yvette, even during their most intimate acts.

He strained to look at the clock on the mantel. It was five thirty. He gently lifted her hand to his lips. Slowly, she looked up at him.

"I didn't realise you were awake," Sean said.

"Why were you kissing my hand?"

"What? Erm – I . . . sorry."

"You did kiss my hand, didn't you?"

"Erm . . . I . . . no."

"Did I imagine it? I've embarrassed you, I'm so sorry."

This might be his only chance to express his true feelings. It was a risk, but regardless of the consequences, he had to tell her.

"Jane, my angel, I love you," he whispered.

She pulled away from him, her eyes wide.

"You love me?"

"I'm sorry – I shouldn't have said anything."

Her voice was a whisper. "I feel the same about you."

He kissed her softly at first, then passionately.

Sean thought he must be in heaven. Surely that was the only way he could be kissing Jane. He might be in heaven, but he'd deserve to go to hell if he let this go any further.

He pulled away. "I'm so sorry, my darling – I shouldn't have done that. I'm a married man. I can't be unfaithful."

Jane nodded. "I understand. You're right. We're both upset."

"I meant what I said, I do love you, but I can't leave Yvette or my sons. I promised Matthew I'd take care of Yvette. As for the boys, I desperately want my sons to grow up in a happy, stable home. And I'd never ask you to be my mistress. To be honest, being so deceitful would destroy us eventually."

"I understand. The last thing I want is to break up your marriage. I'd hate to leave Pierre's education to someone else, but if we can't control ourselves, I'll have no choice."

Sean smiled sadly. "I've been avoiding you since you started working with him. I'm an expert at it. If we're sensible, you'll be with him during the day and gone before I get home from work." Sean could feel his muscles tightening. "I'm going to hate it. But my boys, especially Pierre's welfare, must come first."

Jane used her index finger to blot a tear from the edge of her eye as she spoke.

"It's the only way."

Damn! Now he'd hurt Jane, as well. He should have kept his mouth shut. What was wrong with him?

"I'd better go."

Sean own eyes smarted as he watched her eyes fill. He reached out and lifted a strand of her baby blonde hair that had fallen on her face. His hand froze as they heard Kitty's voice outside the front door.

"Jane, love, it's Auntie Kitty. I need to speak to yeh."

"Quickly! Take your things and hide upstairs," Jane whispered. "I'm coming," she shouted.

Sean grabbed his jacket and crept upstairs, crouching on the landing beside an occasional table housing an oil lamp. What could Kitty possibly want this early in the morning?

"Auntie Kitty! Come into the parlour – you look as though you've seen a ghost. What's wrong?"

Once they were in the lounge, Sean could still hear Kitty's voice. She was evidently struggling to speak.

"I'm sorry, l-love. But I couldn't sleep last night, so I had to come over early and t-tell you myself before you h-heard about it from someone else. It's Charles . . ."

At that precise moment, Milly's kitten leaped on Sean's shoulder. He jumped back, knocking against the table, sending the oil lamp crashing to the floor. Blast! He didn't move for what felt like an age. All he could hear from downstairs was a faint mumble.

"Sean! Get yer backside down 'ere sharpish," Kitty bellowed up the stairs.

Sean pulled on his shoes and made his way downstairs, tucking his shirt in as he went. He didn't care about himself – he was ready to take on anyone's condemnation – but he didn't want people thinking less of Jane.

"What the fluffin' hell have you two been up to?" Kitty's face was livid. "I've come round here to talk to my niece, only to find out that you've taken her down. Turned her into yer bit on the side. Fancy hiding upstairs,

481

yeh bloody coward. If I'd not been in such a state, I'd have realised that were your car outside. What will people think? I oughta kick yer backside for yeh!"

"Kitty, it's not what you think. We love each other. Nothing happened . . . Just a kiss . . . We didn't plan it. I came here to talk – to tell her about Charles. I wasn't aware Milly was away. Jane explained Charles was her brother. She was upset. One thing led to another."

Kitty grasped the back of the chair to steady herself.

"Flaming hell! H-how the flipping heck did you find out he's your brother?" she whispered.

"Sean, let me explain, please," Jane said. "Mam and Dad told Robert and me just before he died. I should never have tried to get close to Charles, but I wanted to get to know my brother," she added.

"Bleeding Nora! Can this day get any worse? Why the hell did they tell yeh?" Kitty made her way to the sofa and plonked down with a sigh.

Jane grasped Kitty's hand as she explained. Kitty looked even more shaken than when she'd arrived.

"If our Milly were here, I'd strangle her! Why didn't she tell me that you knew?"

"She only did it for Dad. It was difficult for her, Auntie Kitty. She didn't want you to know as well because she thought that would change everything."

"I still wish she'd told me. I never would have tried to be yer mam or owt. Wait until I speak to her."

"No. You mustn't. Please, Auntie Kitty – keep it to yourself. She can't know I've told you."

"It all too complicated, all these blinking secrets. Me head is mashed with it."

"Mam's doing her best to keep things as normal as

possible. That's why I didn't tell her I was trying to get to know Charles."

"I told Charles it weren't right, you an' him. If I'd kept me gob shut, he might still be alive," Kitty said.

"Don't blame yourself, Kitty. Charles loved Jane and he'd have needed to be told at some point," Sean said.

"It wasn't your fault, so you mustn't reproach yourself, Auntie Kitty."

"I thought you were smitten with Charles," Kitty said.

"No, it's always been Sean," Jane said.

It had always been him . . . Even in the middle of all this mess, her words warmed his heart.

"I can't take all this in," Kitty said. "But for now, we need to talk about you two."

Sean explained how they were going to keep their distance so Jane could continue teaching Pierre. Finally, Kitty said she'd keep their secret providing nothing happened between them ever again. Not even a kiss.

"I'll be keeping my eyes on both of youse, mind."

"Thank you, Kitty," he said.

"I'm not doing it for you, yeh big gormless lout. I'm protecting Jane."

"I realise that."

Sean had no defence for his behaviour. Kitty was right to be angry.

"You stay away from her," Kitty said, pointing at Sean.

"I don't know how the hell I'll stand it, but I promise," Sean said.

"If you don't, I swear you'll be singing like a choirboy when I've finished with you."

Sean raised his eyebrows. "I won't do anything to hurt Jane – you have my word." He rubbed his temples, the thought of a life trapped in a loveless marriage looming before him. Then his anger flared. "I told you the truth, Kitty. Nothing happened."

"It better be."

"I'd never lie to you."

"Aww, Tatty Head, it's not that I don't care about yeh. I understand Yvette's a right cow. But unless she'll give you a divorce, yeh realise there's no hope for youse two, don't yeh?"

Both Jane and Sean nodded.

"I'm going to wash these glasses. When I get back, I'm taking Jane up to the Hall. Say goodbye to each other while I'm in the kitchen," she said kindly.

Sean couldn't help himself. He pulled Jane into his arms and kissed her goodbye. It brought him such pleasure while tearing at his heart. It was killing him.

He climbed into his car, aware that Jane was watching him. No matter what it took, he would control his drinking. He may rue the day, but he'd do everything in his power to make Yvette happy. To protect his sons and provide for them. As for his happiness . . . well, that would come from doing what he believed was the right thing. From being someone he could respect.

What if he failed? Just because they stayed married wouldn't mean his marriage was a happy one. In fact, it was hell.

Yvette didn't love him, either. She hated him – that much she made evident. All she wanted from him was money and freedom. How could he risk letting Pierre and Joshua grow up in an unhappy home?

He glanced out of the car window. Jane was standing on the doorstep. Slowly, he climbed back out of his car.

"Jane, I'm sorry I have to ask you in this way, but if Yvette will agree to a divorce, will you marry me?"

Jane gulped. "Will she agree?"

"She's as unhappy as I am. Apart from the boys, she can have anything she wants. If her father hadn't bequeathed her inheritance to me, I'm sure she'd have gone back to America straight after Joshua was born. And I'll give her cause to divorce me. I'll take a woman to a hotel and get someone to take photographs. I understand that's how it's done. You won't be named."

Jane nodded.

"Is that a yes?" Sean asked.

"It is. But I'll understand if you can't go through with it. I know the boys mean the world to you. They come first."

"This is for them, too. I've been trying to keep the marriage going for their sake, but things will only get worse."

"Then yes, I will marry you, Sean Kavanagh."

"I wish I could kiss you, but someone might see. And if Kitty catches us, she'll murder me," Sean said as he reached out and touched her fingers.

Jane grinned. "Soon, we'll be able to kiss whenever we want."

Sean drove home in a daze. Once he'd parked in the mews, he remained in his automobile while he composed himself.

This was a turning point in his and his sons' lives. The chance for them to be happy. Jane loved him! For the first time since he'd left New Orleans, Sean felt truly optimistic.

Epilogue

George grimaced as he looked out across the vast tea plantation that stood at the foothills of the Himalayas. Despite the servant boy stood by his side wafting him with a bamboo punkah fan, sweat dripped incessantly into George's eyes. He wiped them angrily. Bloody December and he was sweating buckets.

Things hadn't turned out how he'd expected. After all of his sacrifices, letting that git Moby Dick have Daphne . . . Even the thought of that fat bastard riding her in a few years turned his guts.

Had cancer taken his ma yet? he wondered. It had made it harder for him to leave her, to lie about where he was going, pretending he was heading for Africa. He doubted they'd track him down, but he couldn't take any chances. Life was bloody unfair. All he'd been trying to do was get a decent life. He'd worked hard for it.

But the money he'd got away with was nowhere near as much as he wanted. Or expected to get if he'd had time to help Anne on her way to the graveyard so that Bella inherited half of her fortune. Maybe even all of it, if he'd got rid of Kate as well.

It was all the fault of that swine Max. Sticking his interfering nose in other people's business – he should have stuck a knife in the little git. Why hadn't he? Perhaps he'd become too settled in his cosy life in Faredene. He'd come to care about some of them – it had happened without him even noticing.

What surprised George was that he was missing Bella. Not as much as he was missing Kirby, mind. He'd thought about taking him, but that would have been cruel – he was too old to travel all the way to India.

George, you're a soft sod.

Aye, that was it. He'd been too bleeding soft. But he wouldn't make that mistake again.

"George, darling."

He turned to face the plump, unattractive middle-aged widow.

On board the ship, George had quickly ascertained that she had no family and was travelling to India for the first time to visit the tea plantation her husband had recently bequeathed her. She was the ideal target. Lonely, rich and desperate. Or so he'd thought.

After all this time servicing her needs and living in her home, she'd refused to marry him. Bedding her made his skin crawl – he couldn't help comparing her rolls of flesh to Bella's beautiful, slim sexy body.

"Yes, my precious, what can I do for you?" he said.

"I thought we could take a rest before we change for dinner."

George snaked his arms around her, his lips caressing her wrinkled neck and breastbone.

"My darling, I can think of nothing I would enjoy more. I can't get enough of you."

Bleeding hell. The things he did for money. Maybe he could go back to London and save Daphne. Or to Faredene and throw himself at Bella's feet . . . beg her forgiveness.

She might forgive him . . . She didn't know about Matthew and Sophia – no one did. It hadn't been all his fault. Sophia had been startled by a rat that had run across her feet. All it took was just a little push at that exact moment. They probably would have died on the *Titanic* anyway, he reasoned . . .

Now that you're hooked,
why not try

BEYOND DECEIT

Part of the Faredene Saga

Here's a sneak preview of
Chapter 1 in the third book
in the series

COMING 2022

cൟൟ

Chapter 1

January, 1913

Bella banged the steering wheel as her small automobile hissed and choked noisily along the bustling high street. Although thankful for the anonymity provided by her hat and scarf, she cringed as passers-by stared in her direction. Why did this have to happen on a market day when town was so busy?

Her shoulders tensed as she tightened her grip on the wheel. No, no, no. Please don't give up on me, she thought. If it broke down now, it would set the Faredene gossips off again.

Although Bella and Kate suspected some ladies envied the freedom driving gave them, many regarded it a disgrace. And the last thing Bella needed was more unwanted attention. Despite what she proclaimed to anyone who would listen, she was far from over the pain and embarrassment George's betrayal had caused her. Even after all these months, she dreaded coming into town, especially since her first attack of nerves on Christmas Eve. But she refused to give in. Shame or fear would not stop her from carrying on a normal life. He would *not* rob her of anything else. One day, she'd be as strong as the image she portrayed.

As a loud bang emitted from the engine, two elderly women on the pavement shrieked, one dropping her shopping basket, potatoes rolling into the road, drawing more attention to Bella and her ailing vehicle. Quickly, she yanked the steering wheel, almost colliding with a crowded omnibus, and careered onto Station Road just before the engine ground to a halt outside the large iron gates of Faredene Automobile Repairs.

Bella's hands trembled as she plucked at her hatpin, her heart pounding, her breath coming in gasps as she dragged her scarf from around her neck, throwing it and her navy feather-trimmed hat onto the seat next to her. She clutched at the front of her coat as a searing pain stabbed at her chest.

You're not going to die – you're safe, she told herself as she pulled off her gloves then removed a handkerchief from her bag, dabbing her forehead before using it to rub her sweating palms.

Come on, Bella. Calm down. Breathe.

This was the second attack now. Was she ill? Or was it simply as she feared – a case of hysteria?

Don't think about it – breathe, breathe.

She closed her eyes, willing herself to believe that it would pass . . .

After what seemed an eternity, her breathing slowed and she glanced at her wristwatch. It was eleven thirty. Bella shivered. She must have been sitting here for at least ten minutes – she needed to move.

After taking her compact from her bag, she checked her appearance in the mirror before topping her glossy brown hair with her hat and donning her gloves once more. Ready to face the world again, she stepped onto the icy cobbles, her legs trembling as she negotiated her way through the small yard towards the building.

She wanted nothing more than to go home, but she couldn't just abandon the car. At least the garage owner was one of the few people with whom she felt entirely comfortable. He was a decent man – a widower in his late sixties and with no interest in town gossip.

At the open doors, she smoothed the front of her coat and made her way inside, where she spotted a pair of legs protruding from under a black automobile. He was hard of hearing – if she wanted to attract his attention, there was only one way to do so. Stooping, she tugged at his blue overalls.

The legs jerked. "What the hell!"

A short, stocky man who appeared to be in his early thirties slid from underneath the vehicle. His glasses dangling from one ear, he got to his feet.

"Sorry, miss, I didn't mean to curse. You gave me a fright," he said as he straightened his spectacles.

Bella looked guiltily at the small gash above his eyebrow. "I'm the one who should be apologising."

The man pressed his fingers to the cut. "It's nothing that'll kill me."

"I thought you were the owner."

He smiled, showing his slightly uneven teeth. "And he's as deaf as a post, so that was the only way to get his attention . . ."

Reluctantly, Bella found herself returning his smile. "Exactly."

"Well, what can I do for you, miss?"

"Isn't he here? I'm afraid my car has broken down."

"He retired. I'm the new owner. Richard Yates." After quickly using a rag to wipe off the oil, he offered his hand.

Bella tentatively extended her gloved fingers. "He never said he was leaving."

"It was all quite sudden. He's gone to live with his daughter and her family. As he wanted a quick sale, I got a bargain."

Richard Yates had a friendly face, but she didn't like dealing with men – not any more.

With no thought for how she'd get home or what she'd do about the car, she said, "Right, well, I wish you every success, Mr Yates." She turned to leave.

"Don't you want your car fixing?"

"No, thank you, it's quite all right." She was being foolish, but she needed to get home. "I'll telephone my father," she added.

"Is he a mechanic?"

"No. He's a semi-retired solicitor." Her cheeks burned.

"Perhaps not the best person to help, then. I assume that's your vehicle . . ." Smiling, he pointed to her automobile in the road.

"Yes, but—"

"I'm a first-rate mechanic."

"It's not that. I'm sure you're very competent."

"What's the problem, then?"

"I'm just used to dealing with—"

"Well, if you let me fix your motor, you'll be used to me. I don't want to sound desperate, but if all of his customers take your stance, I'll be out of business in a month – and I don't mind admitting, I've sunk every penny I have into this place."

How would she explain to her father that she'd abandoned the car rather than deal with a man?

Eventually, she said, "It was fine last time I drove it, but this morning it started making a grinding noise." She made a stirring motion with her fist. "And there was a loud bang before it gave up altogether."

Richard smiled again. "Can you leave it with me for the rest of the day? I'll look at it this afternoon."

"I have a couple of errands to run in town, but they won't take long. I was rather hoping you could fix it now."

"Well, if that's the level of service you're used to, Miss . . . ? Sorry, I didn't catch your name."

"Caldwell, Bella Caldwell."

"Right, Miss Caldwell. I'll tell you what – you do your shopping and come back in about an hour. I'll push your motor into my yard and take a look at it now. If it's something simple, it'll be sorted. If not, you may have to wait, but I'll do my best."

"Thank you, Mr Yates," Bella said, backing away, wondering what on earth she'd do for a whole hour in town.

Perhaps after she'd posted her letter and finished her shopping, she could brave the tea shop.

The post office was situated around the corner from the garage, so she joined the small line of customers. The problems with the car had left her jittery and she fiddled with her handbag as she waited to go inside.

As she was served, she kept her gaze to the floor until the post mistress said, "You're looking a bit peaky, Miss Caldwell. How are you keeping?"

"Very well, thank you, Miss Alsop."

The middle-aged woman checked the pearl buttons on the cuffs of her white high-necked blouse, then after wetting the stamp, she used a ruler to align it to the top right-hand corner of Bella's letter before sticking it down.

Finally, she said, "I'm glad, dear. There's nothing wrong

with being a spinster. Don't let the nasty gossips get you down. I never have."

"I, er, won't, thank you."

Bella knew the older woman meant well, but she wished she'd shut up.

"It's good you're not hiding away. I was jilted at the altar, you know. But I hold my head up. Still, I don't suppose it's as bad as what happened to you. At least he didn't take my virtue. Never trust a man, that's what I say, dear."

Bella heard the woman behind her in the queue snigger.

"I won't, thank you," Bella said as she pushed her payment across the counter and scurried out.

Her heart racing, she rested against the wall, breathing rapidly, her head swimming. She'd intended visiting the department store to purchase some new stockings but abandoned the idea. All she wanted now was to be away from the post office before the sniggering customer came out.

Forcing herself to put one foot in front of the other, she made her way back to the garage. As she crossed the yard, her foot slipped. Pain shot through her ankle and tears threatened.

Richard placed his mug of tea on the long workbench that stretched down one side of the garage.

"By heck, that was quick, Miss Caldwell."

Bella stumbled forwards.

"Are you unwell? Hold on a minute while I fetch you a seat." He pulled a battered spindle-back chair from the far side of the room. "It might be a bit mucky, but at least your coat is dark, so it won't show."

"Thank you."

Bella flopped onto the chair, took a few deep breaths and then rubbed her ankle.

"Are you hurt, miss?"

"It's just a sprain."

"I think I'd better call for a doctor. You're as pale as a gallon of clotted cream."

"No, please don't bother. I'm fine, really."

"If you don't mind my saying so, you're far from all right."

Bella's breath hitched and she burst into tears.

Richard hovered uncertainly as she searched fruitlessly in her bag for her handkerchief. Then he pulled a large, clean linen square from his pocket and handed it to her.

As she mopped her face, he said, "I've got just the thing for you." Then he dashed through the door at the back of the workroom into the living accommodation.

He returned holding a glass of dark liquid.

"Sherry – just what you need if you're upset or under the weather. At least, that's what my old mam says."

Bella took the glass, giving him a wan smile. "Thank you, Mr Yates. You don't look like a sherry drinker."

"To tell you the truth, it was left behind in the pantry, but it all goes down the same way."

Bella took a sip. "It *is* rather nice."

"Right, well, if you're not going to let me fetch a doctor, have one of my sandwiches. It's only potted meat. I don't need both and you can watch me while I repair your engine. How does that sound?" He pushed a small plate nearer. "Go on, take one."

"Thank you," Bella replied.

The last thing she wanted was to eat, but he was being kind and she didn't want to offend him. She nibbled at the edges as he worked. Somehow, sitting quietly, no one expecting her to be strong, was surprisingly calming.

After a while, he said, "You're getting a bit of colour in your cheeks now. You can tell me what's upset you, if you have a mind to. I'm a good listener."

Bella dithered. He seemed nice enough. Honest. But then having been taken in by George, clearly she was no judge of character . . . No. She mustn't suspect every man she met. Most of Faredene knew about what had happened between George and her, so he'd find out soon enough, and she'd prefer it if he heard the basic facts from her, not one of the embellished stories that were circulating.

He focused on the engine as he listened. Perhaps that was what made it so easy for her to talk about it. Eventually, he looked up and wiped his hands on a rag that had been hanging over the bonnet.

"Well, my mam says there's a fool around every corner. And it sounds to me that this George fella was the biggest idiot you could meet."

"Thank you. I'm well rid of him, I suppose."

"No doubt about it, if you ask me."

"It's more the loss of what I believed we had that still upsets me. Does that make sense?"

"Yes, it does. I was courting a lass back in Manchester until she died of tuberculosis. It was five years ago now and I often find myself wondering about what might have been."

"I'm sorry. I shouldn't complain. What happened to you was much worse."

"She was taken from me, but I'm not sure that's any worse than being betrayed."

"I allowed myself to be fooled by a charlatan, so I've only myself to blame."

"We've all got to take responsibility for what happens in our lives, but there's no shame in loving someone. Even if they turn out to be the wrong person."

"I thought I was coping with it all, even the gossips, until I had my first attack."

"Attack?"

"Yes. I'm not sure if I'm ill or if I've suddenly become one of those ladies who suffer with their *nerves*." Bella explained about the two episodes where she'd struggled to breathe. "The first time I thought I was going to die, I really did," she ended.

"Best thing you can do is see your doctor. If it's not nerves, you might need some treatment."

"Goodness! You're not suggesting I need locking up, are you?"

"No. Nothing like that. I hear there's a decent fella in town. Doctor Feral or some such."

"It's Doctor Farrell. Actually, he's a family friend."

"There you go, then. Don't your family think you should see someone?"

"They don't know about the first time and the second only just happened. But I'm not going to tell them."

"You're not worried they'll cart you off to one of those sanatoriums? Is that why you're keeping schtum about it?"

Despite how she was feeling, Bella laughed. "Heavens, no. My family would be very supportive. But I don't want to worry them."

"They'd probably prefer to know how you're feeling."

"The thing is that my sister and I run a girls' school.

I've caused enough scandal without people saying I'm unstable or insane if word got out."

He nodded. "See your doctor. He'll keep it to himself."

She suspected there was no need to ask, but said, "*You* won't say anything, will you?"

"Not a word. You can trust me. Mechanics are like doctors – we take an oath to keep secret anything we learn."

She cocked her head to one side, then she laughed as she realised he was joking.

"I'll make us a brew then get this finished. I can do a temporary repair, but I'll need to order some bits to fix it properly."

"Oh, I see."

"Would you like me to come out to the school to put it right when the parts arrive from the manufacturer?"

"Please." She nodded gratefully.

When Bella left the garage two hours later, she felt she'd made a friend and ally.

Next instalment available 2022.

❦

About the Author

Debra Delaney is a qualified coach, therapist and meditation teacher who is fascinated by what makes people think and behave in a particular way. Her knowledge and experience has helped her to build the interesting characters in her novels.

The Faredene saga begins with the arrival of one woman who hides a secret and chronicles the intertwined lives of the inhabitants, both rich and poor, of this small market town. *Lie a Little . . . (to Love a Lot)*, the first instalment in the Faredene series, is full of life, love, strong friendships and tragedy that will make you laugh and cry. *Edge of Despair*, the second in the saga, has lots of humour and anguish that will have you gripped as the characters are charmed and duped as they falter in their efforts to find love and happiness.

Debra lives in Shropshire with her husband. Her biggest daily challenge is indulging in her numerous hobbies while juggling them with her thirst for writing. She is delighted to have completed her first two books and is already writing the third instalment of the Faredene series.

LIE A LITTLE
To Love a Lot

DEBRA DELANEY

Endless years of a lonely, childless spinster's life stretching ahead, Victoria Kavanagh finds an abandoned baby. She knows it's the answer to her prayers. Or is it? Has she stolen him in a moment of madness? She's come close to it before …

Desperate to keep him, she creates a past of her own design and moves to Faredene, but is her new life far enough away from the past she's trying to escape? What a framework on which to build – one of lies and deceit.

Thrust into a world where men are vying for her attention, Victoria has to decide in whom to lay her trust. Can she learn to have faith in her own judgement? First, she must forgive herself for standing by while her father destroyed her mother – her private shame.

Unprepared for the challenges of motherhood and running her own business, whatever the future holds, there's no turning back. Caring for people comes at a cost and her desire to protect a friend sets off a chain of events that has repercussions for everyone whose lives she touches … Her meddling may just be her undoing.

When danger threatens her son, Victoria has to make a heart-breaking choice – but is she ready to let him go?

Made in the USA
Monee, IL
21 April 2024

57303908R00282